THE BEAST EMERGES

The Earthborn Saga Vol. II

Steven Bissett

Copyright © 2023 Steven Bissett

All rights reserved.

No portion of this book may be reproduced in any form without permission from the publisher, except as permitted by U.S. copyright law.

This is a work of fiction. Names, characters, places, and incidents either are the products of the author's imagination or are used fictitiously. Any resemblance to actual persons, living or dead, businesses, companies, events, or locales is entirely coincidental.

CONTENTS

Title Page
Copyright
Chapter 1   1
Chapter 2   25
Chapter 3   59
Chapter 4   82
Chapter 5   133
Chapter 6   164
Chapter 7   207
Chapter 8   239
Chapter 9   276
Chapter 10   309
Chapter 11   352
Chapter 12   398
Chapter 13   453
Chapter 14   495
Chapter 15   533
  547

CHAPTER 1

"Mayday! Mayday! This is imperial vessel Rising Dawn to any human forces in the vicinity of Delta-13. I am in need of immediate assistance! Can anyone read me?"

Captain Galerius Lucan checked the rear-facing cameras on his small vessel and saw a pair of Devourer fighter craft closing fast. Vile green globs of acidic filth shot forth from strange, mouthlike gunports mounted beside their fuselages, narrowly missing his craft. Several had already hit the ship, dealing serious damage to the unshielded vessel.

"I repeat, this is the transport vessel *Rising Dawn!* I need help *now!* For the love of all things holy, somebody help me, please! I have passengers aboard!"

Throwing the clumsy vessel into a lethargic barrel roll, he managed to avoid two of the three blobs that chased after him. The third landed on one of the port engines, burning through its metal housing in seconds and disabling it.

"I've just lost one of my engines!" he screamed into his microphone.

"Imperial vessel *Rising Dawn*, this is Colonel Pinchon of the Black Fang pirates. We have received your distress call, and are coming to help. Hang on."

Stunned that the gravelly voice he heard belonged to a

1

pirate, Lucan was nevertheless relieved.

"Probably rescuing me so they can keep the ship for themselves," he thought, dodging another pair of blasts as he did so. "But at least I'll be alive!"

He saw a pair of nimble fighters form up behind his alien assailants and open fire with their small rapid fire railguns. The first few bursts missed as the pirates found their ranges. Then they zeroed in on one of them, unloading a devastating blast into its sole engine. Instantly the tiny craft exploded, severely damaging its partner and sending it tumbling away from them in a wild spin.

"Colonel Pinchon to *Rising Dawn*, your six is clear. You'd better come with us. They probably let out a distress signal of their own before we took 'em down. They'll be crawling all over this area in minutes."

"Where are we going?" Lucan asked, quickly forgetting his past danger and worried what his rescuers intended to do with him.

"To the only place that's still halfway safe for humans," Pinchon said. "The Black Fang base on Delta-13."

Dubiously Lucan fell in behind his escorts, who cut their speed so the limping transport could keep up.

Far in the distance his scanner showed that the largest Devourer vessels were floating just above the planet. The only ships still in orbit were fighter craft, like the ones that had been on him just moments before. Moving to the opposite side of Delta-13, he descended through a dense layer of clouds and found himself in the middle of a violent snowstorm.

"I-I can't see anything," he said over the radio. "And my instruments aren't showing any base."

"That's because it's camouflaged," replied Pinchon, a smile audible on his lips. "Don't worry, we'll guide you right to it. Just stay on our six."

"Affirmative," he said, clicking off the radio and leaning back in his seat to try and calm himself. The storm beat against the transport, trying to knock it off course. But with effort he managed to stay with his escorts until they slowed into a stationary hover two hundred feet above the ground.

"The landing pad is directly beneath you," Pinchon spoke over the radio. "Begin your descent. I'll let you know if you need to adjust your approach."

"Roger," Lucan replied, flicking the switch to engage landing mode and ever so gingerly lowering the *Rising Dawn* to the pad below.

"A little to your left," Pinchon said. "That's it. Nice and slow. The wind's picking up. Just a tad to the right. A little more. There you go."

Moments later the vessel's landing gear touched the pad, and a green light blinked on to show that the ship was securely grounded. Detaching his harness and leaving the cockpit, he found the dozen passengers nervously talking among themselves, trying to figure out what had happened.

"There's the Captain!" a middle-aged woman said. "He can tell us what's going on."

"Where are we?" a man asked. "This doesn't look like the prison complex."

"It's not," replied Lucan, trying to find the words to inform twelve confused imperial employees that they were now the guests of the most feared criminal organization in the fringe. Before he could elaborate a knock was heard on the hatch embedded in the ship's starboard side. Leaving the passengers to guess among themselves, he turned and walked back towards the cockpit, stopping just short of it. He put his hands on the lever that controlled the door and hesitated for a moment, his mind racing over what his distress call might have gotten them in for. Then he braced himself and gave the old lever a firm twist.

❖ ❖ ❖

"Admiral, all I need to know is what we're doing in response!" exploded the emperor via hologram, slamming his fist down on the armrest of his throne.

Admiral Laura McGannon clenched her teeth at the emperor's outburst.

"Sir, there's nothing we can do at the moment. Our forces have been devastated wherever the aliens have appeared. We're organizing fleets for a counter attack, but it will take time. They've appeared everywhere at once, and we're still working over the best–."

"We don't have *time* to 'work things over!'" roared the emperor. "We must strike now, immediately!"

Nearly sixty years old, and never in good health, the emperor looked twenty years older than he actually was. Despite access to the finest medical care in the empire, he suffered from a rare condition that had proven impossible to treat. His cells aged at a much faster rate than normal, and nowhere was this more evident than in his behavior. The condition worked havoc on his brain, making him erratic and difficult to deal with. Suspicious and impulsive, he distrusted his advisors and sensed conspiracies all around him. McGannon was almost alone in her ability to deal with him on a regular basis without exciting his ire.

Sixty herself, with a thin head of blonde hair that reached down to her ears, McGannon's face looked as though it had been carved out of a piece of granite. Conventional in her outlook on both naval and political affairs, the navy felt she was a suitable agent to ensure their interests were not neglected at court. For this reason she had been appointed nearly ten years before as their liaison to the emperor. Through constant exposure to His Highness her talent had gradually fallen under his eye, until finally he made her his Minister for War. Every other official in the government addressed her as Minister, as suited her office. But the title

'Admiral' appealed more to the emperor for reasons he never chose to explain, and it was in this way that he invariably addressed her.

"First the facility on Delta-13 was destroyed, and now *this!*" fretted the emperor, rising from his ornate throne and pacing the floor nervously. "What's next? Will assassins visit me in my bedchamber tonight?"

"As always, your security is our top priority," replied McGannon, familiar with the routine of calming the emperor's irrational fears as soon as they popped up. Failure to do so would allow them to fester until they became certainties, influencing policy with disastrous results.

"And what of my empire? Are you seeing to the security of *that* as well?" he snapped, waving a crooked finger at her. "We stand on the precipice, ready to be pushed over the edge! Only by drawing together now, into one solid block of humanity, can we possibly overcome these creatures! Oh, *why* did Taegen even bother to warn us years ago, if this was the mess we were going to make of things?!"

Her body imperceptibly tightened at the mention of the emperor's personal mystic and closest advisor. A charming man with mysterious insights that could not be rationally explained, he spoke of a time when a plague would descend upon humanity, the plague of the Devourers. It was his prophecy that had encouraged the emperor, much against his better judgment, to resume the mind control experiments on Delta-13 in the hope of knitting together humanity into a single force that could fight back against the invaders who stood poised to return.

Jealous of his influence over the emperor, many elements in the government had sought to eliminate Taegen at one point or another, but lacked the courage. Fearing they would be found out by his sixth sense, they all treated him with the utmost respect, scarcely admitting to themselves that they wanted him gone lest his clairvoyance should reveal the plots that they carried within.

It wasn't until the military came to see him as a threat that a credible campaign was launched against him. Disbelieving his prophecy, but seeing the utility of mind control for the inevitable conflict with the fringe that was soon to come, they had given it their complete support. Perceiving this difference in purpose, Taegen had striven to keep the mind control project strictly out of the military's hands. This they would not tolerate, and shortly thereafter the transport he was riding on suffered a malfunction and crashed during landing.

At the mention of Taegen, McGannon could never help the twinge of conscience she experienced because of her part in the plot and subsequent coverup. She felt that sooner or later the emperor would have some wild fit of intuition and lay the blame on her.

"I'm sure Taegen would approve of the measures we've taken," she replied confidently, trying to brush aside her guilt. "It's only a matter of time before our forces successfully drive the aliens out of our systems."

"Time, time!" the emperor said, wringing his hands. Throwing himself back into the throne and fidgeting nervously, he stared into space and tried to think.

"I assure you, my emperor, that we are doing everything that can be done," she replied.

"Time, time," he repeated, seemingly forgetting her presence as he mentally withdrew. "Time…"

◆ ◆ ◆

"We cannot sit here and do nothing!" Gromyko said impatiently, pacing the hot floor of the secret chamber. "The planet needs our help!"

"And what would you suggest that we do? Attack

the Devourer ships with clubs?" retorted Wellesley. "There's nothing we can do until the imperial navy arrives, and even they probably can't handle them. There is no more fearsome threat in the entire galaxy than the Devourers. That's why it took a galactic assemblage of sentient worlds to get rid of them the last time."

"There must be *something* we can do," Hunt replied with quiet certainty. "This can't be the way we go out."

"I'll look through the computer for more information," Wellesley replied, willing to humor his friend. "But I don't think we have any options."

Quietly receding from the conversation, the ancient AI began pouring over reams of data in search of an answer.

"I wish *Selek-Pey* was here," Gromyko said after an interval, still pacing the floor. "He might know something."

Doctor Tselitel sat on the floor, her back against the wall. It was so hot that sweat poured off her face and ran down her blouse, soaking it until it clung uncomfortably to her body. Drawing her legs against her chest, her arms glistened as she rested them atop her knees.

"Alright, there is *one* possibility, technically," Wellesley said at long last. "The planets that expelled the Devourers called themselves the Union of Light. Consisting of 496 worlds in all, they were linked together by a psychic communication network that ran through a separate dimension from our present one. This permitted them to communicate with each other and coordinate their efforts. The network is all but silent now, almost none of the worlds possessing the strength to send a signal to the others. Occasionally one will get sent out. But the others usually can't reply."

"How does this help us?" asked Hunt, drawing near to the massive hologram of Delta-13 that dominated the room, watching the alien vessels float menacingly above its surface.

"Well, that's where it gets a little unclear. A world

called *Preleteth* in *Kol-Prockian*, or Epsilon-4 according to human parlance, had been sending out a signal to Delta-13 for ages. Apparently it had foreseen the return of the Devourers, and was desperately trying to warn the other worlds. Delta-13 knew this, but seemingly shut its ears. I guess it was too devastated by the last war with them to face the truth in its weakened condition."

"So it stuck its head in the sand?" asked Gromyko hotly. "Just went about its business while this, this *infestation*, threatened the galaxy?"

"Looks like it," replied Wellesley matter-of-factly. "Epsilon-4 wasn't as strong as Delta-13 when they banished the Devourers. But for some reason it came out of the struggle in better shape. According to translated messages that were put into the computer eons ago, *Preleteth* had some kind of plan for dealing with the Devourers. But Delta-13 wouldn't hear of it."

"What was it?" asked Hunt.

"I have no idea," replied the AI. "All Epsilon-4 ever did was make oblique references to it. And that was in messages that ended a long time ago. I don't think Delta-13 has heard from it in ages."

"I still don't see what this does for us," said Tselitel, getting to her feet and joining them by the hologram. "If we're going to deal with this threat, we need some kind of weapon – something that can take the fight to them."

"I believe that's just what Epsilon-4 had in mind," replied Wellesley. "But we can't be sure until we ask it."

"Ask it?" inquired Gromyko with a cocked eyebrow.

"Of course. With the psychic network all but silent, we'll have to go in person."

"And just how do you intend for us to do that?" asked the smuggler. "We don't have a ship. And even if we *did*, none of us knows how to fly."

"I thought your Black Fang friends might be able to help us," replied the AI.

"I'd hardly call them *friends*," Gromyko said. "And with the collapse of the Underground, I don't have clout anymore."

"You don't need clout, not when you have a temple full of artifacts to barter with," Wellesley said.

"What, hand away all these treasures to the pirates?" exclaimed Gromyko with surprise. "You're the last person I should have ever expected to make such a proposal!"

"Well, as *Selek-Pey* said, sentiment must give place to necessity. And none of these sacred buildings will matter, anyway, if the Devourers tear the galaxy apart. They'll destroy everything that is good and beautiful, unless we find a way to stop them."

"I suppose we can try to raise the Black Fang base on the other side of the planet with the computer," the smuggler said, looking at Hunt. "Provided they haven't been wiped out already."

"They haven't," replied Wellesley. "Their base is well hidden. Besides, the Devourers aren't interested in petty human installations. They're after the planets that banished them."

"Then this isn't just about feeding off Delta-13 and the others?" asked Hunt.

"No, they want revenge first and foremost," replied the AI. "There are other sentient worlds that didn't partake in the battle against the Devourers, and according to the computer they are leaving those worlds alone for the time being. They're zeroing in on the ones who worked against them."

"Does that include Epsilon-4?" Hunt inquired.

"Yes, although fortunately the Devourers didn't reenter our dimension close to it. For some reason they're actually quite a long distance off, though they're moving as fast as they can towards it."

"Then we don't have any time to lose," Hunt said. "Raise the pirate base." Then, looking at Gromyko, "Antonin, time to roll out the old charm."

◆ ◆ ◆

Captain Lucan opened the hatch of his transport and saw a man with a graying, stubbly beard standing before him. Just shy of six feet and on the heavier side of average, his cool blue eyes and air of worldly knowledge instantly commanded respect.

"Captain Lucan?" he asked, half a dozen pirates in uniform standing behind him, each with weapons drawn, though he himself was unarmed. "I'm Colonel Pinchon. Judging by your vessel," he said, leaning back and taking a second look at it, "we reached you in the nick of time."

"Don't I know it!" replied Lucan, eagerly pumping the pirate's hand.

"Permission to come aboard?" he asked with a courtliness of manner that surprised Lucan.

"Please," he replied, gesturing inward and stepping back. Doubtful of his intentions, though hoping for the best, Lucan watched as the colonel entered the craft and strode to the passenger compartment. Seeing that none of the passengers were armed, he gestured for his escort to put away their weapons.

"I'm Colonel Pinchon of the Black Fang pirates," he announced, to the gasps of several of them. "Yes, I expected such a response," he smiled wisely. "But I assure you we mean you no harm. This vessel is of no use to the Black Fangs, and none of you are sought by us. We came to your rescue because humanity is under attack by some unknown race. They've appeared all over the empire, and are assaulting every world they encounter. At a time like this we need to hang together, hence our coming to your aid. The imperial forces that orbit Delta-13 have been destroyed, as has the modest space station. The town of Midway has been destroyed as well, and it won't be long before they take the prison. Imperial forces are gathering in several nearby systems for a counter attack, but there's no guarantee that they'll get here before the aliens have killed every last human in the system. You're welcome to remain at this location until my people have time to repair your craft and send you on your way. But it'll take some time. Yours isn't the first vessel that we've rescued, and you'll have to wait your turn." He paused for a moment and eyed them. "I recognize that you are imperial employees, and that subsequently we are on opposite ends of the law. Please do not interpret our kindness in this matter as an invitation for mischief. Anyone who attempts to sabotage this base's functionality or who interferes with its personnel will be swiftly dealt with. Do I make myself clear?"

A general murmur of assent indicated that his point had been received unambiguously.

With this the colonel gestured for his team to escort the passengers out of the craft, stepping aside and watching as they did so.

"Excuse me, Colonel," Lucan said confidentially as they filed past. "But this is the last thing I expected from the Black Fangs. We *are* government personnel, as you pointed out. I'm afraid I'm at a bit of a loss to understand all this."

"None of that matters now," the colonel replied, to which one of his men snorted his disagreement. "Whatever these creatures are, they mean to wipe us out," Pinchon added pointedly, his eyes boring into the objecting pirate as he strode past. The escort ushered the passengers out into the cold and toward the camouflaged structures of the base, Pinchon remaining behind momentarily with Lucan in the empty vessel. "As you will have gathered, not all of those under my command agree with this course of action."

"Indeed not," Lucan replied.

Mutely Pinchon led the way out of the ship into the bitter cold of the storm. The icy air shocked Lucan's lungs, and it was several seconds before he could speak.

"What are we going to do, Colonel?"

"I don't think anyone is in a position to make long term plans right now," Pinchon replied, his voice barely audible over the howling of the wind. "Just stick by your people for the time being."

"Do you intend to attack those, those *things*?"

"Not if we can help it," Pinchon said frankly. "Our presence here is too small to attack the aliens, outside of brief fighter-to-fighter actions, like you witnessed. No, we'll have to wait for the imperial navy to arrive with the big guns before contemplating anything larger. For now we'll content ourselves with rounding up as many survivors as we can, and gathering intel that might be of use when the time to strike has come. Whoever these invaders are, they won't figure us for much of a threat. That should allow us to get a candid peek at their strength and tactics before the fleet arrives."

"Well, if I can be of any help, please let me know," Lucan said.

"I'll be sure to do that," Pinchon nodded, as they reached a small building a short distance from the pad.

◆ ◆ ◆

"This is Antonin Gromyko of the Underground, calling Black Fang base Omicron. Come in please, Omicron."

The smuggler shook his head doubtfully at his companions, having repeated the same call over a dozen times. He was about to give up when a voice crackled back to him.

"Omicron base calling Gromyko, come in."

"Omicron!" he exclaimed into the microphone. "This is Gromyko! Glad to hear your voice. What is your status? Have the aliens taken an interest in you yet?"

"Negative. They're currently occupied on the opposite side of the planet, evidently boring into the planet."

"Omicron, we need immediate evac from our position. Can you assist?"

The air was dead for several seconds. Crossing his fingers and looking at the others, Gromyko pressed the microphone button again.

"Do you copy, Omicron base? Can you help us?"

"Unfortunately we can't spare any–," began the voice, before it was replaced by another. "This is Colonel Pinchon of the Black Fangs. We stand ready and able to assist. What is your situation?"

"Colonel, this is Gromyko of the Underground. There are four of us in all, plus our equipment. We have a lead on how to stop the Devourers, but we'll need to get off world first."

"Devourers? You mean the aliens?"

"Yes, sir. That's what they're called," replied the smuggler. "We have intel that could be of great importance for the upcoming fight against them."

"Well, I'm not sure about getting you off world. But we can extract you from your present location, provided you're not too close to the Devourers. We can't afford to attract too much attention and put the base at risk."

"I understand, Colonel. But we're days away from the prison. Our instruments show the area to be clean for many miles around."

"Then we'll come and get you," replied Pinchon firmly. "What are your coordinates?"

Quickly Wellesley dug them out of the computer, the smuggler relaying them.

"Alright, we should be able to get you within, oh, about six hours. Sit tight until then."

"Roger, over and out," Gromyko said, stepping away from the computer. "See? The name of Gromyko still opens doors!"

"I noticed that you didn't bring up the artifacts," Wellesley pointed out, a touch of grudging appreciation in

13

his voice.

"Well, why sell the family heirlooms if we don't have to?" the smuggler queried in response. "I don't want to see this magnificent temple ransacked if I can help it."

"That guy seemed pretty friendly," Milo said, joining the other three by the hologram. "Not what I would have expected from a pirate."

"I agree," Hunt nodded. "Wonder what his angle is."

"Right now I don't care," replied Gromyko. "In any event, we'd better hustle. It'll take hours to get back to the entrance from here."

They had barely made it out of the sweltering labyrinth before a high pitched whistle informed them that *Selek-Pey* had rejoined the group.

"Brother!" exclaimed Gromyko, glad to see the misty, undulating form of his friend. "I feared we wouldn't see you before leaving. Where have you been?"

"*Chelek po! Balan trelak suun baya!*"

"They have nearly succeeded! Soon the planet will be dead!" translated Wellesley.

"We know, *Selek-Pey*," replied Tselitel. "We're going to the planet of Epsilon-4 to find answers."

"*Vehren otol Preleteth. Een forran yula samnibo*," uttered the misty cloud in its hauntingly childish whisper.

"*Preleteth* is an imbecile! A dundering, mindless imbecile!."

"Why?" inquired Gromyko. "What are you talking about?"

"*Pasa vel noran*," replied *Selek-Pey*.

"I will say no more," translated Wellesley. "Judging by his tone, I suspect *Preleteth* and Delta-13 weren't on very good terms."

"*Kee*," agreed the mist.

"We have no choice," replied Hunt, ushering the group forward. "The Union of Light is shattered. They can't stop the Devourers."

"*Krol fana deshen. Melen yola venba trelsa fah.*"

"All things end eventually. Humanity, and all other life in the galaxy, have reached their end."

"You mustn't know humanity very well, if you think we're gonna go down without a fight," said Milo.

"*Huuna qerelan mesk valan. Toppah fesa vo.*"

"I have come to say goodbye to my brother, not to argue," said Wellesley.

"But why goodbye?" asked Gromyko.

"Because *Selek-Pey* is just a memory stored by the planet," the AI explained. "When the planet dies, he will go with it."

Gromyko stopped in his tracks on the hot, stony floor, bringing the group to a halt.

"Isn't there something we can do?" he asked urgently. "Download him, or something?"

"With what?" replied Wellesley. "There's no way to interface with the planet. And even if there was, we don't have a device that could possibly store his entire personality. It's too broad and multifaceted, the product of years of daily communion with the planet. No, I'm afraid there's nothing we can do for him. His time has come, just as it has for the world he revered for so long."

"Go on without me," the smuggler said to the rest of the group, handing his pack to Milo. "Wellesley and I will catch up with you later. I need to say goodbye."

"Of course," Tselitel said, putting a hand on his arm.

"We'll see you at the entrance," Hunt said, nodding to his friend and moving quickly onward.

"I hope he'll be alright," Tselitel said, looking over her shoulder as Gromyko shrank into the distance behind them, talking animatedly to the mist.

"Heh, I hope we'll *all* be alright," Milo chimed in. "Don't forget, the planet is under attack right now. I just hope the atmosphere won't evaporate or something when those creatures finish with it."

"I don't think that will happen," replied Tselitel. "Remember, there are plenty of other worlds that support life without being sentient. I think those two faculties are entirely separate."

"I agree," Hunt seconded. "The real question is what they're going to do when they're finished sucking it dry. They might go looking for us. And even if they don't, the *karrakpoi* will. They'll need a fresh supply of warm flesh when the planet is dead."

"Not really making me feel better, brother," Milo said.

"I'm not trying to," Hunt said grimly. "Just stating the facts."

Reaching the entrance hours later, they settled down on the massive steps and waited for Gromyko and Wellesley to catch up.

"I hope he doesn't talk all day," Hunt said to Tselitel, who sat next to him on the steps. "Sometimes that guy has no track of time."

"I'm sure he'll be along shortly," she said, not feeling half so confident as she sounded. Inwardly she fretted that he would hold them up, making them miss their rendezvous with the pirates. Having heard the worst things possible attributed to them, she doubted that patience was among their short list of virtues.

"Might as well grab one last hot meal before leaving here," Milo said, pulling open the smuggler's pack and drawing out the small camp stove. He moved a short distance away so that its heat wouldn't make them uncomfortable. "I'll have this thing going in a snap."

"Milo sure has brightened up since coming here," Tselitel said quietly to Rex, her psychiatric training never at rest. "It's like he was never running at one-hundred percent before."

"He's never comfortable unless some kind of danger is floating over his head," Hunt said, watching his brother work. "He needs it to feel alive."

"He sounds like Antonin in that regard," she replied, putting a hand on his knee and rubbing it affectionately. "I'm glad you're not like that. I don't think I could love a man who was always on the move like that, chasing one thrill after the next. I couldn't possibly keep up!"

"What makes you think I don't?" he asked, a grin forming on his lips despite the strain he was under. "I could be just as bad as they are. After all, it's been one battle after another since you've met me. Maybe my needs are just being satisfied without my having to look after them."

"No, you're not that kind of man," she said with certainty, taking his teasing seriously. "You're much too grounded to go flying after adventure in that way. Only a man who didn't care where the chips fell could live like that. And you never take your eyes off the chips."

"Seems like you know me pretty well," he smiled, giving her a kiss.

"I ought to," she smiled in return. "I carry a little bit of you inside me now, remember?"

"Don't remind me," he said, closing his eyes and grimacing. "Someone as pure as you should never have a touch of darkness enter you, even for humanitarian reasons. I know you were saving my sanity out there in the snow, but I wish there could have been another way. I never wanted any of my darkness to enter you. It was one of my deepest fears, even when I had only seen you in a dream."

"Light needs dark, darling," she said. "The one can't exist without the other. I wish you could see this from my side, and know how I value the little shred of you that now resides in me. It brings me comfort to know that I'll always have you with me. Now I'm never alone."

"Some company," Hunt replied with a roll of his eyes. "If you needed a friend, you could have just taken Wellesley with you."

"Don't be silly," she said. "We have a closeness, an intimacy, that can never be duplicated. Honestly I never believed in finding The One until I met you. Then it was like fate, and I couldn't keep away from you, even if I wanted to."

"Didn't keep you from running after I blasted Milo," he replied, instantly regretting that he'd mentioned it.

"No, it didn't," she murmured. "But I promised that I would never do it again, and I won't. You'll never have to look around for old Lily Tselitel. I'll be right here, by your side."

Touched beyond words, he drew her close and sighed.

Nearly an hour later the smuggler came jogging up after them, short of breath and covered in sweat.

"It's about time you got here," Milo said, laying on his back and peering over his toes. "We've already eaten and packed the kit away again. If you want to grab a bite before leaving, it'll have to be cold."

"We don't have time to eat!" Gromyko exclaimed. "Can't you guys hear that?" he asked urgently, darting up the stairs and pushing the door open. Immediately they heard the faint shriek of a starship's engines in the distance. "Our ride is nearly here! And yet you're all laying around like we're on vacation! Hurry, get on your feet! We have to get outside and signal to the ship when it nears us. He could easily miss us in the trees if he doesn't fly right overhead!"

Heeding his urgency, the group gathered their equipment and dressed for the elements. With the planet in its death throes the storms had gained in ferocity until they could barely be withstood, even within the cover the forest provided. Shoving the door open against the wind that blew upon it, they were nearly pushed back inside by the strength of the gale. Quickly Hunt grabbed Tselitel's arm and pulled her along with him into the cold, her frail form overwhelmed by it.

"Over there!" shouted Gromyko, gesturing emphatically towards a small opening in the trees. "He should be able to see us there!"

The others nodded and followed after him, driving their feet into the massive drifts that had accumulated during their stay in the temple. Forcing their way through snow that reached to their knees, their muscles were burning by the time they reached the place he'd indicated. No sooner had they done so than they heard the transport fly overhead. It was too far away to be seen, the snow being too thick in the air.

"Now what?" asked Milo. "It's not like we've got any flares!"

"Now we wait!" shouted the smuggler over the storm. "He'll have to realize that he can't see us from up there and drop down lower. When he does, we'll be here to wave him down."

"I hope he can see out of the bottom of that thing," Milo grumbled, crossing his arms against the wind and straining his ears for the ship's engines.

Packing Tselitel close against his side as he had on a number of previous occasions, Hunt looked to the frigid sky and waited. He knew there was only a slim chance that the ship would come over that area a second time. There was a broad area to cover, and not a lot of time in which to search it. A brief stop could pass unnoticed by the Devourers. But a prolonged search would raise their curiosity and cause them to dispatch a couple fighters to investigate.

Soon Lily began to shiver. Hunt considered taking her back to the temple to wait until the ship was actually on the ground when Milo suddenly jumped into the air.

"Here it comes!" he shouted. "Over there!"

The ship came so low over the treetops that its scarred hull scratched against them, producing a noise even the storm couldn't drown out. As it passed over the group began to jump and wave their arms, causing it to stop just above them. Waiting until they had moved out of the way, the small vessel descended onto the snow and landed awkwardly on the uneven ground. As they approached the back hatch of the ship opened, and a man in a flight suit popped out. Waving energetically, he didn't try to talk until they were inside and the door was shut.

"Boy, am I glad to see you guys!" he exclaimed with relief, pumping their hands. "I was just about to leave the area when I passed over. I could only risk another couple of minutes on their sensors before turning back. It's gonna be tight as it is."

"With that said, shouldn't we get moving?" prodded Gromyko, eager to leave the region as quickly as possible.

"You're right," said the pilot, a jaunty young man of twenty. "Strap yourselves in, folks! This could be a bumpy ride." With this he turned around and climbed back into the pilot's seat.

The small cargo hold featured metal benches with makeshift straps attached to them. Cold, hard, and uncomfortable, they were not a welcome sight.

"I guess they don't ferry a lot of people in this thing," Milo said, taking a seat on one of the benches and putting the stiff belt over his lap. "I'd hate to think what would happen if we crashed."

"That wouldn't matter," replied Gromyko, following his example. "We'd all freeze to death before anyone could rescue us, anyhow."

"What a cheery thought!" exclaimed Milo.

Ignoring them, Hunt got fastened in the best he could, and then saw to Tselitel beside him. Her hands already numb from her brief exposure to the cold, she sat back and let him finish strapping her in.

"Still helpless out of doors," she smiled apologetically.

"Don't worry about it," Hunt whispered, slipping an arm around her shoulders as the ship shuddered and took off.

"Alright, folks, we're airborne," the pilot called over his shoulder toward the cargo hold. "Hang on tight!"

"What's your name, anyhow?" asked the smuggler, twisting in his seat to throw his voice into the narrow doorway that separated them from the cockpit.

"Bradford! Lieutenant Nick Bradford!" he replied.

"Colonel Pinchon sent me right after we got your message. This little deal is fast," he said, tapping the controls to indicate the ship. "But I still had to come from part way around the planet to get you."

"You mean you got around the world in six hours?" asked Tselitel incredulously.

"Heh, no. I was part of a reconnaissance force that was searching for the wreckage of an imperial destroyer that went down shortly after the Devourers arrived. There were supposed to be some escape pods near the crash site, but they never made it. They'd been damaged before they got free of the ship, and the life support failed before they even touched ground. I was about to head back with the rest of the search team when the Colonel sent me out here for you guys."

"Just one ship? Why didn't he send the rest of the force along as escorts?" asked Milo, feeling terribly exposed in the unarmed vessel.

"He felt stealth was our best asset," replied the pilot, raising his voice to be heard over the engines. "No matter how strong the escort, the aliens could deploy triple our numbers if they wanted to, judging by how many are floating near Midway. Besides, there are a lot of calls for our help going out right now. We can't afford to give everyone the red carpet treatment. Boy, I bet most of them never expected to be rescued by the Black Fangs! But with the imperial forces in the area in ruins, we're the closest thing to a military force. Nobody else stands a chance."

"Do you have any warships? Anything bigger?" probed Tselitel.

"Nothing that can take on those things," he replied, jerking his thumb over his shoulder towards Midway and the enormous vessels that floated above it. "Frankly it'll take the biggest ships in the imperial navy to whip those things, and probably only at double their numbers. I was in low orbit when they arrived. They cut through the local destroyers like they were slicing pieces off a wedding cake."

"So what's the plan?" asked Hunt.

"Gather all the human forces in the area and learn everything we can about the invaders," replied Bradford in the bright tones of an optimistic youth. "We'll throw in with the imperial forces once they arrive."

"Aren't you afraid they'll attack you?" asked Gromyko, unsure if he would be so trusting were he in their place.

"Heh, they're gonna have their hands full dealing with our new friends," he replied with a laugh. "They're not gonna have time to worry about us. Besides, the Black Fangs are the best fighter pilots in the galaxy. They can't afford to throw us away."

At that moment an alarm began to sound from the cockpit.

"What's that?" asked Milo.

"Looks like we've gotten their attention," Bradford said. "Two fighters closing fast. They must have dropped down out of orbit to see what we're doing."

"How long until they get here?" asked Hunt.

"Eight minutes," replied the pilot. "Black Fang vessel VF-29 to base. I am being pursued by alien craft and request immediate assistance. Repeat, this is VF-29 to base, I need help ASAP, does anyone read?"

"We hear you, VF-29. No fighters are in your area at this time."

"Understood, over and out," he said, switching off the radio. "Looks like we're in for a bumpy ride, folks."

"We'll die if we stay out here," Wellesley said in his monotone through the 600G's speaker.

"Who said that?" jumped Bradford.

"An AI friend of ours, a *Kol-Prockian* relic," replied Gromyko.

"You're kidding!" exclaimed Bradford, turning around in his seat to get a look at the ancient construct. Gromyko held the medallion up for him to see. "I never would have believed it! I thought there weren't any *Kol-Prockian* AIs left!"

"Just me, as far as I know," replied Wellesley. "According to data I obtained from the temple, there is an intricate network of caves nearby. They should be just large enough to fit the ship into, provided you can handle this thing in tight spaces."

"Just watch me," replied the lieutenant gamely.

"The caves are just a couple of minutes from here. If we can reach them soon enough, the Devourers won't know which one we've disappeared into, and they'll buzz off. With any luck they'll think we crashed and disintegrated."

Dropping the small ship to just above treetop level, Bradford made best speed for the caves. Soon the ground dropped out from beneath the ship, revealing a massive series of canyons. Instantly he pushed the controls forward, diving into them.

"The scanner's having a hard time keeping track of 'em," he informed them, flying as low as he could. "Hopefully all this rock is working havoc with theirs as well."

"There's a cave coming up on your right, four hundred yards ahead," Wellesley said. "It'll be a close fit."

"I see it," Bradford replied, slowing the craft as he neared the craggy opening.

"You sure that thing is big enough?" asked Gromyko, his aversion to small spaces manifesting itself.

"Absolutely," replied the AI. "Now it's simply a question of the Lieutenant getting us inside without ripping the hull to shreds."

"Don't worry about that," replied Bradford with a smile, deftly guiding the craft into the dark hole. They could hear stalactites scraping on the exterior as they moved inside, several of them snapping off and banging against the ship as they tumbled to the ground. All the passengers craned their necks to see out of the cockpit, the ship's front lights illuminating the black space.

"Hope he's as good at backing out as he is at getting in," Gromyko mumbled. Milo glanced at him and then looked back toward the cockpit, hoping the same thing.

"Just…a little…further," Bradford said tensely, intuiting the vessel's position in the cave and moving it just as far as he could manage. Floating just inches above the ground, he pushed on until a subtle scratching could be heard on all sides. Lowering the craft to the floor, he cut the engines and deactivated all its systems.

"That ought to do it," he said, slipping off his helmet and joining the others in the back. "There's no way their sensors will pick us up with all this rock in the way."

"I wouldn't be so sure about that," replied Gromyko doubtfully. "They're much more advanced than we are, so who can say just how powerful their scanners are? I think our best bet lies in their not being able to get in here and giving up the chase."

"We'll find out soon enough," said Wellesley.

Hunt popped the rear hatch and stepped into the frigid cave, his footfalls echoing loudly off the walls. Tselitel trotted out of the ship and fell in beside him, the others preferring the warmth and cover of the ship.

"Do you think they'll find us?" she asked quietly.

"Guess we're about to find out," he said, pausing halfway between the ship and the entrance as the sound of engines soaring overhead reverberated down the cave. Reflexively Tselitel grabbed his arm and held it firmly, her eyes trying to follow the sound she heard through the rock.

They circled the area several times, trying to find their prey. The rest of the group left the ship and joined Hunt and Tselitel, walking quietly as though the aliens could somehow hear them. Soon the sound died away, and they relaxed.

"Looks like they're giving up," Gromyko said. "Guess you were right, Wellesley."

Instantly upon saying this they heard the vessels' engines screech overhead, along with the discharge of weapons. Several acidic blobs crashed into the top of the cave's entrance, collapsing it and burying the group alive.

CHAPTER 2

Colonel Pinchon stood looking out a window at Omicron base, watching the snow blow over the landing pad.

His landing pad, as he saw it.

Technically the base belonged to the Black Fang organization. But he'd run Omicron for so many years that he'd come to feel a sense of personal ownership over it. Its personnel were his children, and its equipment was his property.

It was irrational, he knew. What the Black Fangs had given, they could just as easily take away. More than once his personal sense of what should be done had crossed the will of the broader organization, leading to conflicts that nearly cost him his post on three separate occasions. At the last minute a compromise would be found, and the issue would pass. That, he knew, was mostly the work of Sedricks Veiss. Though technically third in the chain of command, Veiss had the ear of Chairman Girnius, the organization's leader.

Renowned for his sagacity, the word of Veiss was very nearly law to the majority of his fellow pirates. Though eleven years younger than the chairman, the latter invariably sought his advice before taking any major step. His influence was envied by many, though none would be so bold as to say so. He was closer to Girnius than anyone else, and no one dared to so much as whisper a word against him.

The fact that he was Girnius' brother-in-law didn't hurt his influence, either.

Pinchon knew that his move to indiscriminately rescue human survivors would not be popular at headquarters. Even now he could imagine the campaign that must be gathering for his ouster. Delta-13 was a prime post, intercepting as it did the artifact trade that came out of the Quarlac galaxy. Over the years many jealous fingers had tried to pry it from his grasp. But his record spoke for itself, and his influence at court was unmatched.

That is, until he got a message from Veiss chastening him for his decision.

"I haven't told the chairman yet," Veiss said. "He's got enough on his mind right now. That gives you a *very* limited window to change course. Get those civilians out of there *now*. Especially the imperial workers. Honestly, Philip, I can't imagine what's gotten into you."

"I won't change course," Pinchon said with quiet firmness to the hologram that stood in the middle of his office. "We can't leave these people to die, Sedricks."

"We are a *criminal organization*, Philip, not a charity," Veiss said, never one to sugarcoat matters. "Our goal is to make as much profit as possible from the misery of others. With the imperial navy reeling this is the perfect time to strike. They're leaving entire systems defenseless as they gather up their forces to counter attack. We've never had an opportunity like this before, nor will we again. Even the fringe independence folks are taking advantage of the situation. Word is they'll move to set up a separate confederation within the month."

"What do you think is going to happen once these aliens gain a foothold?" Pinchon asked, his anger beginning to rise. "Do you think they'll settle down to peace once they've finished thrashing the worlds they're now attacking? They've got it out for us, Sedricks. Only by banding together do we have a chance. This is our fight, too."

"No, Philip, it is *never* our fight," replied Veiss. "We *don't* get involved, no matter what is going on. We float on the surface like a thin film over a pond. We roll with the waves and take whatever we can get. That's how we've managed to last this long." Veiss looked over his shoulder and then dropped his voice. "I have to go. Change course *now*, Philip. Or there'll be new management at Omicron." With this the transmission terminated.

A sharp rap at the door was immediately followed by the entry of his second in command, Major Dietrich.

"No word from Bradford, sir," he said, shaking his head. "We lost contact with his ship over the Savanaugh Canyons."

"Guess the fighters got him," he said quietly, turning from the window and facing the major.

"I'm not sure about that, sir," replied Dietrich. "He dropped off our scope several minutes before they reached his area. I think he ducked into the canyons for cover. He's a smart kid, Colonel. If anyone has a chance, he does."

"Is there anyone in the area who can perform a flyby?"

"No, sir. They're all tied up on other tasks."

"Then he's on his own. Provided he's alive at all."

❖ ❖ ❖

"Great idea, Wellesley!" Gromyko exclaimed once the dust had settled. "Hide in a cave! They'll never find us there! But what do we do if they seal the entrance and lock us inside?"

"Knock it off, Antonin," Hunt ordered. "It was the best we could do under the circumstances."

"And what's the best we can do in *these* circumstances?" retorted the smuggler. "Dig our own graves and crawl into them, waiting to freeze or starve?"

"Aw, we'll find a way out of this," replied Bradford, pulling a light from his pocket and striding quickly to the entrance. "Gotta say, though, they've locked us in good."

"Can you push it open with the ship?" asked Tselitel.

"I doubt it," Bradford said, putting a hand on one of the massive rocks that had fallen from the ceiling. "Probably just rip the hull to bits. Still, it's worth a try, as a last resort."

"Not like we have a lot of other options," said Milo. "Not unless you were carrying explosives in that thing."

"Afraid not," replied the lieutenant, leaning against the rubble, his light shining down at his feet.

"If you've all calmed down by now," Wellesley said, "there *is* another option."

"What's that?" asked Gromyko. "Burrow our way out like a band of moles?"

"Why do you think I directed you to *this* cave?" asked the AI pointedly. "It wasn't for the scenery. It's because there just so happens to be another way out. I anticipated that the Devourers might lock us in, so I made sure to find a hideout with a backdoor."

"I didn't see any backdoor," replied Milo.

"That's because you weren't looking," Wellesley said. "Just ahead of the ship there's a tiny path that curves off to the right. You can't see it unless you're right next to it because it all blends together into one large sheet of craggy rock. But get the transport out of the way, and you'll find it."

"Bradford?" asked Hunt, looking to the pilot.

"Already on it," he said, dashing back towards the ship.

They watched as he raised the craft and gingerly backed it out of the tiny slot into which he'd put it. He killed the engines once a small gap had been made between the ship and the wall.

Once they'd grabbed their equipment, Hunt took the flashlight from the lieutenant and approached the rock wall. As Wellesley had said, there was a small path that bent off towards the right.

"Looks like it's going to be single file for a while," Hunt said, flashing the light along the tight corridor.

"Hope there aren't any *karrakpoi* in there," Tselitel said, taking Hunt's free hand and following him inside.

"*Karrakpoi*?" inquired Bradford, as Milo slipped past him, holding the 600G.

"Giant spiders," replied Gromyko. "Take the rear. I had it last time."

Shrugging, the young pilot fell in behind everyone else, scarcely able to see his hand before his face in the darkness.

For two hours they carefully moved down the narrow path, their ears straining for any sounds of danger, particularly from behind. Bradford, the least experienced of the group, consequently moved with the least concern, possessing no real idea of the threat the *karrakpoi* posed. The other members of the group were on tenterhooks in the tight space, aware that the high walls favored the nimble arachnids should there be a struggle.

Seeing a faint glow up ahead, Hunt covered the tiny flashlight with his thumb and slowed down. The rest of the group took his hint and gave him room to move, Tselitel releasing his hand. Putting his hand on her shoulder to indicate she should stop, he moved a little further on and disappeared around a corner.

"Where's he going?" Milo breathed in Tselitel's ear.

"Shh," Gromyko said from behind, worried that the spiders might hear them.

Suddenly Hunt popped back into the corridor, causing them to jump as he shined the light at them.

"It's alright," he said in a calm voice. "Come on. You've got to see this."

"See what?" asked Milo, following closely behind the doctor.

The group filed into an enormous cavern with

massive ceilings. A large structure made of strange, inky black metal surrounded by a number of decaying outbuildings stood a short distance away. Illuminated by numberless glowing mushrooms, the space had a mystical quality that easily played upon the imagination.

"Is this a dream?" Tselitel asked, feeling the strange effect of the place at once. Drawing near to Hunt, she took his hand once more, and together they approached the ancient complex. "This doesn't look *Kol-Prockian*," she observed as they closed the distance.

"You're right, Doctor," Wellesley said. "These structures belong to a race that long predates both humans and *Kol-Prockians*, called the *Voe*. By the time my people came here they were already gone. Only a handful of such sites exist on Delta-13, and even they tend to be well hidden."

"What happened to them?" she asked.

"Honestly I don't know. The ancient priests studied that very question for a long time, but never arrived at anything definite. Even the name *Voe* is just a name my people gave them. It means 'forgotten,' but in a regretful sense, like the faded memory of a beloved childhood home. They were sorry that more could not be known of them, since they were clearly great builders. They seemed to have appeared and vanished within a very short time span. Clearly they were foreign to this galaxy, because there is no visible line of development. They erected structures across the Milky Way for an unknown purpose, and then disappeared without a trace or any sign of a struggle."

"Not that this isn't fascinating," Gromyko said, "but what about getting out of here? I don't want to spend the rest of my life surrounded by mushrooms and ruins."

"Don't worry, I'm sure you would be one of the first to go," Wellesley said tartly. "The lack of stimulation would be the death of you."

"Don't start riding me, Wellesley," Gromyko said, in no mood for wisecracks.

"Wells, just what *are* we doing down here?" Hunt asked. "It looks like a dead end."

"No, there's a path on the other side of the ruins," he replied. "It'll take you deeper into the mountain."

"Deeper?" asked Bradford. "Do we really want to go deeper?"

"Not like we have any choice," Milo said, clapping him on the shoulder and striding into the abandoned metal structure.

"I'm not sure you should go in there, Milo," Tselitel said. "Who knows what's inside."

"Only one way to find out, right?" he asked gamely. "Besides, it'll be quicker than going around." Flicking on the light of the 600G, Milo quickly disappeared inside the structure. "Guys! Guys you need to see this!" he called out moments later.

Hastening in after him, they stopped before a giant, partially transparent figure of a woman. Standing nearly twelve feet tall, and clothed in a dress of pure white, she looked at them with an air of confusion and anxiety.

"You–, you must not–," she stammered, wringing her hands and looking around the room as though she feared some invisible observer would suddenly appear and strike her. "You must not go to Epsilon-4."

"Who are you?" asked Hunt.

"I am Delta-13 in your parlance," she whispered, still looking around. "Time is short. Too short. There can't–. There never was any–. I-I..." her voice trailed, as the fear on her face was replaced by an air of distraction. Without warning she screamed and collapsed to the ground. Milo reflexively rushed to her massive form and extended his hands to her. But they passed through without contacting anything solid.

"Are you in pain?" Tselitel asked. "What's wrong?"

"Th...the ancient consumers have all but finished their work," she lamented, her body convulsing as ghostly tears fell from her eyes. "I-I don't want to die! But it's nothing less than I deserve!"

"What are you talking about?" Hunt asked, trying to inject a little clarity.

"*Please!*" she begged, her massive eyes suddenly fixing on Hunt. "You must not go to Epsilon-4. It-it will endanger you all. I can no longer protect you from the others. You will be–." Instantly her words were cut off by a scream pealing from her lips, an agonized cry. "You have trusted me thus far, Rex Hunt. I have guided your steps with care. But it is too soon. Too soon," she rambled, her eyes growing cloudy.

"Delta, we must have something more specific to work with," Wellesley said in his monotone. "You can't expect–."

"I do not *expect!*" the woman exploded, her eyes clearing. "I *demand!* Rex Hunt will destroy all he encounters if he does not take care. I have carefully guarded him from the dark pool that resides within him. But Epsilon-4 is reckless and headstrong. Its way is the way of hubris. It will fashion a weapon to destroy the enemy, and in so doing produce an even greater evil. Your father could not control the dark power within him, Rex Hunt. You will fail also, without my care."

"You're wrong," Milo asserted, shaking his head. "Dead wrong."

"Oh, I have no *time* to argue with you!" she exclaimed. "I should not even be speaking to you in this forbidden way!"

"Forbidden by whom?" asked Tsclitcl.

"I cannot say," she replied. "Every moment that I speak to you heightens my transgression. As though I hadn't already sinned enough!" The figure released a defeated sigh. "The punishment for the sins of the *Ahn-Wey* is upon us all, from the least to the greatest."

Suddenly the apparition vanished, and the group was left in stunned silence.

"Delta didn't know what it was saying," Wellesley said at last. "It's in its death throes and its mind is clouded."

"I don't know, Wells," Hunt said, walking to where the woman had been just moments before. "Didn't sound like she was off her rocker."

"There's no other explanation for it," the AI replied. "Nothing it said made any sense."

Hunt eyed the ground where the figure had been for another moment, the planet's dark forebodings resonating within him.

"Delta was right about one thing, though," Wellesley added. "Time is short. We'd better get moving.

"Agreed," replied Hunt, drawn from his reverie and gesturing for his companions to follow. Leading them through the mysterious structure and out the back, he found the path Wellesley had spoken of. Following it for nearly an hour, they eventually felt cool air blowing down it towards them.

"Do you guys feel that?" Milo asked. "I think we're getting close."

Rounding a tight corner of jagged rock, Hunt saw dim light at the end of the tunnel. He squinted as the dry, frigid breeze blew stronger, stinging his eyes. He felt Tselitel's hand take his and give it a squeeze, relieved that they had at last found an escape. Filing into the open air, the group instantly missed the cover the cave provided as the wind struck their bodies.

"Back where we came from," Gromyko said. "More or less."

"At least we've got fresh air now," Milo replied.

"What are we going to do?" asked Tselitel, looking above her at the storm as it blew over the canyon, hunching her shoulders against the cold. "We'll freeze if we stay out here very long."

"I brought my radio with me when we left the ship," Bradford said. "If we can get above the canyon I might be able to raise a Black Fang vessel, provided one is close enough."

"Any chance the Devourers will pick up the signal?"

asked Gromyko.

"Oh, sure. But they'll be too busy chasing down the other distress signals all over the planet to bother with our weak little transmission. So far they've concentrated on the big stuff: crashed freighters and whatnot. A portable radio just won't warrant investigation."

"Wellesley, what's the best course out of here?" Hunt asked.

"Straight ahead. There's a low slope to the canyon wall five hundred feet down the path that you can use to get higher. We're lucky: this is about where the canyon begins to peter out and turns to flatland. Otherwise it'd be too steep to climb."

"I would hardly describe our situation as being lucky," replied Gromyko, falling back into his prior morose mood. "It'll be a miracle if we don't freeze by the time we're picked up."

Ascending to the top of the canyon, the force of the wind doubled, blowing the heat out of their weary bones. Standing near a ragged group of weatherbeaten trees, they waited as Bradford attempted to raise a rescue ship.

"Nothing," he said, leaving the open space he'd occupied and joining them by the trees a quarter of an hour later. "This storm is playing havoc with communications. And who knows if there even *is* a vessel in the area."

"Try again," Hunt said, a powerful intuition suddenly washing over him.

"Give it a minute," Bradford said, putting his gloved hands under his arms to warm them. "I gotta get some heat back into me first."

"No, we've got to do it *now*," Hunt insisted, taking the radio and walking a short distance away. "Calling all Black Fang vessels in the vicinity, can anyone read me?"

"This is Omicron base, what is your situation?"

"Lieutenant Bradford and four passengers were forced to put down in some canyons a short distance north of our previous coordinates after coming under attack by alien vessels. Request immediate evac, over."

"This is Colonel Pinchon. Who am I speaking to? Is Bradford alright?"

"He's fine, Colonel. Just a little cold, so I took over radio duty. Now, can you help us?"

"I'm afraid we won't have anything in that area for at least twelve hours. Can you find some kind of cover? Stay out of the elements until we're able to get to you?"

"Yes, I think so," replied Hunt.

"We'll have a ship over your area sometime tomorrow, then. Keep that radio close by until we do. The pilot will call again when he's in the vicinity."

"Alright, we'll hang tight until then. Over and out."

"Who did you get?" asked Bradford, as Hunt rejoined the group. "A fighter in low orbit?"

"No, Omicron base," he replied, handing the radio back.

"But that's impossible!" exclaimed the pilot. "The base is clear on the other side of the planet. This little radio can't possibly reach that far."

"And yet it did," he replied, a cryptic smile on his lips.

"But how?" asked Bradford.

"There'll be time for explanations later," replied Hunt. "Right now we have to get under cover. Pinchon said he couldn't get a ship out to us in anything less than twelve hours, so we'll have to hole up for a while."

"Should we head back down to the cave?" asked Milo.

"No, the canyon will limit the range of the radio too much. We don't want to risk missing a message while we're down there. We need to stay up here somewhere. Fan out and look for a nook or something we can duck into. Antonin, take Bradford and the light and go south. Milo, take Wellesley and go north. Lily and I will go east. Double back in fifteen minutes whether or not you find anything. Go."

With this the team broke up, each heading their

assigned ways.

"I can't believe the planet actually spoke to us," Tselitel said, as she walked into the twilight's gloom with Hunt. "I didn't think that was even possible."

"I suspect we still have a lot to learn about this old galaxy of ours," Hunt said with a smile, squeezing her hand. "But right now let's find somewhere to spend the night. Once the sun goes down the temperature will collapse."

"As if it wasn't cold enough already," she said with a shiver. "But what are we supposed to find? I don't think there's much chance of finding another *Kol-Prockian* shrine."

"At this point even a large snow drift would do. All we really need is something to break the wind and give us a little insulation."

At the end of the time allotted they turned back, barely able to see their own tracks as darkness quickly fell over the land.

"What did you find?" Hunt asked Milo, as he and Tselitel shuffled out of the gloom toward the twin lights of the group.

"Absolutely nothing," he said, shaking his head.

"We found an old bear den underneath a massive tree," Gromyko said. "Not sure we want to take up residence in a place like that, though."

"A bear den?" asked Hunt significantly, for Wellesley's benefit.

"Oh, not one of those again," the AI muttered.

"I don't think it's been inhabited for a long time," Bradford said. "It looked abandoned."

"We'd better hope so," Hunt said, nodding south. "Guess we'll find out, one way or another."

Reaching the den a few minutes later, they found it cramped but sufficient for five people to climb into.

"Think you can fire up that stove without burning this place down, Antonin?" Hunt asked once they'd settled in.

"I reckon," he replied with a grin, busting it out of

his pack and lighting it. The tiny flame proved more than adequate to light the small space, though the heat it cast off was paltry given conditions.

"Alright, now that we've got a little time on our hands," Bradford said, laying on his side and propping himself up on one arm, "perhaps you'd care to fill me in on a few details. For one, how can a planet talk to us? I've heard such things before, but I always thought it was nonsense."

Over the next hour the group's members took turns filling the young pirate in on all they knew about the planet – its workings, intentions, and the dire situation it now found itself in. Bradford listened almost without comment, only occasionally interrupting to clarify some point or other.

"Incredible," he said at last, when the tale was finished. "How long has this been going on? I mean, how long have you known?"

"Not very long," replied Hunt. "Just a few weeks. I was recruited to stop certain experiments that the government was pursuing in the prison. That business ended right around the time the Devourers showed up. Funny, I never realized what a coincidence that was. I wonder if the two events are related somehow."

"And the radio," Bradford said, more interested in settling his own curiosity than following Hunt's line of thought. "How in the world did it reach Omicron?"

"The planet gave the signal a boost," Hunt replied with certainty. "That's how I knew when to try again. I got a powerful urge from Delta-13 that the time was right, and I knew better than to wait around. I raised Pinchon on the very first try."

"Fascinating," Bradford said.

"I'm surprised that the planet stepped in to help us, given that we're still going to Epsilon-4," Gromyko said. "You'd think it would leave us to our fate."

"Guess it couldn't just stand by and let us die," Milo replied, shrugging his shoulders.

"Well, we owe it one, that's all I know," Bradford said, laying back on the ground in his insulated flight suit. "Too bad it couldn't have pointed us to a warmer place to stay while it was at it! It's freezing out here. Frankly I'm surprised you all are handling it so well."

"Oh, we're getting a little help with that," Milo said, reaching into his jacket and pulling out the medallion that dangled below his neck. "Here, try it on. It helps us adapt to harsh conditions."

"No kidding?" asked the pilot, taking the disc and pressing it to his skin. "Hey, you're right! I feel something already!"

"Keep it for a while," Milo said, leaning against the wall of tree roots that stood behind him. "I'll be warm enough once I get a little hot food inside me. Provided Antonin ever finishes cooking it!"

"Aw, pipe down," the smuggler said, poking the little tins with a stick. "It's too cold in here for them to cook very quickly."

An hour later they settled down to sleep. Gromyko shut off the small stove, leaving them in total darkness. The wind beat against the edges of the den, sometimes whistling when it caught a branch at just the right angle. But in the main it provided a background of white noise that most of them found irresistible. Soon quiet snoring filled the tight space.

Hunt was not among them. Laying awake, his back pressed against a bundle of roots, he had his arm around Tselitel. It was comforting to feel her shoulders rise and fall slightly with her breath. She was still good medicine for him, the mere operation of her bodily processes giving him a stabilizing center. Her breathing, her heartbeat, the subtle working of a thousand unconscious impulses that made her who she was – these he had never ceased to crave. They satisfied him deep inside, stroking some indefinable hunger that had always haunted him until he'd known her. It was this, in addition to his love, that drove him to look after her and protect her at all times. If anything should ever happen to her…

"What are you thinking about?" she whispered in the darkness, her mouth against his ear, her very closeness making him shudder.

"How did you even know I was awake?" he whispered back, kissing her temple and drawing her close. "More psychic powers?"

"I wish I could say yes," she chuckled. "But no, the answer is more prosaic than that. I can never hear you breathing when you're awake. You keep such tight control over it that it's inaudible. You only relax enough to be heard when you're asleep. I couldn't hear you breathing, hence you must be lying awake, brooding over some problem."

"Actually, I was thinking about you," he replied.

"Oh, really?" she asked. "I thought you might have gotten used to me by now. We haven't been out of each other's sight in weeks."

"Never," he said adamantly, the point surprisingly important to him. "Nobody could ever get used to you."

"Many have, believe me," she said quietly.

"Now who's running herself down?" he chided gently. "You're always on me when I do that."

"I don't know, maybe it's just the situation we're in. Delta-13 is crumbling beneath us. It can't hold out much longer against the Devourers. And the best plan we've got to deal with them will take us to a world we've never seen before. Frankly, I'm not really sure *anyone* has ever seen it before. I mean, there have probably been archeological digs there and whatnot. But I don't think the empire ever really took an interest in Epsilon-4 from a colonial standpoint. We're gonna be pretty much alone there. If something goes wrong…" her voice trailed.

"We'll handle whatever comes along," Hunt assured her. "You forget, we Deltans are a tough lot. The brothers

Hunt, plus Antonin, will see you through."

"What about Bradford?" she asked, nodding invisibly toward his snoring, unconscious form.

"I have no idea. None of us can fly, so we'll need him, or someone like him, before long. But who knows what the pirates have planned for us once we reach their base. They might help us. Or," he finished darkly, "they might need a little persuasion."

"You'd take on the entire pirate base?" she asked with surprise.

"I'll do whatever I have to do to end this threat," he said determinedly. "I'll break every pirate in Omicron if I have to."

"Yes, I believe you would," she said thoughtfully. Drawing his arm around her neck, she raised the cuff of his glove and kissed his wrist.

"What's that for?" he asked with a smile.

"Just showing a little appreciation. I'm glad you're you," she explained, holding his hand firmly with hers. "You know, you really remind me of your father."

"That's a good way to kill a nice moment," he said flatly, surprised at how totally his mood dropped at the mention of him.

"Oh, I don't mean anything bad," she explained quickly. "But he was so utterly ruthless in his pursuit of what he thought was right. Absolutely nothing could be permitted to get in his way. Even his own conscience. He had become the total servant of what reason had informed him was the ideal course. Whatever personal feelings he might have had about his actions were left behind long ago. I could feel that when he grabbed and began to, well, I don't know what you'd call it. Overwhelm me? I could sense his pain and his anger. But more than that, I felt his complete dedication to the path he had chosen. Every question had been blotted from his logical mind long ago."

"Some path," remarked Hunt. "Dominate the minds of

all mankind? Shore up the emperor's faltering regime?"

"That's not why he did it," she whispered earnestly. "Isn't it obvious? He was trying to prepare mankind for the Devourers. He was attempting to forge us into a weapon that might stand a chance against their onslaught. Hard though it is to believe, he was acting with humanitarian disinterest. He must have known that his course was wrong – no, I'm *certain* that he knew that. But the collective interest of billions outweighed whatever personal guilt he might incur. I could feel that in those few moments that he held me. He had given up on himself as a moral actor, and saw himself as the soulless tool of humanity's salvation. He'd ceased to possess human dignity in his own eyes. That alone is proof of a very active conscience, though one that had been suppressed out of every conscious calculation. It existed only in his unconscious mind, and from there it made his life miserable until he hated himself for what he felt he had to do."

"So in a sense Ugo was right," Wellesley chimed in quietly from the other side of the den. Silently rising from his place, Hunt snatched him from beside his brother and brought him back to Tselitel. "He *was* something of a hero, though a dark one to be sure. Faced with the choices of death or slavery for mankind, he chose the latter, though it destroyed him to do it. No wonder he was such a bitter, vicious man: he took his self-loathing out on everyone around him."

"I can't believe this," Hunt said incredulously. "Are you defending him? You know how he assaulted Lily! And who can excuse what he would have done to mankind?"

"You know what he did after those unfortunate incidents in his youth," Wellesley countered. "After he drove those people mad, he learned medicine and dedicated himself to helping mankind however he could. He was a humanitarian in the truest sense. Not some limp-wristed well-wisher of peace and goodwill, but a man willing to get his hands dirty. Aware that his race was under threat of death, he did the only thing he could to save it. You did the same thing when you killed him – you eliminated a threat to the one you loved. And I did the same thing when I betrayed the *Kol-Prockian* revolutionaries in order to spare my people further bloodshed. Life is not made up of simplistic moral choices, Rex. We each form a judgment about how to best serve the most deserving, and then we serve them. Your father felt that life was more precious than freedom, and he served it – just as I did. And now you are making the same choice, that of life over every other consideration. That is why you would level Omicron base if necessary to reach Epsilon-4. You, your father, and I are each cut from the same cloth. In the end, we stand for life over death."

"I'd say we make a pretty dark trio," Hunt said grimly.

"Not all heroes are immaculate," Wellesley replied. "Someone has to jump into the pile of muck and draw forth a diamond, once in a while."

"That's an interesting metaphor," Tselitel laughed, unable to help herself despite the low mood of the discussion.

"Oh, I'm full of sayings like that," the AI replied, glad to let a little pressure out of the air. "Rex, I'm not equating your father's actions to yours or mine. I'm just saying that the principle is the same. That's all Lily was aiming at, anyhow. I just couldn't help sticking my big mouth into it. I'll be quiet now."

"That's something you'll never be able to do," chuckled Hunt, knowing the ancient AI all too well.

"No, you're right," agreed Wellesley. "But I'll keep quiet for a while. Chuck me back over by your brother, and you two lovebirds can coo to each other in peace."

"Ah," Hunt said in mock annoyance, tossing the medallion and its attached speaker back into the darkness where Milo lay snoring.

"You'd be hard pressed to find another friend like that," Tselitel said, once Hunt had settled in beside her again.

"I know," agreed Hunt. Then, after a moment of thought, "I can't believe I'm saying this, but you're right: dad and I really are cut from the same cloth. I guess I hated what he did so much that I couldn't see that."

"Sometimes the good we strive for blinds us to the facts," she opined. "That's when we need our friends to give us some perspective."

"I guess so," he replied, not really listening as a new thought absorbed him. "Could he have been right?"

"About what?"

"About knitting together mankind into one solid fighting block? Was that the only way to fight the Devourers?"

"Apparently not, given that Epsilon-4 has a plan of its own," she replied.

"*Had* a plan of its own," he corrected her. "Those messages it sent to Delta-13 were from eons ago. Who can say if it's even viable anymore. And whatever it is, Delta sure isn't hot for it."

"I guess we won't know until we get there and talk to it," she said, resting her head against his shoulder and sighing. "Right now it all seems so far away, like something out of a dream. I'd almost think it *was* a dream, and that we've all been running around in a fantasy for the last few weeks, if Bradford wasn't lying over there to falsify that idea at once."

"He seems like a good guy," Hunt commented. "In fact he's outstanding, especially for a pirate. I would have figured him for some bright, up-and-coming navy pilot if I didn't know better."

"He's surprisingly unspoiled, that's for sure," she agreed. "It's like the taint of the organization never rubbed off on him. But he's young. Maybe that will come with time."

"What a cynical idea, coming from you!" he said with quiet energy. "You'd better quit hanging around with low characters like me if you want to keep your sprightly sense of optimism intact."

"I couldn't," she said, leaning back and looking into where she knew his eyes to be. "It would be the death of me.

❖ ❖ ❖

"With a handful of exceptions, our forces are being hammered by Devourer craft along the southern edge of the fringe," Admiral Haslebach reported to Minister McGannon via hologram. "Half a dozen worlds have taken advantage of the situation to declare independence from the empire."

"You must crush them immediately, no matter the cost," McGannon said instantly. "If the rebellion is allowed to fester we'll lose half the fringe planets in weeks."

"Minister, I don't have the forces to battle the Devourers and the–."

"That is why you'll prioritize the subjugation of the worlds in mutiny," she snapped. "Our first consideration is holding together the empire. If it crumbles around us we won't have the means to fight the invaders. Maintaining *discipline* is crucial, Admiral."

"Yes, Minister," he said quietly.

"Report back the moment you have more news. Dismissed."

The admiral sharply saluted and disappeared from view.

Rubbing her tired eyes, McGannon leaned back in her chair, wondering for the thousandth time that day what she was going to do. All across the empire seditious fault lines had erupted into massive divisions the instant the invaders appeared. Many fringe worlds were agitating for independence, heedless of the consequences to themselves and to humanity at large. Failing to recognize that the Devourers were at war with *humanity*, and not merely with the empire, they couldn't grasp the fatal danger of their situation.

"Got to keep them in line," she muttered, pumping her fists and trying to think of a way to impress upon the population the need for unity. "If only Lavery had succeeded."

At that moment she was interrupted by a call from the emperor.

"Yes, my emperor," she said, rising from her seat and bowing low.

"What is our status, Admiral?" he asked.

"Our forces are preparing to counter attack as we speak, Your Highness," she said deferentially. She'd given him the same answer the last time he'd checked in, just over an hour before.

"Good, good," he replied in a distracted tone, his attention wandering. "Tell me, what is the status of the Omega Project?"

"The Omega Project is proceeding as planned, Your Highness," she replied, her cheeks flushing with blood at the mere mention of it. No secret was so tightly guarded in the entire empire as Omega. To speak of it was very nearly an act of treason. It was dangerous in the extreme to discuss it in anything but face-to-face communication, given the prevalence of spies in the government. But there was no way to tell the emperor that.

"Excellent. We need only hang on until Omega is active to stop the invaders in their tracks. Keep me informed, Admiral."

"Yes, Your Highness," she said, bowing again until his hologram disappeared. "Omega," she thought, shaking her head. "How did we ever conceive of something like Omega?"

She knew the project would be either the empire's greatest triumph, or an expensive tombstone that would be placed over its grave. Powerful beyond words, it would either give them the ultimate asset to keep the wavering worlds of the fringe in line and beat back the invaders, or be nothing but a colossal failure, diverting countless resources which could have gone toward bolstering the navy. Possessing no faith in wonder weapons of any kind, McGannon had done all she could to stop the project from ever getting off the ground. But it had caught the imagination of the emperor in a powerful way, and whenever that happened opposition was useless. And dangerous.

She walked to a nearby window and looked out at the night. The glittering skyline of humanity's capital planet presented itself. Millions were going about their business, still unaware of the massive threat that hung over mankind like a dagger. All the news services in the inner worlds were strictly controlled by the imperial government, and they had orders to suppress even indirect indications of the Devourers' presence. Luckily for McGannon, and the other ministerial heads, the invaders hadn't chosen to attack Earth. Yet.

Her mind turned to the emperor, far away at his imperial retreat in the Bohlen system. Heavily fortified, she knew he would be as safe there as he would have been on Earth. Moreso, in fact, since there was nothing to give away the importance of the world save the large garrison. Little more than a village had been built on the otherwise deserted world of Bohlen-7, the emperor preferring to keep the planet's sense of primitive mystery intact. Despite his condition he found peace in the forest that stood near his homely accommodations, and in recent years he'd come to spend almost all his time there. This left most of the daily matters of the government in the hands of his ministers. They preferred this state of affairs, freeing them as it did from the wild whims of an erratic, decaying head of state. Many of them feared that he would assert direct control of the government when news of the Devourers broke upon them, seized by the romantic image of an emperor riding into battle at the head of his legions. But to their surprise he had done no such thing. He was peculiarly passive, as though the invasion had been told to him in a dream. It was terribly important to him, as his constant nagging of McGannon had proven. But the energy to run the war out of his own head had long since left him, the disease having done far too much damage. Ten years earlier, perhaps even five, he would have behaved exactly as his ministers had anticipated. But he was seemingly just a hollow, fretting shell of his former self; a shell that lacked the capacity to act beyond pestering his cabinet.

McGannon sighed in regret of this fact. Sprung from a strongly imperial family, she had always savored the thought of ending her days in glorious fashion in the service of her emperor, whoever he happened to be. Many of her set had cheered the day that Rhemus had ascended the throne in the place of his father Septimus, regarding him as an energetic man who would return vitality to the previously doddering government. But their cheering was soon silenced. Impulsive and emotional in his thinking, he caused as much harm as he did good to the empire during his first decade. Twice he nearly drove the fringe into rebellion through his arrogant high-handedness. But gradually he matured in office, and came to be seen as a flawed, yet more or less effective, ruler by the loyalists of the empire.

That is, until his disease made itself unavoidably manifest in his forty-sixth year. Suffering from fits of rage that alternated with melancholy, it was impossible to tell even an hour in advance how he would behave. Thus his inner circle sought to keep him out of the public eye as much as possible. Sensing a plot to stymie his power within his own empire, he rejected their advice, and even had several of them assassinated out of fear that they were hatching plots. Painfully aware of his slackening grip on reality, he came to spend entire days within his bedchamber. It was at this time that the mystic Taegen appeared. It was on his advice that the emperor sought peace on Bohlen-7 and, to the surprise of all, actually found it. Something about the world eased the symptoms of his condition, allowing him to regain a measure of his former capacity. For this reason Taegen quickly became the ruler's most important confidant and advisor. He gained a powerful, indeed, many felt *decisive*, hold over the emperor, and soon came to direct many of the affairs of the empire.

"And that's why you had to go, Taegen," McGannon thought, pouring herself a drink and downing it slowly. "No one should have the kind of influence you had, no matter the condition of the emperor."

◆ ◆ ◆

"Time to get up, guys," Gromyko said, kneeling beside the flickering camp stove and looking at his comrades in the dull light of dawn. The storm outside screened out much of the morning glow. But enough filtered in through the clouds to permit him to see, even in the abandoned den.

"Antonin, we've been asleep for *six hours!*" exclaimed Milo in a half-awake voice. "Can't you ever leave well enough alone? I think you can't bear to see people resting comfortably if you're not!"

"That's nonsense," replied the smuggler. "I just think we ought to be ready in case that ship gets here early. You can never tell in a situation like this. We might have to–."

Suddenly his words were interrupted by a low growl just outside their shelter.

Bradford sat bolt upright, drawing his pistol from the holster on his hip and cocking it.

"Get away from the entrance," he said, gesturing for Gromyko to leave the stove and move to the back of the small space. "I think the bear has come back to its roost."

At just that moment the creature stuck half its massive body into the enclosure and roared, the sound deafening them in the tight space. Bradford fired two shots at it, but the small caliber rounds only served to anger it. Taking a swipe at the pilot, he raked his claws down his leg, ripping his calf open in one motion. Bradford screamed and dropped the pistol, scampering on his back away from the beast in sheer terror. The bear was about to follow up when a dark cloud of terror flew from Rex's left hand and entered its enormous head, causing it to stumble backward in confusion.

In an instant Gromyko dove for the pistol and pumped the remaining rounds into the bear's exposed side. Dazed by the attack from Hunt, the searing wounds caused it to retreat out of the den and bolt into the forest.

"What *are* you?" Bradford asked Hunt, his eyes wide as the latter crossed the den and knelt to examine his wound. Reflexively the pilot tried to crawl away, unsure what other dark arts he might have up his sleeve. "Are you some kind of magician or something?"

"That's a long story," Hunt said matter-of-factly. "Right now I'm just trying to look at your leg. So quit talking and hold it still."

"Don't see what you can do with it," Bradford said, watching the blood gush from his torn flesh. "Not like we've got a hospital around here."

Despite his pessimism Hunt managed to dress the wound adequately.

"Don't move that thing even an inch," Hunt ordered sternly. "It'll open up again if you so much as look at it."

"I'll try," Bradford said with a grunt, the pain difficult to bear. "Now, perhaps you'd like to tell me what that business with the smoke was all about. I've heard some funny things since coming to Delta-13. But I've never seen something like that before."

"Then you're not native to the planet?" asked Tselitel.

"No, I came here five years ago," replied the pilot, fixing his eyes on Hunt. "What's the story?"

"Some people have gifts. Some of them are positive, like the ability to heal or to gain insight into the nature of others. Some are even psychics who are able to plunge deeply into the minds of those they choose."

"And what's your ability?" asked Bradford, leaning back gingerly so as not to upset his bandages.

"Fear," replied Hunt seriously. "I can inspire fear in anyone I choose."

"Seems to work on animals, too," the pilot observed, nodding toward the entrance.

"It goes back and forth with animals," said Hunt. "Sometimes it confuses them. Other times it enrages them. There's no telling what it will do beforehand."

"And what about the rest of you?" Bradford asked with a grimace. "Can you all do stuff like that, too?"

"Lily can help people sort out their minds," Milo said. "But the rest of us are just ordinary folks." He paused and thought for a moment. "At least, so far. Lily was past forty before she knew she even had a gift. Maybe the same is true of us."

"I think Wanda or Ugo would have noticed if you guys possessed one," Tselitel said, instantly regretting her reference to Wanda when she saw Gromyko's face fall.

"Who are Wanda and Ugo?" asked Bradford.

"Just old memories," the smuggler said, moving to the exit. "I'd better check to make sure that bear isn't still in the area. You got an extra clip for this thing?" he asked, raising the pistol.

"Here," Bradford said, pulling one out of his pocket and tossing it to him. "Aim for the eyes if you see it again. It's probably your only chance with bullets that small."

Gromyko nodded and disappeared into the storm.

"I take it he's not a fan of those two people?" asked the pilot.

"That's a private matter, for Antonin to discuss if he wishes to," replied Hunt.

"Look, I'm not trying to pry. I'm just trying to get my mind off *this*," Bradford said, pointing at his leg. "I'll gladly talk about rainbows if you want."

"Well, maybe you can tell us a little more about yourself," Tselitel said, as Milo took over cooking duties at the little stove. "You said you came here five years ago?"

"That's right. I was on a transport headed for the Quarlac galaxy when the Black Fang folks intervened."

"Intervened?" asked Tselitel.

"That's right. You see, Quarlac isn't too hospitable to humans, and it's hard to get anyone to go out there willingly. So the empire scooped up me and a bunch of others and planned to send us out there whether we wanted to go or not. You might say I'd lived a rough-and-tumble life, even at that early age. The government was glad to get rid of me, especially if they could turn my elimination to their own advantage."

"But you were just a teenager!" exclaimed the doctor.

"Heh, they don't care," Bradford said. "Just so long as you're healthy and you can survive the rigors of the environment for a little while. We weren't meant to last very long, anyhow. Our purpose was to act as a settlement force. You know, hack down the weeds and get some housing set up for the *next* set that would come through. It seems the empire planned to settle Pirac-2 through sheer attrition, just sending more of us undesirables through until we'd whipped it into some kind of shape through our blood and sweat."

"Pirac-2?" asked Wellesley. "That's one of the worst planets currently under human control. What madman would try to settle it? It's nothing but an animal infested, disease ridden nightmare. You'd be better off fire bombing it, if there weren't rich deposits of kantium there."

"So you can see why I didn't want to go," said the pilot.

"But you say the pirates intervened?" prodded Tselitel. "That sounds a little, I don't know, *charitable* for them?"

"It is, for the organization as a whole. But not for

Colonel Pinchon. It was his idea to hijack the ship and resettle the passengers on another world, far from the empire's influence. He really cares about the people out here on the fringe. From what I understand he's gotten in trouble with his superiors more than once for his actions. All I can say is I'm sure glad he stepped in when my ship was flying by this ice cube, because otherwise I'd be dead by now. No one lasts five years on Pirac-2."

"Food is ready," Milo interrupted, serving each of them a hot little tin with his gloved hands.

"You said Pinchon resettled the other passengers," Hunt began, carefully eating his boiling hot breakfast. "Why didn't you go with them?"

"Well, after the Colonel saved my neck the way he did, I figured I owed him. I asked if I could join the Black Fangs and pay back what he did for me. Would you believe it, he tried to talk me out of it! You'd think he'd try to grow the organization, not turn away willing recruits! But when he saw that I was adamant he let me join. He looked after me for those first few years, till I got my feet under me. He pushed me to become a pilot, and even trained me a little himself when he found the time. But mostly I was in the hands of his second in command, Major Dietrich."

"The Colonel sounds like an interesting man," Tselitel mused. "Do you think we'll be able to meet him?"

"Most likely," nodded Bradford. "For all its importance, our base isn't that big, so you can hardly help running into him if you spend any time there. Besides, I'm sure he'll want to meet all of you, after what we've been through together."

"No sign of that bear," Gromyko said, surprising them by suddenly popping into the enclosure. His mood had evened out to all appearances, but he looked distracted by something. "There's blood in the snow leading away from here. I followed it for a while to make sure it was a long way off. Never did see it again."

"After what he did," Bradford said, gesturing toward Hunt, "I can't imagine it will stop running for quite a while. Might even ramble along until it freezes to death, what, with the weather like it is."

"Wouldn't hurt my feelings if it did," Milo chimed in, killing the stove's little flame so it could cool before he packed it away. "Something that big sticks its head in my life, all I want to do is make sure it never comes back!"

Hours later they were sitting quietly inside the den when a weak voice came crackling over the radio.

"Black Fang vessel TR-12, calling Lieutenant Bradford, please come in, over."

"TR-12, this is Bradford. Boy, am I glad to hear your voice! Over."

"Lieutenant Bradford, this is TR-12, please acknowledge, over."

Bradford replied twice more, but received no response.

"He can't hear my signal!" the lieutenant said to his companions anxiously.

"Here, give it to me," Gromyko said, taking the radio. "Probably just need a little better place to try from." With this the smuggler disappeared into the open air once more.

"Time to pack up," Hunt said. "Looks like our ride is nearly here."

A few minutes later Gromyko returned.

"TR-12 will meet us down in the canyon," he said, climbing into the tight space and slipping his backpack over his arm. "The crosswinds are strong up here near the trees. And besides, visibility will be better." With this the smuggler slipped back out.

"Alright, let's get a move on," Hunt said.

"I suspect you'll want this back," Bradford said to Milo, pulling up the medallion by the chain around his neck.

"Nah, keep it for now. You're in worse shape than me. Besides, those things are supposed to deaden pain a little, too."

"In that case, I think I'll keep it forever!" Bradford laughed, his leg still throbbing with pain. "Thank you."

"Don't mention it," Milo said, helping the pilot to his feet and getting him out into the open.

"Once more unto the breach, as they say?" Tselitel smiled quietly to Hunt.

"Absolutely," he replied in a businesslike tone, his mind too serious for sentiment as he pointed for her to leave ahead of him.

Slowly the group retraced its steps and made its way back down into the canyon.

"I hope that pilot is right on the money," Milo said as they reached the canyon floor. "With all this rock around us, we'd be lucky to raise him with that little radio if he was anything less than right on top of us."

"I gave him precise instructions," Gromyko said. "He'll meet us where he's supposed to."

"And where is that?" asked Bradford.

"Right over there," Gromyko said, pointing to a large boulder that stood alone. "He's going to hit the canyon a little south of here and then sweep north until he sees that rock. There's no chance he'll miss us."

"Good, 'cause I don't want to spend a second longer out here than I have to!" said the pilot, ambling along with the help of the younger Hunt.

"A little help, brother?" Milo asked Rex as he shuffled through the snow and wind with the pirate's arm over his shoulders. Twice he'd nearly lost his footing, and he didn't want to risk tearing the pilot's wound open by letting him slip and fall. With an air of distraction on his serious face, Rex got under Bradford's other arm and took his share of the load. Taller and stronger than his brother, Hunt bore the pirate's weight with relative ease.

"Careful, now," Tselitel cautioned, as they helped him down the shallow slope into the canyon, hovering behind them to offer any help she could. In her mind's eye she could see them tumbling down the slope and breaking their necks. It wasn't until they'd finally gained the bottom that she relaxed and walked alongside them once more.

Reaching the boulder, they settled down behind it to get out of the wind. While most of the storm's fury swept latitudinally across the high walls of the canyon, occasional gusts would blow up from the south and steal their warmth. Periodically Gromyko would step away from the rock and pull the corner of his stocking cap away from his ear, straining to hear the slightest sound of engines rumbling in the distance. The third time he did this he nodded to himself and quickly returned to the group.

"He's almost here," the smuggler said. "Stand up and start waving your arms. We don't want to risk him missing us."

"I thought you said there was no chance of that?" Milo replied, helping Bradford to his feet once more.

"Never hurts to make sure," Gromyko said, stepping back to his former listening position and slowly waving his arms over his head.

"I don't see it," Tselitel said with concern to Hunt, as the sound grew louder. "What if he misses us?"

"Give it a minute," he replied.

Moments later the craft emerged from the veil of falling snow that had hidden it. Flying over their heads, it circled around and landed on the other side of the rock. It was the same model of transport as the one they'd lost. The pilot landed facing them, and they could see him energetically waving through the canopy for them to hustle. The rear hatch was already open when they reached it, and they all clambered quickly inside.

"Get yourselves strapped in quickly," he ordered over his shoulder from the cockpit. "We need to get out of here before the aliens notice us."

"Any in the area, Gus?" Bradford shouted over the howling of the wind, just before the hatch was shut.

"Nothing real close by," he replied. "But you can never tell what might be hovering in orbit. I won't feel safe until we're back in range of our fighters."

"You and me both," Bradford replied with feeling.

The instant they were all strapped in the craft lifted off the ground and sped along the ground to the north-east.

"Too bad the canyon doesn't run north for a ways," Gus said. "I wouldn't mind putting a little something between myself and their scanners. Might help keep them out of our hair."

"I wouldn't bet on that," replied Milo.

Tselitel sat shivering next to Hunt, her arms wrapped tightly around her chest.

"No offense, Doctor, but I take it you haven't been on Delta-13 for very long?" Bradford asked.

"No," she smiled. "I've only been here a number of weeks. I'm afraid I was never built for the cold. No body fat."

"I noticed," replied Bradford with an appreciative grin; one that he instantly dropped the moment his eyes met Hunt's smoldering orbs. Clearing his throat and shifting in his place, he suddenly became fascinated by the rivets that held the floor of the hull together.

"Tell me, how long will this flight be?" Gromyko called ahead to the pilot.

"It'll be a while, at least sixteen hours. I have to make another stop before we can head home. A civilian tradeship called the *Sabrina* put down part way between here and Omicron, but way down to the south. Most of the crew are dead. But a handful managed to survive until the Devourers lost interest and flew off. Once we've got them aboard we'll make a beeline for home."

Flying just above the forest to minimize its radar signature, the craft was occasionally pressed downward by a strong gust, causing it to snap the tops off several trees. The harsh crack of shattering wood reverberated loudly within the all-metal ship, causing the occupants to jump whenever it happened.

"Sorry about that!" Gus said from the front after a particularly large one exploded against the hull. "But don't you worry! This old girl is tough. She's got a lot of good years left in her."

"Not as many as she did this morning," Milo muttered, making Tselitel chuckle.

It was long after nightfall that they reached the wreckage of the trader. Landing just short of it, the pilot cut the engines.

"I should just be a minute," he said, throwing a coat over his flight suit and drawing its hood up over his head. "The survivors must have seen us land."

"I hope they kept warm," Tselitel said with concern as Gus popped the rear hatch and stepped out. Through it she could see the pulverized remains of the *Sabrina* lying in the snow. A blast of wind shot into the transport, forcing most of its heat out in seconds.

"We'll help the pilot," Hunt said, squeezing her arm and gesturing for Milo and Gromyko to follow. "Just stay warm."

"I'll keep an eye on Bradford," she nodded, looking back at the emaciated pilot. The journey had proven hard for him, and he looked in terrible shape.

"Yeah, I guess you'd better," Hunt said reluctantly, still annoyed that he'd made eyes at her earlier. Releasing her arm and pulling up his hood, he stepped into the blustery darkness.

With lights they'd gotten from the ship they spread out around the *Sabrina* searching for survivors. Hard, icy flakes flew into Hunt's eyes as he swept the light to and fro, careful not to miss anyone. Reaching the other side he encountered his brother and the smuggler, who had worked their way around from the opposite direction.

"Nobody!" shouted Gromyko over the wind. "Not even any bodies!"

"They must have buried them in the snow!" replied Milo.

Just then a light fell upon the three of them. Turning, they saw the pilot gesticulating.

"What is it?" Hunt asked as they approached.

"Look," Gus yelled, tracing a barely visible path of footprints in the snow. "They must have headed off into the woods!"

"Idiots! They should have stayed with the ship!" said Gromyko.

"Maybe they couldn't," offered Milo. "Maybe something chased them away."

"Like what?" asked the smuggler. "I don't see any tracks."

"I do," said Hunt grimly, shining his light near a small group of trees that had broken the wind and preserved the trail. Striding slowly toward it, he knelt near a succession of long, tube-like impressions that had been left in the snow. "You can forget about the crew."

"What for?" asked Gus, shining his light at the tracks. "What kind of critter leaves a trail like that?"

"*Karrakpoi*," Hunt said, straightening up and shining his light to ensure none were in the area.

"Giant spiders," Gromyko explained to the puzzled pilot, as Hunt walked past him. "Believe me, my friend, they have long since perished. They never had a chance."

Quickly they returned to their ship. In moments it rumbled off the ground and disappeared into the darkness.

CHAPTER 3

"Get him to the medical bay immediately!" ordered Colonel Pinchon upon seeing the barely conscious Bradford in the transport. Gus had radioed ahead shortly before their arrival, and emergency medical staff were on hand the moment they landed. The group watched as the lieutenant was taken away on a stretcher. "Thank you for getting him back in one piece. But for the life of me I can't imagine how he could have been attacked by a bear!"

"It's a long story, Colonel," Hunt said wearily. "Could we talk about it inside?"

"Yes, of course," he nodded, showing the group the way from the landing pad to his nearby headquarters.

"This is a nice place," Gromyko said with approval, as he and the rest were shown to chairs inside the colonel's office. "I wish we could have afforded such surroundings in the Underground. But on the frontlines of the action it was best to keep things bare and minimal."

"Naturally," Pinchon said, taking a seat on the corner of his desk and looking the group over. "I know Gromyko, and I've heard of Doctor Tselitel. But who are you two?"

"Rex and Milo Hunt; brothers," Hunt said.

"Uh huh. And what took you folks so far away from Midway that you happened to survive the onslaught? I imagine you know by now that everyone in town is long since dead?"

"Yes, unfortunately," replied Tselitel. "Although I have hope that a few survived. We have friends–, well, I guess you couldn't call them *friends*…"

"Some past associates of ours were staying outside the confines of the city," Hunt explained. "They were members of the Order. Ugo and Wanda Udris, along with some others."

"I haven't heard anything about any survivors," Pinchon said, shaking his head. "But it could be they're just holed up for the time being, waiting for things to clear up."

"Things aren't *going* to clear up," Milo said. "Not unless we drive the Devourers off Delta-13."

"I agree," Pinchon said, reaching for a cigar box. Taking one for himself, he held it open toward the group, but only Gromyko accepted. "These fellows seem intent on making themselves at home," the colonel continued, lighting his cigar and then the smuggler's. "Right now their fleet is hanging around near Midway. But I expect they'll fan out before long and crush all human forces in the system. For that reason we've been gathering the survivors here and shipping them out on transports as quickly as possible. But I'm certain they'll strike Omicron before we've finished."

"What are your plans in that eventuality?" asked Gromyko.

"Get out of here, just as fast as we can," replied Pinchon frankly. "We don't stand a chance with anything larger than their fighters. Against them we can hold our own just fine, which I imagine is why they've left us alone for the time being. They're just picking up the low hanging fruit right now, defenseless traders and whatnot."

"Like the *Sabrina*," Hunt said.

"Exactly. Speaking of her, what's this business with *karro–, karra–*."

"*Karrakpoi*?" Tselitel offered.

"Yes, thank you, Doctor," he said with a smile. "*Karrakpoi*? What are they? Where'd they come from?"

"I think I can explain that a little more fully than

the others can," Wellesley said in his monotone from Hunt's pocket.

"Excuse me?" Pinchon said, startled by the bodiless voice.

"Here," Hunt said with a grin, holding up the medallion with the speaker attached. "He's an alien military AI named *Allokanah*. I just call him Wellesley. He's our resident knower of all things ancient and alien."

"He's alien, you say?" asked Pinchon, rising from his desk and taking a closer look at the disc that Hunt held.

"*Kol-Prockian*, to be specific," Wellesley said. "My people were the last alien race before man to settle Delta-13."

"You mean there have been others?" asked the colonel, taking a step back and sitting on his desk as before.

'Oh, yes. Many, in fact. There's something about Delta-13 that attracts space faring races to it, like a magnet drawing little particles of metal off the floor. Yet none of them ever seems to hold onto it. It's a hard mistress to please, it seems."

"Apparently so," replied Pinchon. "But you were going to tell me about the *karrakpoi*?"

"Yes, of course. The *karrakpoi* are a race of large spiders that live off the life energy of the planet. Delta-13 is a sentient being, you see, like many other worlds in our galaxy. The *karrakpoi* find themselves caves and cracks in the surface of the planet, as deep as they can, and draw energy from it. The ancient priests of my people used to exterminate them for the benefit of the planet, for they revered it above all other worlds. I recently learned that the *karrakpoi* are not native to Delta-13, but are in fact an invasive species. It appears that the Devourers brought them with them a long time ago and left some behind shortly before their banishment one hundred thousand years ago. Through the work of the ancient priests of *Delek-Hai*, the foul race was nearly exterminated. Unfortunately the Devourers brought even more with them upon their return. I fear the infestation will soon be worse than ever, rendering whole sections of the planet inhospitable."

"Only until the planet succumbs," Hunt said to the AI. "Then there won't be anything to support them."

"Yes, that's true," agreed Wellesley.

"And these spiders killed the crew of the *Sabrina*?" asked Pinchon.

"Yes, there's no doubt about that," replied Hunt. "The crew bolted into the forest, followed by the *karrakpoi*. We left immediately after we saw their tracks, or they would have found us and done us in."

"Poor people," Pinchon said, shaking his head. "These Devourers – what do they want?"

"Revenge on the confederation that banished them," Wellesley said. "Hundreds of worlds, sentient like Delta-13, banded together eons ago. Using their immense psychic powers, they somehow managed to tear a hole in our dimension, bridging the gap to another one. Into this latter realm they exiled the Devourers to stop their consumption of the Milky Way. But something went wrong. Somehow they managed to return, and now they're bent on retribution."

"Against the worlds that banished them?"

"Yes, that's right. That's why their fleet is hovering over Midway as we speak: they're draining Delta-13 of every last drop of life energy it has. It won't be long before their work is complete, and the planet's long life comes to an end. Once they've accomplished that, it's anyone's guess where they'll strike next. But it'll probably be against the other life forms in the system, as you said. The Devourers are parasites – they'll need someone else to feed off of once the planet is dead."

"I guess humans fit that bill as well as anyone," Pinchon said. "They'd probably head for the highest concentrations, worlds where billions of people live. A place like Delta-13 wouldn't hold much appeal for them in that regard."

"I shouldn't think so," agreed the AI. "You don't pass up a juicy steak for a piece of lettuce."

"So these creatures are going to spread across the galaxy, finishing the work they began a hundred thousand years ago?" clarified the colonel.

"Apparently so," replied the AI. "I don't know how they intend to live after they've finished us off. They seem to consume with total abandon. Maybe they'll move on to another galaxy when they've finished with ours."

"A nice thought," Pinchon mused quietly, rolling his cigar back and forth between his fingers as he thought. "So, what can we do about them? I take it that these sentient planets can't help us anymore?"

"I really can't comment authoritatively on that," Wellesley said. "The old confederation that exiled them last time was shattered by the effort. But one of its member worlds, Epsilon-4, seems to have some kind of plan."

"Seems?"

"Yes, it tried to warn Delta-13 about the Devourers' return, and made reference to a plan that it had. But Delta didn't go for it. In fact, Delta tried to warn us off from going to Epsilon, claiming that the world was reckless and would bring all kinds of trouble onto our heads. It was rambling incoherently at times, clearly in agony because of what the Devourers are doing to it. I'd say the old girl's about had it."

"Sounds like it," replied Pinchon with cool self-possession, still rolling the cigar between his fingers as he thought. "What are the odds that the imperial navy can deal with the invaders?"

"Very slim, I should think," Wellesley replied. "Their vessels are unlike any that I've seen before."

"He was a major figure in a massive civil war fought by his people millennia ago," Tselitel inserted to boost the AI's authority.

"Really?" asked Pinchon, somewhat impressed.

"Yes. And judging by the ease with which they cut

through the imperial forces above Delta, and the follow-up fleet that the empire dispatched, I estimate that the navy has approximately a thirty percent chance of success. Naturally that figure is subject to all sorts of inaccuracies. I have to fill in a great many gaps in my knowledge with assumptions. The figure could reach as high as thirty-five percent, under ideal conditions. The computer that the *Kah-Delek-Hai* left behind made accurate scans of every class of imperial warship that has passed this planet since humanity first set foot here. Combining that data with what the computer has observed about the Devourers' vessels, and then cross-referencing that with information from across the empire about each local struggle with the invaders–."

"Leads to a fairly accurate picture," cut in Hunt.

"Yes, if I do say so myself."

"One in three," Pinchon said quietly. He slipped the cigar into his mouth and drew on it before speaking again. "It sounds like whatever Epsilon-4 has in mind is our best bet. Unless the empire has something up its sleeve that we can't account for."

"Like what?" asked Hunt.

"Oh, I don't know," he replied with a slight grin. "You hear rumors about secret weapons and whatnot."

"Don't think we can place any weight on that," replied Wellesley evenly. "We have to work with what we know."

"I agree," nodded Pinchon. "So I take it you're going to the Epsilon system?"

"That's the plan," replied Hunt. "But we'll need a transport and a pilot. None of us can fly."

"I can take care of that," the colonel said. "In fact, I'll fly you myself."

"What?" several of them asked at once, their voices skeptical.

"Aren't you needed here?" asked Tselitel diplomatically, suspecting, along with the others, that he was putting them on.

"Not any longer," he replied, shaking his head. "News has just come down from on high that I've been replaced. The Black Fangs don't feel too kindly about what I've been doing here since the Devourers arrived. They think I should be seizing this opportunity to pillage more than ever, now that the navy is reeling. I made it clear that I would do no such thing, so they put their foot down. My successor is warping this way as we speak. He'll be here sometime tomorrow."

"I'm sorry," Tselitel said, surprised to hear herself consoling a pirate.

"Everything has its season," he said philosophically. "I've had a good run here. Time to move on."

"When do we leave?" asked Hunt.

"Best time would be just a little while before he arrives," Pinchon said. "I'm not going to leave this base without a commander, and the people of this sector need as much help as I can give them. But there's no way he'll let us take a craft out of the sector once he and his escorts arrive. He'd sooner shoot me down."

"Sounds like you know him pretty well," commented Gromyko.

"Heh, I do," he said with a grim smile. "So, I must ask you all to be ready to go at, oh, 0800 hours. That'll give us enough time to warp out of here before he arrives."

"Sounds good," Hunt said, rising from his seat. "Where will we meet you?"

"At the landing pad," Pinchon said, standing himself. "Remember, 0800, on the dot."

"Quite an interesting character," Tselitel said quietly to Hunt once the group had left his office. "He's more complicated than I ever expected a pirate to be."

"Doesn't seem like a pirate at all, not if you ask me," Milo said, following up the rear.

"I've heard many stories about him," Gromyko said. "And they all tend to be to his credit, provided you overlook the piracy present in almost all of them. He's an honorable man making a living in a dirty way, if you can believe it."

"There's nothing I won't believe anymore," Tselitel laughed. "Not after all I've been through since coming here. My life was so simple before this ice cube intervened. Now I don't think it'll ever be simple again!"

"It keeps things interesting, that's for sure," Wellesley said. "So, what now?"

"I say we eat," Milo chimed in. "I'm tired of eating all my meals out of a can. This base has got to have at least a pretty decent place to eat. I mean, it's been here for decades."

"Let's go see," Hunt said, guiding the group toward a nearby building.

❖ ❖ ❖

Morning came much earlier than any of them wished. After so long in the cold, on the run, and under mortal threat, there was nothing they sought so completely as at least thirty hours of uninterrupted rest. Settling for five, they arose long before the appointed time for their departure and, with the colonel's permission, drew whatever equipment they needed for the journey from the base's supplies.

"Glad to see you all are punctual," Pinchon said when they arrived at the pad. Before them stood a modestly sized freighter.

"Is *that* our ride?" asked Milo, pointing at it and feeling the wind go out of his sails.

"Yes, that's our ride," confirmed the colonel. "She's called the *Stella*. We captured her a couple of years ago. She was just a gimpy little affair on her last legs when we got her. But we've patched her up in most every respect, added some armor and a few guns. It's hard to see from here, but we've mounted a remotely controlled turret on the top to fight off pursuers. Don't worry, she'll hold together. You can be assured of that."

At this moment Major Dietrich came rushing out of the headquarters building toward the pad.

"Egan's just arrived in the system!" he said urgently to the colonel. "He's early."

"No, he's on time," Pinchon ground out from between gritted teeth. "According to his own timetable, that is. He must have figured I'd pull something." He turned to the group. "You'd better get aboard and strap yourselves in, folks. It's gonna be a bumpy ride before we warp."

Heeding his instructions, the foursome scrambled into the craft and made for the cargo hold.

"Don't they ever make these things for transporting *people*?" complained Gromyko, distraught to see yet another set of bare benches and simple straps. "We're gonna be cripples before we get to Epsilon."

"We'll be dead, if we don't get off the ground in a hurry," Hunt said, taking a seat along with Tselitel and getting fastened in.

"Ready back there?" Pinchon called from the cockpit.

"Go for it!" replied Milo, just as he snapped the clasp on his belt.

"No, wait a moment!" said the smuggler, his belt half fastened when the craft lurched into the air, quickly leaving the base behind. He slid off the bench, landing on his back with a smack.

"Hang on back there!" the colonel yelled, hearing the clang of Gromyko's lean body against the metal floor. "It's gonna be rough. They're already near the planet."

"*Out of the frying pan, and—*," began the smuggler, his threadbare idiom interrupted when he was thrown to the side as Pinchon dodged an incoming burst of railgun shells from one of Egan's escorts.

"That's too close for comfort!" exclaimed Milo.

"Colonel, how do you control that remote turret?"

barked Hunt.

"The copilot seat!" Pinchon said, pointing energetically at the seat beside him. "Get up here!"

Hunt took off his belt and fought his way to the cockpit, grabbing whatever he could to steady himself as Pinchon's maneuvers tossed the craft every which way. Just as he laid hands on the copilot seat the craft jerked away from a stream of incoming fire, causing him to smack his head against the hull. Dazed, with blood running down his face, he dragged himself into the chair and strapped himself in.

"Button three on the display," Pinchon said, pointing to a computer screen embedded in Hunt's half of the dashboard. "The joystick controls the turret. Everything else is intuitive. Get on it!"

Hitting button three, he saw a pair of fighters closing rapidly on the freighter's rear. Squeezing the bright red trigger on the stick, a pair of cannons on either side of the camera cut loose with a hail of rounds that sent the unsuspecting strike craft spiraling off to either side.

"Didn't see that coming, did you?" Pinchon taunted. "Keep on 'em. We need to hold 'em off until we break out of the atmosphere."

Dropping below the freighter, the fighters cut loose with another burst of rounds, several of which ricocheted off the hull at shallow angles.

"No, you don't!" barked Pinchon, flipping the freighter over so that Hunt could get a shot at them. A lucky round caught one of the fighters in the wing, damaging a subsystem and causing him to pull back. "That's it, Hunt! Just get rid of his buddy and we're home free!"

The second fighter proved elusive, his flying much more skillful than his partner's. Biding his time, he circled around and around the pinwheeling freighter, just out of sight of the turret. For a brief moment the transport fell under its sights, and the fighter's weapons flashed. A handful of rounds crashed into the ship's belly, causing an alarm to blare and a half dozen red lights to flash on the dashboard.

"That doesn't sound good!" yelled Gromyko from the back.

"Doesn't matter," Pinchon said, as the ship broke away from the atmosphere. "Because we're gone!"

Suddenly a blue door of light appeared before the *Stella*. It took but a moment to cover the short distance to it and disappear inside.

"We're alright now," Pinchon said with relief, rising from his seat and heading into the back as the ship cruised down a tunnel of blue light. "We'll be in warp for quite a while."

"What was that alarm we heard?" Tselitel asked as she unstrapped herself.

"A number of subsystems were hit by that last burst," Pinchon replied, leaning against the hull and looking at her.

"Nothing important, I hope," she said, straightening up.

"No, nothing too important. I'll get them fixed before we reach the Epsilon system. For now you folks can relax," he said, as Hunt joined them.

"Darling! Are you alright?" Tselitel asked when she saw the blood running down his face.

"Yeah, I'm fine," he said, still a little dazed from the blow.

"Do you have any medical equipment aboard?" she asked the colonel.

"Of course. We've got everything we'll need for the journey. You'll find them in that container," he said, pointing to a metal box that was fastened to the wall.

Taking Hunt's hand, Tselitel led him to one of the benches and sat him down. Grabbing what she needed out of the box, she sat next to him and dabbed the blood away from the nasty, oozing gash.

"This may hurt," she said, wetting a cloth with antiseptic and applying it to his head.

Silently he grimaced, otherwise keeping the pain to himself.

"I'm sorry," she said, working as gingerly as she could. Bandaging his head when she'd finished, Hunt looked to be in much worse condition than he actually was.

"I don't really need this," Hunt said, fidgeting with the bandage.

"Just keep it on," ordered Tselitel, a little more sternly than Hunt was used to. "We don't want it to get infected. Besides, we need it to heal up before we reach Epsilon-4. Who knows what kinds of bacteria might be floating around there."

"Yes *ma'am*," he said with exaggerated deference that made her laugh. Twisting where he sat, he leaned his back against the hull and rested his throbbing head upon its cold surface. His eyes rolled over to Pinchon, who still stood just short of the cockpit, mutely watching the foursome. "Tell me something, Colonel: why in the world have you believed us? This has got to be some of the craziest stuff you've ever heard."

"I'll believe almost anything, given it's prefaced with a fleet of organic warships bursting into space above my planet from another dimension," he said, heading for one of the benches on the other side of the ship. Taking a seat, he drew a cigar out of his pocket and lit it. Resting one of his booted feet atop the bench, he took a pull on his smoke and continued. "When something like that happens, it's time to throw out your ideas of what is possible and what isn't. Besides, I've always suspected that there was more to that planet than met the eye. I only wonder why it took humanity this long to figure it out."

"The planets don't seem to make themselves known to their residents, not typically," replied Tselitel. "I think they're not supposed to. Delta-13 said it was breaking some kind of rule to talk to us like it was. I think the indirect path is the only one open to them, for some reason or other."

"That seems to be true, Doctor," Wellesley said. "There was no record in the computer of Delta-13 ever addressing either the priests or *Selek-Pey* in that fashion. They always had to meditate and wait for dreams and inspiration. Their communications were more like some kind of mystic ritual than anything approaching the dialogue we had."

"Speaking of that little chat we had," Milo said. "What was that *Een–, Een-Wey–*."

"*Ahn-Wey*," Wellesley corrected.

"Yeah, what is that?"

"According to the computer, it's another term for the Union of Light. I'm not sure what tongue it's from, though. It's unfamiliar to me."

"What, the great Wellesley doesn't know everything?" teased Tselitel with mock amazement.

"Yes, surprising though it may seem, I'm not omniscient. Epsilon-4 might know the answer, though."

"Speaking of that," Milo said. "Do we have to call it 'Epsilon-4' every time? It sounds so boring, like one of the ingredients in a bottle of pain pills. What's the planet's real name?"

"*Strength-In-Darkness-Heeds-The-Call-Of-Everlasting*, if you want the more or less literal English translation. I'm afraid the actual language of the planets would be nearly impossible for the human tongue to replicate. Or the *Kol-Prockian* tongue, for that matter. Like I said back in the temple, we used to call it *Preleteth*."

"*Preleteth*," Pinchon mused. "Got a nice ring to it. Sounds mysterious."

"Funny you should say that, Colonel," the AI said. "Because 'mystery' is exactly what it means. It was discovered by a roving team of ancient priests who were looking for more worlds like Delta-13. You see, the priests of my people used the planet's unique powers to help the willing achieve wholeness. It helped them blend the conscious and unconscious minds into one undifferentiated self. But it was laborious in the extreme to try and get everyone who needed help out to Delta-13. So dozens of teams were sent out across the galaxy to find other worlds that could help the way Delta did. Remarkably, given what we know now, they never found one."

"Incredible," Tselitel said. "I wonder why."

"Maybe *Preleteth* will be able to give us some answers," Wellesley said. "The priests named it 'mystery' because they felt a very strange effect from it that they couldn't understand. Using all the arts they'd learned on Delta they tried to communicate with it. But they never managed to establish contact. After many years of trying they were forced to pack it in and head elsewhere."

"Did they leave anything behind?" asked Hunt. "Any ruins we might be able to use for cover while we're there?"

"I don't know. They visited *Preleteth* long ago, during the heyday of *Delek-Hai*. If they did, there wouldn't have been anyone to look after them. Much like a turtle, I think we'll have to carry our home with us."

"I don't see how we're going to talk to *Preleteth* if your priests couldn't," Pinchon said. "They must have been more skilled in such arts than any of us could ever be."

"Normally, I would agree with you," replied the AI. "But I felt the urgency in its messages to Delta-13. It was desperate to forestall the return of the Devourers. I think that very desperation might be enough to drive it to talk to us now."

"And then what?" prodded the colonel.

"We'll have to see," Wellesley replied.

"I've got to say, that's just about the thinnest plan I've ever heard," Pinchon said, slipping his boot off the bench and standing up. "Do you folks always go off half cocked like this?"

"Nobody forced you to come along," Gromyko said defensively, frowning at the older man.

"Oh, I'm not complaining. I'm just surprised by your

guts, is all. A multi-day warp to a planet none of you have ever seen before is usually prefaced with a little more planning than this."

"I'm afraid there wasn't time," said Wellesley. "Besides, it was the best option available to us. And when you're faced with just one option, you've got to give it everything you've got and hope for the best. It's how we roll. Besides, we're not *totally* devoid of data. A certain amount had been entered into the computer in the great temple. We know *Preletheth* is, or at least *was*, a jungle planet. It's like one giant untended garden from one end to the other."

"Hot climate?" asked Milo, beginning to wilt at the thought.

"Have you ever heard of a cold jungle?" replied Wellesley.

"This day just gets better and better," he mumbled.

"Look at the bright side, Milo," the AI said. "At least we won't freeze to death. We won't run into anything like those blizzards we had."

"Oh, sure. We'll just melt like snowballs in an oven. You've got to remember that Delta is the only thing that Rex and I have really ever known. Antonin, too, for that matter. We're cold weather creatures, no matter how much we gripe about it. Shoot, our blood probably runs ten degrees colder than the average Earthling!"

"I can say from personal experience that that isn't the case," Tselitel smiled, squeezing Hunt's arm with her good hand and recalling the taco. Pinchon eyed the two of them, curious to know the story behind her remark.

"Well, *I'll* be glad if I never feel the cold again," Gromyko said moodily. "I've had enough of it to fill three lifetimes. It takes something out of your heart and leaves you empty inside. It's a cancer that destroys the life that could otherwise thrive on the planet's surface. And it drains the hope from the people who must live in its shadow."

Tselitel's eyes went to the smuggler and she sighed

quietly. She knew he was hurting inside, confused and alone. For the first time in his life, she felt, he didn't have the slightest idea of who he was or what he was doing. *Gromyko, the glimmering hope of the masses* was a fantasy that had died with the Underground. Perhaps he could have clung to a few wispy vestiges of it wherever his prior legend was known. But with Midway destroyed by the *karrakpoi*, and the planet rapidly succumbing to the Devourers, it was as if his entire past life had been erased from existence. His clout, his importance, in fact, his very purpose for being, had been swept away. There was nothing for him now, save whatever he could manage with his own two hands.

"How long until we get there?" Milo asked Pinchon, breaking Tselitel out of her reverie.

"It's going to be days," he said, moving toward the cockpit. "You folks had better get settled in for a long wait."

The time passed slowly for the passengers, the walls of the freighter quickly becoming a prison for Milo and Gromyko. The latter took to staring out of the cockpit into the stream of blue that surrounded them, lost in thought. Several times Tselitel attempted to engage him in conversation, trying to draw him out of himself. But he was too morose to respond in anything but monosyllables.

"I can't get anywhere with him," she said quietly to Hunt on the third day of their journey. "He's clammed up, shutting everything else out. I'm afraid he won't recover from this."

"He will," Hunt said with certainty, looking at the smuggler from where he sat. "Antonin is resilient; he had to be to lead the Underground for all those years. He'll bounce out of it, eventually."

"I hope you're right," she said, taking his hand with her bad one and instantly grimacing. Resting her left, she reached across her lap with her right and retook his hand.

"How's the left doing?" Hunt asked. "I noticed you could use it pretty well when you bandaged me up."

"Oh, it's not too bad if I'm careful," she said, holding it up and flexing her fingers gingerly. "It's healing pretty fast. It must not be as bad as I first thought."

"Good, 'cause I don't think I could go with a woman who has only one good hand," he teased, kissing her forehead and putting his arm around her.

"Hey, I forgave you for hitting me with that tree, remember?" she laughed delightedly, the first real levity she'd felt in days. "That's got to count for at least one broken hand. Or two feet – they're less useful, you know," she said, wiggling her toes in her socks.

"You know, for a tall woman, you've got very small feet," he said, snatching her left up and pulling it over his knee. "What are they? Sixes?"

"Six and a half," she said, as he began to massage her foot. "Ooh, that feels good."

"Oh, this," he asked, gripping her ankle with his right and tickling her with his left.

"Ah! Stop!" she screamed with laughter, trying to pull her foot out of his iron grasp. "Uncle! Uncle!"

"Surrounder won't save you!" he laughingly taunted.

Rolling onto her back on the bench, she pressed her other foot to his shoulder and tried to pry him off. But it was no good.

"My kingdom! My kingdom for a respite!" she giggled uncontrollably, writhing on the bench, her face turning red with glee.

"I don't want your kingdom!" Hunt replied. "I want your psychiatry practice!"

"Fine! Fine! My practice for a respite!" she wheezed, running out of breath as he released her. With mock anger she jerked her foot back to her side of the bench and scowled at him. "You're always picking on me."

"Only because I like you," he laughed, putting his hand behind her back as she sat up and rubbing it.

"For the life of me I can't imagine why you'd want

my psychiatry practice," she replied in a more normal tone, straightening her ruffled clothes. "My reputation is laying in bits back at the–," she stopped. "Oh, Rex, do you think *any* of them survived? Sadie? Poor Vilks?"

"Probably not," he said with grim frankness. "I don't see how anyone could, at least not long term. The security doors in the prison could probably hold back the spiders for a while, to say nothing of the armed guards. But sooner or later I expect the Devourers would open fire on the prison, busting a hole for the *karrakpoi* to pour through. That, or they'd just pry it apart with those big tentacles of theirs."

"A terrible way for their stories to end," she mused sadly, leaning up against him with a sigh.

"A lot more will end that way if we don't stop them," Hunt replied with determination in his voice.

"I agree," Tselitel said quietly.

Looking over his shoulder from the pilot's seat, Pinchon watched Hunt and Tselitel quietly talking to each other, unable to hear what they were saying.

"Your friends sure are a couple of lovebirds, aren't they?" Pinchon asked Gromyko, straightening up in his seat and watching the blue sail past.

"Uh huh," the smuggler replied. He had one leg pulled up in the seat, his arms wrapped around it, his chin upon his knee. An expression of the sheerest disinterest in his surroundings on his face, Gromyko looked as though he hadn't slept in days. As far as Pinchon knew, he *hadn't* slept in days, choosing instead to maintain a constant vigil in the cockpit.

"You know, you can't just watch this stuff stream by forever," the colonel said, gesturing toward the bewitching tunnel of light. "It makes you batty if you stare at it too long."

"Uh huh."

Seeing he could get nowhere with the morose smuggler, Pinchon patted him on the shoulder and went back into the cargo hold.

"He's in bad shape," the colonel said quietly to Hunt, jerking a thumb over his shoulder. "You shouldn't let him stay up there too much longer."

"Not much I can do about it," Hunt replied. "He's in some kind of mood, and only he can snap himself out of it. Maybe *Preleteth* will be able to help when we get there; give him something else to think about."

"I don't know," Pinchon said. "I've seen cases like his before. His past life is dead and gone, and he doesn't see a reason to go on any longer. When they get that bad you've got to beat 'em within an inch of their lives to remind 'em that they want to live. It activates all the old instincts that are lying dormant at the back of the mind."

"That's brutal," Tselitel said with shock.

"It works, ma'am," Pinchon said with a shrug. "Right about the time a man starts feeling that life is too much of a burden, you've got to remind him that life is the only thing worth struggling for. It's worth *any* burden; *any* sacrifice. You've got to keep swinging, even when you don't think you can. Or, like in his case," he said, glancing over his shoulder once more, "when there doesn't seem to be a point."

"I don't think 'death therapy' is the answer," Tselitel said disapprovingly.

"Well, you could be right. I don't know him as well as you folks do," he said, looking between them. "But I'd plan on doing something about it, and soon. He's only gonna get worse if he stays on his present course. Something outside of him has to knock him in the right direction. And if one of *us* doesn't do it, it'll probably be something twice as bad from his environment – something he isn't prepared to deal with." He stood up. "Just wanted to pass that along."

"Thanks," Hunt said, watching him turn and move slowly back toward the cockpit.

"The colonel is from the rough-and-tumble school of psychiatry," Tselitel observed..

"Sometimes that's the best one," Hunt said. "It gets

results."

"Provided it doesn't leave the patient in worse shape than he's already in," she replied, nodding toward Gromyko. "I don't think he needs tough love right now. He's out of sorts and confused, like a compass that's spinning and spinning and can't find north. What he needs is guidance, direction; not a good drubbing."

"A good drubbing can give you direction like nothing else can," replied Hunt, stretching his arms over his head with a yawn. "It forces your instincts to rise up from the depths and speak to you with greater clarity, like Pinchon said. I suppose our ancient ancestors never were out of touch with their instincts long enough to miss them. But most of us have lived predictable, stable lives for so long that we never hear from them anymore. It takes 'death therapy,' as you called it, to remind us that we're just as much body as we are mind. Moreso, I think."

"But Antonin has been in mortal peril for years," countered Tselitel. "If 'death therapy' was the answer, it would have worked its magic by now."

"No, that's not what I mean," replied Hunt, shaking his head. "Being under *threat* is largely mental. You're *aware* that danger is nearby. You plan for it and try to forestall it. But what I'm talking about is actual, immediate danger, like when that bear burst into the den days ago. But even that was the mere *threat* of danger. It didn't rake its paw down Antonin's leg like it did Bradford. What our dashing friend needs to experience is the palpable, immediate *fact* of death staring him in the face. As long as it is a *possibility* it won't have the same force. It won't reach him the way it needs to. He has to *feel* it. Probably nothing short of jumping him and clamping my hands around his neck will suffice."

"What! Strangle your own friend!" exclaimed Tselitel louder than she'd intended. Milo, sitting on the far end of the cargo hold, looked up from the book he'd been leafing through and shot her a puzzled look. "You can't just *do* things like that, Rex," she continued, dropping her voice. "You can't take psychiatry, literally, into your own hands."

"Why not?" he countered. "If it works, it works. Antonin will understand the reason for it after I've finished. He'll be the first to trumpet the 'death cure' for anyone who's lost hope. In fact, he'll make a nuisance out of himself over the subject, if anything. He won't mind."

"You can't treat people that way, darling," she said with quiet earnestness. "You have to respect their dignity."

"Only the rich and secure can afford dignity," Hunt said with a dry laugh. "Out here," he began, before remembering where he was. "Well, back on Delta-13, something either worked or it didn't. Oh, we had pride. But we didn't stand on ceremony over the propriety of a given course of action. It either worked, or it wasn't worth talking about. And if it did work, the only question was why we'd lacked the courage to do it sooner."

"You're a hard man, Rex Hunt," Tselitel said. She'd long been aware of that fact, but his personal tenderness towards her made her forget it most of the time. It was only when they discussed actions of one sort or another that she saw the cool pragmatism of his ethics. In his view, a legitimate aim carried its own justification. His moral conceptions stood atop each other like a pyramid that stacked upward toward the sky: some aims were *more moral* than others, and held precedence. In such a case, the lesser moral questions didn't have to be balanced against the greater: they were simply eliminated according to the crisp arithmetic of his mind. If a course was good, it was to be pursued, no matter how many other moral precepts had to be stepped on in the process. It crossed her mind that Lavery had shared the same approach to moral questions.

"I think we're going faster," Wellesley said, breaking her train of thought.

"Faster?" asked Milo, hearing the AI's monotone from where he sat.

"Yes. I wasn't sure at first, since sometimes traveling by warp is subject to a certain amount of variance in speed. But our velocity has increased by twelve and a half percent in the last six hours. That's too much for the touch of wobble that sometimes comes into the picture."

"Is that dangerous?" asked Tselitel, as Hunt arose and made for the cockpit.

"Not at present. Though it does raise the question of why we're accelerating at all. That's not supposed to happen."

Leaning on the back of Pinchon's seat, Hunt looked at the dashboard, trying to find some kind of speedometer.

"I heard what your AI said," the colonel said, tapping on a digital display whose number was slowly ticking upward. "And he's right. More than that, the rate at which we're accelerating is increasing rapidly. In another six hours we'll be traveling fifty percent faster than standard."

"How much can the ship handle?" Hunt asked.

"That's something we'll get to find out together," Pinchon said. "I've never flown more than ten percent above standard. People have been real cautious about tinkering with warp travel ever since the Gradetsky Incident."

"What happened?" asked Gromyko, temporarily stirred out of his melancholy.

"Ask me again sometime and I'll tell you," Pinchon said, not wishing to relive the memory of that famed disaster at just that moment. "But I've got a better question for you than how fast we can go."

"What's that?" asked Hunt.

"Just *what* is making us go so fast?" the colonel asked. The ship began to shake as he said this, making him and Gromyko bounce in their seats. "You'd better head back there and get strapped in. This could get rough."

"What's going on, brother?" asked Milo as Hunt rejoined them.

"The colonel says to buckle up," Hunt replied. Snatching Wellesley off of the bench he'd been resting on, he took a seat beside Tselitel and strapped himself in.

"We never catch a break, do we, Rex?" asked Wellesley. "I think you and I were born to be in danger. It chases us everywhere we go."

"I couldn't agree more."

A sudden jolt reverberated through the craft, causing the contents of several metal containers strapped to the hull to jump and produce a nerve jangling clang. Tselitel gripped Hunt's hand with her right until the knuckles turned white.

"I've never liked flying of any kind," she admitted quietly, another jolt passing through the ship. "I like my feet firmly on the ground."

A bright red light flashed from the cockpit just as an alarm started to blare.

"It's alright, folks," Pinchon informed them calmly from the front. "Just a minor subsystem. Nothing essential."

"Then why did they install it?" Tselitel asked in a whisper, his breaths becoming quick and shallow.

The lights in the cargo hold flickered for a moment and then went out.

"Is it too late to buy flight insurance?" Wellesley asked from the darkness, as the craft barreled faster and faster down the tunnel of light.

CHAPTER 4

"Minister McGannon, the alien vessels near Delta-13 have returned to orbit," Admiral Makarovich, commander of the sector that included the beleaguered planet, reported via hologram.

"What are they doing?" she asked. "Effecting repairs? Preparing to move out?"

"According to long range scanners, they aren't doing anything, Minister. They're just floating up there."

"I see. And what is the state of things planetside?"

"That's what I wanted to speak to you about," Makarovich said with a touch of hesitation. "For days the invaders' vessels had their...tentacles embedded in the planet. This provoked significant seismic activity, along with a worsening of the storms that were already pummeling its surface."

"I don't have time for a long explanation, Admiral," McGannon said irritably. "Just cut to the point."

"Minister, something happened to the planet shortly before they returned to orbit. An enormous earthquake shook it down to its very core. It was like some kind of death rattle. The storms lost their intensity, and the already low temperature started to plummet. After that the ships released their hold of it and resumed orbit."

"What are you trying to tell me, Admiral?" she asked, disturbed by the news, though she didn't show it.

"I believe they have some kind of geo-weapon that can assault the very essence of a planet. If so, only a handful of their ships would be required to reduce a world of billions. And seeing the way they leveled the ships we sent against them–."

"What I need are *facts*, Admiral, not what you *believe* to be the case," snapped McGannon, more shaken by his hypothesis than she cared to admit. "Continue to gather data on this question, but don't speak of it to another soul. Report back when you have something I can use."

"Yes, Minister," the admiral said, just before she shut off his hologram.

"Sounds like we need a weapon of our own, something that can take the fight to them," a man said behind her. She closed her eyes and silently drew a breath before turning to face him.

Eglis Krancis was the will of the emperor personified. A man feared above all others, he had the power to act in the emperor's name without responsibility to anyone save Rhemus himself. Perceiving himself unable to handle the affairs of the war alone, and increasingly unwilling to trust the ministers that he himself had chosen, he appointed the shadowy figure as his personal fixer. Cold, crisply rational, and utterly ruthless, Krancis was everything that the emperor was no longer capable of being. Tall, lean, with gaunt cheeks and a pair of piercing eyes that missed nothing, he moved silently wherever he went. Fanatically loyal to the emperor, he had been chosen in one of Rhemus's rare moments of clarity to ensure his will was being done. Preferring the smallest footprint possible, he was simply known as Krancis to all save a close circle.

"You're hinting at the Omega Project," McGannon said, rotating her chair and eyeing the almost spectral figure who stood half a dozen steps away.

"My sources indicate it is our only chance," Krancis said in a thin, precise voice that contained just the slightest trace of menace.

"Our forces have not truly engaged the enemy yet," McGannon said calmly, determined to keep her cool in his presence. "Only now have they gathered into effective battlegroups. Soon we'll launch the counter attack that will drive them back."

"I don't share your assessment," Krancis said, taking a framed award off her wall and examining it for a moment. "My sources estimate that the navy has a twenty-nine percent chance of victory. Not very good odds, Minister."

"I would be more than willing to have your sources check with those of the navy, to ensure we are both working with the most accurate information possible," she said with studied politeness. Riled beyond words by Krancis' involvement, she nevertheless had to treat him with the utmost deference. Only a slight nod from his vulturelike head would be necessary to have her declared a traitor and executed immediately. She wondered what madness could have possibly possessed the emperor, causing him to entrust his entire authority to a man almost no one knew. It was enough to make her wonder if he was being held hostage at the imperial retreat, forced to act against his will. But she knew that was impossible, guarded as he was by a sizable detachment of naval personnel that she herself had chosen for the task.

"No, only Omega has a chance of retrieving our fallen fortunes," Krancis said, hanging her award back on the wall. "I can only think, Minister, that the project would have been farther along had it enjoyed more enthusiastic support from you. But I know how you fought the reallocation of resources from your precious navy to a project that you never truly believed in."

"Omega has enjoyed my wholehearted support from the start," she said, only keeping an edge out of her voice with effort. "I was thrilled when the emperor asked me to personally oversee the initial stages of its development."

"And yet, he did not ask you to remain with the project for the long term," Krancis said insinuatingly. "Naturally, given your well-known aversion to Taegen, it would only make sense that a weapon intended to act against a threat that he alone foresaw would not excite much enthusiasm on your part. Of course, now that he has been proven correct..." he let his voice trail, walking to the window of her office and looking out upon the base that surrounded her headquarters. "The emperor has the utmost faith in Omega, Minister. And thus we, as the agents of his will, must have an equal measure of faith. This is no time to fall back on conventional measures. The navy has already failed in its duty to protect the empire from those who threaten it. Indeed, it has allowed them to penetrate the very core of the emperor's domain and lay siege to his possessions. Such failure reflects upon those who have the ultimate responsibility for conducting war in the emperor's name. Namely, it reflects badly on *you*, Minister."

Despite herself her cheeks flushed. She knew this was what he'd been working around to ever since he'd entered her office. But to hear the words actually roll off his lips struck fear into her heart. It was a long moment before she could collect her thoughts enough to speak.

"I assure you, Krancis, that I will–."

"The emperor is not interested in your *assurances*, Minister," Krancis interrupted, turning from the window, his eyes boring into her. "He wants results. And he wants them *immediately*. Don't forget that we serve in his name, Minister. Failure to deliver will be interpreted as a lack of zeal for his cause."

"I will deliver results," she said, fighting to keep her voice steady as he made for the door.

Laying his hand upon the knob, he paused and turned toward her again.

"Finish Omega," he said in a quiet voice. "No matter what you have to do; no matter what you have to sacrifice:

finish Omega."

❖ ❖ ❖

Hunt could hear Tselitel muttering prayers in the darkness next to him as the freighter tore its way down the tunnel.

"We are *rapidly* approaching our destination," Pinchon called from the cockpit. "But the controls are dead."

"What do you mean?" asked Hunt.

"I mean I'm not flying this bird," the colonel replied. "We're no longer warping under our own power. We're being *dragged* to our destination by force."

"Just what I like to hear," Wellesley said sarcastically.

"How can you joke?" asked Tselitel, her nerves tighter than a bowstring. "We could die any second now!"

"I've been in too many life-or-death situations to even blink anymore," the ancient AI replied. "Death will come when it will come. Besides, I don't think this is the end for us."

"Why not?" she asked.

"Call it an intuition," he said calmly.

"Hold on to something, folks!" Pinchon said. "We're about to break out of warp!"

Just as he said this the ship dropped into normal space, traveling at tremendous speed.

"Colonel, what's that we're heading towards?" asked Gromyko, pointing at a massive green orb that grew alarmingly larger with each second.

"That's Epsilon-4," he said, unfastening his restraints and bolting out of the seat. "And we're about to crash into it like a bullet."

"Well, stop us!" exclaimed the smuggler.

"I can't. Even if I could turn the ship around and burn the engines on full blast, we'd never lose enough momentum to keep from crashing. Our only hope now is the escape pods." Tapping a few keys on the dashboard, a series of small doors opened on the inside walls of the freighter. "Get into the pods!" he ordered the others.

"But we'll starve down there!" Tselitel protested.

"Each pod is equipped with a survival kit and a radio," explained Pinchon quickly. "Now get in!"

In a flash they were all strapped into the human-sized pods. The colonel entered his only after he'd made sure the others were secure.

"It's gonna be close," he said over the radio. "Eject immediately!" With this he pulled a bright red handle that hung from the top of the pod, and instantly he was blasted into space.

The others followed suit, and five small pods fluttered away from the doomed freighter.

"The pods are programmed to automatically fly to the safest location," Pinchon told them, his voice crackling as interference from the planet affected his radio transmission. "They're outfitted with small rockets that will guide us to *Preleteth*."

"But will they slow us down enough?" asked Gromyko.

"Oh, yes. Don't worry about that," the colonel said. "We're home free now."

"Home free? Floating over an alien world, our supplies lost to us?" asked the smuggler. "How are we supposed to survive down there? Shoot, are we even going to land in the same region? We're floating apart already!"

"One thing at a time," Pinchon said sagely. "The pods will ensure that we land within fifty miles of each other. The radios will keep us in contact until we can meet up and make a plan. But remember, if we *do* lose contact, make for the tallest point you can see. It will give us a rallying point if we all hit the ground near each other. And if we don't, it'll help boost our radio signals so we *can* get together."

Soon they hit the atmosphere, the pods becoming incredibly hot as they scorched their way to the planet below. The rockets fired to slow them down and guide them toward a common landing zone.

"I see some kind of obelisk down there, in a clearing," Pinchon said, his voice half obscured by crackling. "No matter what: make for that obelisk! That is our rally point!"

As the ground loomed up before them each of the pods deployed a trio of parachutes to slow their descent. Hunt could see the other pods disappear into the trees just before his broke into the dense canopy. He heard branches snap under the weight of his pod as it embedded itself in the boughs of an ancient tree.

"Remind me never to skydive," Wellesley said from his pocket. "I'll take my thrills on the ground."

"You and me both," Hunt said, pressing the release for the pod's door and shoving it away from him. The metal panel clattered to the ground below him. "Uh, we've still got a ways to go yet."

"How far?"

"About fifteen feet," Hunt replied, craning his neck around the outside of the pod. "I might be able to climb down one of these branches."

"Do it. But don't forget the emergency kit first."

The kit consisted of several days of rations, basic medical supplies, a handheld radio, and a handgun with two spare clips.

"This is Hunt. Does anyone read me?" he asked over the radio. "Hunt to group, please respond."

"Maybe they landed farther away than the colonel thought."

"Yeah, could be," Hunt said, clipping the radio to his belt. Jamming the other supplies into his pockets, he slipped the pistol into his waistband and was about to climb out onto a nearby branch when Wellesley stopped him.

"Not that it isn't fun to ride around in your pocket," the AI said. "But how about slinging me around your neck, like the good old days? Then I can consistently see what's going on. Besides, I'll finally be able to stop talking in this dreadful monotone."

Popping the speaker from the 600G off Wellesley, he looped the medallion's golden chain around his neck and worked him under his shirt.

"Somehow it always comes back to just you and me, doesn't it?" he asked Hunt, as the latter looked once more at the ground below. "Well, isn't that a pleasant sight."

"Yeah," Hunt said quietly, carefully reaching for the closest branch and clambering out onto it. Wrapping his legs around it, he crawled along it to the trunk. The tree was old, enormous, and terribly crooked. But its long and chaotic growth had left plenty of handholds for Hunt to use on his way down. No sooner had his boots hit the soft dirt than the pod slipped from its place in the branches and clattered noisily to the ground.

"Hope nothing nasty heard that," Wellesley said, as a brightly colored snake slithered over an exposed root a short distance away.

"Yeah, hopefully not," Hunt agreed, drawing the pistol from his belt and cocking it.

"Expecting trouble?"

"No way to know what to expect on a rock like this," Hunt replied, getting out from under the tree's low hanging branches. He moved around, trying to find the obelisk. But the canopy above him was so dense he could barely even see the sky.

"Probably gonna be dark in a few hours," Wellesley commented in an idle tone. "Of course, it's hard to say for certain, never having been here."

"Any idea how to find that obelisk the colonel mentioned?" Hunt asked.

"Climb a tall tree? Seems like about the only way to get

above all this greenery."

"Thought of that," Hunt replied, wiping the sweat from his brow that had already begun to gather in the hot, moist wilderness. "I was wondering if you had a *better* idea than that."

Suddenly he heard a gunshot echo out across the jungle, causing all the birds in the area to take to the sky with a deafening racket. Instantly Hunt bolted in the direction of the shot.

"A little to your left," Wellesley said after he'd covered some two hundred feet. "You're curving off course."

Shifting his path slightly, Hunt ran until his lungs ached and his muscles burned.

"Must be…close…" he said between gasps, resting his palms on his knees. The moment he could move again he took off, fueled by the fear that one of his friends was in danger.

"Move a little to the right now," he heard Wellesley inside his head, as his ears pounded with the sound of his heart. It felt ready to burst out of his chest. Unused to exertion in such hot temperatures, his body was protesting in every way it could muster. Sweat poured into his eyes until he was half blind, forcing him to stop and wipe them with his already damp sleeve. Leaning against a tree to catch his breath, his abdomen cramping from running, he was about to ask Wellesley if he'd missed his target when another shot rang out, this time very close.

"Through those bushes!" Wellesley said excitedly, as Hunt burst through a wall of tall bushes with sharp thorns that drew blood from his exposed forearms.

"Where are you?" Hunt called out, pistol in hand.

"Rex?" a voice said from thirty feet ahead, muffled by the foliage.

"Lily!" he exclaimed, rushing to the sound of her voice. She was propped up against a narrow tree with spiky bark, her pod nowhere in sight. Her hair tousled, her clothing soaked with sweat, she smiled weakly when she saw him, grimacing with pain.

"What happened?" he asked, feeling her arms and shoulders with his hands as though to intuit her injury. "What's wrong with you?"

"I've been asking myself that question…my whole life," she said with a dry laugh, wincing immediately after.

"Oh, very funny," Hunt said. "This is serious! How did you get here?"

"The pod got stuck in a tree," she said, gesturing with her gun a short distance ahead. "I smacked my hand on the inside of the pod when it crashed. I broke it up real good this time." She held up its discolored form for him to examine, drawing a sharp breath the second he touched it."

"Yeah, I'd say you're right," he agreed, sitting down beside her and brushing the hair out of her eyes. "But how did you get over here?"

"Well, I tried to climb out of the tree," she said, shifting painfully where she sat. "But with just one good hand I slipped and fell, oh, probably ten feet."

"Better let me check her over," Wellesley said. "If she's punctured anything inside, we need to know right away."

Quickly Hunt slipped the AI off his neck and into Tselitel's hand. Anxiously he watched her face for any sign about her condition. About half a minute later she sighed with relief and handed Wellesley back.

"He says I'm okay. Bruised and bloodied, but otherwise alright."

"Good," Hunt said, putting the AI back around his neck. "Why did you shoot? Did something attack you?"

"No," she said, shaking her head. "Like an idiot I left the radio in the pod. I don't know, I guess I just wasn't thinking straight. I heard your voice come over it after I hit the ground, so I knew you were close by. I figured a shot would let you know where I was." She smiled. "Looks like I was right."

"Smart girl," he said, kissing her dirty forehead and squeezing her shoulder with his hand. "I haven't heard from the others. They must be too far away."

"Or..." she started to say.

"No, the odds are against it," Hunt said, cutting her off. "Two out of five survivors is beyond unlikely."

"I hope you're right," she said, handing him her gun. "Take it. I've never been any good with those things anyway."

"Too bad," he said, tucking her pistol into the back of his waistband. "Never hurts to have another shooter on the team."

"Hey, this is me, remember?" she asked with a faint smile. "I'm no good out of doors."

With half a grin on his lips he raised his hand to her cheek, brushing a little dirt off with his thumb.

"We'd better get a move on," he said. "Wellesley says it's gonna be dark in a few hours." He paused. "I don't suppose you got a look where the obelisk is?"

"Uh huh," she said, nodding behind her. "That way. My pod was facing it as I came down."

"See? Not so useless after all," he said, helping her to her feet. "Can you walk?"

"Not if you'll carry me," she teased, her sense of humor slowly filtering back in.

"Sorry, the pack mule service has closed for the day," he laughed, watching as she took a few hesitant, painful steps. "Are you good?"

"Yeah," she said, nodding slowly. "I'm good."

Taking her hand, they set off in the direction she'd indicated.

"Have you seen any animals yet?" she asked quietly, her eyes darting around as they pushed further into the jungle. "This is the most savage, wild place I've ever seen."

"Nothing yet," he replied confidently, his eyes periodically panning their surroundings. "But the sound of our pods crashing probably scared them away. And if that didn't, your gunshots probably did. Provided no one else has visited since the ancient priests, none of the animals have heard civilized noises for thousands of years."

"Would you try the radio again?" she asked, climbing over a fallen log. "I'd like to know if they're in the vicinity."

With a shrug he unclipped the radio from his belt, certain they hadn't moved far enough to pick anyone up but willing to humor her.

"Hunt to Pinchon, Milo, Antonin: come in, please." Waiting a few moments, he tried again. "Nothing," he said, putting the radio away. "Maybe when we get a little closer to the obelisk."

"They ought to be close enough to pick up the signal," Wellesley said, the skin contact produced by their clasped hands allowing both to hear him. "I wonder if the planet is interfering with the signal somehow. There *was* a lot of static on colonel Pinchon's radio as we neared the surface."

"That's true," Tseliel seconded. "When I heard you after I fell out of the tree you sounded very faint and crackly. But what could possibly be interfering? This planet is uninhabited. It's not like trees give off electrical signals."

"Well, someone had to build that obelisk," Wellesley pointed out. "Perhaps there's other forms of infrastructure around here."

"But that was the *Kol-Prockian* priests, wasn't it?" asked Tselitel. "Wouldn't their general adherence to a life of poverty preclude advanced infrastructure?"

"That obelisk wasn't made by the priests," the AI said." They had no use for obelisks. Many peoples have found them significant down the annals of time. You humans built quite a few of them, from what I understand. But they simply had no purpose within *Delek-Hai*, so they were never built."

"Could it have been built *before* the priests came here?" asked Hunt.

"I doubt it. There was no indication of intelligent life on *Preleteth* recorded in the computer. I mean, they were here to study the planet, not relics left behind by other races. So it's *possible* that they didn't bother to mention it."

"But unlikely," Hunt said.

"Just so. In any event I wouldn't worry too much. Whoever was here probably left a long time ago."

"We can only hope," Tselitel said doubtfully, glancing once again at their surroundings as they moved.

Unseen animals chittered and ran under the bushes, keeping track of their progress but never revealing themselves. They sounded small, no bigger than a large cat. Yet they made the most unusual noises. Tselitel's fears began to run away with her as she imagined all kinds of ferocious, rabid little beasts that were just waiting to sink their teeth into her legs. Hunt saw the worried look on her face and gave her a little nudge as they walked.

"Don't worry," he grinned, drawing the pistol to calm her nerves. "They'll have to get through me first."

After nearly an hour an opening appeared in the canopy and they caught sight of the obelisk in the distance.

"Don't seem to have gotten much closer to it," Hunt said, offering Tselitel a drink while he eyed it. "Looks like it's made out of metal, like that structure in the cave."

"I noticed that, too," Tselitel agreed, handing the small pouch of emergency water back to him. Seeing something dark on the edge of her vision, she gasped and jerked her head toward it. To her surprise there was nothing there.

"Another one of our little friends," Hunt said, following her eyes. "Come on, we'd better keep moving. I want to get as close to that obelisk as possible before we lose daylight."

"You know that wasn't one of our 'little friends,'" Wellesley said to him once they'd resumed walking. "It's a lot bigger than that."

Mutely Hunt nodded.

"I'll keep my ears pricked up for any more signs of it. I don't think we've seen the last of it."

❖ ❖ ❖

After nightfall Milo was picking his way through the jungle, his small flashlight illuminating only a tiny portion of his surroundings. The darkness was alive with creatures all around him. Whether climbing in the trees above him or dashing between the small green shrubs that everywhere obscured his view, the strange planet presented a cornucopia of life unlike he'd ever seen before. Used to the sterile winterland of Delta-13, his senses were overwhelmed with a thousand sounds and smells that he'd never encountered before.

"Gah!" he exclaimed, tripping over an unseen log and smashing his face into the moist ground on the other side of it. His flashlight flew from his grasp, landing half concealed under a plant. "I'll be glad not to spend another second here than I have to," he muttered, getting to his feet and brushing the damp soil from his clothes. The air was so close and humid that it felt like a steam bath. Groping under the plant for his light, he found something wet and scaly that moved at his touch. Instantly jerking his hand back, he heard it chitter and scamper away. "I'll die of fright, if nothing else," he thought, his heart rate slowly ticking toward normal as he grabbed his light and shined it around, ensuring nothing else was near him.

Sitting on the log he'd just tripped over, he drew the radio from his pocket.

"Milo to Antonin. What's your status?"

"The same as when you asked me ten minutes ago," the smuggler replied irritably. "Why don't you leave me alone? Stop bugging me."

"Come on, Antonin; you can't tell me that you're not a little lonesome out here tonight, too," Milo said, getting to his feet and slowly walking toward the bright green peak of the obelisk in the distance. It had begun to shine once the sun had dipped below the horizon. "This place is creepier than anywhere on Delta-13. Out there you had *honest* animals that would eat you outright. Bears and whatnot. But here everything looks like it wants to sting or stab you to death! I'm certain I'm gonna step on some snake or lizard and get a leg full of venom before I ever reach the obelisk."

"Yeah, if we're lucky," Gromyko said. "Then I won't have to listen to you anymore."

"Aw, you don't mean that," Milo said, moving slowly around a large boulder that stood in his path. Peeking cautiously lest something was hidden behind it, he reached the other side and let out a sigh of relief. "How far away are you from it now?"

"At least an hour yet," he replied. "Now get off the air."

"Fine," Milo muttered to himself, slipping the radio back into his pocket and picking up his pace. Fingering his handgun but leaving it tucked in his belt, he wished he'd had more experience using one.

Half an hour later he heard a voice crackle over the radio.

"...Col...chon to anyone who...Come in, please..."

"Pinchon? Colonel Pinchon? Can you read me? Over."

"Affirm...Where are you?"

"I, uh," Milo said, struggling to find the obelisk's light through the ceiling of flora. "I'm thirty, maybe forty-five minutes away from the rally point. Over."

"Under...My radio was...on impact...Can't..."

"Colonel? Colonel?" Milo asked urgently after several seconds of dead air. "Do you read me, Colonel?"

"Something is out..." Pinchon said. Suddenly a gunshot rang out over the radio, nearly making Milo jump out of his skin. "Double time it for the obel..." Another gunshot. "There isn't..." Then the air went dead.

"Antonin?" Milo asked.

"I heard. The shots were close to me. I'll try to help him if I can."

"Be careful," Milo said, drawing his pistol and cocking it. "I'll meet you at the obelisk."

◆ ◆ ◆

"What *was* that?" Tselitel asked Hunt, as they hastened through the jungle. She'd only seen a snatch of it, but it was enough to tell her it wasn't good. "It looked so, so *strange*! Like something out of a nightmare."

"Let's keep moving," Hunt said, pulling her with his left hand, a flashlight in his right. The guns were snugly tucked into his belt, as he knew they wouldn't do any good against what was following them. Whatever the creature was, it hated light. Moving with lightning quickness from one side of them to the other, it constantly strove to find a dark approach by which to near them.

Hunt had to drag Tselitel along, the pains from her fall increasing with each passing hour. It was with difficulty that she moved at all.

"Behind you, Rex!" Wellesley suddenly called out.

Flashing the light behind him, he saw an inky black creature of shadow rear up and howl. Darker than midnight, it looked like a ghoulish, distorted impression of a human form. Nearly seven feet tall, it raised its arm to shield itself from the light as it turned and darted for cover.

"Aaahh!" screamed Tselitel on seeing it, the memory of the figures Bodkin called up in her mind instantly rushing back and filling her with terror. Ripping her hand away from Hunt's, she took off running.

"Stop her!" Wellesley barked, just as Hunt bolted after her. Within a dozen steps he'd reached her, taking the back of her belt in his powerful grasp and pulling her to a stop.

"No! No, keep them away!" she shrieked, dropping to the ground and covering her face with her hands. "No more! No more of the demons!"

"I won't let them hurt you," Hunt growled, dragging her to her feet and setting off again, flicking the light every which way. Thrice he saw the creature, each time on a different side of them. Soon they burst into an open space, the obelisk standing a modest distance away. Twisting around and flashing the light, he saw the face of the creature poking out of the leaves and branches. Squealing hideously, it drew back into the jungle.

"How can such things even *exist*?" asked Tselitel, panting beside Hunt. Slipping to her knees, her muscles burning with fatigue, she glanced between him and the jungle. "Rex?"

"I don't know," he replied, looking at the glowing orb at the top of the obelisk. "But I have a feeling we're going to find out."

"Look! Over there!" she said urgently, pointing toward a little dot of light that grew as it neared. "It must be one of the others!"

"Are you two okay?" asked Milo once he could make them out in the gloom. "You look like you've seen a ghost!"

"Not far from it!" Tselitel said, using her good hand to push off the ground.

"Some kind of…dark creature was chasing us," Hunt said, nodding to where it had disappeared. "Fast, aggressive. Like some kind of–."

"Evil spirit?" asked Gromyko, approaching unseen from the side. In a flash Hunt had the light and one of his handguns leveled on the smuggler's smiling face.

"Antonin!" Tselitel said, putting her arms around his neck and hugging him as Hunt lowered his weapon.

"Could have gotten your stupid head shot off, pulling a stunt like that," Hunt grumbled, sliding the pistol back into his belt. "You should have shined your light at us."

"Can't. I lost mine."

"Lost it?" asked Tselitel, pulling away from him. "But…those creatures only back off when a light is on them! You could have been killed, or worse!"

"That's why I lost mine," he grinned cryptically.

"What have you got up your sleeve?" asked Milo, crossing his arms, an inquisitive look on his face.

"Well, one of those creatures cornered me in a cave," Gromyko began casually, cocking onto one leg. "I managed to outwit it and get *it* backed into the corner it had chosen for me. Last I knew it was wailing under the beam of my light, unable to get out."

"So you trapped it?" Tselitel asked.

"Uh huh," he said, brushing a little dirt off his arm. "It was not the first one to learn that you cannot corner Gromyko! I am quicksilver! A shadow dancing upon the wall!"

"Don't say shadow," Tselitel said, shivering at the thought. "But what are those things?"

"They are death personified," the smuggler said. "Some kind of evil that surpasses all our understanding."

"What makes you so sure?" the doctor asked.

"This does," he replied, raising his arm to show the underside. A glimmering scar of sheerest black made her gasp. "All the cells are dead. The instant it touched me I felt the life go out of them. It's a miracle that I got away as luckily as I did. It merely grazed the surface, killing only the first layer of skin. I can't imagine what it would have done had it seized my head."

"You mean a whole bunch of those things are rambling around out there, just waiting to jump us?" Milo shuddered, looking around with his light.

"Don't worry," Hunt said, handing Tselitel's light to Gromyko. "With three lights they won't be able to get close. Just keep an eye out: they move fast."

"That's not what I mean," his brother said. "Half the

time I was walking without mine on! I didn't want to get spotted by any, I don't know, *natives!* But the whole time one of those things could have snuck up and drank my blood, or whatever it is they do!"

"You might have been better off that way," Hunt replied.

"What, bloodless?" asked Milo incredulously.

"No, without your light on," Hunt said. "It could be the lights that are attracting them."

"I don't care if they do," Milo said, gripping his until his knuckles turned white. "I don't think I'll ever shut mine off again!"

"Don't worry, Milo," the smuggler said, slapping a hand on his shoulder and turning toward the obelisk. "You are with Gromyko! What can possibly go wrong?"

"A great deal, apparently," he replied, stabbing a finger toward the black scar.

"Oh, that is nothing but a scratch, something to remind me that I am alive. In fact, I'm glad for it."

"You're nuts, you know that?" asked Milo, as the pair began to walk forward.

"Looks like the colonel was right," Tselitel said quietly to Hunt as they followed up the rear. "He needed some kind of brush with death to remind him how sweet it is to live. If he's right, it was quite *literally* a brush with death!" Darting her eyes around, she suddenly blurted out, "Oh my! What about Pinchon?"

"I don't know," Milo said, shaking his head. "Antonin and I heard him on the radio earlier. The reception was bad, but it sounded like something was after him. He cracked off a couple of shots, and then we lost contact."

"He was close to me when he cut loose," Gromyko said, making a finger gun and pumping his thumb a few times. "But I never saw a trace of him. I found a couple of shell casings on the ground along with some tracks his boots had made in the dirt. But before I could follow them one of those creatures found me and chased me into that cave. After that I made for the obelisk, and then you all, when I saw your lights."

"Then he's dead?" asked Tsclitcl as they neared the obelisk..

"I doubt it," Gromyko replied. "He is a resilient man, used to danger. He probably has the best chance of all of us of making it off this rock alive."

"I've been thinking about that," Milo said, carefully scanning the ground nearby with his light. "Just how do we plan to do that? The ship was smashed into a thousand pieces when it hit. And those pods are a one use affair. Are we stuck here?"

"Oh, we'll find a way off," the smuggler said confidently.

"Why?"

"Because fate would not have brought us here without a plan to take us off again," he explained. "You don't go through that much trouble just to maroon five people."

"Fate is just superstition," Milo grumbled, having hoped for something more concrete on which to base his hopes.

"Fine, call it the 'will of the *Ahn-Wey*' if you like," Gromyko replied. "Clearly we're caught up in something bigger than ourselves. First Delta-13 goes through all the trouble of piecing us together, welding us into a team. And then Epsilon-4 drags us through slipspace at an incredible rate of speed because it wanted us here *immediately*. This is where we're *supposed* to be. I'm sure of it."

"For all we know, Epsilon was trying to *kill* us!" exclaimed Milo. "If it wasn't for those pods we'd be puree of human right now! And within hours of reaching this miserable place we're jumped by death monsters! No, Antonin, I *don't* think we're part of some grand plan. I think we're jumping from one frying pan into another. Shoot, you've already been scorched once."

"Love taps," the smuggler grinned, tapping his arm. "Just a little message to remind me to live."

"Enjoy it while it lasts," Milo muttered gloomily, as they drew ever farther into the circle of light that descended from the massive pillar. Soon their lights became superfluous and they shut them off, except for Milo.

"Turn it off," Hunt said to his brother. "Save the battery."

"These things last for months," he replied.

"Yeah, and who knows how long we'll have to be here," Hunt replied firmly. "Shut it off."

Drawing near to the ancient monument, Gromyko let out a low whistle.

"This thing is enormous," he said, pressing his palms against it. "Funny," he added, pulling his hands away, "it's as cold as ice."

"You're right," Tselitel said, pressing her good hand to it for a moment. "But how can that be? It must be ninety degrees fahrenheit right now."

"I was wondering the same thing myself," Pinchon said, making them all jump as he walked around the massive structure. "You people shouldn't talk so loud. I could hear you from a mile away."

"Pretty sure the local animal life knows we're here already," Milo said. "And the local spectral life, too."

"What makes you think they're the only things out here?" asked the colonel rhetorically. "We've been here for less than six hours, and already we've established that someone other than the priests have been here," he said, laying a hand on the obelisk. "Moreover, we've seen a creature that is unlike anything humanity has encountered before. Now is not the time to make assumptions."

"How did you know about the creature?" Tselitel asked. "None of us have mentioned it."

"Simple, I saw the mark on his arm," Pinchon replied, nodding toward Gromyko. "I've got one on my leg that matches," he added, reeling up a bit of his cuff to show them. "Looks like we both got lucky – nothing but surface wounds. Next time I think they'll dig a little deeper."

"Agreed," nodded Gromyko. "We must be careful."

"Right now I'd like to know where we're supposed to spend the night," Tselitel said, glancing uncomfortably over her shoulder despite the luminous glow of the obelisk. She felt the creatures could return at any moment, and wanted to put something between herself and them.

"Inside the obelisk, naturally," replied Pinchon.

"And how are we supposed to get in there?" asked Milo. "Beat our way in with rocks?"

"Well, I was thinking we could use the door on the back," Pinchon smiled. "But we can try your method instead, if you'd like."

"Come on," Milo said with a frown, feeling stupid. "Let's see if it's even warm enough to sustain life. It might be just as cold inside as it is outside."

On the back they found a door just large enough to admit them without stooping. Laying a hand on the simple handle that protruded from its surface, Hunt opened it without difficulty, the door swinging as easily as if it was brand new.

"Not like the ancient doors on Delta-13," Wellesley commented to him, as he looked inside.

Within it was dark. Hunt drew the flashlight from his pocket and shined it around, revealing a narrow hallway with a series of doors on either side. The inner walls were made of the same material as the outer structure, and their cooling presence left the temperature pleasingly mild. Unexpectedly, the floor consisted simply of dirt.

"Pretty comfortable in here," Milo said, flicking his light to and fro. "Be nice if there were some lights, though."

"That's what I was thinking," Tselitel said quietly, taking Hunt's hand with her good one and staying close. "Do you think any of those creatures could be inside?" she whispered, afraid one might hear her.

"Probably not," Pinchon said, striding ahead of the group. "Those things seem to roam the countryside. I don't think one would get trapped in here."

"Only one way to be sure," Gromyko said, grabbing one of the doors and thrusting it open. "Nothing. Just an empty room."

They checked all of them, but with the same result.

"I wonder what this place was," Tseliel said, looking up at the high ceilings. "What purpose could it possibly have?"

"Might have been a beacon of some sort," Hunt offered. "Help guide people who are in the area. It doesn't seem to have any equipment other than that light. And it's against commonsense to build something this massive just to house a dozen or so rooms. You could do it with a lot less material."

"It could be a beacon," assented Pinchon, nodding slowly. "But these walls make me think it's something more."

"Well, whatever it is, it'll give us shelter for the night," Gromyko said. "I suggest that we take a few of the rooms and get whatever sleep we can, breaking forth as soon as the sun has dawned. We're going to want to have as much light on our hands as possible when we search the area tomorrow."

"Search for what?" Tselitel asked as he walked past her.

"Why, for what we came here for," he grinned. "A way to save the galaxy. Now, why don't you and Rex take this room. Milo and I will take the one next to it."

"Shouldn't we stick together?" Milo asked. "I'd rather have as many lights around as possible."

"Oh, don't be a baby," Gromyko said with a careless wave of his hand. "The light outside will keep those creatures at bay. And if you like, we can leave one of the lights shining at the door. But there is no way I'm sleeping more than two to a room. These spaces are too small for half a dozen people to draw breath in them without producing a stinking swamp of human odors by dawn."

"I'll keep an eye out by the door," Pinchon said. Then looking at Gromyko and Milo, "One of you can take over in a few hours."

"I'll take the second watch," Hunt said.

"No, you stay with her," the colonel said, studying the careworn look on Tselitel's face. "She's been through enough for one day. Between the three of us we'll keep it covered. Goodnight." With this they filed out of the barren room and closed the door.

"Want something to eat?" Hunt asked, kneeling on the floor and busting out one of the emergency rations he'd put in his pocket.

"All I want to do is sleep," she said, her arms wrapped tightly over her chest, her hands trembling from anxiety against her sides. "But I don't know if I'll ever be able to sleep again."

"You will," he said, taking her arm and pulling her gently down to the space beside him. "Just get a little something into you first. It'll help you relax."

"What *was* that thing?" she asked again, unable to get the ghastly image out of her mind. "I can't believe how much it reminded me of the figures I saw in my apartment. Not an exact replica, of course. But the *spirit* was the same." She closed her eyes after saying this, regretting her choice of words. "Do you think they can come through the walls?"

"No, or Antonin couldn't have trapped one with his light," replied Hunt matter-of-factly as he chewed on an emergency ration bar. "Whatever they are, they're bound by the material world. You saw the one that chased us maneuvering around obstacles like any normal creature. Whatever they are, they're still subject to the laws of physics."

"That's something, anyway," she said, laying on the floor, propping herself up with her arm. "Strange that the people who built this place left the floors made out of dirt.

You'd think they'd cover them with something."

"Maybe they ran out of money," Hunt quipped. "Spent it all on that shiny light."

"Somehow I doubt that," she smiled faintly.

"Oh, maybe this place is a combination beacon and refuge for weary travelers like us. After all, there aren't any locks on the doors, so it isn't any kind of permanent residence. It wouldn't do to freeze their visitors with ice cold floors."

"I don't suppose so," she replied, finally taking a piece of the ration he'd opened. "Still," she said, munching on it, "I can't figure this place for a hotel. There's got to be something more to it than that."

"We'll probably find out in time," Hunt said, emulating her posture and looking into her eyes. "Are you alright?"

"I don't know," she said honestly. "I was until we saw that beast tonight, despite everything we've been through already. But…" she let her voice trail, her eyes searching the walls as though to see through them.

"Hey, I've got you," he said, taking her arm in his hand and rubbing it. "Nothing is going to get in here tonight. Just take it easy."

"I'll try," she said, enjoying his touch. "This is a far cry from where we met."

"It is," he agreed. "And I don't think our journey is over yet. I think it's barely begun."

"So do I," she said, her eyes climbing the shiny black walls around her, her mind wandering back to the creature.

"That's enough worry for one night," he said, reading her thoughts from her expression. Rolling onto his back, he drew her onto his chest. Her head resting just below his chin, she let out a long sigh.

"I'm sorry I bolted tonight," she said, her mouth half muffled by his shirt. "I put us both at risk when I did that."

"That's alright," he said, rubbing her back with his

hands.

"I just don't know what came over me! I couldn't help myself. I'm not usually such a coward."

"There's *nothing* cowardly about you, darling," he said, caressing her cheek with his hand. "Coming here has proven that."

"I think whatever that woman did to me left some kind of lasting damage," she continued, as though he hadn't spoken. "First *Selek-Pey* reminded me of them, and then that creature tonight. I mean, how ridiculous can you get? There's a world of difference between those two! *Selek-Pey* was a kind, benevolent friend. And that demon tonight–."

"That's the second time you've said that," he cut in. "Why *demon*? Why something immaterial?"

"I don't know. I guess it just seems appropriate."

"I don't think that's an accident," he said, gently stroking her hair as he thought. "That's right, earlier in the jungle you said 'no more of the demons.' Doesn't that strike you as an odd choice of words? 'No more' of them?"

"Sorry to intrude," Wellesley said, still slung about his friend's neck. "But I think Rex has a point."

"See? The 'brilliant war AI' agrees with me," he said lightly, hoping to put a smile on her lips.

"You're never going to let me forget that, are you?" he asked with a sigh.

"Probably not," he grinned, relieved to hear a quiet chuckle escape the woman who lay partially atop his chest.

"Back when you were under attack in your apartment, I noticed a strange quirk in your mental activity. I didn't mention it at the time because I didn't have the least idea what it meant. Frankly, I still don't. But in all my time with you, Rex, and even reaching as far back as *Koln* and *Kalak-Beyn*, I have *never* seen anything like it. Only when she was attacking you, and then again tonight, did you exhibit this kind of activity."

"What do you think it means?" she asked, concern in

her voice. "Am I going nuts?"

"No, nothing like that," he said reassuringly. "But it's significant that it has only ever been present during encounters with the 'dark side,' for lack of better words. It's as though you recognize something in these figures; something that makes you recoil as fast as you can."

"Well, they *are* nightmare figures, both sets of them," Hunt said. "That wretch outside her apartment was there to scare her out of her wits, drive her from the planet."

"But it's more than that," Wellesley insisted. "A lot more. Lily has a peculiar sensitivity to others. Most of her life she thought it was just a matter of intuition. But the experience on Delta-13 proved it to be the psychic tenderness of a natural born healer. She has a vulnerability unique to her. It's buried under a half dozen layers of rationality, psychiatric training, and cultural programming. But it's there all the same – inescapably manifesting itself. Her sensitivity to Milo's situation proved that."

"What's your point?" asked Hunt.

"Hey, don't interrupt him," she said with a little laugh. "I was just starting to feel good about myself."

"You should always feel good about yourself," he said, kissing her forehead. "Wellesley?"

"I agree."

"No, I meant, what are you driving at?"

"Oh. Well, you understand that this is a preliminary assessment. Naturally, without any information besides–."

"Wells," Hunt said, a touch of impatience in his voice.

"Fine, I think the figures she saw in her room were real."

"What!" exclaimed Tselitel, nearly jumping off Hunt's chest.

"That's pretty far-fetched, old friend," Hunt said, drawing Lily back down.

"Not so much as you might think," he said, warming to his subject now that it had finally been thrust into the open. "Consider *Selek-Pey*: he was just as real as you or I. And yet he was nothing but a memory stored by the planet. A virtual presence that was as lively and dynamic as the original version, that misty recollection interacted with his environment as though he was the *only* version. I think these sentient worlds have a great deal more capacity to interact with their residents than we ever imagined before."

"You're losing me," Hunt said.

"Okay, uh," the AI said, digging around for words. "I suspect that they can, and do, maintain detailed recollections of some of their residents. *Selek-Pey* is the most notable example we're aware of. But there's no reason to think they haven't done it with others, perhaps even on a large scale. The figures that Lily saw ground her to powder with fear – they bore a reality that she couldn't possibly escape. Now, from our experience with *your* gift, this doesn't tend to be the case. Milo saw his own guilt paraded before him and turned over a new leaf, but otherwise hasn't shown any ill effects. From what you told me, the people you struck in the basement that night with Antonin were terrified out of their wits, like animals that had some deep seated terror thrust before them. And like animals they tried to crawl away from it, senselessly trying to press themselves *into the concrete*. Their rationality had totally deserted them for a time. That never happened to Lily. She was scared, literally, to tears. But she never lost conscious hold of herself like they did, reduced to mere instinct and the fight-or-flight response."

"I still don't see your point," Hunt said.

"According to Ugo, your power consists of drawing up unconscious fears in the person you strike, which was the same power that woman had. But who is to say that's all it can do? Lily has been subtly different ever since the attacks. It's as though her sensitivity has been cranked up several notches. Even physical phenomena seem to hit her harder than before, though by her own testimony she was never a terribly robust person."

"So you think..." trailed Tselitel.

"I think the attacks kicked open the doors of your gift and made you perceive faint memories still held in mind by the planet," Wellesley said. "I think the figures were real, but just scarcely perceptible. Rex, remember that night in the snow with her, when you said you felt a presence of some kind watching us?"

"Uh huh."

"I believe that was just such a figure. You've never noticed any such presence before. Yet the very first time you did was with Lily, during direct physical contact. I don't believe those two factors are a coincidence. I think she enabled you to perceive what she was only unconsciously aware of herself. Later, when she was under attack, those unconscious perceptions were brought to the fore, terrifying her but not blinding her the way the others seem to be affected."

"Then what were those figures?" she asked, her fear increasing the more she thought of them as real. "And why did *Selek-Pey* frighten me at first? He wasn't like them."

"I can't say on either score," Wellesley replied. "Maybe the planet's memory of him was clouded with other, less pleasant memories. But the fact that the creature we saw in the jungle tonight evoked the same kind of mental activity in you that they did makes me think that they're similar."

"But how could mere memories attack us?" countered Hunt. "You saw the scars on Antonin and the colonel."

"I don't know that, either," the AI said patiently. "I don't have all the answers – just most of them. Perhaps when we get in contact with the planet we'll learn more."

"*If* we get in contact," Tselitel said glumly.

"Oh, I think we will," Wellesley said with confidence. "I agree with Antonin: the planet wants us here. Now it's just a question of how to communicate with it. But I expect *it* will answer that question for us, in its own time."

"So what do we do in the meantime?" asked Hunt.

"In the meantime we stay alive, try to secure some kind of food source, and don't stay out after dark."

"I don't suppose you have a plan for the first two?" prodded Hunt.

"There are plenty of animals roving the jungle. With nearly a half dozen handguns to our name we ought to be able to keep from starving once the emergency rations run out. Naturally that's not a long term solution. But the Devourers aren't gonna give us time to worry about that."

"That's right!" Tselitel exclaimed. "I'd forgotten entirely about them! I've been so busy just surviving that I haven't had the headspace to think about them."

"Well, maybe their impending arrival will work in our favor," Hunt said. "It'll give *Preleteth* a reason to cut to the chase and get with us immediately. Remember, its neck is on the line just as much as ours is. More, perhaps."

Hunt awoke early the next morning with Tselitel beside him. She was sleeping tensely, her breathing tight. With care he got to his feet and slipped out the door without waking her.

"She still asleep?" Milo asked, as his brother approached him by the obelisk's outer door.

"Yeah," he replied, stretching his arms over his head. "But just barely. Anything new here?"

"Silent as the grave," he said, the door ajar so he could peek out. "That green light is still shining, even with the sun about to come up. I haven't seen or heard from our nightmarish friends all night. They *must* know we're here, so it seems that light does just as good a job as any other at keeping them away. Funny that it's green, instead of some more normal color."

"I'm gonna take a look around," Hunt said, walking past him.

"You sure that's a good idea?" Milo asked, seizing his arm lightly to stop him for a moment. "We don't know what else might be lurking out there. After all, that light only stops those creatures. It won't work against normal predators."

"I'll keep my eyes open," Hunt said, drawing the pistol from his belt.

"Alright," Milo replied, releasing his arm and stepping back. "Just call out if you get in trouble, and I'll come running."

Nodding, Hunt slipped out the door and glanced around. Everywhere the ground was bright. Streaks of light colored the clouds above, signaling the impending rise of the sun. Striding a short distance from the obelisk, he turned around and cast his eyes up and down its massive form. He hadn't noticed it the night before, but it stood in a grassy clearing completely devoid of larger plantlife. The jungle surrounding it had a sharp cutoff, as though it had been deliberately pruned back only a month before. The total absence of any kind of markings on the ground, however, negated that idea. Something was holding it back, keeping it from growing.

"I suspect that obelisk keeps more than just those creatures at bay," Wellesley said, thinking along a similar line. "Can't imagine why, though, unless the people who built it really didn't like plants."

Without commenting Hunt kept walking until he'd reached the north side of the clearing. Just as he was about to step into the wall of jungle before him, the AI spoke again.

"Are you sure about this? It might be better to wait until the others are up. Strength in numbers, and all that."

"I don't think so," Hunt said, following a strong intuition. "I think it might not work if the others are here. Might scare it away."

"Scare what away?" Wellesley asked, as his friend pressed through the vibrant green leaves into the dark, humid space beyond.

"I don't know."

"So we're risking our necks because…" trailed the AI.

"It's just a feeling that I woke up with, Wells," Hunt said, pausing for a moment. "I can't explain it. But it feels just like the intuitions that Delta-13 sent me about meeting Lily. Now, if you want to help, keep your mouth shut and your ears open. I don't like this any more than you do."

"Alright," he replied dubiously. "Just let the record show that I've got my doubts."

"Not half as many as I've got."

Moving cautiously, Hunt paused every little while to stop and listen. The jungle was dark, mysterious, forbidding. The thick canopy above kept out most of the dawn's early light, masking his surroundings in shadows. He kept his flashlight at the ready but switched off, taking to heart Milo's experience of the night before. Besides, he was sure that Wellesley would alert him if one of the creatures drew close.

For nearly an hour Hunt pushed deeper into the jungle, aware that each step carried him farther from help. Quietly he cocked his pistol, determined to throw as much lead as he could if something should jump him.

"They'll be worried about us," Wellesley said, as his friend splashed through a weak little stream. Kneeling beside it, he washed the sweat from his face with handfuls of the water.

"I know," he replied regretfully, thinking especially of how it would make Tselitel fret. "But I've got to follow this through. It might lead to what we came here for in the first place." He thought for a moment. "You *have* been keeping track of our path so we can find our way back, right?"

"Of course," replied Wellesley. "I wouldn't be a 'brilliant war AI' if I didn't attend to such minutia, would I? Well, would I?"

But Hunt didn't respond. Remaining perfectly still, he listened as someone quietly moved behind him, about a dozen paces off. Their footfalls were perfectly silent. Only the brushing of large, flappy leaves against their shins gave away their presence. Carefully Hunt slipped his finger inside the trigger guard of his pistol, flicking the safety off with his thumb. The hair stood up on the back of his neck as he heard whoever it was drawing closer. When they were half a dozen steps away he twisted onto his back, facing them with the gun firmly held between both knees.

"What the?!" he exclaimed, when his eyes fell upon his visitor.

"Your weapon is unnecessary," a figure of bright blue light said. It looked like a woman, but a very strange one. Her features were recognizably human, but distorted, as though she'd been the victim of genetic manipulation. Her jaw, mouth, and nose were unusually small, yet her cheekbones were broad and her eyes round and large. Only five feet tall, with neatly cut hair and garbed in a skin-tight covering of blue, she drew close, extending her hand to him. "I am *Alleehavah*."

Cautiously Hunt got to his feet, tucking the pistol back into his belt and taking her hand. Cold to the touch and as smooth as glass, it felt otherworldly.

"My name is–."

"Rex Hunt," she said with an impish smile. "Yes, I know. The worlds of the *Ahn-Wey* have long been aware of you. You should be very proud of yourself. Never have we beheld one grow so quickly in the fulfillment of his destiny."

"Destiny?"

"Of course," she replied. "To destroy the Devourers once and for all. You were born to this task, and only you can accomplish it. It is for this reason that this world drew you to it. They are coming. Indeed, the consumers of all life are now close at hand. Time is short, and you have much to do and learn."

"I don't understand," Hunt said. "Who are you, really? And how am *I* supposed to stop the Devourers? I'm just one man."

"One man is all it takes," she smiled. "As long as he is the *right* man. There is still one hope left for the galaxy. It will require courage and sacrifice, along with an enormous amount of risk. But rest assured, *you* are what is needed in this dark hour of humanity's journey. Come, walk with me. We have much to discuss."

"What about my friends?" he asked, reluctantly falling in beside her.

"They will be taken care of," she said with a reassuring motion of her hand. "As we speak two of my kind are approaching their camp within the obelisk. They will be told where you are, and that you are alright."

"And who is 'we?'"

"Why, we're *you*, of course," she smiled. "Humanity has long been within this galaxy. Yours is not the first civilization of man to take its place among the other great races of the Milky Way. Eons ago we were the absolute masters of all we beheld. It was we who first spoke with the living worlds, learning their wisdom. In peace we trafficked with all the other races of this galaxy, and with those who stood far beyond."

"What happened?" Hunt asked. "How did it go wrong?"

"The Devourers came upon us, much as they came upon you. It was evident that they came from another dimension, but that information was of no use to us. We armed for the conflict, but they swept aside our forces and those of the allies who came to help us. They ravaged our worlds, draining their precious life and killing our people wherever they found them. This galaxy," she said, waving her hand over her head, "was once *teeming* with living worlds. Now it is mostly barren. The Devourers have left only death in their wake. Never again shall this galaxy know the vibrant life of those forgotten days. Were it not for the action of the *Ahn-Wey* in banishing them, there would be no life at all here today. But that victory came at a terrible cost."

"You mean the death of most of the *Ahn-Wey*?" he asked.

"And now they have returned," she said, evading his question. "There is not strength in this galaxy for a second banishment. Only the second way remains."

"What way is that?" he asked.

"Why, your way," she said, looking at him as they walked. "The dark worlds of this galaxy have found their way into your family, Rex Hunt. It is they who cultivated the gift you bear, and that of your father. Indeed, it was through him that they sought to dominate mankind, preparing the way for the Devourers. When this failed they brought them through as quickly as they could, determined to stamp out the Earthborn before you were too strong to stop."

"This is all going by a bit fast," Hunt said, shaking his head. "You mean these dark worlds brought the Devourers?"

"Yes. I'm sorry," she smiled apologetically. "I am so used to the tale that I've skipped around. Before the *Ahn-Wey* there was a league of all the living worlds in the galaxy. Together they thrived with mankind. We took care of them, and they took care of us. It was a symbiotic relationship. However, many of the worlds grew jealous of our prominence in the galaxy and sought to cast us out. A great conflict grew within the planets of the league. Finally the league was shattered by a secret cabal led by the planet *Eesekkalion*. It seduced many worlds to join it, promising them glory from the ashes of mankind. Forming a league of their own, which they called the *Prellak*, they began to scour all the dark corners of the universe in search of a scourge they could let loose upon mankind. Finally they discovered the Devourers. Long ago banished to another dimension, they waited in silent anticipation for the time of their release. Through *Eesekkalion*'s great wisdom they managed to slice a hole in the wall that separated our dimension from theirs, thus allowing the parasite to descend upon our galaxy."

"But that would be suicide," replied Hunt. "The Devourers would consume the *Prellak* worlds as well."

"No, at the slightest provocation they could send

them back, though at a cost similar to that suffered by the *Anh-Wey*. Holding this over their heads, the Devourers were forced to do their bidding. After countless ages in their prison, they were glad to. Appearing everywhere at once, just as they have this time, they surprised the good worlds of the former league and devastated them. Those who survived the first attack reformed themselves into the *Ahn-Wey*, determined to fight alongside humanity against the parasite. But it was no use. The invaders were too strong for us, even combined. It was then that Delta-13 formulated the plan that ultimately drove them from the galaxy."

Silently they walked for a few moments.

"You must still have many questions," she said, stopping and looking up at him. Then she smiled. "You are such an attractive man. It is a pity that your clan took so long to develop."

"My clan?" he asked.

"Yes. You see, humanity used to be divided into a great plethora of clans. We were united by a common confederation that led us into the stars. But under that great unity were many subdivisions. Sometimes a single world, but more often a collection of star systems. Led by ancient families of high standing, each clan sent a representative to the *Eelay*, our governing body. Well, if they were developed enough, that is. I'm afraid there is no polite way to say this, but the Earthborn clan was the most backward of all the families of man. Physically robust, they lacked the mental powers of the other families. Your world was long regarded as the backwater of the human race, and consequently very little attention was paid to it. We were aware of your existence, but you were scarcely aware of ours."

"But how did we come to reach Earth if we were so primitive?" asked Hunt. "We must have had some kind of development to reach there in the first place, if the rest of you didn't start there."

"I am afraid this is another topic that cannot be

worded politely," she said, a shy smile on her gently glowing lips. "But your people descended from a ship that was loaded with poor, unintelligent laborers. In fact, they were prisoners. The vessel crashed on Earth and was not deemed of sufficient value to justify a rescue operation, so the laborers were left to shift for themselves. Your subsequent expansion into the stars has proven that assessment inaccurate."

"But we're still the dumb cousins, eh?" Hunt asked.

"Oh, your people are not dumb!" she exclaimed quickly. "Please don't get me wrong. All humans possess an intelligence that sets them apart from the vast majority of races that inhabit the universe. But compared to the rest of ancient humanity…" her voice trailed.

"Compared to them, we're not the brightest stars in the sky," he said.

"I'm afraid that is correct," she replied, smiling shyly once more. "But you have many other advantages that help to balance that trait out! Take myself, for example. I am not so attractive as you, nor as tall. And yet I am one of the finest specimens of my clan, renowned for both my appearance and my stature. The humans of Earth were some of the strongest, hardiest survivors of our race. And they have a great capacity for independence of thought, initiative, and unorthodox thinking. These are all faculties that the rest of us generally lacked. Intellectual and unwarlike, we were easy prey for the monsters that invaded our territories. Now you, the 'dumb cousins,' as you characterized yourself, stand a greater chance of holding out than the rest of us did."

"That leads to a question I have," Hunt said.

"Please, I am eager to answer any questions you may have," she replied generously.

"Why did we survive? And what happened to the rest of you? Or is that a part of the 'terrible cost of victory' that you mentioned earlier?"

"You're very perceptive," she said approvingly. "Yes,

you are precisely correct. The worlds of the *Ahn-Wey* were able to send the Devourers back to their prison, but only with our help. They expended the psychic energy of their resident populations along with their own in the great exertion that tore open the wall separating us from the dimension which had imprisoned the parasite. And in so doing killed every human who dwelt upon them."

"What!" exclaimed Hunt, both shocked and angry. "But how–. How could they do such a thing? Expend human lives like so much ammunition in a gun? Wipe us out as a race?"

"I assure you, they did not expend us," she said soothingly, laying a cool hand upon his arm. "It was with the full consent of the clans that they did so, for we recognized that the only hope for the survival of all life in our galaxy was the removal of the parasites. Unless this was accomplished all races would fall, and none so quickly as man itself. Everywhere our overmatched forces were crumbling before their onslaught. There was no choice, no second option."

"And yet, we have a second option now?" asked Hunt, regaining his composure.

"Yes, and that is for reasons that are unique to your clan as well. Your people possess a strong inclination toward the dark energy of the universe. In this there is both power and danger. Your ancient relatives, both my people and those of the other clans of our confederation, had no such tendency toward shadow. In this form of energy there is both incredible might and the perpetual hazard of unimaginable destruction. We were peaceful, passive, and intellectual. Our capacity to destroy was pitiful in comparison to yours, due to our affinity for the energy of light. But do not mistake my words," she added quickly, just as he was about to speak. "Light can be just as destructive in other races as darkness is in humans. But it does not work upon our kind in that way. Even now there are races that prowl the galaxy who are strongly aligned with light. And yet they would destroy all who cross their path."

"So the effect is specific to humans," Hunt said.

"Precisely. And the unsavory beginning of your clan contains the seed of your future development. The prisoners who crashed on Earth were not well in the mind. Your intellect appears to us a jumble of contradictions."

"You're saying we're broken?" asked Hunt, cocking an eyebrow.

"You have such a decisive way with words," she said, appreciating that fact and also uncomfortable because of the lack of room it gave her to maneuver diplomatically. "But yes, you are correct. There is great anger, great hatred in your clan. You are torn apart, each of you individually, by challenges that were unknown to us. Insecurities, longings, a thousand forms of suffering. It makes you weak, and it makes you strong. It forces you to develop the faculties needed to overcome it."

"School of hard knocks," he summarized quietly to himself.

"Again, your words cut to the heart of the matter without flinching," she said, a smile stretching from ear to ear. "Oh, I hope I don't embarrass you with my appreciation," she added quickly, noticing a change in his expression. "It's just that I have never had the pleasure of speaking with one of your clan before. And you are so crisp! So – so *decisive!*"

"You keep saying that," he said, a puzzled grin forming on his lips. "Is that important to you?"

"The people of my clan were not decisive," she said regretfully, her face falling at once. "We were confused and lost when the parasite descended upon us. If we'd only been more resolute in our actions…" she trailed.

"The parasite would have worked its will all the same," Hunt said with certainty. "There's nothing you could have done. They were too powerful. Even the imperial navy is reeling from their blows."

"You comfort me," she smiled appreciatively, as he

glanced away to look at a small creature which had scampered under a nearby bush. "I understand why your woman loves you."

His head snapped to her at this, surprised for reasons he couldn't explain.

"Are you surprised that I speak of love?" she giggled. "It is said that the people of your clan are great distrusters of love. They awkwardly approach it, like an animal uncertain of what it has found."

"Ha!" burst out Wellesley.

"I'd say that's right," Hunt nodded.

"My people long thought your clan was incapable of love; of the sacrifice necessary to stop the Devourers when they returned. They said only the other clans were capable of surrendering their lives to spare the galaxy from ruin. Many believe it was our great burden, the purpose for which we had risen in the first place."

"I imagine our people have been a disappointment to yours," Hunt said evenly, factually.

"To many, yes. But not to me," she said eagerly.

"And why is that? We seem to be the black sheep."

"Because all things in life must have their counterpoise, their balance," she said. "It was our very softness, our benevolence and generosity that permitted the Devourers to savage the Milky Way. Had we been stronger, more aggressive, we could have resisted them, as the people of your empire are now striving to do."

"It isn't my empire," Hunt replied grimly.

"But it rules over you, does it not?" she asked with confusion.

"It tries, by force and manipulation," he explained. Then, tapping a finger on his heart, he said, "But not in here. In here I maintain my own government."

"Wonderful!" she exclaimed. "You truly are the descendent of your ancient forebears! Even in your political attitude there are divisions! Separations! We were never capable of such independence. Even I am not, though I appreciate it. You are an incredible human being, Rex Hunt."

"No," he replied with certainty, shaking his head. "I'm just one man trying to survive."

"Each word confirms my understanding!" she said, clapping her hands and taking a little leap in the air. "No thought of the common good! *Just one man, trying to survive!*"

"Is…that a good thing?" he asked dubiously.

"You must understand my context," she said. "Of course we must all serve the common good if we are to abide as a race. Without thinking of the rest of our species we shall surely fall. But at this time we need the hardness, the independence of thought that you demonstrate without effort! Without even being *conscious* of it, so natural is it to you! That is what makes you remarkable, quite aside from your terrible gift."

"This is quite literally fascinating," Wellesley said to Hunt. "But don't you think we ought to ask her about *Preleteth*'s plan?"

"*Alleehavah*," Hunt began.

"Yes?" she asked quickly, looking up into his face. "Another question?" she asked with anticipation. "Oh, I love questions! I never have anyone to talk with besides the planet, and it knows all that I do, and much more. Through you I get to experience ignorance again! I get to see the broadening of a worldview and participate vicariously in it! Oh, it's glorious!"

"Indeed," he chuckled, unable to help himself. "Many years ago this world communicated with Delta-13, warning it of the return of the Devourers and hinting at a plan–."

"Yes, the Key of Dissolution," she said eagerly.

"I'm sorry?"

"For what?" she asked.

"No, I mean I don't understand – what is the Key of Dissolution?"

"You mean, Delta-13 hasn't told you?" she asked, her

face again a picture of confusion. "But why wouldn't it?..." she trailed, more to herself than to him.

"You're losing me again," he said.

"Oh, I'm sorry. The Key of Dissolution was a plan to deliberately shatter a minor dimension which stood adjacent to the one which contained the Devourers. The hope was to establish a kind of firewall that would prevent the parasite from ever crossing back into our domain again. But this plan was fraught with risk, the possibility of it doubling back on us considerable. For many years this world tried to convince Delta-13 of its obvious necessity, but to no avail. A majority of the *Ahn-Wey* agreed with this course, but they wouldn't act without the consent of their once great leader. Thus the plan was deadlocked, until it has now become superfluous."

"Superfluous?" he asked in shock. "Then Epsi– I mean, *Preleteth*–."

"You may use either term," she said peacefully. "I'm familiar with many forms of communication, and with the generally accepted naming conventions of many races, including the regrettably vanquished *Kol-Prockians*."

"But we came to *Preleteth* because it said it had a plan!" he exclaimed. "We thought it would be able to help us stop the Devourers."

"It can help you," she said. "But not in the way you think. The age of the *Ahn-Wey* has come to an end. Every hour that passes sees another of their member worlds reduced to barrenness. They no longer have the strength to fight back, even to save themselves. No, humanity will have to resolve this crisis on its own. It is now to the clan of the Earthborn that the galaxy looks for salvation."

"But what can we do?" he asked, anxiety filling him. "Our ships were crushed by the Devourers as soon as they appeared."

"*Preleteth* will prepare you for the struggle to come," she said. "And I will help you in any way that I'm able to."

"How can you help if even the *Ahn-Wey* are powerless

against them?" he asked, growing exasperated. "There's nothing we can do to them! They'll sweep us aside like dust!"

Pausing in her walk she turned to him and laid a hand on his arm.

"Look within *yourself*, Rex Hunt. There you will find the answer. The gift that the *Prellak* implanted within you can be turned against them. There is time, and there is *hope*. You need only to believe that."

"I'm not one for belief," Hunt said.

"Yes, you are," she said, resuming movement. "It was your father who was not. And you are not him, Rex Hunt. Not by any stretch of the imagination. He was dominated by the darkness of the *Prellak*. They channeled more into him than his soul could handle. Though essentially a good man, he was clouded by the dark power and could no longer see the true course. That is not true of you. You are a stronger man than he was."

"I have surrendered to the power before," he said, recalling the fight in the ancient room. "I killed my father with it. I could have killed my friends with it, too."

"But you *didn't*," she said earnestly.

"Only through the intervention of Lily," he replied, briefly explaining what had happened. "Without her I would have become the terror of Delta-13."

"She was only able to help because you *wanted* her to," *Alleehavah* said. "Her gift cannot force itself on another. It may only guide and assist the motion already present within. She gave you succor and support at a desperate moment. But that act only succeeded because *you wanted it to*. She is not capable of forcing you, or anyone, with her gift. It is benevolent and kind, unlike the one that you carry."

"She says the nicest things," Wellesley remarked.

"I still don't understand how I came to possess it in the first place," Hunt said. "Nor my father, for that matter, How could the dark worlds *implant* a gift in us?"

"I'm afraid I spoke imprecisely when I said that,"

Alleehavah said meekly. "It is not that they *implanted* it in you. Rather they drew to the fore a power that had lain dormant in your family for generations. They knew he would become a brilliant man and sought to turn him to their cause. But his power was limited. Recognizing this, they turned their attention to his young son, hoping to awaken in him a greater darkness than they had managed in his father. But before this work could be completed, you were both, along with your brother, exiled to Delta-13. There the planet buried the darkness deep within your unconscious mind until such a time as you would be strong enough to handle it. Realizing the tremendous asset the *Prellak* had inadvertently put into its hands, the planet watched over you, helping you grow and assiduously managing the dark power they had stimulated within you. Aware that you needed more help in order to control it, the planet brought you into contact with another."

"Ugo," Hunt muttered.

"Ugo?" she asked. "No, I mean Lily. She is the counterbalance needed to maintain the power of your mind over the shadow within. At least she was. You have grown very strong. Only the greatest exertion can unsettle your mind now, the most desperate struggle."

"But how can this gift be used against the *Prellak*?" he asked. "I call forth the fears of the unconscious mind. What good can that possibly be against a confederation of planets?"

"Truly you have much to learn, Rex Hunt," she said with surprise. "Is that really all you think yourself capable of?"

"Isn't it?" he asked.

"No, by no means. That is the most natural channel for the darkness within you to express itself. But it can pour forth into myriad directions, manifesting as all sorts of gifts. But it will have to be developed, grown into something mature and multifaceted. It will require training."

"And who will train me?" asked Hunt. "You?"

"Oh, of course not," she laughed. "I have no such capacity to instruct. I am only the assistant to this world. No, *Preleteth* will teach you itself. In fact, it is ready to begin now."

"But how can it instruct me?" he asked incredulously. "I thought the worlds of the *Ahn-Wey* were forbidden direct communication."

"They are," she replied with a shameful look on her face. "But there is no longer any time to worry about that. The Devourer threat must be eliminated, no matter the cost."

"What cost?" he asked.

"I'm sorry, there's no more time to explain now," she said, pressing a finger to her temple. "The planet wishes to speak with you at once. Follow me."

Silently she led him through several hundred feet of dense jungle, her small, sleek body slipping past the grasping foliage with ease. Hunt, his frame larger and his clothes inclined to get caught on sticks and thorns, fell further behind until he lost sight of her.

"Hey, hold up a minute," he called when she didn't stop. "I'm still back here."

"Oh, I'm sorry!" she said through a wall of green, quickly doubling back and standing before him.

"How much farther do we have to go?" he asked, pressing his way through a thornbush that drew blood from his arms.

"You're bleeding!" she exclaimed, taking his arm in her gentle blue hands, her touch strange upon his skin. "Do you need medicine?"

"Oh, that?" he asked casually, turning up the underside of his forearm and looking at the half dozen rivers of red that trickled toward his elbow. "That's nothing. Don't worry about it."

"Are you sure?" she asked with concern, her large eyes wide. "I'm supposed to ensure your safety heading to and from your meeting with the planet. If you should be hurt…"

"No, it's nothing to worry about," he said, wiping the blood off on his other sleeve and holding his arm up again for her to see. "Just a few scratches, is all. Now, how much farther is it?"

"Not very far," she said dubiously, looking at his arm once more and then brightening up. "Just another few minutes."

"Lead the way," he said, gesturing forward and falling in behind her once again.

"Solicitous little critter, isn't she?" Wellesley asked, as her lightly glowing form brightened the leaves and branches that slid over her body. Soon she stopped before another obelisk, this one much smaller than the first.

"It is within such structures that *Preleteth* may manifest itself for a period of time. Do not open the door for any reason, until you are instructed to do so by the planet." She opened it and gestured for him to enter.

"Aren't you coming with me?" he asked, stopping just inside as she began to close the door.

"No, that is not my place," she said. "*Preleteth* must speak with you alone. Please, go at once."

Without another word she shut him in.

"Why don't I like the looks of this?" Wellesley asked, as Hunt drew his pistol.

Carefully Hunt worked his way inside, checking each room for inhabitants but finding none. The space was much smaller than the first obelisk, but the walls were made of the same ice cold metal, and the air was correspondingly cool and refreshing after his jaunt in the jungle.

"Something doesn't feel right, Rex," the AI said. "I think we ought to get out of here before–."

"Do not be alarmed," a deep, booming voice said from behind Hunt. Jerking around, pistol held at shoulder height, he scanned the smooth walls of the structure but saw nothing. Reluctantly he lowered his pistol.

"Where are you?" he asked.

"I am all around you. In the tongue of your friend, I am *Preleteth*."

"Then you can hear me speak?" Wellesley asked.

"Of course. But there is little time for us to talk. The parasite is nearly upon us, and then my time will end. They know of the place I took in the last struggle against them, and they are determined to exact retribution. Many of the *Ahn-Wey* have already fallen before them."

"How long do we have until they get here?" Hunt asked.

"Several days at the most," *Preleteth* replied. "Their warp technology is advanced. Yet I am able to slow their progress through interfering with the dimension through which they are traveling. But they are crafty, and I must continually change my tack in order to frustrate them. They are ingenious at circumventing the methods that I use to slow them."

"Then it was you who increased our warp speed?" asked Wellesley.

"Indeed."

"But why?" asked Hunt. "You could have killed us! In fact, you nearly did."

"It was never my intention to harm you," *Preleteth* said. "But I had to hasten your advance, or you would never have had time to complete the training before the parasite arrived. I am sorry that I failed to slow you adequately before your vessel rejoined this dimension. But the struggle to frustrate the Devourers' journey distracted me for a critical moment, and I was unable to help. However, I had faith that your native ingenuity would save you from disaster. Clearly my faith was not misplaced."

"Clearly not," Hunt said, dismayed by the haphazard methods of the planet.

"*Alleehavah* told us that you have no plan to deal with the Devourers," Wellesley said.

"That is correct. The methods available to me are

inadequate to stifle this threat. The future of the galaxy rests with humanity now. We are no longer capable of protecting our fellow creatures from the abominations that surround us."

"But what can we possibly do?" Hunt asked. "We're outgunned!"

"Indeed, I estimate the humans have approximately a thirty percent chance of victory against the invaders," Wellesley seconded. "Everywhere imperial forces are in the retreat. It won't be long before their reserve fleets are smashed, and they are reduced to hit-and-run tactics."

"The estimate you form is accurate," *Preleteth* said. "But only on the basis of the information you have available. In secret the empire is laboring to ready a weapon – one of such power that it can stem the tide. Indeed, it is in the concealment of this weapon that the worlds of the *Ahn-Wey* are spending their final strength, and in that, rendering their last service to the galaxy. The *Prellak* are bent upon finding this weapon with all of their might. For years they have striven to discover its location. Only through perpetual exertion have we been able to hide it. In this we have been aided considerably by the servants of the emperor, particularly a human named Taegen. Regrettably he has fallen, a victim of jealousy at the hands of his colleagues. But others have risen in his place who continue his work. They have kept secret the location of the weapon through innumerable acts of devious manipulation. At this time there are no less than fourteen false locations into which equipment and personnel are being funneled; all with the aim of deception. The true location is known to only a few."

"What is the weapon?" asked Hunt.

"I cannot tell you. Not yet. There will be a time when you shall know, for it will become a necessity that you should. But until that time your curiosity will have to linger. We cannot risk its being discovered by telling even one soul unnecessarily. The hopes of more than just humanity rest upon its successful completion. There will be no life in this galaxy unless the Devourers are stopped."

"I understand," he replied, nodding.

"And now the time has come to continue your training. You have grown strong, Rex Hunt, though the teachings of the Order are merely a starting point. Nevertheless they were a necessary foundation, one upon which we will build. Indeed, it was for that purpose that Delta-13 guided you to one of their better operatives."

"Ugo," Wellesley said.

"That is correct. Though difficult, as you have learned, he was quite intelligent. Naturally there was much which his patron world did not teach him, for he was not ready. Hence I will teach you of things that he never even dreamed of. His nature was too intense – too easily swayed by emotionality to entrust with the most powerful secrets of the elemental realms. In that he was very much an archetype of your people. The ferocity of your ancient forebears shone through in his spirit. The ease with which he could become unsettled ultimately kept him from attaining the heights his intelligence and insight entitled him to. He simply could not be trusted to hold steady, as you do."

"I am easily unsettled as well," Hunt replied, wishing the planet to know fully who it was getting. "I'm not ideal for this sort of work, either."

"In that you are mistaken," *Preleteth* replied. "Unlike most humans, you possess a tremendous will and intensity, though it has been buried by your mode of living. It ennobles you, protecting you from the petty quarrels and fears of your kind. You must take this aspect of your nature and add to it all that your clan is capable of. In this way you can bring an end to the parasite that has descended upon us. The other clans were not capable of such work, and thus they fell. Nobly, it is true. But all the same they fell, unable to care for the galaxy that should have been their responsibility once the *Ahn-Wey* had finally slept among the stars. Now it is to *your* people that all life in the galaxy must look. It is upon your kin that the burden of guardianship has now been placed."

"We are not ready," Hunt said. "I fear we never will be. We are too willful – too weak and petty and given to strife. There is nothing great in humanity, no wells of nobility from which we can draw strength. We will fail you, *Preleteth*. The burden is too great."

"In this also you are mistaken," the voice said slowly, confidently. "Your people will be great. But only when the consciousness of this high purpose finally bursts upon them. Until that time they will stumble and fall. Indeed, even after they will still falter. But they will rise again, redeeming their mistakes, righting their wrongs. The greatness you require is in you, Earthborn. You need only look for it. The noblest features of your brother clans are with you, though they are hidden. Seek them, and you shall know them."

"I will try," Hunt said doubtfully.

"You will learn to see these truths in time," *Preleteth* said. "But now the time to train has come. Your abilities have been brought from the raw matter of your unconscious by the labors of the Order. But we have far to go before you will constitute a threat to the Devourers and their *Prellak* masters. With the limited knowledge we passed along to them, the Order was capable of developing the gifts of the descendants of your clan. Now I shall take you farther than they ever could have. Indeed, in no other human would it be possible, had not the *Prellak* taken an interest in your father, and yourself. For they molded the unformed depths of your mind until you both had the potential to be great weapons. But they only developed him to a point, so that he would be a threat to his fellow men but not to them. We shall carry your strength onward until you will be death to all who oppose you. None shall be able to stand against you."

"But how can you trust me with this responsibility?" Hunt asked. "You must know what I told *Alleehavah*, about what happened in the battle with my father. I lost control. But more than that, I *surrendered* control. I let the darkness well up within me until I could destroy my own father with it. How can you possibly entrust such incredible power to a man like that?"

"Because you are our only hope, Rex Hunt," *Preleteth* said. "The people of your clan give power to those who rule badly over them, because it would be worse to live with no ruler at all. Indeed, when we banished the Devourers the first time there were incalculable consequences. Yet the choice had to be made. We must concern ourselves with solving the problem of *our* time, and not seek permanent solutions, for they do not exist. Besides, we have great faith in you, and in the one who accompanied you here. She will be with you, to keep you steady even if you are not able to do so yourself. Trust in yourself, and trust in *her*."

"I agree," Wellesley said. "Come on, Rex: these guys have had a long time to think about this, and they're a lot more plugged into the situation than you or I. They've got the best shot at being right about this."

"He must settle his own mind," *Preleteth* said. "Only if his heart is with us shall we succeed. None can coerce him."

"My heart is with you," Hunt said decisively. "With doubts, but to lack doubts would make me more than human."

"I am glad you recognize that fact," *Preleteth* said, a smile in its voice. "We do not seek perfection, but simply the best your clan is capable of. And none is so capable as you, Rex Hunt."

"I'm ready," he said.

"As am I," *Preleteth* said. "Now we shall begin."

CHAPTER 5

"Minister McGannon, our fleet has engaged the invaders besieging Komia-2," a pretty female AI said via hologram. "Admiral Nelson wished me to inform you of our progress."

"How goes the battle?" she asked, her attention riveted by the first major counterattack against the Devourers by the imperial navy.

"Our forces have already downed several of their ships, though with great losses. At this rate, our casualties will be at least twice those of the enemy by the battle's end. But with our superiority in numbers, we ought to carry the day."

"Have they dealt any serious damage to Komia-2?" she asked.

"The planet appears to be enduring severe environmental disturbances," the AI replied in a serene, artificial voice. "It is evident that the invaders are manipulating its weather systems to wreak havoc on the population. But there's something odd about their use of such manipulation – other planets in the system, though under siege like Komia-2, aren't being subjected to this treatment."

"Very interesting," McGannon said, thinking back on what Admiral Makarovich had told her days before about a possible geo-weapon.

"Minister, I'm sorry to report that we have just lost Admiral Nelson's flagship, the *Tremendous*," the AI said, breaking in on her train of thought.

"The *Tremendous* was a super carrier," McGannon exclaimed in shock. "How could we possibly lose it so quickly?"

"The invaders crashed into it with one of their capital ships, severing it in two and emerging on the other side. This vessel is enormous, Minister, fully thirty-eight percent larger than the *Tremendous*."

"And Admiral Nelson?" she asked.

"Lost, Minister, along with most of the hands," the AI replied. "His second in command, Admiral Bannon, has assumed command from the bridge of the *Intrepid*."

"She's an imbecile," McGannon mumbled to herself, immediately regretting her words when the AI tilted her head, clearly hearing her. "Not a word of that leaves this room. Do you understand me?"

"Yes, Minister," she said, her voice still calm and incongruously serene. "I'm afraid threat appraisal has been changed. I now estimate our casualties at three times those of the enemy."

"Are there any other forces nearby that can assist?" McGannon asked, striving to stay calm, clenching and unclenching her hands below her desk where the AI couldn't see them.

"All imperial forces in the area are concentrated in the battle fleet that is currently engaged," she said. "The closest elements we could call on are several days away. I'm afraid the battle will be over by the time they arrive."

"Bannon will have to sweat it out," McGannon said grimly. "Pull up a display of the battle. I want to see how this looks."

"Of course, Minister."

Suddenly the pretty AI was replaced with a tortured glowing ball of broken vessels, spiraling dogfighters, and massive capital ships battling it out with all their might. The line of battle had quickly been shattered by the confrontational tactics of the Devourers. Getting in close to their assailants, they used their enormous tentacles to smash through their hulls with troubling ease while fuming green shells crashed against them, burning holes. Like vultures tearing through warm, soft flesh, they ripped armor plating from their hulls and let it drift off into space. The tentacles plunged deeply into the exposed decks, smashing crew members like gnats and dealing incredible damage.

"Only fifty-three vessels against our hundred and sixteen capital ships?" McGannon asked rhetorically. She'd already known the relative strength of the combatants, but she was shocked to see how well the invaders were grappling with the vastly superior numbers of their foes.

"Yes, Minister," the AI replied, about to continue when McGannon held up a hand for silence.

Leaning in closer to the chaos that floated above her desk, she saw imperial fighter craft gang up on their nimble opponents, trying to hold them away from the over-matched capital ships. Slipping away from their pursuers, they easily flew into the massive gashes that their own capital ships tore into those of the imperial navy, firing globs of death into their vulnerable insides.

"Keep them back," McGannon muttered, trying to will the battle to turn more decisively in their favor. "Hold back those fighters..." her voice trailed unconsciously.

"Minister, I'm afraid we may lose our connection," the AI said. "The ship I'm currently–."

With that the transmission cut out.

"Sounds like they're in a bad way," Krancis said from behind her, once again slipping in without notice. "You should have sent more forces with them."

"I sent everything we could manage," McGannon said without reservation, her shock making her forget to whom she spoke. Instantly she spun her chair around and faced the emperor's right hand, seeing in his face that he had registered her remark but that he wasn't inclined to make anything of it. She arose respectfully and waited for him to speak.

"It is clear that the imperial navy isn't capable of effectively grappling with the invaders, and that they will shortly be swept aside," Krancis said, taking several steps toward her. "Therefore I have decided to oversee the final steps of the Omega Project personally, to ensure that it is operational before that occurs."

"You?" she asked in surprise, immediately regretting her words.

"Yes, Minister," he said quietly. "The emperor feels that we have not seen the worst that the Devourers are capable of. As the navy has just demonstrated, it is not yet ready to withstand the fierce tenacity of their philosophy of warfare. They assault without restraint, without the slightest thought of sparing themselves harm. Like bullets shot from a gun, their only thought is to destroy their target. Such selfless fanaticism is outside all our conceptions of civilized warfare, and thus our technology is not ready to cope with it. Our vessels are designed around hammering an opponent that keeps itself at a distance, attempting to minimize loss to themselves. The suicidal tactics of the invaders destroy the whole tempo of our combat doctrine."

"We will learn to grapple with them quickly," McGannon said, venturing as much assertiveness as she felt capable of in his presence.

"No, we are not going to waste any more vessels on battles that cannot be won," Krancis said, raising his voice slightly. "We must save our strength, keeping our fleets intact to protect Omega. For the time being the invaders do not know its location, but it is only a matter of time until they figure it out. When they do, they will throw everything they have at it. We *cannot* afford to exhaust our forces before that fateful day arrives. We must have the strength to hold them back until its completion."

"But we can't leave the empire unprotected!" she exclaimed, her sense of duty overcoming her better judgment. "The invaders will be able to run free if we do that. Our people expect us to protect them, to save them from this onslaught!"

"And the emperor expects obedience to his *will*," Krancis said in a tone of quiet menace. "Those who do not conform to his will *shall be replaced*." He eyed her for a moment. "Do you believe you can better serve humanity in your present post, or in a ship headed for the kantium mines of Quarlac?"

"You wouldn't!" she said.

"I will do anything in the service of the emperor," Krancis said. "This is your last chance, McGannon. Either order the withdrawal of our forces from Komia-2, or I will immediately appoint someone who will."

"But we can win!" she pleaded. "If we pull out now, the Devourers will replace their losses and continue the siege of the planet! Then all those who have died up until now will have lost their lives for *nothing*. Don't forget that Admiral Nelson was a favorite of the emperor, and that his vessel was one of the first lost."

"The emperor has no favorites in an hour as dark as this," Krancis said, his face cold as a wall of stone. "He knows where his duty lies, and that the protection of humanity as a whole must take precedence over any concern he may feel for the memory of one man. Do you have such an awareness of your duty?" He eyed her for a moment, and then began to walk away.

"Colonel Johnson," she said into her intercom, causing Krancis to stop just short of the door.

"Yes, Minister?"

"Get in contact with the third fleet," she said reluctantly, eyeing the man before her. "Order an immediate retreat."

"Minister?"

"You have your orders!" she barked, switching off the intercom and looking at Krancis. "You have your retreat, Krancis. I'll send out the necessary orders to keep our forces disengaged from the invaders. Rest assured," she said, her eyes narrowing bitterly, "I know where my duty lies."

"That's good," he said casually, laying his hand on the doorknob. "Because it would be awkward to replace you just now. It's never good to change horses midstream."

She watched him slip out the door, closing it quietly behind him. The instant it was shut she ripped a paperweight off her desk and hurtled it across her office, smashing a hole in the far wall. Trembling with rage, her face flushing with blood, she smacked her fist on the desk, sending a bolt of pain up her arm as several objects clattered off of it onto the floor. Then, drawing a sharp breath, she strove to control herself.

"Those poor people," she muttered, thinking of the lives that had been fruitlessly lost over Komia-2. "I hope somehow they can forgive us."

❖ ❖ ❖

"You must understand that the darkness within you can be channeled in many directions," *Preleteth* said. "With it, you can manipulate matter, striking objects with your will just as easily as with your fist."

"With his will?" Wellesley asked.

"Of course. It should have been obvious to you that the bridge between your mind and the world around you can be expanded to bear more than just the capacity to inspire fear."

"I guess I never thought of it," Hunt said, standing in a hidden room beneath the obelisk that *Preleteth* had shown him. It was a vast, empty space, gently illuminated by a faint glow that seemed to possess no place of origin. Following the planet's instructions, he had left his light and weapon behind. "Can the living worlds strike matter in this way?"

"No, it is not within our power to act in that manner," *Preleteth* said. "Such a capacity would have made us unstoppable deities to all other forms of life. And that was never intended."

"Intended?" Wellesley asked.

"There is no time for further questions," *Preleteth* said. "You must push all such queries from your mind, focusing it *entirely* on the task at hand. Without your total concentration you will fail."

"I understand," Hunt said, taking a moment to clear his mind of everything except the space in which he stood. "What now?"

"Look behind you," *Preleteth* replied.

Slowly Hunt turned, seeing a dark creature like that he had seen in the jungle the night before. Instantly he raised his left hand and cut loose with a stream of smoke from his gift, striking the creature in the chest. It wailed ferociously, but showed no sign of harm.

"What is that thing doing in here?" demanded Wellesley, as the beast shifted on its feet. "Are you trying to kill Rex?"

"No, I am putting him against the greatest terror known to mankind – death itself. Upon this target he will learn to develop his powers. The lights in this space will keep it in check. You can see how it doesn't rush him. It is paralyzed, unable to advance or retreat because of the glow."

"Scanty protection indeed," Wellesley commented.

"Your opinion is neither sought nor welcome, *Kol-Prockian*," *Preleteth* snapped. Then, in a calmer voice, "You can see, Rex Hunt, that the creature is not susceptible to your gift as it now manifests itself. The ability to conjure fear, while of enormous power against your fellow humans, will be of no value in the fight ahead of you. Only the direct power to attack your target will answer in this conflict. You must not compel the force within you to express itself in the mode you have been taught by the Order. You must give it freer rein, letting it spill upon your victim as it will."

"But how?" Hunt asked, completely at a loss.

"I will guide you," *Preleteth* replied. "Raise your hand, and follow the channel I carve."

Raising his hand toward the creature as he was told, Hunt could intuit a path unfolding in his mind. It had a reality he could almost touch, though he couldn't see it. He could feel his spirit flowing out before him, as though to touch the creature. Instinctively he pulled back, lest it seize the psychic flow and follow it back to its source.

"No, let it touch the creature," *Preleteth* said. "It cannot use this channel to harm you. It lacks the capacity to convey its dark form in that manner. Only through direct physical touch can it poison another being."

Allowing it to flow outward once more, he felt the psychic channel make contact with the creature, causing it to snarl and claw the air in front of it.

"Do you feel it reaching out from you?" *Preleteth* asked. "Like another appendage extending from your chest?"

"That's a nauseating image," Wellesley commented. "Oh, excuse me, I forgot. I'll just sit in my corner."

"I can feel it," Hunt said quickly, hoping to distract the planet before it grew angry with his impudent friend. "But I haven't the faintest idea how to *attack* with it."

"Patience, Rex Hunt," *Preleteth* breathed heavily. "Patience. What you are doing now is opening a link between your mind and the outer world. Once you have grown comfortable with this action we will start pouring some of the darkness within you onto the target. That will be the true beginning of your offensive power. But you will have to surrender to the darkness, allowing it to flow through the channel you set for it."

"But won't it dominate me if I give it free rein?"

"Normally it could," *Preleteth* said. "But I will restrain

it to prevent that from happening. Once you've learned how to channel the darkness into the outer world there will be no risk of it spilling over into the rest of your psyche, and you will be safe from harm. The same thing happened for you back on Delta-13. That world restrained the darkness until the Order taught you to channel it into fear. You see, it is *crucial* that the dark power be channeled, else it will infect your mind. The Order gave you a potent, though limited, method through which to do this. I will teach you one that is vastly more destructive, harnessing the elemental power itself."

Drawing a deep, slow breath, Hunt reached out yet again and touched the creature. Viciously it tore at the air, trying to reach him as the bridge between them held firm. Wellesley could detect his friend's heart rate climbing as it did so. Rationally he knew that the creature couldn't hurt him. But on an instinctual level he saw a threat, separated only by a half dozen paces of open air, and his body responded accordingly. After nearly a minute Hunt severed the bridge.

"That's good," *Preleteth* said encouragingly. "That's very good. Often it takes students a great deal longer to establish a connection to their target. Clearly the *Prellak* knew what they were doing when they chose to develop the power within you. You have the clarity of mind to advance more rapidly than any of your kin. But this is only the first step. Now you must allow the darkness itself to begin to well up so that it may flow down the channel into the target. Let it pour over you like rain falling from the sky, filling every nook of your psyche."

"But I thought you said that would overwhelm me," Hunt replied.

"Normally that would be correct. But I will carefully manage it so that it cannot. The darkness will be permitted to flood through your mind without submerging it. You will be able to feel it. Indeed, you'll nearly be able to *taste it*. This is a necessary step because it will enable us to hasten your training by many, many weeks. Perhaps months."

"Isn't this just a bit risky?" interjected Wellesley. "What if you goof up?"

"The living worlds do not 'goof up,' *Kol-Prockian*," the ancient being said with annoyance.

"Oh, so that time that you nearly *killed* us yesterday by crashing our ship simply didn't happen?" the AI prodded, undaunted. "Remember what Delta said before we came here, Rex? It said that *Preleteth* was reckless. Do you really want to risk your sanity by trying to shave entire weeks off your–."

"How *dare* you cast aspersions on my capacity!" the world exploded. "What competence does a gadget such as yourself have to judge me?"

"As you might have noticed, had you been paying attention, I merely quoted what Delta said about you," Wellesley replied tartly.

"That diseased old rock was out of its mind," *Preleteth* scoffed. "Racked by pain inflicted by the parasite, it uttered pure nonsense."

"It's your call, Rex," the AI said. "Just wanted to be sure you had every angle clearly in view."

"Thanks, pal," Hunt replied, taking a few steps away from the dark creature and thinking for a moment.

"Well?" prodded *Preleteth*.

"I'm game for it," he said.

"Good. Now, you must open a channel toward the creature like before. Once this is done, allow the darkness to well up inside you, spilling into every quarter it wishes to fill. I will hold it back from dominating you. Of *that*," the world added sharply, for Wellesley's benefit, "you may be certain."

Breathing deeply once more, Hunt formed another bridge with the creature and closed his eyes. He could sense the pool of darkness undulating in the back of his psyche, just waiting for the chance to spill over. The fear that it would overwhelm him flashed through his mind, followed by the temptation to channel its terrible power in the manner the Order had taught him. But he dismissed this at once, aware that he must cast away the old crutch and learn a new method for controlling his shadowy inheritance. Choosing to trust *Preleteth*, he permitted the pool to rise until it penetrated every portion of his soul. A sensation akin to drowning struck him as the processes of his mind came under its influence. Unable to help it, he began to panic.

"Calm," *Preleteth* said soothingly, perceiving his inner struggle. "Remain calm. The power will not hurt you."

Taking heart from its words, Hunt relaxed. It was then that the planet allowed the inner shadow to wash over him, blotting out the outer world and plunging him into a sea of mental darkness. He perceived an incredible power. Dominant and absolute, it possessed the power to master all it encountered, including the one who bore it. A hundred sensations crowded his mind, each one telling him something about the gift he carried. Yet his power of description was defeated by what he experienced. Something akin to a smell arose within his mind, it being his psyche's feeble attempt to understand what it beheld. The scent was acrid, foul, and incredibly strong, like rubber boiling in a bubbling pool of sulfurous water. He perceived at once that the darkness he possessed was a weapon like no other.

In that instant *Preleteth* lowered the floodwaters and allowed his psyche to reemerge.

"You lying, deceptive, manipulating," Wellesley began in as angry a tone as Hunt had ever heard.

"Hold o-on, Wells," Hunt said unsteadily, confused to find himself lying on his back and trying to catch his breath as though he'd been drowning for real. "I'm-I'm okay."

"No thanks to this blundering orb of sheer stupidity!" he exploded. "You collapsed right after it spoke to you. I kept trying to pull you out of it, but I couldn't."

"It's okay," Hunt said, shivering as he got to his feet. "I learned what I needed to. I understand the darkness now."

"Are you satisfied *now, Kol-Prockian*?" asked *Preleteth* in a superior tone. "Clearly your friend is fine, and has profited from the experience."

"Apparently," Wellesley replied dubiously.

"What do we do next?" Hunt asked, the chill quickly leaving his bones. "Do I attack the creature now?"

"No, there is something else that you must do," the planet said. "You have come to appreciate the peculiar nature of the darkness, which is the second step in your journey here. Next you must experience the strength of your people. It is in your ancestral fortitude that you must find the power to channel the energy within you against the enemies of your kind. Should you omit this step, the shadow cannot fail to overwhelm you once my hand is no longer present to control it. You will descend into the collective memory of your people, and there perceive their struggle and their strength. This will harden your mettle, permitting you to master the force that now strives to master you."

"Do it," Hunt said.

"Wait!" Wellesley objected.

"What is it *now*?" asked the planet in exasperation. "If you intend to keep cutting in like this I will be forced to–."

"Oh, calm down, will you?" the AI retorted. "I was just going to suggest that Rex lay down first, instead of *falling down* like the last time. Or don't you care if he splits his head open?"

"Thanks, Wells," Hunt chuckled, quickly dropping to the floor and stretching out.

Closing his eyes, pictures started to float before him. He saw ancient humans laboring, striving against the odds, determined above all else to survive. Their struggle filled him with pride; a pride he had always dimly felt but never internalized. He could feel their courage, their hope – and their despair. At once he perceived that he was not a mere disconnected atom afloat in a sea of chaos. Instead he was part of a continual stream of beings, each of them connected to their forebears and their descendants by their collective struggle to survive. He felt a destiny within this stream of beings; for he owed it to the ancestors that he should continue their work; and he owed it to the descendants that they should have the fruit of his sacrifices to build upon.

Long he lay on the floor, the strength of his people flowing into him. Finally the vision passed and he sat up.

"How do you feel?" Wellesley asked, as he got to his feet.

"I feel good," Hunt said in a strong voice. "But strange, too. I'm-I'm unsettled."

"The experience is transformational, Rex Hunt," *Preleteth* said. "Within a handful of hours you have perceived the continuity of your people. Now you must rejoin your friends, consolidate what you have learned, and rest. The ancestral memories were not shown *to* you, but rather drawn *from* you. That act has fatigued you more than you presently know. Very shortly your strength will fail and you will sleep deeply. Do not fight this, striving to stay awake. Allow the recuperation to come upon you totally, without reservation. Soon – perhaps not today, but soon – you will see things that will complete your transformation; personal things that will settle your mind and clarify your purpose."

"But there's no time for rest!" Hunt protested. "You yourself said that the Devourers are nearly upon us–."

"Then there is none so qualified as I to speak on the matter," cut in *Preleteth*. "But even if a thousand of their vessels now floated in orbit above us, still we would have to pause. I have given you more insight into the hidden workings of the Earthborn mind than any of your kin have ever experienced. The demand placed upon your faculties has been incredible, and they require replenishment. No matter of necessity can overcome that fact. You have not perceived it, but our time together has been long. Dusk is nearly upon us, and you are far from your friends. *Alleehavah* will guide you back to them. Ensure that you return early tomorrow, for we have much work to do. May your steps be safe."

With this Hunt felt the presence withdraw from the room. Glancing around him, he saw the room was empty. Unbeknownst to him, *Preleteth* had at some point removed the dark creature.

"That was fascinating," Wellesley said. "And off putting. *Preleteth* is terribly high handed."

"You've got to remember it's under the gun," Hunt said, leaving the hidden room via a narrow staircase. "That's enough to put anyone on edge. Otherwise I'm sure it would've been more agreeable."

Retrieving his flashlight and pistol, Hunt left the obelisk.

"*Preleteth* wasn't kidding about dusk being close," he said uneasily, scanning the gloomy jungle around him. "It's halfway dark already. I hope those creatures won't come out until the sun is *actually down*."

"Don't worry," *Alleehavah* said from behind him, making him jolt and jerk around. "You will be among your friends before darkness falls."

"Don't do that," Hunt said, his heart slowly climbing down from between his ears. "You scared me half to death."

"Oh, I'm sorry!" she said quickly, consternation on her face. "I had forgotten that the people of your clan perceive danger in the unknown. Naturally, not recognizing that it was I who spoke, you imagined me to be a threat. Me! A threat!" she giggled, her short blue form walking past him. She stopped a few feet ahead, turning back and beckoning. "Come on!" she said encouragingly. "You want to get back to your friends, don't you?"

"Didn't your people jump when someone surprised them?" Hunt asked, falling in beside her, walking at an easy pace.

"No, mostly not," she said casually. "Such a notion must seem strange to you. But we were not wired to consider the unexpected as a threat. We were not combative, as your clan is."

"Fascinating," Hunt said. "I thought it was just a natural sort of thing that anyone would do."

"Oh, it is natural – to your people. And that is the only context you have ever known. So it is logical that you would draw your conclusions from that base of data."

"Do you always speak so technically?" he laughed. "Most of the time you talk like any contemporary human. But then you drop into sheer gobbledegook."

"Does this surprise you?" she asked in a voice that almost purred, keeping her eyes on the path beneath her gently glowing feet.

"Yeah, a little I guess," he replied.

"You must remember that I do not speak your language as a native. So I must translate my thoughts into a form you will comprehend. Sometimes my style becomes too…technical, as you put it. This is particularly pronounced for someone from your background, lacking both education and social experience outside of a very low social strata."

"Ouch," Hunt muttered, looking away.

"Did you hurt yourself?" she asked, looking at him with puzzlement. "Perhaps you stepped on something?"

"No, I–," he began, stopping with a chuckle. "Nevermind."

"Oh! I see! My words hurt you!" she said quickly, an apology written on her face. "I'm so sorry! I forgot that your clan often takes factual comparative statements as insults!"

"You seem to forget a lot of things about us," Hunt grinned, making eye contact for a moment. Bending down as he walked, he snatched up a small stone and chucked it into the distance.

"You must remember that I am merely a projection of the planet, a memory. With *Preleteth* so distracted by its effort to slow the Devourers, to say nothing of its other responsibilities, my processes are sometimes given a lower priority. I can't always draw upon my whole base of knowledge at once."

"Don't worry about it," Hunt said, grabbing a dead stick from a nearby tree and snapping it.

"Why did you do that?" she asked frankly, her eyes open and curious.

"Do what?"

"First you tossed the stone," she said, looking over her shoulder and pointing at where he'd picked it up. "Then you broke that stick without purpose, casting its two pieces aside. Are you feeling weak? Does the manipulation of your environment help you regain a sense of control? Oh, such a question must sound very naive to your ears!" she giggled. "It is probably the most normal thing to people of your clan."

"It *does* sound naive," he said. "But it is an intelligent question, all the same. To answer it, yes, I suppose I *do* feel a little weak right now, out of my element. The things I've learned today," he said in a confidential tone, jerking his thumb over his shoulder at the obelisk. "Well, I guess they've turned my world upside down. I must admit, I feel very small right now. Though perhaps humbled would be a better word."

"You should not feel small: you are the greatest of your clan. It is with ease that I trust you with the fortunes of our people, for I perceive the greatness in you. I only regret that one such as you was not present when the Devourers first came upon our galaxy. Then we could have fought against them. Oh, and I could have introduced you to my family!" she added happily. "Although I suspect you would have intimidated them! They were intellectuals, and not used to the rigors of strife, as you are."

"Was your family prominent?" he asked, feeling a little awkward and trying to divert the attention away from himself.

"Indeed they were. I belonged to the family of *Bharr*, chiefest of the families of the clan of *Ooel-Rhee*. I was the youngest of two daughters. I had barely reached adulthood when the Devourers were banished, destroying our people in an instant."

"I'm sorry," Hunt said with feeling.

"It was a necessary sacrifice," she said simply. "I have long been reconciled to it. Though – hehe, no," she giggled, stopping herself.

"What is it?" Hunt queried.

"I only wish I could have experienced…love, before the end," she said, darting a glance at him and then looking away. "That is my only regret."

"Many of my clan never know love, not really," Hunt said, hoping somehow to reassure her with that fact. "It's rare, like a flower growing at the top of a mountain. Only a lucky few ever know it."

"Because of your distrust for each other?" she asked.

"I don't know, maybe," Hunt said. "I guess there's a lot of reasons it doesn't work out. Mostly because we don't really understand love."

"Don't understand it?" she laughed, gleeful incomprehension in her face. "How could you not understand it? Doesn't love hold your families together, your communities?"

"I think that's mostly instinct, not love," Hunt said. "The survival impulses handed to us from our ancestors guide us constantly."

"And these impulses, are they good?"

"I imagine. They've kept us alive this long, haven't they?"

"But do they not constantly cause division as well, separating you from one another?"

"They also separate us from the *bad* among us," he said knowingly.

"In such a short time you have taught me much about

your clan," she said appreciatively. "I wish we could have met before this, when I still would have had time to reflect on your words. Now I shall scarcely have time to digest your teachings before my end."

"Your end?" he asked with alarm.

"Naturally. When the parasites destroy *Preleteth*, I shall be destroyed as well."

"Oh, of course," he uttered regretfully.

"You will mourn my passing?" she asked hopefully, looking up at him furtively.

"Yes, absolutely," he said firmly.

"Again! Such decisiveness!" she enthused, laying a hand on his arm and keeping it there until he looked at her. "Do I…make you uncomfortable?" she asked, withdrawing her hand.

"No, not at all," he said.

"Then why do you look at me for touching you? Oh, is it that you perceive me as a threat?" she asked, narrowing her eyes as though to see the answer. "Your clan is often careful of touch, I have heard. There are many rules regulating when it is appropriate, correct?"

"Yes, that's correct," he replied. "But no, I didn't see you as a threat. You just reminded me of someone."

"Your love?" she asked eagerly.

"Yes, that's right," he nodded.

"How long have you been in love with her?" she asked.

"Oh, I don't know," he shrugged. "With all that's happened, I haven't kept track of the days. But it feels like my whole life. The part that's been worth living, anyway."

"Life is always worth living," *Alleehavah* said with quiet resolution.

"Not to my clan," Hunt said.

"Oh, how I wish we could talk more!" she said. "You could teach me so many things that *Preleteth* has never been able to about your clan. It has given me a broad overview of your people. But from you I learn such subtleties! There are so many nuances that I've never known before! I regret not being able to absorb more of your teachings."

"I would hardly call what I've said 'teachings!'" he laughed. "The curmudgeonly ramblings of a backwater hick, perhaps. But–."

"Shh," she said, turning toward him and laying a finger on his lips. "You must not speak ill of yourself, not even if you want to. The hopes of all our kind rest with you now, and you will need all your strength for the fight to come. Undermining yourself is a betrayal of your purpose."

"A fact is a fact," he replied simply. "And the fact is I *am* from a backwater. Or rather an ice pond. No amount of positive thinking or good intentions will change that."

"The world we inhabit is the one we create for ourselves," she replied serenely, resuming movement. "Our perception of our lives is the only thing separating the happy from the unhappy, the confident from the timid. It is an act of choice to fit ourselves into the context that we desire. We are not passive victims in this. You must not see your background as something that *disqualifies* you from speaking upon life, as you have just done. Hailing from a unique, forbidding world gives you a perspective that is sorely lacking in the empire today. Those with power have been entitled to it from birth, growing up in soft surroundings which have only served to strengthen their sense of entitlement and subsequent distance from the rest of your people. The upper levels of the empire are filled with people who, while intelligent, have never known the desperate pain of hunger, cold, and insurmountable loneliness. They have never been thrust back upon themselves so totally as you have. You can do more than any of them can, because you have suffered more than any of them."

"You've got a very strange way of building a guy up," Hunt said with a chuckle, regarding appreciatively the figure beside him. "I never quite know what you're going to say, but it always makes me think."

"I am glad," she said, her cheeks bunching up in an adorably childish smile. Suddenly alarm flashed through her eyes, and her smile was replaced with a grimace of anxiety. "The *kals* are abroad. Night is almost upon us. We must hurry." With this her pace quickened into something just short of a run.

"What are *kals*?" he asked.

"Those dark creatures that assaulted you and your friends last night," she said. "They favor the jungle above all other spaces. We must reach open ground soon, or they will be upon us. Oh, I've been so stupid!" she fretted, slipping into a run. "Here I have been satisfying my curiosity at your peril! Oh! I should be punished!"

Before Hunt could speak she sped up even more, forcing him to save his breath and bend all his attention simply on keeping up. Her sleek, glassy body slid past the grasping branches and sharply edged leaves of the vegetation around them. But they impeded his progress and sliced at his exposed skin until blood was pouring from a dozen wounds as before. A sharp stick that he failed to see in the failing light until the last moment jabbed him just below the right eye, puncturing the skin and snapping against the bone.

"Gah!" he exclaimed, clutching his face with his right hand. Taking his eyes off the tangled path beneath him, he tripped over a vine and tumbled to the ground, smacking his head glancingly against the truck of a large tree.

"Rex Hunt!" *Alleehavah* said urgently, hearing him fall and doubling back. He felt her smooth hands on his arm as she tried to pull him upright. "There is no time to see to your wound," she said in a distracted voice, her attention seemingly elsewhere. "Hurry! You must get up at once!"

With a growl Hunt pushed through the dizzy haze that clouded his mind. He wiped warm blood from his check with the back of his right hand as *Alleehavah* took his left and dragged him forward.

"They do not know where we are yet," she said in a forceful whisper. "They feel we are close. They can sense your life force, Rex Hunt, and they hunger for it. Stealth is our only ally now."

"Can't you do anything to them?" Hunt asked. "Call upon the planet, or something?"

"That is a complicated matter, best suited to another time," she replied quietly. "For now, empty your mind, focusing solely on the present. It will take all of our wits to reach your friends without incident."

Moving cautiously through the chaotic growth around them, they carefully worked over fallen logs and around dense walls of vines. The trees and other plants were so tightly packed in this part of the jungle that many of the paths that *Alleehavah* chose proved too small for Hunt to follow, forcing her to double back and find another way.

"Oh, we must move faster," she fretted. "Several of them are nearly upon us."

That moment they heard a ghostly howl off to their left, followed by several more. With a gasp *Alleehavah* drew Hunt's hand against her side, her eyes staring openly into the bushes. There was nothing to see, but she stood transfixed until Hunt moved past her and gave her hand a tug. Recovering her presence of mind, she quickly moved on silent feet ahead of him.

"Not much farther," she said, her fear turning to hope as the jungle thinned out and shreds of the setting sun managed to pierce the thinning canopy above them. "Just another few moments and we'll–."

Suddenly a *kal* threw itself across their path, howling with desperate fury. Instantly Hunt flashed his light at it, sending it bolting into the jungle.

"Hurry!" *Alleehavah* screamed. "They've found us!"

Breaking into an all out run, the pair tore through the remaining hundred feet of jungle, bursting into the open just as three *kals* caught up with them. The fastest of the trio reached out a dark hand, dragging its claws across *Alleehavah's* back, making her scream and tumble to the ground.

"*Alleehavah!*" Hunt exclaimed, twisting around as he felt her hand slip out of his. Shining his light on the creatures as they snarled and tore at the air just within the cover of the trees and vines, he drove them away, hearing them clamber noisily in retreat.

"*Alleehavah*, are you alright?" he asked, kneeling beside her. She lay face down in the grass. Rolling her onto her back, he saw her face twisted with pain, her body almost completely paralyzed.

"I...will be fine," she gasped. "You...must go. Before the light grows...too dim."

"No, I'm not leaving without you," he said, taking her up in his arms and looking around. "Which way?"

She pointed off to his left.

"Another small growth of jungle separates us...from your friends," she said, biting her lower lip as his steps jostled her back. "This clearing is west of...the one you found...last night."

"What happened to you back there?" he asked, his eyes everywhere at once as he searched for more *kals*.

"The deathly ones have infected me," she said. "Even now their plague works its way to my deepest essence."

"Will you die?" he asked through gritted teeth, his breathing growing labored as he moved for two.

"A memory cannot die," she smiled faintly, slipping her arms around his neck to ease his burden just as she felt his strength beginning to wane. "But they have contaminated me. It will take time for *Preleteth* to divest me of the sickness they have put into me."

"Can we help you?" Wellesley asked.

"Oh! Your friend speaks through the skin!" she enthused. "What did you–."

"Just answer the question, honey," the AI replied with

firm kindness. "You can satisfy your curiosity later."

"*Preleteth* must take me to itself again," she said.

"How?" Hunt asked.

"In the obelisks," she said. "They are the greatest connection to the planet. Inside it will reabsorb me at once, clearing out the infection and rendering me whole. But only if we hurry. If the infection spreads too far–."

"That's not…going to happen," Hunt said. As the clearing came to an end, and trees loomed up before him, he stopped and put *Alleehavah* down. "Just give me…a sec…" he panted, resting his head on the ground beside her, his hands clutching fistfuls of grass as he willed energy to return to his body. Already the words of *Preleteth* were proving themselves true, and at the worst possible time. A deep fatigue was reaching up from the depths of his soul and covering him like a blanket. His awareness of his surroundings was diminishing rapidly, a feverish cloudiness blunting his thoughts.

Affectionately *Alleehavah* stretched out her barely functioning hand and ran its glass-like fingers through his hair. With a start he jerked his head upward, his fevered mind not recognizing the touch as friendly at first.

"Oh," he said with relief, as he saw her faintly smiling face looking back at him. "I thought you were one of them."

Just then a howl pealed out a hundred yards behind him. Turning his head heavily he saw two *kals* trying to force their way into the open. They were being held back by the almost vanished light of twilight.

"Another couple of minutes and those turkeys are gonna be on top of us," Wellesley said. "You've got to move now, Rex."

With great effort Hunt stood up. Bending over to pick up *Alleehavah*, he nearly lost his balance and fell over her. Fighting to keep his footing, he smacked his head to knock some clarity into it and got her into his arms once more. Feebly her arms returned to their place around his neck, offering little assistance.

Miraculously the *kals* hadn't anticipated their line of retreat, and they managed to slip through the narrow tongue of jungle that separated the two clearings from each other before they were hemmed in.

"Just a little further," Wellesley said, as Hunt's eyes fell upon the obelisk in the distance.

"Please...Rex..." *Alleehavah* said faintly, her grip slipping. "I...I can't...." With this her arms fell awkwardly away from her, dangling helplessly in the air.

Hunt closed his eyes and uttered a low growl, dragging up every last ounce of strength still within him. The blue arms began to jerk violently as his pace quickened into an awkward, bouncing jog.

"Just...a little...further," Hunt said to himself, as though chanting a mantra. "Just...a little...further."

Halfway to the obelisk he tripped, falling to the ground on top of his charge. Her body felt stiff and unresponsive. He knew the poison had nearly completed its work.

Rising once more, he took her rigid arms in his hands and pulled her up, throwing her over his shoulder. Desperately he pumped his burning legs across the final stretch, dropping to the ground once more just outside the obelisk's door.

"Help!" he cried feebly to anyone inside. "Please, help!"

Receiving no answer he dragged himself to the door, his consciousness of where he was slipping away. Indeed, his whole environment seemed to recede before him, leaving only himself, the door, and the faintly glowing body just behind him. Shoving the door open with his hands, still laying on his belly, he called out one last time. His sight failed him just as he heard footsteps approaching.

◆ ◆ ◆

"Your Highness, I would like to report that I have taken direct control of the Omega Project. I am certain that it will be completed on time."

"Good, Krancis," the emperor said to the hologram before him, sitting in his private chambers at the imperial retreat. "But why does it take so long? Omega was supposed to be finished long ago."

"Your Highness, the engineers assure me that they are working as fast as they are able," Krancis said in his thin, precise voice. "Having examined every report they have produced within the last three years in minute detail, I stand personally convinced of that fact. There is no lack of zeal among the personnel doing the work."

"Then *why* is it taking so long?" he repeated. "Omega was supposed to be completed long before the mind control project, rendering that abominable last resort utterly needless."

"We are lacking some final element," Krancis said, regretting the effect he knew his words would have on his sovereign. Indeed, within moments the latter began to fidget anxiously. "The engineers have studied every inch of the weapon, but cannot determine what is missing. All the pieces seem to be in place, down to the last bolt. But still they cannot activate it."

"It is as though Omega does not want to be used," the emperor said quietly, his mood shifting suddenly as it often did. Looking wistfully away from the hologram for a moment, he added, "It is our last resort, dear friend. Our only hope. Our every energy must be bent upon its activation."

"Yes, Your Highness," Krancis said sincerely. "For this reason I have allocated more resources than ever toward the project. Additionally, I have ordered the imperial navy to avoid combat with the invader, nursing our strength to protect Omega from direct attack should its location be discovered before it can be activated. This will ensure we have the time to finish it."

Slowly the emperor's face clouded over.

"You have done...what?" he asked, doubt mixing with outrage. "My people must be protected!"

"That is what I am doing, Your Highness," Krancis said, maintaining his composure. "Even the most optimistic estimates–."

"The navy must be redeployed at once," the emperor cut him off. "Across the board! I don't want to leave the invaders a moment of peace! They must *suffer* for the death they have already inflicted upon my domain, my people!"

"Your Highness, the navy doesn't stand a chance against them," Krancis said in a voice that began to harden. "There is no hope of defeating them in a conventional struggle. The battle of Komia-2 alone would have been a pyrrhic victory of extraordinary proportions, and that was being fought with some of our best forces."

"Was?"

"Yes. I recalled our fleet before the battle was finished."

"Imbecile!" exclaimed the emperor ragefully, slamming his fists on the table. "How can we ever succeed against our foe unless our people have the courage to stand and *fight*? There will be no victory in cowardice!"

"Your Highness, I ordered the withdrawal to *preserve* your forces so that they could protect Omega," Krancis said. "We have the strength to win limited engagements with our present forces. But in a protracted conflict our casualties will far exceed theirs, leaving us defenseless. No, it is only through the careful application–."

"Do you *presume* to lecture me?" the emperor demanded.

"I would never presume any such thing," Krancis said calmly, his self-possession unshakeable.

"Then carry out my wishes!" he shouted, smashing

the button that controlled the hologram with his fist, making Krancis' apparition vanish. "Weaklings! Imbeciles!" he bellowed, rising from his seat and walking to the covered porch at the back of his retreat. Standing upon a hill, the rustic abode looked down across a forest that stretched for thousands of miles. Invisibly the emperor's elite bodyguard stood watch, patrolling every inch of ground around the imperial complex. Resting his hands on the railing he looked upon his peaceful surroundings and wondered how a galaxy that contained a place so beautiful could also, at that very moment, hold something as vile and destructive as the Devourers within its confines.

"Are you well, Your Highness?" an old woman asked from behind him, making him jump and turn around.

"Oh, Elasha," he said with relief, gazing upon the forest once more as she moved with gentle steps to his side. "Why did it come to this, Elasha? Why, when we are already suffering such difficulties, did such a foe have to come upon us? And why did the blow have to fall only *after* the death of your brother Taegen!" He raised his trembling hand in the air between them, the ravages of his disease making it increasingly unsteady. "I would trade my right arm for but one word of advice from his wise lips."

"Your Highness," she began soothingly. "The first word from my brother Taegen's lips was always that you should trust your own judgment. But now I must speak the truth to you, though it will make you hate me."

"Nothing could make me hate you, dear Elasha," he said, taking her hand in his and squeezing it firmly.

"Taegen warned me that a time such as this would come. Indeed, he spoke of it just before he lost his life."

"Oh, Taegen!" the emperor burst out, his emotional control failing him. "The loss of a hundred worlds would not have been too great, had it spared your life to counsel me in this dark hour!"

"He foretold the worsening of your condition," Elasha

went on resolutely. "And now I must deliver his parting counsel."

"Yes, yes please!" he said desperately, taking her hand in both of his, hoping for some miracle that would spare his domain. "I will do whatever he advised, though it cost me half my empire!"

"He said that in a time not far off, your disease would render you unable to command the empire," she said. "That time has come, Your Highness. You must relinquish control, and leave the conduct of the war to others."

"Traitor!" he bellowed, smashing the back of his hand against her delicate face, sending her sprawling to the ground. "Taegen never advised any such thing! You are in league with those who wish to destroy me! You think you've deceived me, but you're wrong! I'm aware of your machinations, how you seek to separate me from the power that is mine by right! But no matter: I will stand strong!" He watched savagely as she rose to her feet. "It is only out of the memory of your brother that I do not–."

At this moment she seized both his hands with hers. Closing her eyes and opening her mouth, she let out a low moan and caused a vision to pass before him.

Suddenly he stood alone atop a hill covered in grass. A bitterly cold wind blew against him, robbing his warmth and bringing with it a dense fog. In moments he was hidden within it, unable to see more than a foot in any direction.

"Elasha?" he pleaded at once, crossing his arms over his chest and hunching his shoulders. "Where have you gone, Elasha?"

Desperately he ran into the fog to search for her, but with no result.

"Don't leave me, Elasha!" he cried. "I-I was wrong. I shouldn't have hit you. Oh, please come back. Please don't leave me!"

"Elasha has not left you," a familiar voice said from behind him. "You have left her."

Instantly the emperor turned around, beholding only a dim silhouette in the fog.

"Taegen?" he asked. "Is that you?"

"It is I, Your Highness," Taegen replied, drawing closer and revealing himself. "Why have you struck my sister? She did only that which you bid her to do."

"But she told me to surrender the empire!" he pleaded. "And I…I cannot…" he sputtered, unable to find his words as his face began to twitch. "I…I will not…"

"She has advised you with love, as I have always done. Though now you disturb my peace, yet I must come forth to speak once more with you, guiding you as I have always done."

"Yes! Yes, Taegen," the emperor said, nodding emphatically. "I will heed *your* advice!"

"It is that which Elasha has given you, for she has spoken only that which I asked her to speak before my death," Taegen said. "You must obey her words. All of humanity stands ready to fall. We are strong, but our strength is tenuous. On a single error all may fall into the abyss, never to be redeemed. We must be cautious – guided by the most capable minds. And there is none so capable as Krancis."

"Krancis is wrong!" the emperor exploded. "He would sacrifice my entire domain because he is afraid to fight!"

"You, my emperor, are the one who is wrong," Taegen said sharply. "You doubt your friends; you *curse* those who love you! Were it not for my love of our people I should not answer you again."

"But, *Taegen–*." pleaded the emperor, immediately remorseful.

"No. You will heed my advice. Only then may the empire stand. You must relinquish control at once, Highness. You must trust Krancis with all your might, committing the conduct of the war fully into his wise hands. Do not interfere with him anymore. Otherwise you shall shatter our only hope for success."

"I...will do as you advise," the emperor said in a defeated voice.

"I'm glad," Taegen said with visible relief. "Do not call on me again except in the direst need. I must go."

"Wait! Please don't!" the emperor begged as the vision faded. He saw Elasha standing before him, a bruise rapidly forming on her cheek. "Elasha, I'm sorry!"

"It is alright, Your Highness," she said soothingly. "The only thing that matters now is that you contact Krancis at once. Reassert his total conduct of affairs immediately, as my brother told you in the vision."

"Yes, yes I will," he said eagerly, moving into his chambers at once, leaving her alone.

"I am sorry to abuse your memory this way, my brother," she said quietly, looking up at the sky as faded streaks of dusk's last light played across the clouds. "But it was the only way to convince his diseased mind of what must be done."

Halfway across the galaxy Krancis sat in his office at the site of the Omega Project. One leg tossed over the other, he reflected on the order from the emperor instructing him to engage the Devourers wholesale.

"I can't do it," he said, his voice firm as he spoke the words of treason. "For the sake of the empire." He arose from his chair and walked to the window. Below him stood the enormous creation upon which all of the empire's hopes had been pinned. He drew a deep breath, letting it out slowly. "Perhaps in time he will see the necessity of this," he added quietly, clasping his hands behind his back as he watched workers move to and fro. Suddenly a bleep from his computer told him of an incoming hologram.

"Krancis?" the defeated-looking form of the emperor said.

"Yes, my emperor?" he asked, bowing deeply upon seeing him.

"I am rescinding my last order to you," he said in a

hollow, distracted voice. "I–I trust your judgment fully in conducting this war. Fight well. Fight in my name with honor."

"That I shall always do, Your Highness," Krancis said, bowing deeply once more. Before he had time to look up the hologram was gone. "That didn't take long," he remarked to himself, sensing the hand of Elasha at work.

CHAPTER 6

Shadowy dreams filled Rex's fevered mind as he slept. Ancient visions from humans long dead paraded before him. Many of them had a message, it seemed, crafted specifically for him. He saw shamans and other ancient medicine men look at him through the foggy expanse of time that separated them. He felt a connection, a oneness with these people, as though he knew them intimately. In a sense he did – their warnings were meant for him just as much as they were meant for anyone. A sense of ownership, even of pride in what their descendents would accomplish, was implicit in the warnings they passed along.

Each message bore the peculiar characteristics of the unconscious mind. Highly symbolic and at times confusing, they played out before him like plays in an ancient amphitheater. They varied widely in terms of detail and duration. Indeed, some lasted for only a few seconds before giving way to another. But they all held one common element that fused them together: they each warned of an external danger, something so monstrous that it must occupy all the time, energy, and ingenuity that humanity could bend upon it. Perpetually unclear as to just what the threat was, the shamans, medicine men, and, eventually, priests, all agreed that it was a mortal danger, a peril that would sweep humanity away, erasing the final clan to survive the original war against the Devourers.

As time passed and this interpretation emerged, details became more specific. He realized that he was absorbing the message stored in the unconscious memory of the race, and, that being the case, his mind was able to focus on more minute aspects of the collective memory than had been the case just hours before. The threat seemed to the progenitors to be something beyond ancient, beyond all conceptions of age that any contemporary race could contemplate. It bore a subsequent scorn for all it observed. And yet a peculiar impotence stopped it from reaching forth its hand and crushing those it despised directly. It had to move in the shadows, manipulating them toward their own destruction; or otherwise working through agents, like the Devourers, to accomplish its purpose. Like a specter it haunted humanity. Hunt suspected that the shadow that had fallen over mankind must be upon other races as well, driving them to strife and chaos.

As he reflected on these things the visions began to fade. Soon the smooth, cool walls of the obelisk were apparent around him. He groaned slightly, trying to find his voice. Instantly Tselitel dropped to her knees by his side, her good hand caressing his cheek.

"Darling, are you alright?" she asked quietly, as the faces of the others crowded his view. "Can you hear me?"

"Ye–," he began, his voice a strange croak. Clearing it, he tried again. "Yes, I can hear you," he said with a nod, glad for the touch of her gentle hand. "Is *Alleehavah* alright?"

"Allee-who?" asked Milo, chewing on one of the protein bars from the emergency rations.

"He means the blue girl we found," Gromyko said with casual ease. "We cannot say for sure, my friend. She disappeared almost as soon as we got her inside. It's funny how all these glowing people look! Like some kind of far distant relative, you know? It makes me wonder if–."

"She *is* a relative," Hunt cut in, the smuggler's avalanche of words making his head buzz. "I'll explain later."

"Of course," replied Gromyko. "You should have been here! We had visitors of the strangest sort!"

"I'm sure Lily can tell me all about it," he said with quiet significance. Pinchon, who stood a little way off silently watching, nodded to himself.

"Alright, let's give him a little time to recuperate," the colonel said, gesturing for the other two men to come with him. "He'll be quite alright in the good Doctor's capable hands."

She smiled at the pirate as he stood by the door, waiting for the other two to file out before closing it quietly behind him.

"I see Antonin is back to his old chatty self," Hunt said regretfully, closing his eyes and swallowing hard. "I almost wish he was still feeling glum, except I wouldn't wish what he was feeling on anyone." Opening his eyes and looking into Lily's gray ones, he smiled. "Hi, babe."

"Hi, yourself," she chuckled, leaning down and giving him a gentle kiss. "How have you been?"

"Busy," he said, rolling his eyes and drawing a breath as his mind raced back. "Terribly busy. Delta-13 had nothing on *Preleteth* when it came to speed. That old ice cube moved like a glacier compared to this one. It's got me progressing faster than I thought was possible. And *farther* than I thought possible. Why, you wouldn't believe–," he began, growing excited.

"Just calm down for a little while," she said, pressing her long, thin finger to his lips. "You need to rest now. You've been through quite an ordeal."

"Tell me about it," he sighed, rolling his head back and forth on the emergency blanket that served as a makeshift pillow. Then he grinned. "Doctor's orders?"

"Yes," she laughed, kissing him again. "Doctor's orders." She leaned back and laid out on the floor next to him, resting on her elbow. "Is there anything I can do for you? Are you thirsty?"

"Yes," he nodded, turning his head to look at her. "But more than anything else, I just want you to touch me for a little while. I feel like I've died and come back to life again, and I want to feel a little life, a little love."

"That'll be easy," she said in a warm voice, twisting and laying her head and shoulders upon his chest. "Looks like we've come full circle again."

"Looks like it," he said, touching her head affectionately.

"Is Wellesley alright?" she asked, her voice suddenly tightening with concern.

"I'm here, don't you worry," he said. "I just didn't want to break up all the warm fuzzies."

"You're so thoughtful," she said lightly.

"I know."

"How have things been here?" Hunt asked, craning his neck to look at her briefly. "I heard that you had visitors."

"Yes, a pair of beings named *Kowla* and *Rheef*. They told us that *Preleteth* was talking to you, and not to expect you until late. Then they filled us in on what was going on, generally speaking."

"Good," Hunt said, closing his eyes. "I don't think I have the energy to give you all the details myself." Suddenly they snapped open. "Or the time! What time is it?"

"Don't worry," Wellesley said. "We've still got a couple hours until dawn. You weren't asleep *that* long."

"After that two day stint in the sack after our raid on the pirate base, I don't trust my internal clock anymore. Not while sleeping, I mean."

"You have plenty of time to relax," the AI reassured him. "Just take it easy."

"What, I've got *two* doctors telling me what to do now?"

"She's the doctor," Wellesley said. "I'm just a brilliantly talented hobbyist. Besides, it never hurts to have a second opinion, especially for you. You need all the help you can get."

"Don't I know it!" Hunt laughed dryly.

"What's that mean?" Tselitel asked, raising her head above his chest and looking into his eyes.

"You don't miss much, do you?" he asked warmly. "Oh, nothing much. Just that my life – or what I amusingly *thought of* as my life – has actually been a small piece in a puzzle of galactic proportions."

"I'd hardly call the decisive role in something this large a 'small piece,'" Wellesley said. "You've got to leave all that 'poor, downtrodden scavenger' stuff back where it belongs: buried in the snows of Delta-13. Your horizons are infinitely larger than that now."

"What do you mean 'the decisive role?'" asked Tselitel.

"Well, the gist of it is this," Hunt said. "The *Prellak* worked on my dad to turn him to their purposes. Apparently my family has a deep river of darkness running through it. The *Prellak* sought us out for cultivation, trying to make us into weapons. When their plans didn't work out the way they wanted for dad, they turned to me. But then we got shipped out to Delta-13, and the planet stymied their efforts. They had big plans for me, until that poor old world got in the way. Recognizing the weapon I had the potential of becoming, Delta took care of me, eventually guiding me to Ugo and the Order. You know everything that came after that. But more specifically, it guided *us* together, so you could serve as a counterbalance for me. It knew that at some point I would be overwhelmed by the darkness within, and that I needed you to pull me back again."

"People talk about being 'destined' to come together," she laughed. "In our case we have definite proof!"

"And how!" he laughed with her.

"So the dark worlds sought you two out for their own purposes," she said, resuming the thread of conversation. "I bet they're surprised to find you arrayed on the other side of the battle now. And angry."

"I should think so," he said. "Funny, I hadn't thought

about that."

"Your mind has been occupied lately," she said, giving him another kiss and laying her head down as before. "So what happens now?"

"Now I go back to the obelisk in the jungle," Hunt said. "Or rather in a few hours. I have more training to do, and precious little time to do it in. Frankly I don't think we can get it done before the Devourers arrive, not with all the ground we have to cover."

"I'm sure *Preleteth* has a plan for them," Tselitel said.

"I don't think it does," Hunt said dubiously. "I think it's just throwing everything it can at the problem and hoping for the best. Best for the galaxy, anyway. It seems to have accepted the idea that its days are sharply numbered. *Alleehavah* sure has."

"And just who is *Alleehavah*?" she asked, her curiosity rising. "I saw her briefly as the others brought her inside. Then she disappeared like a mirage."

"She's a memory held by the planet. Like *Selek-Pey*, I suppose, though somehow physically real as well. She's all that's left of an ancient human of the same name. She acts as the planet's assistant, and guided me to and from my rendezvous with it. Filled me in on a lot of background details, too."

For the next hour Hunt talked, telling Tselitel everything he'd learned. He knew he should have been sleeping, but he was too excited to rest. Finally, nearing the end of his tale, his eyes started to grow dry and his lids became heavy. Seeing this, Lily once again laid a finger on his lips.

"That's enough out of you for now," she said with a fond chuckle. "You need to sleep before your next session with *Preleteth*."

"I guess you're right," he said with a yawn, patting her warm, thin form affectionately. "One more thing, babe?"

"Uh huh?"

"Grab me some water, will you?" he asked. "I could use that drink now."

"Sure," she said, slipping off his chest and standing up. Back moments later, she was unsurprised to hear him snoring quietly as she opened the door. She shook her head with a smile, closing the door and leaving him alone.

"Rex!" he heard his father shout, making him almost jump out of his skin.

"Wellesley, did you hear that?" Hunt asked. "Wellesley?"

Looking down at his chest, he saw the AI's medallion wasn't there. It was only at that moment that he became aware that his surroundings consisted of nothing but darkness.

"Rex!" he heard his father say again, this time from behind him. Jerking around, he saw Maximilian Hunt standing before him, young and vibrant – the man he'd known before he was consigned to prison. "I did it for us, Rex!" he said, drawing near, his voice pleading with him. "I never wanted to use mind control. It was just the only option left open to us. The Devourers will take everything we can throw at them, and more! I did it to weld us into one solid form that might have a chance against them. You have to believe that I did it for the greater good!"

Hunt saw the desperation written on his father's face. More than anything he wanted his son to believe in the nobility of his purpose, no matter how low his methods had fallen.

"I believe you, Dad," Hunt said, nodding slowly. "No matter what you did, I know you did it for the right reasons."

Instantly immeasurable relief flooded over his father.

"Now I can rest easy," he said, fading slowly away.

"Wait!" Hunt cried out, suddenly desperate to keep him near for even a few seconds more. "What are you? Where did you come from?"

"I'm just a memory, Rex," the apparition said,

becoming opaque again. "It was in that moment when you touched me, just before I passed. A little shard, a little snapshot of myself, got lodged in your unconscious mind. I saw in that brief instant what I had become, and I had to let you know I was sorry. I don't know how, but I willed it, and here I am. Maybe there's more to this gift of ours than just fear! Somehow it gave me the power to do something constructive for the first time in years." He eyed his son for a moment. "You were terrible in that moment, Rex," he said, shaking his head with wonder. "An agent of pure woe."

"I was a weapon," Hunt said grimly. "Just as I was meant to be."

"Yes, I know," his father said. "You became something powerful – something terribly dangerous. Yet you came back from it! You overcame it!"

"Lily helped me with that," Hunt said, smiling faintly.

"She's a good girl," he replied, putting a ghostly hand on Hunt's shoulder. "She's just what you need. She's what *any* man would need in your position. You've got a dark path ahead of you, son. I don't envy you for it, though your part in the conflict is going to be glorious. I don't know how you'll manage it, but I'm sure you'll turn around all our fortunes. It was what I tried to do, but failed." He looked down at his feet regretfully for a moment, his face covered in shame. "I *never* wanted to do it, Rex. It was just the only way I could see forward."

"I know," Hunt said. "You followed the best course you could see. That's all any man can do."

Maximilian looked up and smiled at his son.

"You're a better man than I ever was. No matter what happens, I want you to know that," he said with feeling, slowly fading into mist.

"No, I'm not," Hunt said, his eyes moistening. "Don't leave me, Dad. I can't do this alone. It's too much for me."

"No, it isn't," Maximilian said, reasserting his form until it was half visible. "You have all the inner strength that you need. We were chosen by the *Prellak* in part because we are *strong*, Rex. We can handle this work, the burden set before us. I tried to do my part for our people until a greater laid me low," he said. "I'm glad, if it had to be anyone, that it was you."

"I never wanted to do it," Hunt said.

"I know you didn't," he said, putting a hand on his shoulder once more. "But when a father goes astray, who better to guide him back except his son?"

"Father…" Hunt began, struggling for words as tears ran down his cheeks.

"Goodbye, Rex," he said, smiling once more. "And thank you."

"Father? Father?" Hunt called, looking all around him, but to no avail. "Don't leave me," he said quietly..

"I'll always be with you…" he heard in a faint whisper on the wind, as the dream began to evaporate. "Inside you."

Soon he found himself in the obelisk once more, the glowing face of *Alleehavah* looking down at him.

"Oh, I had hoped you'd awaken soon!" she said happily as he got to his feet and took a couple steps away from her. "We have much to do," she continued, looking at his back as he thought. "But I didn't want to disturb you. *Preleteth* made it quite clear that you needed all the rest you could get. It said you must keep your strength up."

"My strength is fine now," Hunt said in a voice that was settled and confident. Looking a little upward and closing his eyes, he nodded to the shard of his father. "*Thank you*," he said internally. Then, opening his eyes, he turned and faced *Alleehavah*. "I'm ready to go whenever you are."

"Marvelous!" she said happily, clapping her hands together. "We'll leave at once."

"Why doesn't *Preleteth* teach me here?" Hunt asked. "It's just another obelisk, right?"

"Oh, no," she said emphatically. "I'm afraid the two structures have very different properties. The planet is not able to risk manifesting in an environment like this."

"Not able to *risk* it?" Hunt asked. "What could possibly go wrong? It's just me and my friends here."

"I'm afraid I can't go into that now," she said evasively, glancing away for a moment. "But rest assured, the other obelisk is your only option for addressing the planet directly. To continue your training, we shall have to repair there at once."

"Then that's where we'll go," Hunt said, willing to let the issue rest for the moment.

"Aren't you forgetting something?" Wellesley asked as he made for the door, *Alleehavah* in tow.

"Like what?"

"Like *breakfast*, perhaps?" the AI prodded. "This lovely creature and myself may be able to live upon the air. But you're going to have to grab something to eat if you don't want to collapse while you're learning how to save the universe."

"Galaxy," Hunt corrected, reaching for the door. "Just the galaxy. The universe is next week."

"What, your sense of humor is back?" asked Wellesley. "What's happened in the last few hours?"

"Ask me again sometime and I'll tell you," he said, emerging from the room and seeing the others in the main hall.

"Where'd she come from?" Milo asked, startled to see *Alleehavah's* glowing form among them.

"Haven't you been paying attention?" Gromyko asked. "This structure acts as some kind of superhighway for these glowing people. They can pop in and out at will."

"Good morning, everyone," Hunt said, as they all looked over his guest thoroughly. "This is *Alleehavah*. She's been helping me with my training."

"Oh, I wouldn't say *helping*!" she said quickly, her little five foot frame shrinking meekly. "I've merely been assisting *Preleteth* in its work."

"Hello, *Alleehavah*," Tselitel said warmly, extending her hand. "I'm–."

"Doctor Lily Tselitel, love of Rex Hunt," she said quickly, taking her hand in her glass-like grasp and shaking it energetically. "I'm honored to speak with the one who shares his heart."

Tselitel blushed at this, while everyone except Hunt shifted uncomfortably.

"Have I said something wrong?" *Alleehavah* asked, looking from one awkward face to the next. "Oh! I see! How stupid of me. I forgot that your clan only speaks of such matters in special circumstances, usually after a long period of emotional preparation. I wish to apologize profusely for any–."

"That's okay, *Alleehavah*," Hunt cut in with a chuckle. "Don't worry about it. We could all use a little loosening up on matters like that."

"Oh, okay," she said happily, clasping her hands behind her back and smiling broadly. "Your clan's ways fascinate me. Defensive one minute and generous the next! Very exciting!"

"Our clan?" Milo asked, as his brother went to where they'd piled up their emergency supplies, taking several bars and a small flask of water. "Do you mean family?"

"No, she means *clan*," Hunt said, stuffing the provisions in his pockets and rejoining the group. "It's a long story, but Lily can fill you in while we're gone." He looked at his small companion. "Are you ready?"

"Mhm!" she said in a chipper voice, nodding happily.

"Alright. We'll be back before dark," he said to the group, kissing Tselitel and making for the exit.

"Cute couple," Pinchon said, watching the mismatched pair slip out the door.

"I wouldn't call them a couple," Milo said disapprovingly.

"You never know," the colonel replied, taking out his

pistol and checking the ammunition. "Stranger things have happened. You can see that little gal is over the moon with your brother."

"But he isn't over the moon with *her*," Milo said, growing warm. "He'd never do that to Lily."

"Can't be too sure," Pinchon uttered, sliding the magazine back into his pistol and tucking it into his belt. "Love is a fickle thing. You feel it one moment, and it's gone the next. You can't depend on it."

"Ah, you've been a pirate too long," Gromyko said with a wave of his hand. "You think that everyone is trying to cheat everyone else. Where's the trust, the belief in honor?"

"It was trust and belief in honor that destroyed the Underground," the colonel replied. "Don't forget that. Fedorov was only able to work against you because he was in your blind spot. A less trusting man would have seen him a mile away."

"As a matter of fact, they did," admitted the smuggler. "But I've known Rex Hunt for ages! He could no more hurt this dear lady than fly!"

"Then why did she take his hand just as they got out the door?" the pirate asked.

"She was probably just appreciative for what he'd done for her yesterday," Tselitel said calmly. "I have no doubts about Rex."

"Nice to have no doubts," Pinchon said, taking a flask and a bar for himself and heading for the door.

"Where are you going?" Milo asked.

"Well, we've got to have something to eat, don't we?" the colonel said, turning momentarily. "I'm going to shoot us some fresh game. Get together some wood for a fire. We'll cook it as soon as I get back."

"Alright," Milo said sullenly, not wishing to take orders from the pirate but aware he was right all the same.

"I'll go with you," Gromyko said, following close on his heels.

"It's a one man job," Pinchon said. "I don't need any help."

"Oh, I insist," Gromyko said, laying on all the charm at his disposal. "Besides, if you nail something big, you might need help carrying it back. No sense wasting all that good meat, eh?"

The pirate frowned but acquiesced, aware that he couldn't get rid of the smuggler in any way short of shooting him.

"We'll be back before you know it," Gromyko said, turning around and winking on his way out the door.

"Milo, does the colonel seem a little…strange to you today?" Tselitel asked once the duo had gone.

"Like how?"

"I don't know," she said, looking for the right words for the vague feeling she had. "Like…something else is moving him? I mean, I realize that a pirate isn't going to be the most trusting person in the world–."

"Ha! You're right about that," Milo cut in emphatically. "Half the time Rex was gone yesterday he was casting aspersions."

"Right, exactly," she said. "But it seems like more than just that to me."

"Well, the guy has got to be a mess inside, losing his command and all that back on Delta," Milo said in a reasonable tone. "On top of that, he's probably wondering how we're going to survive, now that the *Stella* has been smashed into a thousand pieces. Frankly, I'm a little curious about that myself."

"I'm sure the planet has some kind of plan for that," she said, nodding her assurance. "It wouldn't make a lot of sense to train Rex just to leave us stranded here, and with the Devourers practically on our doorstep, no less."

"Yeah, I guess you're right. Still, I wouldn't worry too much about Pinchon. He's hardly the first man I'd want to be stuck here with, but he's far from being the last. So far he's been nothing but good sense personified."

"But that's what's so *strange* about all this," she said, lowering her voice into a confidential hush. "After keeping such a cool head during the escape from Delta-13 – to say nothing of getting us all off the *Stella* safely – it's odd to see him act this way."

"Well, I'll keep an eye on him, if it'll make you feel better."

"Thanks, Milo," she smiled. "It would."

◆ ◆ ◆

"Your woman is very beautiful," *Alleehavah* said in a chipper voice as she walked with Hunt across the clearing and into the jungle that surrounded it. "Such elegance of form! Such a long, distinct bone structure! I'm afraid the people of my clan lacked such precision in their makeup. Our virtues were mental, not physical."

Glancing at the distorted face of his companion, he was inclined to agree but too polite to say so.

"All peoples have their virtues," Hunt said, the small blue hand still holding his tightly. Despite what he'd said about loosening up back in the obelisk he found the luminous girl's touch uncomfortable. He knew that nothing but innocent affection motivated it, but it was hard to separate it from the mature love he'd felt through Lily's touch. The vague sense that he was betraying the latter flashed through his mind, but he instantly shoved it away. At that very moment the most important thing was the mission. And if *Alleehavah did* happen to feel a touch of infatuation, well, that should just be tolerated so as not to add friction to a relationship that was vital for all mankind.

"What are you thinking about?" she asked, noticing

the serious, withdrawn look on his face. "Does something trouble you?"

"Only my own doubts and suspicions," he said cryptically. "Nothing worth worrying about."

"Is it something I can help with?" she asked eagerly, squeezing his hand a little tighter, unwittingly contributing to the problem.

"Heh, no," he said with an awkward laugh. "I've just got a lot on my mind."

"That used to happen to me all the time," she said, happily swinging their joined hands between them. "Before the conflict destroyed our people I used to meditate all of the time. It was the only way I could organize the jumble that passed through my mind constantly. Have you ever tried it?"

"Ha!" exclaimed Wellesley.

"Is this funny?" she asked, a puzzled look on her face.

"No, it's just that you don't know Rex like I do," the AI said. "He's not the sit-and-reflect sort. Now, *me* on the other hand–."

"Well, it's natural for you," she cut in matter-of-factly. "Being physically impotent, you have no other way to fill your time than with reflection. But Rex Hunt is a man of action, and his thoughts must give way to his actions. We each live out our function as is most natural to us, and that results in a natural one-sidedness. The cure we most stand in need of is the reversal of our predilections. We must not be ourselves in order to heal ourselves from being ourselves."

"That's a mouthful," Wellesley said, a little chagrined at her unintentional insult.

"Oh, I can express it differently if it will–."

"No, that's fine," he said. "I think I'll just be quiet now."

"Do *Kol-Prockians* often act this way?" she asked Hunt in a confidential whisper. "Honestly I have very little background with their kind."

"Oh, don't mind him," he smiled, glancing down at the medallion that slid side-to-side upon his chest as he walked.

"He's just a little temperamental at times."

"I see," she replied, her eyes narrowing as she thought. "Could it be old age? After all, he must be very ancient, by your standards, to still be among us. Ooh, how old is he?" she asked with excitement. "Does he date from the early days of their civilization? He must know more about their society and people than, well, any living being today outside of the *Ahn-Wey*!"

"A lady never tells her age," Wellesley said with an audible roll of his eyes.

"But you're not a lady..." she said, her voice trailing. "Oh! You're joking!" she said in a bright voice. Then her face clouded over. "Oh, you're using humor to deflect an uncomfortable question. Does the subject of your age bother you because–."

"My age doesn't bother me at all," he snapped.

Jumping from the sharpness of his outburst, she walked a few steps with a nervous charge to her steps before settling down once more. Giggling quietly, she looked at Hunt and mouthed a question.

"Temperamental?" she asked, her eyes wide.

He replied with an exaggerated wink and a nod, to which she giggled again, covering her mouth with her hand. Wellesley, seeing everything that Hunt did, replied with a ragged sigh, but said no more.

"Your friends seem nice," she said, abruptly changing the topic to spare the AI any more embarrassment. "They were very gentle when they carried me inside the obelisk. I regretted that I was too weak to thank them for their efforts at the time. But the planet had to assimilate me at once to halt the spread of the *kal* poison. As it was, I barely survived in my present form."

"I've been meaning to ask you about that," he said, stepping over a fallen log and giving her hand a little tug to help her over it. "How can they threaten you? As you said, you're a memory held by the planet. They can't *kill* you, right?"

"No, they can't kill me," she said. "There's nothing to kill! But they could corrupt my memory, making me into something dark and horrible like they are. Or at the very least filling my form with confusion, rendering me useless to *Preleteth* and to you."

"Then you're not sure what effect it would ultimately have?" Wellesley asked, his curiosity stimulated.

"Honestly, I am not," she said, her face screwed up in thought as she reflected. "I don't think a being like myself has ever actually succumbed to an attack by the *kals*. We've been hurt a number of times, like I was last night. But we've always managed to reintegrate with the planet before lasting harm was done."

"Never? In over a hundred thousand years of history?" asked Wellesley. "That seems like pretty long odds."

"Oh, you must understand that we rarely walk abroad like I am now," she replied. "I'm sorry, I should have explained. We dwell within the planet almost exclusively, only venturing forth on the rarest of occasions. I have spent more time in this form since meeting you than I have in the last century. Most of the time there just isn't a reason to manifest myself."

"Interesting," Wellesley said. "Tell me, do you remember when a delegation of priests from my people came here many years ago?"

"Yes," she replied hesitantly.

"From what I understand they were never able to make contact with *Preleteth*, though they tried for years to do so. What went wrong?"

"I–I don't know," she said. "Perhaps the planet did not consider them worthy."

"It's hard to imagine a more worthy set of people!" exclaimed Wellesley, surprised by the idea. "They dedicated their lives to helping others achieve wholeness. The galaxy has probably never seen a more pure, selfless group than the priests. Their greatest success was found on Delta-13, where the planet worked actively to–."

"We must hurry," she said, cutting him off and pulling her hand away from Hunt's. "Daylight is precious if we want to avoid another encounter with the *kals*."

"What's the matter, *Alleehavah*?" Hunt asked, jogging to keep up with her.

"The day is wasting away, and here we are talking and strolling!" she said in a tone of self-reproach. "The planet will be angry with me if I don't get you to the obelisk promptly. It already took me to task for the trouble we ran into last night. If I fail again I will probably be replaced by another of its assistants. And I – I don't want that," she said, glancing at him. "Please hurry, for my sake."

"Alright," Hunt said, letting the issue drop.

"There's something funny going on around here," Wellesley said, communicating freely now that physical contact with *Alleehavah* was broken. "This isn't the first question she's evaded, and I'm certain it won't be the last, either. And there's more: I get the distinct impression that *Preleteth* is hiding something from us. I suspect we're part of a bigger game, Rex, and that we don't see all the pieces on the board. Yet."

Mutely he nodded, *Alleehavah's* back still turned as she hastened through the vines and leaves ahead.

"I'm glad you agree with me," the AI said with a touch of relief. "Frankly I was beginning to think this little minx was turning your head." Wellesley paused for a moment. "Of course! That's exactly what she's been doing! Ah, I feel your temperature rising. But before you toss me into the jungle, I want you to know I *didn't* mean turning your head away from Lily. Only an idiot would think such a thing was even possible. No, I mean something more prosaic. You've been so fascinated by her adorable, naive little sister routine that you haven't bothered to really step back and think about how deftly we're being manipulated. You heard what she said: the planet has *other* assistants. So why did you get *Alleehavah*? Especially after the danger she put us in yesterday when she botched our trip back to camp, nearly getting you killed. You'd think the planet would immediately give us someone else to work with, out of respect if nothing else. And yet, here we are, traipsing through the jungle with *her*."

Unable to answer but intrigued by the AIs words, Hunt slowed momentarily as he walked behind his luminous escort and contemplated her slender form. Wellesley was right, he reflected: there *was* something peculiar about the treatment he'd been getting. Like he was being given so much to think about that he wouldn't have time to ask too many questions. No sooner had he learned one thing than something else was being jammed down his throat. It made him curious. And suspicious.

"Here we are!" she said in a bright voice at last, the smaller obelisk emerging from the trees before them. "Please go in at once. It is waiting for you."

"Will you be here when I get out?" he asked needlessly, just buying a little time to think before spending hours with *Preleteth*.

"Oh, of course," she smiled broadly. "And this time we'll leave nice and *early*, so that we get back without any trouble."

"Good, glad to hear it," he said in a distracted voice. Turning away and reaching for the door's handle, he paused momentarily. "Keep thinking about this," he said to Wellesley.

"What else would I do? I'm 'physically impotent,'" he said sarcastically.

"What was that, Rex Hunt?" *Alleehavah* asked, as he pulled open the door and disappeared inside.

"I am glad to see you well," *Preleteth* said in a thunderous voice moments later. "An encounter with the *kals* is usually fatal."

"Yeah, we made it through alright," he replied.

"Though only barely. Just what are those things?"

"There will be time for questions later," the planet replied. "For now you must meet me downstairs so that we can begin our work for the day."

"Later, always later," Wellesley said, as Hunt opened the secret door that led down into the structure.

"Don't forget that I hear all that you say, *Kol-Prockian*," *Preleteth* said with irritation. "You are truly an AI made in the image of your creators."

"Nice of you to say," Wellesley said tartly, making Hunt grimace.

"Rex Hunt, I will not train you while that…construct is in our presence," *Preleteth* said. "It casts a baleful shadow of doubt across all that we are trying to accomplish here. Only an open mind can receive the training necessary to overcome the parasite. I insist that you take him outside and leave him with *Alleehavah*. She will look after him."

"Like she looked after Rex last night?" retorted the AI. "Look buster, I don't know–."

"Enough, Wellesley!" Hunt said. "Just keep your mouth shut."

"I'm glad you see reason," *Preleteth* said. "I will wait for your return."

"You won't have to, because I'm not leaving," Hunt said. "Either we both stay, or we both go."

"Your petty sense of personal loyalty will be your undoing," the planet warned darkly. "This conflict is much bigger than you and your friends."

"Now *where* have we heard that line before?" Wellesley asked, thinking of Ugo.

"*Kol-Prockian*, if you say *one more word*…" *Preleteth* rumbled.

"He'll keep his comments to a minimum," Hunt said, aware that he could honestly promise nothing more, given the AI's salty character. "But I will not stay here one moment longer unless he can stay."

"Consider your path carefully, Rex Hunt."

"I have," he said coolly. "I suggest you do the same. The Devourers are nearly upon us. And I am the only one capable of bringing us victory in this struggle."

A long moment of silence ensued.

"*Preleteth*?" he asked at last.

"The AI may remain," it said grudgingly. "Provided it *remains silent*."

"You have my solemn word," Wellesley said sarcastically.

"Good enough," Hunt said, stepping in before the spiral of recriminations began anew. "What are we going to do today?"

"We are going to take the first steps toward making you a genuine weapon," *Preleteth* replied slowly, anger still in its voice. "Yesterday you learned to reach out with the gift within you. We are going to strengthen that capacity today, and try to give it offensive power."

"How?"

"Watch and I'll show you," the ancient being replied with annoyance. "Now, I'm going to manifest a series of targets," it said, causing a number of large round wheels of hard light to appear a dozen feet away from Hunt. "First you will reach out and touch them as you did yesterday."

Fixing his eyes on the center target, he drew a deep breath and released it slowly. Then, recalling what he did the day before, he slowly formed a bridge of psychic energy between himself and the target. He held it for a moment, and then began to draw it back.

"Good job, Rex," Wellesley said, as the finger of energy retracted.

"Perhaps *you* would like to teach him?" *Preleteth* snapped. "It was a good effort. But you must be quicker. Here, I will guide you."

A moment later Hunt snapped out a connection, retracting it immediately after.

"That is the kind of pace you have to set," *Preleteth* said. "You must be quicker than lightning. It must be instinctual, immediate, merciless. Like stretching forth your own hand to pick a stone off the ground. There can be no hesitation. Do it again for the other targets."

With the planet's help he quickly flicked each target from left to right.

"You must develop the capacity to act that quickly," *Preleteth* said. "Because then you will have the mastery necessary to channel a load down the bridge you've formed."

"But what good is this going to be against the Devourers?" Wellesley asked. "They have enormous ships in space, not tiny detachments of soldiers. What difference does a few spirit zaps make in the equation?"

"These 'spirit zaps' have nothing to do with the weapon Rex Hunt must become," the planet said in a smoldering tone. "His gift is not intended to be used this way. These are merely exercises to put him in the right frame of mind. I am not trying to turn him into one of your handguns."

"Handguns seem about as useful against the Devourers right now…" Wellesley's voice trailed quietly.

"What now?" Hunt asked quickly, before the AI dug himself any deeper into trouble.

"Now we begin to pass a payload of the darkness you carry within down the 'zap' you're emanating."

"In order to hurt the target?" Hunt asked.

"Stop thinking in such linear terms," the planet chided him. "Just follow as I guide you."

Again Hunt reached out to one of the targets. A moment later, still following *Preleteth*'s lead, he felt a deep well of darkness open within him. It traveled down the bridge and poured onto the target. The hard light disk darkened until it exploded.

"What the–," exclaimed Hunt, reflexively covering his face with his arms as bits of dust coated him. "What happened?"

"You increased the darkness quotient of the object until it shattered," *Preleteth* explained.

"'Darkness quotient'?" Wellesley asked.

"What are you, a composite being?" asked *Preleteth*. "Is it possible to deal with one without the constant interference of the other?"

"Well, two heads *are* better than one," the AI quipped.

"We have a long established dynamic," Hunt explained. "Now, what about this quotient?"

"The nature of matter is such that it can only bear so much darkness or light before its essential structure degrades, causing it to disintegrate. Light and dark are energies that exist in a balance within all the creatures of the universe. Organisms tend to show an affinity for one of these energies over the other, and their destiny is aligned with it. Many feel that one or the other is better, but looking from an abstract perspective they are both simply a part of nature. Twin rivers, flowing down the mountain of history beside each other, their natures shape those who bear them. Generally speaking, an organism can only sustain so much of one energy or another before its structure is overwhelmed. At that moment it disintegrates, as you have just seen."

"Then my goal is to upset the balance of energy until a given enemy can no longer exist?"

"Exactly. The excess of dark energy will destroy them."

"Then how do the *kals* manage to survive?" Hunt asked. "They are the purest darkness I've ever seen."

"Unfortunately there isn't–," *Preleteth* replied.

"Time?" asked Wellesley. "And just when will there be?"

"Perhaps when three dozen Devourer vessels *aren't* bearing down on us at best speed?" snapped the planet. "I'm tired of this little game of cat and mouse we're playing, so I'll be upfront: we have at best a week until they get here.

Probably more like three days, judging by how good they're getting at dodging my interference. During that time I must make a master out of one who was no more than a high level initiate upon arrival. I am likely the only being capable of performing this work, now that the other worlds of the *Ahn-Wey* have reached their mortal hour. No matter how important your curiosity is *to you*, the galaxy has bigger concerns than having it satisfied. He must be ready to perform the delivering work necessary to end the parasite once and for all. For this reason all of our time together must be dedicated to preparing you."

"Good enough," Hunt said.

"I knew I could convince you," *Preleteth* replied. "But you're not the one who keeps sticking his finger into the middle of this. The question is, will the *Kol-Prockian* keep impeding our progress?"

"I'll be a good little boy," the AI replied. "For the time being."

"It's no wonder your people were broken and carted away," the planet sighed in exasperation. "Your opinion of your own importance had to get you in trouble eventually. The war of *Krelen-Gar* was initiated by your race, quite needlessly I might add. It was little more than an opportunity to strut and show your power. But it came back on you, didn't it?"

"Don't you *dare* speak of *Krelen-Gar*!" exploded Wellesley, his voice so loud it staggered Hunt. "No honest being could–."

"*Enough!*" Hunt exploded. "There's no time for this! Not anymore! We have to get back on track before the Devourers get a hold of us! Now, what is our next step?"

For the next hour Hunt practiced shattering the hard light targets that the planet placed before him. Dialogue was kept to a minimum, both sides of the previous argument silenced by his outburst.

"This is too easy," Hunt said, still fuming. "Give me

something harder."

"As you wish," *Preleteth* said, causing a massive shield of hard light to appear before him. "This has five times the mass of the previous targets. Try to overcome it."

"Overcome it?" Wellesley asked in a more or less cooperative tone.

"Yes. Hard light is the ideal target because it actively fights his influence with its very essence. Being made of light itself, its structure belongs to the opposite side of the spectrum. Instead of passively receiving the darkness he channels into it, the target pushes back. A target as large as the one now before him will represent a real challenge for his nascent abilities."

Hunt spread his feet a little, bracing himself for the contest. He raised his hand to begin, but the planet stopped him.

"Lower your hand," *Preleteth* ordered. "That is an instinctual aid that you must do without. It helps you focus your mind, but it unconsciously directs the darkness down an offensive path. It channels it into something like a psychic spear, which, while sufficient for human targets, is woefully inadequate for the Devourers. You must let it well up naturally without trying to guide it. Form the bridge as before, and then pour the darkness along it. Your role is that of a vessel that pours water, and not that of a pugilist who balls up his fist. You must *spread* the darkness, and not *throw it*."

Keeping his hands at his side, he felt the bridge proceed from his chest and connect with the massive sheet of hard light. Then the darkness began to build, filling up his psyche until it felt ready to burst.

"Release it now!" the planet said. "Stop holding it in!"

In a flash a giant load of darkness traveled down the bridge, spilling onto the target and spreading across half of it. The light receded before it, temporarily overwhelmed. But quickly its progress slowed, and the ground it had taken was lost. Moments later the target stood as before, a perfectly pure square of bluish-white light.

Panting, Hunt dropped to the floor, trying to catch his breath. His entire body felt drained, as though he hadn't slept in days.

"What did I tell you about letting it flow out?" *Preleteth* lectured him. "You may have lowered your hand, but your approach was just the same as if you'd kept it raised. You tried to build a *payload* of darkness to overwhelm the target with! That is contrary to what I told you! Your darkness must flow forth into the target, taking it over until there isn't a shred of light left to stop it. By building up a payload you overloaded your own psyche, making it impossible to channel more! If you'd kept your output more reasonable you could have poured it on continuously!"

"But...I would have run out of...darkness," Hunt countered, shifting to his back, his chest rising and falling. "I could feel it. There wasn't enough!"

"You only *feared* there wasn't enough!" corrected *Preleteth*. "The darkness is part and parcel of your people. You can't exhaust it. But you can overload your own psyche by trying to put out too much at once. You need to recognize your own limits and *respect them*, not *fear them!*"

"He gets the message, *Preleteth*," Wellesley said, recognizing his friend was too tired to want to speak. "Give him a quarter of an hour, and he'll be ready again."

"No, not today he won't," the planet said bitterly. "Thanks to his fear we now have to wait until tomorrow. His psyche won't be ready to bear another load until then. The better part of a day has been lost."

"It won't do to chew on him," Wellesley countered. "A student always makes mistakes. Otherwise he'd be the master."

"Thanks, Wells," Hunt said, struggling onto his elbow and looking at the massive target before him. "It's awfully big," he said in a dejected voice.

"Not nearly so big as the threat that stands on our doorstep," *Preleteth* replied sourly.

"Since we can't do any more today, why don't you answer some of our questions?" Wellesley queried, trying to be constructive.

"Do you think training Rex Hunt is the only matter that requires my attention?" asked the planet.

"I imagine not," replied the AI.

"Far from it. Now that he has wasted this day, I must bend all my energies upon slowing the Devourers' advance. Perhaps I can redeem some of the time lost."

"*Preleteth*?" Hunt asked a few moments later, sensing that the planet's consciousness was no longer with them. "*Preleteth*?"

"Guess it's gone for the day."

"Yeah," Hunt strained, getting to his feet with effort. "Boy, that didn't go as I expected."

"We all fail our teachers once in a while," Wellesley said philosophically.

"But not usually with so much riding on our *not* doing so," Hunt said in self-reproach, reaching the stairs and climbing them slowly. "I don't know what came over me. I heard what *Preleteth* said about letting it pour out naturally. But all the same I ignored it and tried to build up a payload."

"Humans tend to stick to habitual ways of thinking whenever they're faced with a novel problem. It feels safe. Fact is, most of the time it *is*. When they are faced with a new situation they try to fall back on the tried and true – the most familiar. They don't like to add two unknowns to the mix at the same time."

"Was that true of *Kol-Prockians*?" he asked in a distracted voice, his mind replaying the scene of his failure over and over.

"Heh, no. My people were a more reckless set than that. It's why I was programmed to be so conservative. By their standards, anyway. I was supposed to balance out the equation. But you must remember the savage beginnings of your people – what they were up against. It makes sense that humans would be an overall conservative race because of the millennia during which they barely held on to life at all. It made them cautious, wary. Well, I mean they already *were* like that. But experience made them more so."

Reaching the top of the stairs, Hunt pushed open the little door that hid the stairwell and passed through it, not bothering to close it behind him. Walking down the small hall past the empty rooms on either side, he reached the obelisk's main door and opened it. After the gloomily dim illumination of the training room, the daylight outside hurt his eyes, making him blink. After a moment he saw *Alleehavah* sitting on a large rock a half dozen paces away, her legs dangling over the side.

"What? You're done already?" she asked, jumping down. "Oh! What wonderful progress!"

"No, not *wonderful progress*," Hunt said flatly, annoyed with himself. "I blew it, and *Preleteth* said we had to stop for the day."

"Oh," she said sympathetically as he walked past. "But you will make double the progress tomorrow! Your dedication to fix today's error will drive you to greater achievement."

"I guess so," he said grouchily.

"Where are you going?" she asked, as they walked southward from the obelisk. "Your friends are to the east."

"It's not like we don't have time until sunset," Hunt said. "I feel like walking for a while. Maybe I can shake a little of this gloom away before reaching camp."

"I'll walk with you," she said, trotting after him and falling in beside him. "I don't want you to get lost."

"I'm sure that's what *Preleteth* would prefer right now," Hunt said. "He's pretty mad."

"Oh, the living worlds don't have genders," she corrected. "They're just–."

"It was a figure of speech," he snapped, looking at her angrily. "Look, if you're just gonna correct me, then stay behind!"

Silently she lowered her head, looking at her feet and walking gingerly. Several minutes passed before he spoke again.

"I'm sorry, alright?" he said in a half-combative tone when he saw her still drooping beside him.

"Oh, it's okay!" she said, trying to sound bright but not feeling it. "I know your people often react with anger when they feel helpless. It is a normal behavior among your clan."

"Don't dissect me," Hunt said irritably.

"But I would never hurt you..." her voice trailed, confused by his expression.
Oh! Another figure of speech!"

"Yeah," he said, not looking at her.

"Tell me," she said, glancing at him. "Are there many–."

Alleehavah's words were cut off by her tripping over the massive exposed root of a nearby tree. Tumbling into a heap, she looked up at Hunt and then laughed.

"I need to watch which way I'm going," she said, a smile reaching from one cheek to the other. Dusting off the few particles of dirt that had managed to adhere to her smooth body, she extended her hand toward Hunt. "A little help, please?"

Reaching down he clasped her slender hand with his strong, rough one, pulling her to her feet in one powerful motion.

"I see why your woman appreciates your touch," she said, holding on for a moment longer than necessary. "You're strong and protective. You make me feel safe, even though I cannot truly die."

"We all have our little talents," he said, smiling faintly in spite of himself.

"Your talents are by no means meager, Rex Hunt," she

said, switching the hand which held his and walking beside him. "There is a reason that the worlds of the *Prellak* chose you and your father. You are both potent men. Or were, in his case." She looked up at him with round, doe-like eyes. "I'm sorry for your loss."

"Thank you," he said, nodding and looking away as he recalled the visit he'd had from his father's memory.

"You both are protective men," *Alleehavah* continued. "It is why he would work such a monstrous deed in the name of his race. He would never have acted thus for his own benefit. Only a man who was truly disinterested could make such a sacrifice of his conscience for the sake of others. At no point in his journey was he motivated by self-seeking. And neither are you. It is for this reason, among others, that the *Prellak* chose you."

"Are there others among my clan that have been chosen by the *Prellak*?" he asked.

"No, only you and your father were suitable vessels," she replied. "Long ago a dark seed was planted within your family. Well, not a *seed*," she corrected herself. "That's just–."

"A figure of speech?" he smiled.

"Yes!" she giggled. "Again, the darkness was already present in your clan. But your family was chosen to be the special exponents of this heavy principle. Through thousands of years of cultivation your ancestors were linked to other people in your clan through marriage in order to produce the most pure expression of this element possible"

"You mean they were *bred*? Like *cattle*?" asked the heretofore mute AI.

"If you like, yes," *Alleehavah* said, not grasping the implication.

"I don't like," Wellesley said. "Not by a long shot. Just who felt they had the right to genetically engineer this particular family among the humans? Some gaggle of fiends with a god complex?"

"Shh!" exclaimed *Alleehavah* instantly, twisting

toward Hunt and pulling him to a stop. "You must not speak that way! Never allow such words to leave your mouth, Rex Hunt." Anxiously she searched the holes in the canopy above them, trying to get a look at the sky. "I hope you haven't been heard. No, no, I'm sure you haven't," she said, sighing with relief. "I forgot – your friend speaks through the *skin*. And there's no way he could have been heard." Closing her eyes and sighing again, she relaxed and pulled him back into their walk.

"What was that all about?" Hunt asked incredulously.

"You shouldn't ask me about that," she said, looking away from him as they walked. "I-I can't talk about it. Too dangerous."

"*What* is too dangerous?" he persisted. "And just what could hear us?"

"Please, Rex Hunt," she pleaded, stopping again and taking his other hand with her free one. "You mustn't ask such questions. There are things that cannot be told. Were I to utter even a word about, well, about such matters, *Preleteth* would punish me! It would probably destroy me! I am privy to secrets that I am not at liberty to disclose. Please, I'm begging you, do not press me further." She looked away shamefully for a moment, and then looked up at him again. "I-I couldn't long hold out against you. I would have to tell you. And that would be my end."

"What, are you in love with him or something?" asked the AI with surprise.

Averting her eyes and releasing his other hand, she pulled him for a second time into a walk.

"Then that's it!" Wellesley exclaimed. "You've got the hots for him!"

"Let it alone, Wellesley," Hunt said, seeing how uncomfortable it made her. "*Alleehavah*, I won't push you further."

"Don't bet on it," the AI interjected. "Rex, there are things we need to know, and this blue chick is–."

"In enough trouble as it is," Hunt cut him off. "We're not going to add to her problems by grilling her."

"Oh! Thank you!" she exclaimed, jumping up and wrapping her thin little arms around his neck. She hugged him for a long moment and then slipped back to the ground. "Please, if there's *anything* I can do to compensate for not being able to discuss–."

"I doubt it," Wellesley said acidly.

"Well, you could tell us about the *kals*," Hunt said. "Just what are they?"

"They are me," she said after a moment.

"Look, if you don't want to tell us, just say so," Wellesley replied pointedly. "You don't have to make up nonsense."

"No, I mean it!" she said earnestly, looking up at Hunt. "Not literally, of course. They obviously couldn't be *me* in reality, or *I* wouldn't be me."

"You don't say," the AI said, his eyes audibly rolling.

"I am using a figure of speech," she smiled. "You remember when my people joined with the *Ahn-Wey* to banish the parasite from our galaxy?"

"LIke it was yesterday," Wellesley said tartly.

"Yes, *Alleehavah*, we do," Hunt said.

"Well, as I told you before, the living worlds required our psychic strength as well as their own to complete the task. The act destroyed all the human clans of the Milky Way save your own. But there is more to it than that. We weren't merely destroyed: we were *bonded* with the living worlds. Well, a handful of us were. But in a distorted, limited form. In the moment that our energy joined with that of the planets, an imprint from a fraction of us was stored. Sometimes it was positive, as in my own case. But very often it was negative. The act of banishment took all that we had, leaving only a slight residue. Even the people of my clan bore darkness, Rex Hunt, though not such a generous amount as your own clan possesses. When our energy was taken from us, often only that tiny element remained. It was that which passed into the planet's memory. And it is those memories that you see when the darkness falls with the setting of the sun."

"But why doesn't *Preleteth* stop it?" asked Hunt. "If they're just memories, it should be able to assimilate and neutralize them, right?"

"No, it can't do that. Not without risking the corruption of the other memories it holds," she explained. "The consciousness of the planet is not subdivided, Rex Hunt. There are no walls behind which it can hide. Were it to assimilate the *kals* it would endanger both memories of light, such as myself, and also other elements a thousand times more precious. So it must tolerate their presence, allowing them to roam free on its surface, causing terror to whom they will."

"But they're really your people?" asked Wellesley, still getting used to the idea.

"Yes. A terribly corrupted form. Honestly they are more like a sliver than a true representation. All that was dark, destructive, and deathly in my clan manages to live on in them. It is as though one drew forth cancerous cells from an individual, and then multiplied them in a laboratory until they were more or less assembled in the shape of a human being."

"A horrifying image," the AI said.

"Indeed. You can readily see why the *kals* are such terrible creatures. No longer human, but not in any way spirit, either, they travel the surface of *Preleteth* in search of life they can devour. The animals in the jungle have learned to stay away from them, and manage to flourish in spite of them. Though the occasional sick one among them still falls prey to their depredations."

"Is this true of other worlds?" asked Wellesely, his curiosity growing. "I mean, are other dark memories stored from that great outpouring of psychic energy?"

"Of course," she replied simply. "All surviving worlds of the *Ahn-Wey* contain such memories, though not always in such a clear form. Some can only faintly manifest them. Like a shadow dancing on the wall they are present, but unnoticeable save to the most perceptive."

"Like Lily!" Wellesley exclaimed. "I was right, Rex! The figures she saw on Delta-13 *were* real!"

"Then she was haunted by visions of ancient *humans*?" he asked, his skin crawling for her sake.

"Oh, more than just visions," *Alleehavah* corrected serenely. "They were as real as you or I. But the planet was far too weak to do anything more than show them, and even that, it sounds, was on the most subtle level possible. Your woman is most sensitive if she is capable of detecting them."

"She has a profound gift," Hunt said, his mind racing back to the terrible sight of Tselitel coming apart from the attacks of Bodkin. His teeth ground as he thought upon it. He wished he could kill Bodkin a second time over for exposing Lily to such horrors. "Could they have hurt her?" he asked suddenly, his voice flat, low, and deadly serious.

"Not physically," she said. "It seems that Delta-13 was too weak to manifest anything that distinct. And in the absence of physical contact, it is doubtful that they could have formed the necessary connection to hurt her any other way. If they *could* have made some kind of juncture, they would have drained every last ounce of light from her soul, rendering her as dark as they are."

"*That's* why she was horrified by them, Rex," Wellesley said conclusively. "She could feel what they were capable of, and recoiled from them. It's a miracle that she didn't go mad from what she saw."

"Many have gone mad on Delta-13 from the influence of the *kals*," *Alleehavah* replied helpfully, supporting his point without feeling its personal implications for her hearers. "As I understand it, that unfortunate world possesses a reputation for psychologically damaging its residents."

"Some of them," Hunt replied grimly.

"But it also assisted the ancient *Kol-Prockian* priests in their strivings for wholeness," Wellesley added. "I wonder that they never detected the influence of the *kals*."

"Delta-13 was an unusual world," *Alleehavah* replied uncomfortably.

"But I thought it was the chief of the *Ahn-Wey*?" asked Hunt, surprised out of his introspection by her unexpected words.

"Oh, it was in a sense," replied *Alleehavah*. "But it always had a peculiar illogic in its approach. Often resisting necessary steps that disagreed with its impulses, it had the most unusual way of prioritizing its efforts. After inviting the scourge upon us by teaching the living worlds to meddle, it formed the *Ahn-Wey* to drive them out. This done, it opposed the only action that could prevent their return. Somehow it had second thoughts, and sought to bury its attention beneath the snows that covered it. For millennia it lay dormant, until the *Keesh'Forbandai* came to our galaxy and raised it from its stupor."

"I've never heard of the *Keesh'Forbandai*," Wellesley said.

"In your tongue they were known as the *Voe*," she replied.

"Oh! The forgotten ones!" the AI said. "Remember, Rex? They were the ones who built the subterranean structures we found on Delta-13 inside that cave."

"They built many structures across the Milky Way," *Alleehavah* said. "The obelisks are their doing. As are many other things that you have yet to discover in your travels. They are a race like no other, far surpassing all the clans among our people, Rex Hunt. And yours as well, *Allokanah*."

"You know my name?" he asked with surprise.

"Of course," she smiled.

"You *are* a brilliant military AI, after all," grinned Hunt. "Your fame must be spread far and wide."

"Oh let it die, will you?" Wellesley asked with mild annoyance. "One chance expression shouldn't be held against me."

"Yes, but it summed up your self image too well to be discarded," Hunt replied. "Go ahead, *Alleehavah*."

"Uh, okay," she said, releasing his hand and walking a little quicker ahead of him.

"What are you doing?" he asked with confusion, causing her to stop and turn toward him.

"Going ahead," she said simply, a puzzled look on her face.

Shaking his head, he took her hand in his once more and resumed walking.

"No, I meant continue what you were talking about," he said.

"Oh! Well, the *Keesh'Forbandai* are not from this galaxy, as I said. Where they came from I do not know. But they helped the remnants of the *Ahn-Wey* to reorganize themselves and nurse what strength they had left to hold the *Prellak* more or less in check. They built the obelisks to allow worlds like *Preleteth* to speak directly yet in secret with their inhabitants. They performed a great many other works and then departed, vowing to return but never doing so."

"Did they say why they were leaving?" Wellesley asked.

"I imagine so. But *Preleteth* has never told me."

"So it keeps secrets from more than just us," the AI mused dryly. "Wait a moment. Did you say that Delta-13 taught the other worlds to *meddle*?"

"Oh! I've said too much!" she said in a voice filled with angst. "I only hope the planet doesn't punish me!"

"We won't tell it," Hunt said crisply. He wasn't sure if it could have heard her already, but he hoped to calm her enough to get more information out of her. "How did it teach them to meddle? By interacting with humans?"

"I can't say more," she said emphatically, shaking her

head side-to-side as though to cast the notion out of her mind. "Already I have roused your suspicions towards things that ought not to be uttered. Oh! If only I had kept my mouth shut! But I am such an idiot!"

"No, you're not," Wellesley said. "We're your friends, *Alleehavah*. You can tell us about it."

"No," she said, shaking her head again. "Absolutely not. I must keep my word! I must keep silent! I know things that I am not supposed to, and *Preleteth* agreed to let me manifest only if I kept such matters to myself. I have put myself in peril by speaking so loosely. I *must not say more!*"

"Alright," Hunt said in a calming voice. "Alright, no more. And don't worry about *Preleteth*. I'm sure it would have blown a blood vessel already if it knew."

"That's a figure of speech," Wellesley cut in quickly, tired of all the mixups. "He means–."

"I understand what he is driving at," *Alleehavah* smiled. "And I believe you're right."

"Good," Hunt said, giving her hand a little squeeze.

"What else can you tell us?" Wellesley asked. "You said the *kals* are the corrupted memories of ancient humans. Are there other such memories in the galaxy?"

"No, I don't believe so," she said slowly, thinking for a moment. "Our people were the only ones to join with the *Ahn-Wey* in their struggle against the Devourers."

"I can't imagine that to be the case," the AI said. "Surely other races must have seen the necessity of destroying the parasites."

"Oh, of course," she said quickly. "I'm sorry, I spoke imprecisely. Many races fought the invaders. But only our people were capable of joining with the living worlds in driving them back into the realm from which they'd been drawn. This was facilitated by the symbiosis that we enjoyed – the deep psychic union we had formed. No other race possessed such a connection, and thus it was not possible for them to help."

"I see," Wellesley replied. "What a cruel burden for one race to bear alone."

"Indeed," she said solemnly. "What a terrible price to redeem our actions."

Hunt opened his mouth to inquire further into this cryptic comment, but Wellesley cut him off.

"It's remarkable that the *Ahn-Wey* managed to survive the ordeal if they had to draw psychic energy from their inhabitants," the AI said musingly. "I should have thought they would have exhausted themselves in the struggle, and then, to speak terribly crudely, drawn upon the humans more or less as batteries. But I suppose they did the best they could."

"Oh, certainly," *Alleehavah* said. "As *Preleteth* told me, the calamity was too great for our people to bear. Indeed, our clan was not so hardy as yours, Rex Hunt," she said, smiling at him appreciatively. "Perhaps if we had been of your stock we could have borne the blow. But then we'd have lacked the peculiar sensitivity that makes such a transfer of psychic energy possible to begin with! So I guess it was just the way it had to be."

"Indeed," Wellesley said quietly.

❖ ❖ ❖

"Alright, smuggler, what's your game?" Pinchon asked Gromyko some hours later as they rested near the cool waters of a small brook.

"I'm sure I don't have the slightest idea what you're talking about," he replied, flashing one of his thousand watt smiles.

"You came with me because you don't want to let me out of your sight," the pirate explained. "You're loyal to your friend, which means you think I'm going to try and pull something while he's away from camp with his little blue girlfriend. What do you think I'm going to do? Try to murder him?"

"Who can say?" the smuggler replied offhandedly. "You've become quiet and suspicious of late. And now all of a sudden you're casting aspersions on my truest friend. I don't think you'd stoop to murder. Besides, what purpose would that fulfill? But the fact that you even brought it up tells me something that you haven't otherwise mentioned yet."

"And what's that?" the colonel asked, taking a sip of water from his canteen before refilling it.

"That you consider him a threat," Gromyko said, watching carefully for a response.

For a split second the pirate froze. Then he drew the canteen out of the stream and put the cap back on.

"Why would I consider him a threat?" Pinchon asked.

"I don't know," the smuggler smiled. "Why don't you tell *me*?"

"It's surprising that I should have to tell *you*," the pirate said, laying aside the canteen and looking his unwelcome companion in the eye. "After all, you know better than anyone what he did inside that old base of ours, when he drove a half dozen of my people mad."

Gromyko's face instantly flushed, the memory of that moment washing over him. He could see the pirates as though they stood before him – consumed by fear, tearing each other to pieces. The recollection was not a pleasant one, and he blinked his eyes to brush it away.

"I see you remember it," the colonel said with grim certainty. "A man with that kind of power has to be watched carefully. Why do you think I volunteered to pilot you all? It wasn't out of the goodness of my heart. That man is dangerous. He seemed alright at first, so I was inclined to give him the benefit of the doubt. But when he showed up last night, exhausted with that blue girl lying a few feet behind him, I knew something was up. The planet is working on him, Gromyko. Frankly I never should have let him out of my sight since coming here."

"Rex is solid to the core!" the smuggler protested. "He's no danger to anyone!"

"Are you sure of that?" he asked with quiet intensity.

Another unwelcome memory passed Gromyko's mind: the terrible sight of Hunt about to destroy his friends right after he'd finished his father. His black eyes, the cold inhumanity of his voice, the strange, alien word he uttered just as he was about to unleash his gift on Tselitel: all of it shook his assurance and froze his normally hyperactive tongue.

"So you're not quite so sure of him as you like to make out," Pinchon said, reading the doubt on his face. "Then why should I be any more certain of him? You've known him for years, as I understand it."

"Yes, I have," the smuggler said quietly. "But–."

"But what?" countered the pirate. "Look, we're on a planet that can manipulate the speed with which ships can travel through warp. Blue beings made of light are walking around, to say nothing of those black things that clearly want to sink their teeth into us." Here he slapped his leg, indicating the wound he'd received during their first night on the planet. "I'd say we're in a pretty unprecedented situation. Who's to say what kind of influences your friend is being subjected to right this minute? And what do we have to protect ourselves with if he *does* go bad? A few handguns? My people in the cave had those, too."

"Wellesley is keeping an eye on him," Gromyko said.

"What? A piece of jewelry?" Pinchon retorted. "And what's he gonna do? Talk him to death? No dice, friend. If a half dozen of my people weren't able to handle him, an ancient piece of alien tech isn't gonna do the job."

"I guess it's just a question of faith, then," the smuggler said.

"It's that kind of thinking that destroyed the

Underground. It's what separates your lot from ours. And it's why we're still around, and your people *aren't*. Take a piece of advice from someone who has been in the business of reading people a lot longer than you have: when a man is as dangerous as Hunt, no matter how good his intentions are, you've got to watch out. I think your friend stands on the edge of a knife right now, and he could go either way. If everything turns out alright, then he could be a great asset in the fight against the parasites. And if not–."

"Rex Hunt is as solid as they come," Gromyko reiterated, assuring himself as much as the colonel.

"But are you sure this power isn't too much for him?" the pirate inquired further, aware that the smuggler was still uncertain. "It seems a lot for any man to bear. And, like I said, we don't know what kind of influences he's under right now. The planet could be pushing his buttons as we speak, brainwashing him."

"These planets don't do things like that!" exclaimed Gromyko, surprised at the very idea. "They're benevolent!"

"These worlds aren't gods, they're simply another kind of being. As such, they have motivations and aims that probably aren't too different from our own. All we really know about them is what a handful of wide-eyed believers have told us, and what the planets themselves have chosen to impart. That's no basis for trust."

"What else can we do? We're precious short of allies right now, my friend. And these beings seem to have the only possibility of a path forward. We can't just turn our backs and walk away."

"I'm not suggesting that we should," Pinchon replied. "I wouldn't have brought you all here if I thought that. But that's no reason to dump your friend in their lap and let them do whatever they want with him. And make no mistake, smuggler, this old rock has got him dialed in pretty well. Why do you think it's sicced that little blue girl onto him? He feels protective of her, and that's got him distracted, which is just what the planet wants. You saw those two that visited us yesterday – they were neither naive nor young. In fact I got the distinct feeling that they felt themselves far superior to us."

"Well, you have your answer, then," Gromyko shrugged. "For someone as important as Rex you roll out the red carpet. You don't send someone to meet with him who dislikes his kind from the start. That's just bad tactics."

"Don't you see what I'm talking about?" asked the pirate, growing annoyed. "That only helps to prove my point. Treating him differently from us indicates he's being manipulated."

"I don't agree," the smuggler replied simply.

"So what are you gonna do now?" asked the pirate with exasperation. "Tell him and the others?"

"No, I'm not. We've got enough problems already without adding to the tension in the group. But I'm not going to let you get in his hair, either."

"Fine. But just remember this: I've got my eye on him. If he starts to go loopy, I'll take him down without hesitation. I'm not gonna have a repeat of what happened in that base on my hands here."

"It won't come to that," Gromyko replied, shaking his head. "You may be assured of that."

"Good to know."

A few moments passed awkwardly during which neither man looked at the other. Then Gromyko spoke up.

"One question."

"What's that?" Pinchon asked.

"Why would a Black Fang pirate care about the danger Rex supposedly poses?"

"Let's say I'm a humanitarian, and I'm looking out for my fellow man."

"That's the thinnest excuse I've ever heard," laughed the smuggler.

"It's all you're gonna get for now," Pinchon replied

sourly.

"Fair enough," he nodded. "Well, since we're out here anyway, why don't we actually go look for something to eat? There's no telling how long we're gonna have to stay on this rock, and our supplies won't last more than a few days."

Mutely the colonel got to his feet and stepped across the little stream, Gromyko right behind him.

"Just one more question," the smuggler uttered after a few minutes.

"What?" the pirate asked, pushing a leafy branch out of his way and letting it snap back in Gromyko's face.

"How did you know Rex was the one who leveled your people in the caverns?"

"The Order isn't the only organization to employ members with gifts," he replied cryptically, his tone indicating that he would say no more.

CHAPTER 7

"Goodbye for today, Rex Hunt!" Alleehavah said happily, waving at him from the edge of the jungle. "I'll see you tomorrow!"

"Alright," he waved, returning half her smile and turning toward the massive obelisk that loomed in the distance. His face darkened with thought as he put his hands in his pockets and slowly walked back to camp. Through bits and pieces of information that *Alleehavah* had accidentally dropped he began to paint a very dark picture in his mind of what stood in the way of humanity's continued existence in the Milky Way.

"Doesn't look good, does it?" Wellesley asked, reading his quietness with his usual accuracy.

"No, it doesn't," Hunt agreed, looking down at his feet as he walked. The sun was setting, casting painful rays of light into his eyes as he walked towards it. "But I admit that I've only got dark inklings. I had to keep the conversation going half of the time, keeping her off guard. You were in a better position to piece together what's really going on."

"Is that an invitation to theorize?" the AI asked.

"It is."

"Very well. Well, first off, it's clear that some other big player is a part of this drama. Whatever, or *whoever* it is, must be incredibly dangerous. You saw the way that *Alleehavah* jumped out of her skin and started staring at the sky."

"I did," Hunt nodded.

"Yeah, well, whoever it is, they can inspire fear even in the *Ahn-Wey*. She said that the *Keesh'Forbandai* built the obelisks, in part at least, so that *Preleteth* could speak to its inhabitants in secret."

"Can't be the Devourers," Hunt mused as he walked. "The *Keesh'Forbandai* came to *Preleteth* after they'd been banished."

"That's right. Besides, why would *Alleehavah* be afraid of the Devourers hearing what I said earlier? They're already on their way here now anyway."

"Right."

"So someone else is a part of this, and *Preleteth* is trying to keep us in the dark about them. And there's more. Something…darker."

"As if there wasn't enough of that already," Hunt laughed dryly.

"Yeah, it seems to be part and parcel of our age."

"Go ahead."

"Okay, I admit this is where I start climbing out on a limb," the AI said with a touch of hesitation. "But I think–."

"Hey, Rex!" Gromyko called from off to his left, making him jump. "Give us a hand with this thing, will you?"

The smuggler and the pirate were part way to the obelisk, dragging a large animal. It had something of the appearance of a buffalo about it, but it was much leaner and less shaggy. Two men could drag it, though with great difficulty.

"Where did you shoot this thing?" Hunt asked as he approached, eyeing the bloody fur at the base of its neck. "You look like you've been dragging this thing for miles."

"I think we have!" the smuggler said, dropping the hind leg he'd been pulling and wiping his brow with the back of his hand. His clothes were soaked through with sweat, and parts were stained with the animal's blood. "I'll tell you, I'm about done in. Grab a leg, will you?"

With a nod to the mute Pinchon who stood next to the smuggler, Hunt grabbed the creature's two front legs and wrapped them under his arms. Together the three of them hefted it the rest of the way to the obelisk, dropping it beside a modest pile of wood that Milo had left near the door.

"We're gonna need more than that to cook this thing," Pinchon said with a shake of his head. "What did he think we were gonna catch? A couple of rabbits?"

"I'm sure he wasn't expecting anything this bountiful," the smuggler said, proudly patting the limp head of his prize. "Not bad for someone who's hardly used a gun before."

"You mean *you* shot this thing?" asked Hunt.

"Absolutely," he grinned, as Pinchon strode off. "Where are you going?" he called after him.

"To get some more firewood," he replied. "Since Milo screwed up his end of this, someone has to get more. And it had better be quick," he said, stabbing an angry finger toward the half-set sun in the distance. "We've got maybe half an hour before those things come out, looking for blood."

"I'll go with you," Gromyko said, genuinely concerned that the colonel would get jumped in his absence. "Keep an eye on this thing, alright?" he asked Rex as he hastened after Pinchon. "Tell Milo about it!" he shouted as he moved farther away. "With all his time in the wilderness, he's got to have some idea how to butcher fresh meat!"

"We probably should have thought of that before spending our precious ammo like that," Wellesley said, as Hunt opened the door to the obelisk and went inside.

"Hello?" he called, shining his light around the dark space. "Lily? Milo?"

Hunt searched each room but found no trace of them. His heart began to race as he went back outside, casting his eyes around the quickly darkening environment.

"Where could they be?" he muttered under his breath. "Lily! Milo!"

"What is it, Rex?" the latter asked from behind him, having just rounded the obelisk.

Instantly Hunt turned around, gun in hand.

"Hey, take it easy!" Milo said, gesturing for him to lower the pistol. Tselitel was right beside him, a bundle held tightly in her arms. "We come in peace!" he laughed.

Shoving the pistol into his belt, he neared them both.

"Where have you two been?" he asked with a mixture of concern and censure in his voice, looking at his brother. "It's nearly dark. Or hadn't you noticed?"

"Oh, we stayed close to the clearing," Milo said with a dismissive wave of his hand. "Besides, we're packing too, you know," he said, pulling aside his light jacket to reveal his handgun. "Don't forget that I used to live for months on my own, out in the wilderness of Delta-13. I think I can handle anything this place can dish out."

"Provided they respond to bullets," Hunt said, moving to Tselitel and kissing her cheek. "What have you got there?" he asked, putting a searching hand on the bundle she carried.

"Milo and I went looking for something to eat in case Antonin and the colonel didn't come up with anything," she explained, laying the bundle on the ground and unwrapping it. Within were held massive clusters of berries and other small fruits. "Now, we're not familiar with what's edible on this planet and what isn't. But we thought Wellesley might have some idea."

"Those red ones are all bad," he said instantly to Hunt. "And the little purple ones, too."

"Red and purple have got to go," Hunt said.

"What!" exclaimed Milo. "That's most of our haul!"

"They're all descended from the same family," the AI explained. "They cause intense hallucinogenic effects before leading to paralysis and finally asphyxiation."

"What a waste," Tselitel said, dumping out ninety percent of their haul once Hunt had relayed the AI's words. "Good thing I insisted on waiting until we'd asked about them."

Milo stared at the pile of berries, his face flushed.

"Milo..." Tselitel said quietly, concern growing in her face. "You *didn't* eat any, did you?"

"No," he said. "But I nearly did." He pulled a handful of them out of his pocket. "I was gonna sneak a few when you weren't looking." Tselitel eyed him with a censorious look. "What? I was hungry!"

"It's a wonder he's survived this long," Wellesley said to Hunt.

"Milo, have you got any experience with butchering game?" Hunt asked.

"Sure," he said offhandedly. "But there's no way I'm gonna butcher *that* much game!" he added, pointing at the dead beast. "Do you know how much work that is? I'll be at it all night!"

"Then I suggest you get started," Hunt said. "There's a knife in the emergency kit."

"Yeah, I know that," he replied sullenly, striding past his brother and muttering.

"How have you been?" he asked Tselitel, who was kneeling before the handful of berries that had been okayed by Wellesley, carefully checking for any juice that might have spilled onto them from the poisonous ones.

"Oh, I'm alright," she smiled faintly, some of her hair stuck to her perspiring forehead.

"Are you sure?"

"Absolutely," she said, forcing a greater smile. "It's just..." she began. But she was cut off by Milo emerging from the obelisk with the knife, still muttering. She waited until he walked past. "Well, I couldn't help but feel that something was out there, watching us as we poked around for berries. I couldn't put my finger on just what it was. But it felt like it was all around us. And it felt..." her voice trailed.

"Felt what?" Hunt prodded, as her eyes got a far off look in them.

"Well, it felt *nasty*, unfriendly." She leaned close to his ear. "I don't want to say this," she whispered almost inaudibly. "But I feel like the planet is watching us, and that it's attitude is far from friendly."

"Wellesley has been thinking something similar," Hunt replied quietly, taking her good hand and giving it a reassuring squeeze. "He thinks it's hiding something from us. And I agree."

"Then I'm not going nuts!" she laughed quietly. "But I thought *Preleteth* was supposed to be a friend!"

"So did I," Hunt said.

"Then it's some kind of enemy?" she asked, her eyebrows raised.

"No…no I don't think so," Hunt said, shaking his head slowly. "But I don't think it's doing anything more than using us for its own purposes, either. We're just a tool, as far as it's concerned."

"Nice thought," Tselitel said reluctantly, popping one of the safe berries in her mouth and chewing it. "Yuck!" she said, screwing up her face. "These things taste horrible!"

"I said they were edible," Wellesley uttered to Hunt. "Not that they were tasty!"

"I can only imagine what Wellesley is saying right now," she said with a playful roll of her eyes. "Probably something terribly logical."

"You can bet on that," Hunt laughed.

"I guess one of us had better get that fire going," she said, rising to her feet and making for the pile of wood when Hunt took her left wrist and stopped her.

"How's this hand feeling?" he asked, standing up and holding it close to his face to examine it.

"Bad as ever," she said, wincing as he gently felt it. "I think I smashed it up worse than I did the first time."

"*You* didn't bust it the first time," Hunt quietly corrected her. "Antonin did."

"But it wasn't his fault," she protested mildly. "It was

just an accident."

"Sure," he said, drawing her hand gingerly to his lips and kissing it. As the sun sank lower beneath the horizon and the temperature began to subtly drop, he felt glad to have Tselitel with him. His growing suspicions about *Preleteth* and *Alleehavah* had put him on edge, and it was with relief that he gazed into the eyes of the one person he knew he could trust without any reservation at all. "Have I told you lately that I love you?"

"No," she giggled quietly, glancing toward Milo to ensure he hadn't heard. But he was too busy complaining to himself to hear anything except the sound of his own voice. "As a matter of fact," she said, drawing a little closer, "you've never told me that."

"What? Never?" he asked with quiet earnestness. "I must have at *some* point."

"Not that I'm aware of," Wellesley chimed in. "You've never said it to her while I've been in your presence."

"You're a big help, Wellesley," Hunt said with mild annoyance.

"Always glad to pitch in," he smirked audibly. "Naturally she knew it, of course, even if you never said it."

"But it's still nice to hear it," she smiled. "But I'd better go," she said, reluctantly pulling her hand from his grasp. "Someone needs to start that fire."

"Oh, sit down, silly girl!" he laughed, guiding her back to the patch of grass beside the berries. "Rest that hand of yours. *I'll* take care of the fire." Bending over and kissing her on the forehead, he went inside the obelisk for one of the emergency lighters.

Ten minutes later a modest fire was slowly growing in intensity, Hunt adding more wood to it periodically. Soon the orange light flickered brightly, competing with the green glow that descended from the beacon above them.

"That thing must have some kind of special properties to it," Tselitel said, craning her neck upward. "All day Milo and I worked around the edge of the clearing to find these berries," she said, ruefully regarding the poisonous pile for a moment before continuing. "The jungle is equidistant from the obelisk on every side. Like someone measured it off with a ruler."

"It's funny," Hunt said, following her eyes and looking upward for a moment. "*Alleehavah* said that the obelisks were built to allow the planet to communicate in secret with its inhabitants. But for some reason *Preleteth* can't manifest itself in this one. I have to trek halfway across the jungle to another, smaller one, just to talk with it."

"Maybe the *Keesh'Forbandai* built this one to keep the planet out of their hair," laughed Wellesley.

"Heh, could be," Hunt chuckled.

Tselitel was about to ask what the AI had said when her attention was drawn to Pinchon and Gromyko. They rounded the corner of the obelisk with armfulls of wood.

"That ought to be enough to cook most of that thing," Gromyko said with a satisfied sigh, dropping his load next to the fire.

"Next time you're given a task, Hunt," Pinchon said, putting down his pile and looking at Milo, "finish it! We barely got out of the jungle before those creatures started howling for blood."

"Hey, someone had to go with Lily to make sure she was alright," Milo protested. "She wanted to look for something else to eat in case you guys didn't turn anything up. I couldn't very well let her go rambling around here alone, what with a broken hand and all!"

"Doesn't look like you two have much to show for your little adventure," the pirate said disapprovingly, eyeing the small pile of berries next to Tselitel. "Doctor, leave the survival tasks to those who have made a profession of getting out of tight scrapes. We'll leave the mending of broken minds to you. Deal?" Without waiting for a response he trudged into the obelisk to deposit his equipment.

"Ah, don't worry about him," Gromyko said, squatting down beside his two friends, his eyes flashing brightly in the firelight. "He's just bent out of shape because I shot our dinner, and he didn't. But, when you go hunting with Gromyko…" his voice trailed.

"Why don't I believe that, Antonin?" Hunt asked, cocking an eyebrow.

"What do you mean?" the smuggler asked, raising both of his.

"A man like Pinchon doesn't get upset over something as petty as that. There's something else on his mind. Something you're not telling us."

"Ah, are you psychic as well?" Gromyko laughed, shifting on his feet momentarily to take his eyes off Hunt. "The truth is–."

"The *truth*, Antonin?"

"The truth is he doesn't trust you," the smuggler confided in a whisper. "He left this morning right after you did, intent on following you. I went along with him to keep him from bugging you, or worse."

"Worse?" probed Tselitel.

"Yeah," nodded the smuggler. "He, uh, heh, he *knows* that you're the one who took out his people in the cave, back on Delta-13. I don't know *how* he knows that," he added quickly, as Hunt shifted uncomfortably, "but he does. Said something about some of the Black Fang people having gifts too, but he didn't give any details. Maybe they have psychics on the payroll. It would make sense, if you think–."

"What is *worse*, Antonin?" persisted Tselitel. "Do you think he'd try to hurt Rex?"

"I can't say," Gromyko said honestly. "He might. So far he's been as cool as a mouthful of snow about the whole business. Doesn't seem to hold it against you at all," he said, looking at Hunt. "But ever since you've been going off with that blue girl–."

"*Alleehavah*," Hunt cut in.

"Yeah, *Alleehavah*. Well, since then, he's been all eyes and ears, watching everything you say and do. He's worried about what influences you might be under. He's not a big one for trust, my friend, so he's naturally suspicious when you start spending entire days away from the group with some funny little chick who's made out of light. These pirate types are all the same," Gromyko said confidentially, leaning closer. "Even when they've known a man for years they still wonder if he will turn against them one day. They live in a savage world with one moral rule: maximize profit. Funnily enough, that tends to keep their behavior pretty solid most of the time. After all, you can't make much money if nobody trusts you! But their belief in honor, in integrity, is absolutely nil. For this reason he believes your head could be turned by your little friend. He suspects that it's happening already."

"He's right, Rex," Tselitel seconded. "Just this morning he was trying to sell us on the idea that you and *Alleehavah* were having an affair."

"Sounds like he's trying to spread doubt," Hunt replied in a low voice that began to growl, eyeing the door through which Pinchon had entered the obelisk.

"Ah, he's been on the wrong side of life for so long that he doesn't know how normal people behave anymore," Gromyko said dismissively. "We'd see his type in the Underground from time to time. Let me tell you, I *never* trusted them with an ounce of authority. Oh, sure, on the outside they're all put together and responsible. But their inner world," here he thumped his chest with the flat of his palm, "it's *packed* with dark suspicions and imaginary plots. They fancy that everyone is out to get them, sooner or later. Just let it roll off your back, Rex. Don't pay any mind to him."

"You have to mind what a man thinks when he's got a gun tucked into his waistband, Antonin," Hunt said quietly, as the colonel stepped back into the open air and walked to where Milo was slicing thick cuts of juicy red meat from the dead animal. "Though he's right to have his suspicions of

Alleehavah and the planet. Wellesley and I have our own."

"Do tell," the smuggler said, leaning in closer.

"I don't have anything real definite yet," he said quietly, his lips barely moving. "But it's enough to justify Pinchon's suspicions. Not of me, of course; but that there's a plot of some kind brewing."

"Interesting," Gromyko said, glancing over his shoulder toward the pirate. "Maybe I judged him too quickly."

"Yeah, maybe so," Hunt replied, picking up a small stick and absentmindedly scratching the ground with it as he watched the colonel and his brother talking quietly together.

"What are you going to do?" Tselitel asked, following his eyes.

"What do you mean, babe?"

"Well, about the–," she paused and dropped her voice even lower; "about the *planet* and all. If it *is* working some kind of conspiracy, how can you trust it?"

"I don't see that I have a choice," Hunt replied in a low grumble. "Our backs are up against the wall. And there's no doubt in my mind that it *is* developing me as a weapon. I'm more powerful now than I've ever been before. Believe me, I don't think it's an *enemy*. But I think it's playing us."

"I wonder if that distinction is meaningful," the smuggler mused aloud, rubbing his chin. "After all, if it's trying to spend our lives for a purpose we're not intentionally serving…"

"The only cause I'm trying to serve now is the *human* cause," Hunt said. "And anything that helps me do that I'll welcome with open arms."

"Thought you weren't much of a cause man," Gromyko grinned.

"Times change," Hunt said with a shrug. "That, and the company has improved in the meantime," he smiled at Tselitel beside him, giving her a little nudge. "I'm no longer just running around with renegade smuggler types."

"Ha!" laughed Gromyko, slapping his leg. "Yes, I

suppose the moral quality of your social circle has improved considerably from where it was even two months ago."

Late that night Hunt lay in his room with Tselitel beside him, looking up into the darkness that surrounded him. He'd lain there for nearly an hour, unable to sleep as his doubts about the planet grew ever larger. Tselitel's breathing had long since evened out beside him, and he concluded she was asleep.

"Rex, do you think we should tell Lily that the figures she saw *were* real?" Wellesley asked. "I mean, the last thing we said about it was that I *supposed* them to be real."

"I don't think there's any reason to scare her with that," Hunt whispered almost inaudibly.

"Scare me with what?" she asked, shifting where she lay and putting her good hand on his stomach. "Darling?" she persisted, after several moments of silence.

"Guess the cat's out of the bag now," the AI commented.

"I didn't want to tell you this," Hunt said reluctantly, hearing her draw up beside him and rest on her elbow, her breath warming the air just above him. "The figures you saw in your room...were real."

"Oh my!" she exclaimed, her good hand shooting from his stomach to her mouth. Instantly the haunting memories of those terrible nights returned, and she began to shiver uncontrollably. "Rex!" she pleaded, burying her face in his chest as he turned on the flashlight.

"Darling!" he said, taking her in his arms. "They're not here! I promise you: they're not here! Open your eyes and look!" he said, shining the light around.

"I can't!" she cried, a fierce panic attack seizing her. "Oh, Rex! I know they're out there! I just know it! Following me around! Watching me! I-I can't take it! Every night I can barely sleep. I try to be brave–."

"You *are* brave," Hunt said firmly, squeezing her tight against him.

"No, I'm not," she sobbed, the fear crawling into every nook of her psyche. Tears began to wet his shirt as her chest convulsed. "You don't understand," she said, raising her mouth to his ear so she could whisper, her eyes squeezed shut lest the figures pry them open and make her behold them. "I-I take medication for anxiety. Or I *did*. Every six months I get injected with a pellet that slowly releases my medicine. I was coming close to due for another one before I left for Delta-13. But when the announcement of my appointment came I had to move quickly, and with everything that I had to do before leaving I just forgot. Oh, I know the medical facilities on Delta could have accommodated me. But what would that have done to my reputation? They were already looking for anything that could undermine my authority as an investigator. They would have *drooled* to get their hands on that little tidbit of data. *Doctor Lily Tselitel is on anxiety meds!*, the headlines would have read. It would have undermined everything I was trying to do there."

"That's why you were beating yourself up for not being a stronger person the night Rex rescued you from that woman," Wellesley said. "You said they should have sent someone else in your place."

"Yes, that's why," she sniffled, her tears running off her cheek and down Hunt's as she held him close.

"Why did you hold out on us, Lily?" the AI asked. "You didn't have to bear that alone."

"I-I couldn't let you know," she said. "I *shouldn't* have told you. Now you know what a weak little dummy I am." She drew her face above his and laughed at herself. "Ha! The famous Lily Tselitel! A cowering little child who has… who has to draw her self-assurance from…from a tiny little *pellet*," she quavered, holding up her thumb and forefinger to indicate the size of the pellet. "I'm a fraud, Rex," she said, her eyes as red as her hot, flushing cheeks. "I rail against the 'pill pushing school of psychiatry,' and I try to take a natural approach with my patients. I try to guide them into greater self-command and self-knowledge. Yet I've never had command of *myself!* I've never conquered my own fear! I'm not a strong person, Rex," she said, burying her face in his neck. "I never have been. I never will be."

"Darling–," he began, but she cut him off.

"Why do you think Milo and I went hunting for berries today?" she asked, raising her head again. "It was because I had to get away from this place! I had to get away, to keep moving all the time. I couldn't spend more than a few minutes in any one place or the...the fear would come and seize me. So I found where Milo was picking up wood and told him what was going on. I was just going to follow him around since I can't really haul wood with this bum hand," she said, raising her left. "But he knew that engaging my attention would be better, so he suggested hunting for something to eat instead. It was sweet of him to cover for me with Pinchon later on, making it sound like it was his idea to stop scavenging for wood and hang out with *me*. But the fact is it's all my fault. It's my fault that Pinchon and Antonin had to go hunt for more wood, putting them at risk. If I wasn't so *soft!* So...so *stupid* I could just–."

"No more of that!" Hunt ordered forcibly. "Not a syllable. "I won't hear the smartest woman I've ever known running herself down that way."

"Oh, I'm not strong like you," she sobbed, lowering her head once more. "I shouldn't be here. I-I never should have come to Delta-13! I've been a liability ever since I met you. I nearly cost you your sanity when that woman fought with you! I nearly froze you and Antonin and Milo when you had to keep stopping for me when we walked through all that snow together! Rex, *you killed your own father for me!* I've nearly cost you your mind and your life! And if that wasn't enough, I drove you to patricide!"

"I've made my peace with that," Hunt said. "And so has my father."

"Oh, I don't think I ever can," she said, her voice

shaking as her chest began to convulse again. "It's too terrible to think about."

"Wellesley?" he asked.

"I'm reading multiple chemical imbalances in her brain," the AI replied calmly, authoritatively. "Whatever problem she was suffering from before has been exacerbated by the medication. It was suppressing her problem, naturally, and not fixing it. Now that it has run out, the problem has doubled. It'll take time for her to come out of it."

"Oh, I'm not going to come out of it," she said. "Why do you think I was on medication in the first place? Because I couldn't handle this on my own! Oh, I tried! I really did! It's why I became such an authority on the human mind in the first place. I was trying to solve my own problems before anyone else's. But it didn't work. In the end I needed meds. I was just too *weak*," she said, grinding out this last word with desperate scorn.

"So what if you were weak?" Hunt asked.

"Oh, baby," she gasped, crying even harder.

"Answer me," he said with firmness. "So what if you *were* weak?"

"Then I ought to pack it in and call it a day," she said, not daring to look up. "I should just accept that I'm a human fortune cookie – something waiting to get snapped in two. I'm just not worth the time, Rex! I'm not worth the effort. I should quit wasting people's time and get out of society! Go become a gardener or something!"

"You don't have to be strong to be worthwhile," Hunt said.

"That's not true," she sniffled, looking up at him. "You can't believe that, not with your background. Delta-13 was a hard mistress. You yourself said that you had to be strong to survive. It was why you had all those harsh rules, remember? The ones that Milo punished himself almost to death with? That's the reality of life – the way things are when there aren't cushy surroundings to wrap yourself in.

That's when we're truly human: when we have to stand against the elemental forces that would lay us low and strive to overcome them. But I can't do that. I'm…I'm not strong enough. You tolerate my weakness because you love me," she said, putting her face down yet again. "But nature wouldn't be forgiving. If I was living back along with our ancestors I would have been ground to powder in an instant. I never could have borne the burden."

"No," he said. "Because I would have been there. And I would have protected you."

"You're sweet," she said quietly. "But I don't deserve you. That's why I couldn't tell you before. I-I couldn't bear to lose you. But now I have to. I can't hold you back anymore. You have an important mission to do. I can't possibly–."

At this he growled and took a fistful of her hair in his hand, wrapping his free arm around her middle. Rolling her onto her back, he kissed her forcibly until her sobs stopped and her tears ceased rolling down her cheeks.

"I can't do it, Rex," she said when their lips finally parted. "I–."

He kissed her again, even more powerfully than before. Nestling her head in his arm, he covered her ears to blot out every other sensation that might distract her. Slowly, thoroughly, he probed every inch of her mouth with his tongue, sending one message loud and clear.

"No matter where you'd go," he said, pulling his mouth away from hers, "no matter how long I'd have to travel, I'd find you. And I'd bring you back to *me*, understand? Nothing is going to separate us."

"Rex, I–."

Again his lips silenced her, pressing hard against hers until she finally moaned and wrapped her arms around his neck.

"That's not fighting fair," she laughed despite herself, a faint smile on her tear-stained face. "You know I can't resist you."

"That's why I did it," he smiled in return. "I don't want you to."

"But Rex," she began, pressing a finger to his lips with a chuckle. "And let me get this out this time, *please*. I'm not the girl you need. Really, I'm not. One of those hardy types from Midway is what you need for a job like this. Your destiny is going to carry you across the galaxy, battling a foe greater than mankind has ever conceived of before. You need all the help you can get. All the *strength* you can get. You need *strong* people around you, like Antonin and Wellesley. You can't afford any deadweight. Ah!" she said, putting a finger to his lips again. "I'm almost done. And then you can do anything you want. But just hear me out. Our people rose from the dust *because they were strong*, Rex. You're a true representation of our people, not someone like me. And you're going to need all the strength our race can give you if you're to succeed. Sure, I'm feeling good right now – you've practically kissed my socks off! But tomorrow I'm going to be a trembling mess. I'll do my best to hold it in, but inside I'll be doing this," she said, making a waving motion with her good hand. "And you can't afford to worry about that; you *can't* have a burden like that on your mind. Your head has to be clear for whatever *Preleteth* has in store for you."

"Are you finished now?" he asked.

"Uh huh," she said.

"Alright, then I've got a few words for you," he said, shifting slightly where he lay, still half atop her. "First of all, I wouldn't be alive today if it wasn't for you. Ah!" he said, laying a finger on *her* lips. "Just hear me out, okay, Doctor? It's time for *you* to take a little of your own medicine. We're a team, see? We go together like one hand inside another, because we're *meant* for each other. And you never find that in people who are of the same sort. To reach that true, deeper level of connection you have to be *different*. I could never bond with one of those hard Midway girls you think so highly of because they'd never let me in. They'd never have the *vulnerability* to trust. Their guard is always up, and that kills it. Sure you're fragile and you're scared – I wouldn't have it any other way. Because that's *who you are!* Don't you see that? You're built to be a worrier, to be sensitive. Now, something along the way aggravated that until it became something you couldn't manage. But we'll find that answer in time! I'm not giving up on you, no matter what. I can't. You're inside me. You're part of who I am now. You might think leaving would be the best thing for me. But it would be the cruelest step you could ever possibly take, so put it out of your head, if you have the slightest regard for my well being."

"There's nothing I care about more," she said quietly, talking past the finger that was still on her lips. "Nothing at all."

"Then get rid of all this nonsense about leaving," he said.

"But I'm not *worth it*, Rex," she pleaded earnestly. "Don't you see that? You've been *chosen* to lead us to victory. As long as we were a couple of renegades on the run from the authorities on Delta-13, I could kid myself that I deserved you. But what right has a silly little psychiatrist like me got to be with you now? What right does *anyone* have? Your task is inconceivable – extraordinary. It's beyond anything in human experience. You deserve only the best."

"That's what I've got," he said. "The best for me."

"Do you believe that?" she asked seriously. "I mean really? Deep down in your heart?"

"Yes, I do," he said sincerely. "With every ounce of my being."

"And you know I'm not always going to be like this?" she asked. "Steady, I mean? I can come unglued again like I did before. Especially if I think about–."

"Then don't!" he said quickly, cutting off her train of thought. "Just look at me; think about me."

"That's easy," she smiled. "But I *need* you to know what you're getting yourself in for. You already have such a burden to carry, Rex. Are you sure that you want this?"

In response he kissed her again. Not passionately, but slowly, warmly. His first kisses were meant to show her that he would be aggressive with her if he must; now he wished to demonstrate that he would be tender if he could. The choice was hers which one it would be; but the arm wrapped tightly around her side left her with no doubt that she couldn't shake him, no matter how hard she tried. Smiling as she kissed him back, tears of happiness began to well up in her eyes.

The next morning Hunt awoke early. Tselitel was resting quietly by his side, her breathing indicating that she was just barely asleep. With infinite care he slipped away from her and got to his feet, creeping like a thief out the door and into the main hall. To his surprise Milo was still out front, butchering the massive animal Gromyko had shot.

"Don't you have any sense at all?" Hunt asked his brother as he stepped into the growing light of dawn. "Even if we cook all this stuff it won't last more than a few days in the open air. Frankly I'm surprised Antonin even bothered shooting something this big."

"A simple good morning would do just as well," Milo said tartly, wiping the blood smeared back of his hand across his sweaty brow. "And the truth is I *didn't* stay with this thing all night. I fell asleep partway through."

"It's as well to leave the rest of it now," Hunt said, squatting down beside him and looking over the mangled carcass. "I take it you haven't done this in a while?"

"No, I haven't," he replied irritably. "And I was never much of a hand at it, anyhow. I probably haven't butchered more than a dozen animals in my life. And most of them were a lot smaller than this."

"Then what was all that business about surviving in the wilderness all alone, living off the land?"

"Oh, it was true enough," Milo said, putting a pair of bloody hands on the ground and shoving off with a grunt.

"But I might have exaggerated how long I had to rough it a bit. Most of the time I ate out of a can." He surveyed his work for a moment and then gestured to the pile of roughly cut, overcooked steaks that stood in a pile by the fire. "But as you can see, I can manage."

"Yeah, we won't starve for the next few days." Glancing back over his shoulder toward the door, he drew closer to his brother. "Thanks, Milo, for helping Lily yesterday."

"Anytime," he said quietly, a faint smile on his lips as he rinsed his hands with water from one of the canteens. "But I'm surprised she told you about it. She made me swear up and down to keep it a secret between us. In fact, I think she was more scared of you finding out than she was about those shadow things she saw back on Delta. It's odd. I thought you two didn't keep any secrets from each other."

"Yeah, so did I," Hunt said with a quiet touch of disappointment in his voice, looking back toward the obelisk again.

"Well, don't be hard on her," Mil said, drying his hands on the back of his shirt, it being one of the few parts of his wardrobe to remain relatively clean. "She's not used to living on the run like we are. It turns some people upside down, makes 'em scared of things that they shouldn't fear."

"She's off her meds, too," Hunt said confidentially. "Did she tell you that?"

"No," he shook his head, lowering his voice. "No, she didn't."

"Yeah," Hunt crossed his arms, turning to keep a constant eye on the obelisk's door. "Don't spread that around. I shouldn't have told you, either. But someone has to keep an eye on her while I'm gone. Be ready for anything. She could come unglued at any time, at least until the withdrawal symptoms wear off."

"But I never saw her taking any meds," Milo said, a puzzled look on his face. "How did she keep it a secret all this time?"

"It was a pellet," Hunt said, making a finger gun and discharging it into his own side. "An injectable. Said she only needed one every six months or so. She was coming close to due for another one when her assignment to Delta-13 came through, and she had to scramble."

"I get it," Milo nodded. "Any idea how long she'll take to normalize?"

"None whatsoever," Hunt replied. "I don't think she does, either. We'll just have to keep our eyes open, take things one step at a time. And try not to leave her alone while I'm gone. Being around others helps a lot."

"I'll keep close," he nodded. "Not like I've got a lot else to do, anyhow. I'm sure Antonin will keep an eye on our Black Fang friend."

"Doubtless," Hunt said. "Keep an eye on him, too, while you're at it. I don't like what he's been saying lately."

"Yeah, me either."

"Alright," Hunt said, punching his brother in the arm. "Thanks."

"You bet."

"What do we do now?" Wellesley asked, as Hunt walked past the obelisk into the other half of the clearing. "Soak up the dawn's early light?"

"No, now you tell me your theory about–."

"Good morning, Rex Hunt!" *Alleehavah* said in a chipper voice from some distance.

"Is fate trying to keep us from talking?" Wellesley asked in a voice that mingled humor with frustration. "Well, it'll keep. Can't keep our little blue friend waiting."

"Did you sleep well, Rex Hunt?" she asked as he drew near, a hopeful look on her face.

"More or less," he replied, looking around at their dimly lit surroundings. "*Alleehavah*, isn't it dangerous for you to be out this early? The *kals* could have caught you in the jungle. It's still pretty dark in there," he said, peering over her shoulder into the almost impenetrable wall of greenery that stood behind her.

"Oh, I spent the night under the glow of the obelisk," she said in a simple, obvious voice, pointing at the green beacon. "I wanted to stay close so that we–, I mean, so *you* could leave for your training as soon as possible."

"Well, we can't go yet," Hunt said. "It's still too dark."

"Oh, I know," she nodded vigorously. "I wasn't going to come and get you until it was safe to depart. But when I saw you just now I had to say hello."

"She's in a good mood," Wellesley said quietly. "Charm her. Maybe we can learn something more."

"Would you like to walk with me, *Alleehavah*?" he asked, pushing aside the naggings of his conscience as he followed the AI's advice. "We'll be alright as long as we stick to the clearing. I'd like to stretch my legs; get a little exercise."

"Would I?" she asked excitedly, taking his proffered hand quickly and falling in beside him. Instantly his heart went into open rebellion against his course of manipulation. He knew it was a mean, dirty, low trick. But he *had* to learn what the planet was up to, and she was his best bet.

"I'm sorry that the Devourers will be here soon, *Alleehavah*," Hunt began, trying to find his footing. "I'm going to miss you."

"Oh, I'll miss you, too," she said in a warm tone. "But all things must end. My life with the planet has been long – longer than anything either of our clans could possibly ever hope to achieve, despite all of our technology. Nearly one hundred thousand years have I watched the galaxy go about its business. Civilizations have risen and fallen; innumerable wars have begun and ended; the workings of the Unseen Ones–," suddenly she paused, glancing up at him furtively and then changing topics. "I hope I've been helpful to you, Rex Hunt."

"Oh, you have," he nodded, smiling at her as sincerely as he could manage. "You've shown me a whole new world.

I can see why *Preleteth* chose you to accompany me. We're so suited to each other. Who knows, perhaps if it had been another time, another place…"

"You think that, too?" she asked urgently, searching his eyes for confirmation.

"Yes," he said, matching her gaze with difficulty, his honest soul revolting at his lies.

Instantly she leapt into his arms, pressing her cool, smooth lips to his. The sensation was strange, alien, disturbing – almost as though he was kissing someone who was dead. The realization that he *was*, in fact, kissing the mere memory of a woman who had died eons before unsettled him all the more, and it took all his fortitude to simply stand there as she kissed him. But she was so carried away by her enthusiasm that she didn't notice his lack of reciprocity, and moments later she drew her head back, satisfied beyond words.

"Oh, it's better than I imagined!" she said. "I've never kissed anyone before. Can you believe that? In over one hundred thousand years of living! Never once! Your lips are so warm!"

"I'm…glad…" was all he could manage, glancing quickly over his shoulder to ensure that no one from camp had seen what she'd done. When he turned back to her he saw she was watching him, concern on her face.

"Do you regret what we've done?" she asked, her joyful eyes instantly wary. "Oh, I'm sorry!" she said suddenly, pulling her hand away from his. "I-I forgot! Your people don't–, I mean, even *my* people didn't. I mean–," she sputtered, trying to find some way to process what she'd done.

"*Take her hand!*" Wellesley barked instantly. "Soothe her! Calm her down! We need to get her guard down if we're going to learn anything."

"No, *Alleehavah*," Hunt said with a smoothness of voice that made him loathe himself as he reached for her hand and grasped it. "You haven't done anything wrong. Nothing at all. It's just–," his tongue froze, trying to find words as she peered up at him, her open eyes trustingly taking in everything he said. "I–."

"It's an old custom among Rex's people that they have only one *physical* relationship at a time," Wellesley threw in, trying to bail out his friend. "I can assure you that his heart is with you, *Alleehavah*. Why just last night we sat up late talking about you. But he's made his promise to Doctor Tselitel, and he must remain true to her. But nothing can ever take his heart from you."

"Oh, really?" she asked, her eyes filling with tears of happiness.

"Yes," the AI said with perfect calmness. "Absolutely."

Instantly her face fell.

"I never should have kissed you!" she said quickly. "I-I made you break your word to your beloved. The woman you love." Her naive face clouded over. "But, you just said you love me. How can you love both of us?"

"The heart of the Earthborn is complex," Wellesley said. "Even I don't pretend to understand it. The fact is *they* don't understand it, either. But I can assure you of his feelings."

"Oh, Rex Hunt!" she exclaimed happily, squeezing his hand in both of hers. "As you said, if only it had been a different time and place."

"Yes, exactly," he said, nodding stiffly, his cheeks blushing until they were ready to burst. "The, uh, the *sun* is just about up, I think. When will the *kals* be out of the way?"

"Any minute now," she said, pulling him into a walk toward the western end of the clearing. "They retreat to their caves and holes before it's truly up to avoid any risk of exposure. Come on! Let's take a look!"

Giggling she broke free of his grasp briefly and trotted to the edge of the jungle to peer inside.

"'*Uh, I think the sun is coming up soon,*'" Wellesley said

in a mockingly deep voice. "What kind of sweet talk is that?"

"I don't know who I hate more right now," Hunt ground out from between gritted teeth, speaking in a constricted whisper. "Me or you."

"Oh, shut up," the AI said. "This is no time for moralizing. She's our only avenue for answers."

"There is so much wrong with this that I can't even–."

"I think it's bright enough!" she exclaimed, turning from the giant leaves she'd pushed aside in order to peek. "There shouldn't be any of them–."

Suddenly her words were cut off by a large black hand clamping itself over her mouth, its long, cruel fingers digging into the surface of her blue cheeks. With a muffled shriek her tiny hands grasped the dark wrist, trying to pull it off. The hand lifted her off the ground, her legs dangling freely as a sharp saber of black was thrust into her back and out through her abdomen. The sinister face of an enormous *kal* emerged from the foliage momentarily, a vicious, evil smile upon its lips. Indifferent to the light of the rising sun even as it began to make the surface of its dark skin smoke, the creature laughed its scorn at the man who stood ten paces away in shock and withdrew into the jungle.

"No!" screamed Hunt, rushing forward as the *kal* and its victim disappeared behind the wall of green. Exploding through that wall, his eyes took a moment to adjust to the semi-dark he found within. He saw the *kal* carrying *Alleehavah* on the ghastly sword it had made of its own arm. The creature felt the exact moment Hunt's eyes fell upon it. Emitting a low, slow laugh, it thrust *Alleehavah* upon the ground and turned toward him..

In a flash Hunt discharged two bolts of fear, each of them striking the *kal* in the chest. It paused momentarily, looking down and watching for ill effects. When none manifested it reeled up its cheeks in a grotesque smile and began to plod steadily toward its target.

"Remember what *Preleteth* said," Wellesley coached

him calmly. "Don't try to strike it. Form a connection and *pour* darkness into it. Let it flow out."

Hunt drew a deep breath as the *kal* closed the distance. The psychic bridge extended out toward the creature, touching it and making it pause once again as it tried to grasp what was happening. The darkness in Hunt rose quickly, mingling with the fear he felt for *Alleehavah*, who lay writhing on the ground.

"*Now*, Rex..." Wellesley said with quiet urgency, as the beast resumed movement.

A massive eruption of darkness burst from Hunt, slowing the *kal* until it barely moved. Hunt fell to the ground as the blast left him. He saw the creature somehow grow darker than it had already been. Desperately he fought his way to his feet just as its motions began to normalize.

"Nail it again, Rex, or we're goners!" Wellesley shouted. "The effect is wearing off!"

Forming another connection bridge, Hunt cut loose with everything that was left in him. Like a sack of concrete the blow struck the *kal* in the chest, dropping it to the ground and shattering it upon impact.

Falling to his hands and knees, Hunt gasped for air as he tried to retain consciousness. His limbs growing weak, he collapsed to the soft soil of the jungle floor.

"You did it, Rex!" Wellesley said. "Now just stay with me until we can get out of here. There must be more of those things around."

"Can't leave...*Alleehavah*," he panted, his lips pressed against the dirt.

"Rex, she's gone," the AI said. "Nobody could have survived that assault."

"I...I can't," he gasped, struggling to his feet with the help of a tall, thin tree that stood beside him. "I can't...leave her here," he said, fighting his way forward, leaning on every branch and tree that presented itself. His ears rang and his head swam as he moved, his awareness of his surroundings rapidly dropping until all he could perceive was the still form of *Alleehavah* a short distance away.

"*Allee...havah?*" he asked, dropping to his knees behind her, nearly falling across her as he did so.

"Yes, Rex Hunt?" she asked, rolling over with difficulty and smiling faintly. "I'm afraid I must–," here she sharply inhaled, her face screwed up with pain. "I'm sorry," she said, beginning to weep. "I let them get me."

"No," he said, shaking his head wearily. "It's not...your fault. Don't worry. I'll-I'll get you to the...obelisk. *Preleteth* can help you." He tried to slip his arms under her back and knees to lift her up when she stopped him.

"No," she said. "There isn't time." She looked down at the grisly wound in her abdomen. "Look at it. You can see the darkness spreading, like little...fingers of death."

Reluctantly he followed her eyes. Like an infection the *kal's* frightful venom was passing into the rest of her system.

"Soon I'll be like one of them," she said painfully, her teeth gritted in agony. "I-I can't be that, Rex Hunt. I *won't* be that. You...you have to destroy me."

"I can't do that!" Hunt exclaimed, the shock of her statement energizing him momentarily. "How can you ask that?"

"There isn't time to–," she paused, drawing another sharp breath. "*Please*, Rex Hunt," she gasped. "I could never be a horror like they are."

"Do it, Rex," Wellesley said. "One final kindness."

"*Please*," she begged, her eyes wide momentarily. "If you love me, then do this for me. Let me end my days...as I truly am."

Looking between her pleading eyes and the darkness that spread farther through her body with each passing moment, he nodded wearily.

"Kiss me once more," she said. "Just let me feel your warm lips one last time."

Leaning over, his arms barely strong enough to hold

him up, he pressed his dirty lips to hers and closed his eyes. Moments later he pushed off the ground and stood over her small form.

"Now I can die happy," she said, closing her eyes and smiling through the pain. "Goodbye, Rex Hunt."

A knot began to form in his throat as he bridged the distance to her battered body. Lacking the strength to go further, he cut it and found a bent tree to lean against, taking most of the load off his wobbly legs. Connecting once more, he followed the advice of the planet, allowing the inner darkness to flow out instead of blasting it out in an instant. Slowly the darkness filled her body until it reached the base of her skull.

"Goodbye, my love!" she called, just as it crawled up her jaw and across her face. For a moment she was all black, a vision of midnight. Then she shattered into dust, her body no longer able to sustain its own existence.

With a sigh Hunt slid from the tree and fell face first into the fine powder that moments before had been *Alleehavah*.

"Rex," Wellesley said reluctantly. "We've got to go. It's not bright enough to stay here."

"I know," he mumbled, tears rolling out of his eyes and into the powder. "She left this life believing a lie, Wells. And for what? We didn't learn a…single thing from her."

"We did the best we could," the AI replied, as his friend struggled upward once more, his mind in a haze.

"No," he said, shaking his head exaggeratedly. "We did the *worst* we could. I just hope we'll be forgiven for it someday."

Shambling through the forest half in a dream, Hunt made his way to the clearing just as the sun poked over the eastern trees and bathed the land in daylight. Squinting against its brilliant rays, Hunt made for the obelisk but fell to the ground part way there.

"This is it, Wells," he groaned, rolling onto his back as

he began to lose consciousness. "I'm spent."

"That's alright," the AI replied, as he heard Milo shouting excitedly in the distance for the others to come out of the obelisk. "We're safe now."

❖ ❖ ❖

Admiral Claus Von Ortenburg waited patiently outside Minister McGannon's office, carefully examining a painting that hung from one of the walls. The minister's assistant, a young woman named Vicky Gleeson, eyed the admiral with undisguised admiration. Barely fifty, his closely cut hair had prematurely turned snow white years before. The lower part of his left arm had been lost decades earlier during a fierce battle with a fanatical set of fringe separatists. This feature was balanced by the loss, years later, of most of his right eye during a training accident, necessitating its removal and subsequent replacement with a black eyepatch. His loyalty to the emperor beyond all doubt, he held the command of the ninth fleet.

"The minister will see you now, Admiral," Gleeson said deferentially, rising to open the door for him both out of respect and to get a look at him up close.

"Thank you, my dear," he said with a charming air of culture, nodding slightly as her bright, curious eyes scanned every inch of his face, determined to make a permanent imprint of it. The moment he'd disappeared inside the minister's office Gleeson sighed and returned to her desk.

"It's always a pleasure to see you, Admiral," McGannon said with a smile as she returned his salute. Von Ortenburg stood stiffly before her, his hat held tightly under his arm. "Please, make yourself comfortable."

"Thank you, Minister," he replied, his stance barely

easing as he shifted slightly on his feet.

"What brings you to Earth, Admiral?"

"There's a matter of the gravest importance that I must discuss with you, Minister," he said in a low tone.

"Yes?" she asked, sitting on a corner of her desk and crossing her arms. "What is it?"

"Ma'am, I regret to inform you that several high officers in my command have secretly formed a cabal, the intention of which is to mutiny against the order to stand down. They have been in talks with officers who are sympathetic to their aims all across the empire, and my impression of their combined strength is not good. I estimate that nearly thirty percent of the high officers are in league with them, and that more are falling to their way of thinking every day."

"I am aware of the unpopularity of the order to stand down," McGannon replied. "I don't see why you had to come here personally to tell me this."

"Because, ma'am," he said, drawing closer, "nearly sixty percent of my own officers have decided to mutiny. It was only by agreeing to come here and present their case in person that I was able to hold them off. Even now they're awaiting word from me."

"Do they intend to hold Earth hostage if I refuse?" she asked coolly, contemplating the general strength of the ninth fleet as it hovered in orbit near the shipyards above Mars.

"No, Minister," he replied, shaking his head. "They explicitly wished me to tell you that was *not* their intention. If their demands are not met, or I fail to return promptly, they will take command of as many vessels as they can and make for the nearest battle with the invaders. Many of their homeworlds are under attack as we speak, Minister. They will risk anything to come to their aid."

"Their intentions speak well of their fighting spirit," McGannon said with a touch of pride in her voice. "If not their military discipline." She drew in a deep breath and let it out slowly. "Inform them that I will not take action against any officer who has spoken of mutiny, so long as they quietly return to their duty. But should any of them actually *take* that fatal step," she said, her voice lowering, "then I shall order all loyal vessels of the imperial navy to hunt them down and destroy them. I shall give priority to their destruction over that of the invaders, even if the latter lay siege to Earth itself."

"Yes, Ma'am," he replied. He was about to turn and leave when he hesitated. "Minister…why are we standing down?"

"Are you questioning your orders, Admiral?" she asked quietly.

"No, Minister," he replied calmly. "I have long since demonstrated my loyalty to the emperor," he continued, raising the stump of his left arm. "And I loyally follow all orders issued in his name. It is simply that I do not *understand* my orders."

"No one in the navy today deserves to know the truth more than you," she replied sincerely. "But I'm not at liberty to discuss the reason. Rest assured that it is a good one, and that soon all will be made clear."

"Yes, Minister," he replied with a salute, withdrawing from her office.

"A good reason indeed," she said scornfully to herself, sliding off the corner of her desk and making for the window. She looked to the sky, thinking of the ninth fleet as it floated over Mars, its loyalty hanging by a thread. She hoped her threat would be enough to keep them in line. In truth it was a mere bluff, for the admiral's figures had been conservative. Her sources indicated that nearly *half* the high officers were ready to rebel against an order that she herself felt was senseless. Any attempt to have one fleet fire upon another would have only strengthened their cause, convincing them that some lunacy had seized those at the top and that mutiny was the only sane course of action. The fleets would then coalesce under an independent command and do their best to drive back the invaders. Secretly she almost wished they would, for she had no more faith in Krancis' plan than Von Ortenburg's disobedient subordinates did.

Meanwhile, countless lightyears away, a man dressed completely in black sat inside his office watching the workers buzz about the Omega Project like ants.

"Sir, our fourth examination of Omega's subsystems is complete," a woman said to him. "We still can't determine what's wrong – why it won't start."

"Did you have a different team perform each examination?" he asked calmly, almost indifferently as he sat with his forefinger pressed to his temple, his elbow on the armrest of his chair.

"Yes, sir. Each of them found no error. We–," she hesitated momentarily. "We suspect something is wrong with Omega itself, sir."

Slowly Krancis swiveled in his chair to face her.

"The emperor has faith in Omega, Lieutenant," he said quietly. "Do you lack faith in his vision?"

"No, sir," she said quickly. "But we're up against a wall. We can't find what's wrong."

"Then perhaps nothing *is*," he mused, more to himself than to her.

"Sir?"

"Bring me all the documentation that has been written about Omega since the inception of the project," he ordered, rising from his chair and walking past her. "Dismissed."

CHAPTER 8

"Rex?" Tselitel asked, cradling his head in her arms, her legs folded under her. "Rex, darling?"

"He's exhausted beyond belief," Milo said, leaning against the wall of the obelisk to cool off after hauling his brother back to camp. "I've never seen him like this before."

"I have," Tselitel said, thinking back to the battle with Bodkin. "Wellesley, what happened to him?"

"He got into a fight with one of those creatures," the AI replied briefly. "The battle drained him. I'm afraid *Alleehavah* is dead."

The sound of her name filtered into his unconscious mind and startled him awake, causing him to jerk upright.

"Easy, honey," Tselitel said. "Easy. You're alright now."

"Where…How did I…" he asked in sentence fragments, his half alert brain trying to piece together where he was.

"You're safe now, Rex," she reassured him, gently grasping his shoulders and drawing him back into her lap. "Just rest."

Looking around, he saw Milo walking toward him; Gromyko and Pinchon were a few feet away, eyeing him curiously.

"What happened, brother?"

"*Alleehavah* got jumped by one of the *kals*," he said,

licking his lips and unconsciously swallowing. Instantly he leaned over and spat vehemently, remembering that the powder he tasted was in fact *Alleehavah* herself. With regret he wiped his hand across his mouth, feeling keenly the shame of his final lies to her. "She, uh," he said, thinking how he could trim the story down to its bare essentials. "She was infected and dragged into the jungle. I jumped in after her and got the *kal's* attention. I managed to destroy it with what *Preleteth* has taught me, but it left me exhausted. By the time I reached *Alleehavah* she was nearly dead. She passed moments later."

"Oh, that's terrible," Tselitel said, brushing the dirt from his face with her good hand. "I'm so sorry, Rex. She was so sweet."

"Yes," he said. "She was."

His heart about to burst, he struggled to rise but failed, falling back into Lily's arms.

"What's the rush?" asked Gromyko. "You need to rest, my friend. You look awful, like you haven't slept in days." He winked at Tselitel. "Just let the good Doctor here nurse you back to health."

"I can't," he said, rolling his head out of Tselitel's lap and getting onto all fours. With a grunt he pushed off the ground and stood up straight, wobbling on his feet. "I've got to get to *Preleteth's* obelisk. I have to continue my training."

"How?" asked Milo. "You look like you've been run over. I doubt you could handle it."

"When I want your opinion I'll *ask* for it," Hunt snapped, pushing away Tselitel's solicitous hands and striding quickly toward the jungle.

"Let him go," Gromyko said, as his friend walked away. "When his mind is made up there's no changing it. He's got to carry out what he's planned to do."

Hunt got under the cover of the trees and then looked back to ensure no one was following him. He could see the three men going about their business, but Tselitel stood watching where he'd disappeared into the vegetation. He looked at her for a moment, and then turned away, walking deeper until his strength finally gave out and he collapsed onto a large rock.

"How could we do that, Wells?" he demanded, tears of bitter shame running down his cheeks. "Lie to that poor girl?"

"We did what we had to do, Rex," the AI replied with cool rationality.

"How can you be such a machine?" he barked. "We led that little thing on until she didn't know which way she was going! It's probably our fault that she got jumped by that *kal*! If her head hadn't been in the clouds over how she *thought* I felt she would have noticed it! But instead we got her run right through the middle! What a savage death for a sweet, pure being!"

"Beating yourself up isn't going to help," Wellesley replied. "If it was *our* fault for distracting her, it was also hers for not paying attention. Shoot, the *kal* is the one ultimately responsible for killing her. No one made it assault her like that. What was it doing out so late in the morning, anyway? We had no reason to expect it to be there. *Alleehavah* herself said they slink back into their holes before the sun is really up."

"Your rational gymnastics won't work this time," he said, his face twisted into a scowl of self-reproach. "Nothing is ever going to wipe away the look of surprised agony on her face when that monster impaled her. I can see it before me like it just happened. That's a memory I'll always carry with me, like a brand of shame burned into my soul."

"I've had those, too," Wellesley said softly. "More than I dare to remember. I've lived a long life, Rex, and I've done a lot of nasty things. *Alleehavah* isn't the first pure little dear that I've tried to twist. But it's always been for a higher purpose. You must believe that, no matter what else you decide to take away from this. Neither of us did it for our own selfish purposes. *Preleteth* has been holding out, and she was the only way we could learn more. But we had to *trip* her into giving up her secrets: she wasn't going to hand them away willingly. We had to bury her thinking in a fog, get her so confused that we could extract the truth before she really knew what was going on. It was the only way. Ultimately she was just a casualty of war; a war that began eons ago when the Devourers first attacked this galaxy. You heard what she said: the *kals* are the charred remains of the darkness contained in her own people, the shadowy residue of their psychic presence. She fell as her whole race fell: fighting the invaders. There was no more apt way for her to finally depart this life and join her people in sleep. And to fall while still in possession of her mental purity, by the hand of one she *loved*, no less: that was better than she could have expected, what with the Devourers nearly on our doorstep."

Hunt turned around and sat upon the rock that he'd heretofore lain across. Drawing a deep breath, he exhaled it slowly, feeling some of his inner tension flow out of him.

"My father said something like that," Hunt said. "About being glad that he fell by my hand instead of anyone else's."

"Yes," Wellesley said. "When you get as corrupt as he did, it's better to fall by the blow of a pure man than to go on living. The same would have been true of *Alleehavah*. If you hadn't destroyed her she would have been a menace to every living thing on the surface of this planet. It was her time. Someday it will be ours, too."

"Yeah," Hunt said, looking at the ground beside his feet for a moment as he thought. "But to lie to her that way," he uttered quietly, shaking his head. "I can never forgive myself for that."

"She would have, had she known," Wellesley said.

"Perhaps," he replied, rising from the rock. "But it doesn't matter now. Her story has ended. Soon I'll close the book on those who have brought this darkness to our galaxy in the first place."

"Attaboy," the ancient AI said. "What are we going to do first?"

"Talk to *Preleteth*," Hunt said grimly. "It's time we got some answers."

❖ ❖ ❖

Admiral Claus Von Ortenburg stood just behind the pilot and copilot seats in his transport, watching as his flagship, the battleship *Victory*, loomed ever larger before him.

He'd turned over in his mind a thousand times what he would do when he was finally in the midst of the officers who had spoken to him as the fleet had neared Earth, persuading him to make an unscheduled stop and speak to Minister McGannon. He considered lying to them, weaving a tale of a brilliant counter attack that would take the invaders by surprise after they'd been lulled into a false sense of security by the empire-wide withdrawal of the fleet. But he dismissed this almost as soon as it had crossed his mind. His simple, honest heart could do no such thing to those who had entrusted their lives and honor to him.

He held their respect; that he knew for a fact. They would think of no violence against his person. But they would probably put him right back on the transport he was currently riding, getting him out of the way before warping.

"Battleship *Victory*," the pilot said over the radio, breaking the admiral's train of thought. "This is transport vessel BT-niner-four-one-oh-two, requesting permission to dock, over."

"Permission granted, BT-niner," a woman replied. "Proceed to docking bay four."

"Roger. Over and out," the pilot said, flipping up the

microphone on his helmet and turning to the admiral.

"Sir, we're about to dock," he said solicitously.

"Of course, Lieutenant," the admiral replied, getting his meaning and heading back into the passenger area to strap himself in. Several other people were back there with him, most of them furtively glancing at him, trying to get a glimpse of the famous victor of the battle of Theta-2. Normally he appreciated their attention. Indeed, on numerous occasions he'd signed autographs for those bold enough to ask for one, though that was frowned upon by those on high. But this time he barely noticed his fellow passengers, so absorbed was his mind by the problem before it. Soon he felt the rattle of the ship docking with the *Victory*, followed by the voice of the lieutenant over the intercom announcing the conclusion of the trip. Distractedly he unstrapped himself and made to follow the mass of departees. But the instant they saw him behind them they moved with one consent respectfully to either side, giving the hero of Theta-2 plenty of room to pass down the middle.

"Thank you," he said. At bottom a humble man, he had never quite gotten used to the treatment his fame brought him. Often he chose to ignore it, and at no point did he ever attempt to capitalize on it. This raised the esteem he was held in still higher.

Moving quickly through the lower levels of the ship, he gradually made his way to the command deck. Halting just before the closed door of meeting room number three, he closed his eyes and muttered a silent prayer. Laying his hand on the knob, he twisted it open and stepped inside.

"Attention!" cried one of the officers, snapping a crisp salute as the admiral entered. Instantly all in the room followed his example, nearly three dozen individuals in all.

"At ease," Von Ortenburg said, once he'd returned their salute.

"Admiral," began Colonel Alexander Crito, the ringleader of the mutineers on board the *Victory*. "What did

Minister McGannon say?"

"She made it clear," the admiral said, eyeing the room before continuing, "that any action to rebel against the authority of the emperor would be met by swift and unyielding force. She said that she would give priority to the destruction of mutinous vessels over that of the invaders."

"What?" demanded Crito, his face flushing. "We're under assault all across the empire, and we're supposed to roll over and play dead, letting those things have their way with our homes? What kind of madness is this, when the servants of the emperor are considered a greater threat than his enemies simply for defending his worlds?"

"She also told me," Von Ortenburg continued, "that anyone who has spoken of mutiny will not be acted against, so long as they return to their duty at once."

"Duty?" asked Major Eva Roarty. "Our duty is to our people, to those who depend on us to protect them! None of us joined the imperial navy so that we could stand by and watch as our worlds are savaged and our families are killed!"

This outburst was met by a general clamor of assent from those in the room.

"Admiral, which way do you go?" asked a third. "Are you with us, or with McGannon?"

"Minister McGannon serves in the emperor's name," Von Ortenburg said with calm authority. "It is by his will that she holds the post she has long filled, and filled well."

"Admiral, this insane policy cannot possibly proceed from the emperor!" exclaimed a fourth. "He must be out of communication, or worse! It could be the invaders have found and killed him already, trying to crush our resistance through killing our leader!"

"Indeed, how else can you explain the feckless policy of the naval ministry?" asked Colonel Crito. "There's no way that the emperor would ever stand for this! No one knows better than yourself the vigor with which he responded to the various rebellions of the fringe worlds. Why, every cadet in the navy knows the story of your action at Theta-2. The emperor *personally* ordered that battle, though our forces were outnumbered and outgunned. The navy did not disappoint his faith that day. Nor would we now, if the ministry only allowed us to fight!"

"We need that kind of audacity now, Admiral," Roarty seconded. "We can't run and hide, trying to save our strength! We have to fight, even if *none* of us come back alive. We owe it to our people."

A further clamor of assent went through the room.

"Our minds are decided, Admiral," Crito said, drawing closer and lowering his voice respectfully. "We don't want to act without you, sir. But we'll do what we have to."

Looking around the room, he saw three dozen pairs of apprehensive eyes upon him. They all desperately wished that the navy's greatest living hero would go forth with them to battle. Indeed, many felt that the only way they could succeed was through his strategic brilliance and inexhaustible courage.

"It was at the battle of Theta-2 that I lost my arm," he said slowly; "in the service of my emperor. Though the entire empire should fall before the invader, I will never doubt he who has been a father to us all. I will gladly lose my other arm in his service. Indeed, my life is not too great a price to pay to spare him insult at the hands of those who have sworn fealty to him." He looked the room over once more, the many pairs of eyes now downcast. "Do what you will, my fellow officers. But I will do what I must." With this he turned and left the room.

Moments later a trickle of shamefaced officers began to file out of the room. The trickle soon became a flood, each one silently returning to their posts, all thought of rebellion permanently driven from their minds.

◆ ◆ ◆

"There is no *time*, Rex Hunt," *Preleteth* said, once the former had told him of *Alleehavah's* death and demanded answers. "The Devourers are nearly upon us."

"You've been saying that for days," Wellesley cut in.

"Because it has been *true* for days, *Kol-Prockian*," snapped the planet. Then, in a softer tone, "Rex Hunt, I am sorry that *Alleehavah* should have perished before your eyes. I could sense a great attachment growing between you two, and it is a terrible accident that you should have beheld her demise."

"An accident?" roared Hunt, his scarcely contained emotions spilling forth like a hot river of lava. "How can you call that an *accident*? She was murdered by one of those devils! I–."

"An unfortunate end for such a dear being," the planet cut in, trying to calm him. "But her end was in sight, as is mine. Once the parasite arrives there won't be anything left except the foul creatures that follow in their wake."

"The *karrakpoi*?" asked Wellesley.

"Yes, if you must use that language," the planet said in a scornful tone.

"And just what's wrong with my language?" demanded the AI.

"What's wrong with it?" retorted the ancient being. "I'll tell you what: it belonged to a backward set of renegades, that's what! Oh, the humans might not have much going for them. But at least they have the sense to act in concert! Your people, on the other hand, carried individuality to its most logical extreme! Nothing meaningful could ever be done with that lot of imbeciles because they were always too concerned with their own petty little desires. It was even reflected in their government! Their internal divisions left them so weak that their foes carried them away into slavery piecemeal! Even in the great final conflict that swept them away they failed to act in unison!"

"Every race meets its end someday," replied the AI.

"Indeed. But some meet it much sooner than others."

Suddenly an enormous roar burst in the sky overhead, the deafening sound reaching even into the lowest level of the obelisk.

"What was that?" Hunt asked, looking fruitlessly at the ceiling above him.

"The Devourers," *Preleteth* said. "They have arrived."

"What do we do now?" asked Hunt.

"There is nothing further that we can accomplish here," the planet said in a tone of fatal resignation. "Within hours they will embed their fierce claws into my surface and begin draining my essence. The *karrakpoi* will spread across the land, killing everything they find. You must leave now. Ships have been hidden some distance from here for your use. Take them and go."

"But my training–."

"Will do you no good if you're dead," the planet cut in. "Soon their fighter craft will establish a blockade, cutting off your escape. You must leave *immediately*. Travel due south from the obelisk that your group has taken for its camp. There is a hangar in which you will find a pair of vessels."

"But–."

"There are no *buts!*" exploded the planet. "Go! Now! Gather your friends and depart *immediately*. Remember what you've learned and build upon it, Rex Hunt. The fate of the galaxy hangs in the balance. Go!"

Without another word Hunt bolted to the stairwell, climbing the steps three at a time. Bursting into the daylight outside, he tore through the jungle toward the obelisk.

"I hope they're smart enough to bundle up camp ahead of our arrival," Wellesley said, as Hunt ran for all he was worth. "There's no way they missed the appearance of our friends."

Glancing up through the canopy above him, Hunt was

relieved to see no ships.

"No, they won't be that close yet," Wellesley said, intuiting his thoughts. "They'll float in orbit for a little while first. If we're lucky, we can reach those ships before the fighters start searching the planet's surface for occupants."

"How are…we gonna fly…the ships?" Hunt asked between breaths.

"I haven't the slightest idea," Wellesley replied. "They're bound to be something other than the average imperial transport. We'll just have to cross our fingers, I suppose."

The vegetation around him was a green blur. Suddenly it ended, and he broke into the clearing, his heart beating loudly in his ears.

"Need…a break," he said apologetically, dropping to his knees and touching his head to the ground. Breathing heavily, he felt the sweat pour off the top of his back down his neck and onto his head. It had been hot and terribly humid inside the jungle, the closeness nearly suffocating him as he ran. Used to the bitter cold of Delta-13, the stultifying heat of Epsilon-4 drained him of his strength, leaving him lethargic despite the state of near panic that he was in. Moments later he fought his way to his feet and trudged as quickly as he could toward the massive obelisk.

"Just a few minutes and we'll be there," the AI said encouragingly. "Keep it up."

"Never got…our answers," Hunt observed, swallowing hard as his mouth filled with the sweat that poured down his face and around his upper lip.

"No, we never did," Wellesley said matter-of-factly. "Somehow it seems we're always a little late in that regard."

"Yeah," Hunt replied, forcing himself into a jog until he reached camp.

"What in the world is going on, Rex?" Milo asked, as his brother, red and exhausted, dropped to the ground outside the obelisk.

249

"Are you alright?" Tselitel asked, rushing to him and hitting her knees. "Are you hurt?"

"Devourers," Hunt gasped. "They're here."

"I knew it!" exclaimed Gromyko. "I knew that sound couldn't be anything except some warning of woe! I'm glad to see my old intuition is still up to snuff." The smuggler looked at Milo. "And *you* doubted me!"

"Glad you're…happy, Antonin," Hunt said dryly.

"Oh, I'm not *happy*," the smuggler said quickly. "I just–."

"What are we going to do?" asked Pinchon, approaching the group.

"There are ships," Hunt said, still catching his breath as Tselitel held him. "*Preleteth* told me about them." He pointed past the obelisk. "Miles south of here. Due south. We've got to…go now."

"I told them to gather the supplies as soon as we heard that noise," Pinchon nodded knowingly. "We'll be ready to move in three minutes."

"Good man," Hunt said appreciatively, as the pirate went back inside to finish his work. "The rest of you follow suit. We need to get off this rock before they spot us."

Tselitel kissed him on the cheek and followed the other two inside.

"Glad we've got Pinchon here to run things when you're gone," Wellesley said, as Hunt struggled to stand up. "Antonin would have spent all his time gawking at the sky, trying to prove he was right while arguing with Milo. And poor Lily is too busted up to be effective at a time like this."

"Yeah," was all Hunt could manage as he walked inside, hunched over as his stomach cramped from his exertions.

Two and a half minutes later the group departed the obelisk for the last time, heading straight south as they had been instructed.

"What are we gonna do if it gets dark before we reach

the ships?" asked Milo as they pressed their way into the wall of leaves and vines that separated the jungle from the clearing. Looking around anxiously, he tried to figure out how many hours of daylight they had left. "This place will be crawling with those dark creatures before too long."

"All Epsilon said was to head south," Hunt replied, finally catching his breath.

"But what if–," Milo began.

"Then we keep moving until we reach it!" snapped his brother. "Now shut up and keep moving."

Mutely Milo moved toward the front of the group, following just behind Pinchon. Gromyko had the middle, while Tselitel stayed close to Hunt in the rear.

"Are you alright?" she asked as quietly as possible, not wishing to embarrass him in front of the others but forced to speak over the crunching of sticks and the brushing of bodies against leaves.

"It's not every day that you kill someone," he replied bitterly.

"What?" she asked, a confused look on her face. "I don't understand."

"One thing at a time," Hunt replied, shaking his head side-to-side to dismiss what he'd just said. "Just focus on what we're doing now. We'll be lucky to get out of this alive."

She squeezed his arm with her good hand and then pulled ahead of him, sticking to the narrow path the other three had already carved in the jungle.

"It wasn't your fault," the AI assured him quietly after a few moments.

"Just leave me alone, Wells," Hunt said quietly.

Scarcely an hour passed before a Devourer fighter screamed overhead, the gust it generated rustling the tops of the trees.

"It's alright," Pinchon said once the noise had begun to subside. "They don't know we're here. They're just looking."

"And what makes you so sure of that?" Milo asked,

scanning the canopy above and ready to duck should he hear incoming fire. "They were able to find us inside a *cave* when we flew into one with your man Bradford."

"No, they found your *ship*," corrected the pirate. "Their scanners can't pick up individual humans."

"How do you know that?" prodded Milo, pushing a branch out of his way with annoyance.

"We didn't waste any time feeling out their capabilities once they'd reached Delta-13," the colonel replied. "That included the capacities of their various subsystems. You don't think we'd neglect to check their radar, do you?"

"Very efficient," Gromyko said approvingly. "Let's just hope they don't find those ships and torch 'em before we even get to them."

"Yes, let's," agreed Pinchon without turning around.

"I can't imagine what vessels *Preleteth* has in store for us," Wellesley said to Hunt. "To my knowledge this rock has never really drawn the attention of the empire. Even the pirates haven't spent much time here. Who do you think could have left ships behind?"

"Guess we'll find out," Hunt replied glumly, pushing aside a heavy vine that hung in his path.

Silently they strode through the stultifying jungle, innumerable insects biting them. All throughout the day Devourer fighter craft passed overhead, searching fruitlessly for them.

"I just realized something," Tselitel said the instant the thought crossed her mind. "There's no way the Devourers' radar will miss the escape pods. That's probably why they keep passing over this area: they know that someone managed to get off the *Stella* before it crashed."

"I agree," Pinchon said grimly, the thought having already occurred to him. "That's why we won't stop until we reach those ships."

Eventually the lengthening of the trees' shadows

became unmistakably clear, causing Milo to carefully search his left and right flank every few moments.

"Do you guys think we should bust out the flashlights?" he asked hesitantly.

"What for?" asked the smuggler casually. "Those things don't come out yet. It'll have to be pretty close to dark for that. Sunset is still a long way off."

"How long off?" asked Tselitel.

"Oh, probably another two hours," Gromkyo replied, searching for the sun through the foliage and finally finding it. "Maybe a little less."

She looked over her shoulder to Hunt.

"Oh, goody!" she mouthed, shaking her head with dismay before turning back to watch where she was going.

"She's taking this well," Wellesley opined. "Without the meds I thought she'd come apart to learn the Devourers were finally here."

"She's stronger than she thinks," Hunt replied.

"Yeah, you can always count on Lily to be sensible when the pressure is on," the AI agreed, hoping to divert his friend's attention by talking about his favorite subject. "Honestly that's one of the things I like the most about her. Just a solid, dependable girl."

"She's a bit old to be a girl, don't you think?" Hunt replied in a distracted tone, his mind still back with *Alleehavah*.

"Well, when you're as old as I am, everyone is young," Wellesley laughed. "You know, it was kind of odd for me back there, talking to *Preleteth* these last few days. I'm not used to being merely the *second oldest* being in the room. Kind of threw off my balance a couple times."

"Wouldn't know that from how you went after it," Hunt replied. "I doubt it's been told off like that in recent memory."

"Yeah, probably not," chuckled the AI. Then, switching topics to keep the ball rolling, "I wonder what this silly old orb has against *Kol-Prockians*, I mean *really*. Sure my people were a little…chaotic. But this rock's scorn sounded personal, like it had been burned in some way."

"I wouldn't know," replied Hunt without interest.

"Guess that's why the priests never made contact with it," Wellesley mused. "Can't have a conversation if only one of you is talking."

"Yeah."

"Hardest thing in the world," the AI said, stifling a laugh.

"Uh huh."

"Yeeeaaahhhh," Wellesley dragged out.

"Wells, why are you so bound and determined to keep me talking?" Hunt asked.

"Who, me?" he asked innocently.

"Out with it."

"Oh, it never ends well if you get too self-absorbed," the AI replied. "And I know how you're gonna rake yourself over the coals because of what happened to that poor little thing back there."

"Did you ever think that maybe I'm *processing this*?" he asked. "People do that sometimes, you know."

"Not you," Wellesley replied with instantaneous certainty. "You know your own mind better than anyone I've ever known. You already know your position, of that I have no doubt. I'm just trying to keep you from sinking too deep into it."

"Doubt you can prevent that," he replied sourly.

"Rex, she wasn't a real girl," Wellesley said, unable to let the point go so long as his friend was suffering. "*Alleehavah* died a hundred thousand *years* ago. We were talking to nothing but a memory, like *Selek-Pey*. We never knew *Alleehavah* – just the psychic imprint she left on the planet. If the real *Alleehavah* could somehow come back to life this very moment, she would know *nothing* of us because we've never met her."

"You're right," Hunt said reluctantly. "Guess I'm being silly."

"No, you're just being *human*. Or, *organic*, I guess I should say. A *Kol-Prockian* would have done the same thing in your situation. The vivacity of her personality, combined with a humanoid physical form, tells all your instincts that she's a living, breathing person. The tiny part of your behavior that's actually *rational* takes time to catch up with the rest of your impulses, and by then you've convinced yourself that she was a human being. It'll take time to work her out of your heart."

"Not sure I want to do that, to be honest," Hunt said quietly, glancing at Tselitel to ensure she couldn't hear. "She was so *sweet*, so naively trusting. I don't think they make people like that anymore."

"I suppose you find one here or there," Wellesley replied. "But they're few and far between, to be sure. Judging by what she told us, I reckon they were more common among her people than among yours. Guess that's why they let themselves be used by the *Ahn-Wey*."

"Is that what you think?" asked Hunt, his attention instantly captured.

"Yeah, that's what I think. I've been around this miserable old galaxy of ours for too long not to know a rat when I smell one. I think *Preleteth* kept dodging our questions because it *couldn't answer them*. I think the answers were too horrid for us to hear and continue working with it."

"Alright, professor," Hunt said. "For once I don't think we'll be interrupted. Lay out your theory, start to finish."

"With pleasure. Alright, the story we've been fed so far is that the *Prellak* brought the Devourers into this dimension to punish your human cousins for stealing their thunder. Finding the parasite insurmountable, the old human confederation joined with the *Ahn-Wey* and drove them back into their prison through a self-sacrificial act."

"I wouldn't say we were *fed* that story," Hunt replied. "I don't think *Alleehavah* would lie to us."

"Nor do I," agreed the AI. "But who do you think she learned it from?"

"Oh."

"Yeah. Right now I wouldn't trust *Preleteth* any farther than I could throw it." He paused momentarily when Hunt chuckled. "Don't think about that statement too closely. You know what I meant."

"Uh huh," he replied. "Alright, then what?"

"Well, this is where it gets a little sketchy."

"Just go for it," Hunt said. "The last time you started prefacing things we got cut off by Antonin and his trophy."

"What, are you getting superstitious?" asked the AI.

"No, but it's tempting sometimes," he replied. "Go ahead."

"Well, I don't buy that bit about the humans having to die the way they did. On some planets, perhaps. But why did other worlds like Delta-13 and Epsilon-4 have enough energy to last for a hundred thousand years if they *had* to drain their populations? I don't think that they did. I think they drained their populations to save their own necks."

"What?" exclaimed Hunt, causing the rest of the group to look over their shoulders at him. Too fascinated to explain, he just waved them forward and watched his feet until they lost interest.

"Think about it, Rex," the AI continued. "*Alleehavah* told us that the *Keesh'Forbandai* brought Delta out of a stupor it had fallen into. Well, I don't think it was in a *stupor* at all. I think it was so guilt-ridden by what it had done that it buried itself in a haze, trying to forget. I think the *Keesh'Forbandai* made it face up to its responsibilities and got it back on track, more or less."

"Why would they do that?" he asked.

"Search me. Just a random, benevolent impulse? In any event we *know* that Delta had human residents before, because of what Lily saw. And think about this: why was Delta going on about having already 'sinned enough?'"

"You're right," Hunt agreed. "And it said something about the *Ahn-Wey* having to receive punishment over their sin."

"Exactly!" Wellesley exclaimed excitedly. "Now, as far as we know, it was the *Prellak* that brought the Devourers into our galaxy. This shattered the old league and led to the formation of the *Ahn-Wey*. But Delta didn't say *the living worlds* would be punished for their sin, which would make sense if it meant the initial act of bringing the Devourers here; it said the *Ahn-Wey*, the so-called 'Union of Light.' And to our knowledge, the only act they've undertaken together was the expulsion of the parasite. Why would Delta speak of that as a sin, if it was only a regrettably necessary act of self-sacrifice?"

"You think they were killed," Hunt mused quietly. "Murdered."

"Yes, I do. I think that when the *Ahn-Wey* had their backs against the wall, they sacrificed those poor, trusting people first and only used their own psychic energy once they'd already been dissolved."

Hunt felt a dark rage growing inside him that he could barely control. Unable to imagine what the ancient humans were like, he simply took what he knew of *Alleehavah* and multiplied her billions of times over, spreading her across the galaxy in his mind. He imagined all those sweet, trusting faces joining with the *Ahn-Wey* in the honest belief that they would expend their life force equally, sharing in the sacrifice. It never would have occurred to them that they would be wrung out like oranges.

Sharply Hunt stopped and looked behind him, his mind racing back to the small obelisk that he'd spoken to *Preleteth* in. He felt the darkness well up inside, along with the desire to exact justice from one of the worlds that had betrayed his ancient kin.

"I know what you're feeling," Wellesley said. "But there's no use. Your powers aren't great enough to threaten an entire planet."

"Something must be done to avenge those people," Hunt said, as the rest of the group became aware he had fallen behind.

"Darling?" he heard Tselitel call from ahead.

"Something *is* being done," the AI replied. "The Devourers are about to go to work on it. In a couple of weeks, maybe less, this place will be just as dead as Delta is now."

"A fitting end," Hunt said implacably.

"Yes, I think so," Wellesley agreed, as Tselitel came bounding through the vegetation, her hair sticking to her sweaty forehead and cheeks.

"Oh, there you are!" she said in relief, brushing it from her eyes. "I thought we'd lost you."

"Nope," he said, nodding for her to resume walking.

"Are you okay?" she asked reluctantly, a faint hint of darkness visible in his eyes.

"I'm fine. I was just talking to Wellesley."

"Hey! You guys alright back there?" they heard Milo yell as he tramped through the brush toward them.

"Yes!" Tselitel called back. "We're coming!"

"Alright," Milo replied uncertainly, halting where he stood a short distance away.

"Go ahead, baby," Hunt said, the shadow leaving his eyes. "I'm right behind you."

"Okay," she said, looking at him for a moment and then proceeding.

"I hope they take it slow, Wellesley," Hunt growled. "I hope they make this world *suffer* for what it has done."

"I think they will," the AI replied. "They've had a hundred thousand years to build up an appetite."

As time passed and darkness began to fall around them, it was another set of appetites that filled their minds with anxiety. Slowing their pace to cut down on noise, their eyes constantly searched the dense foliage around them. Every shadow was double-checked; every little dark patch scrutinized with care. Even with five of them walking together they didn't feel safe. The only exception was Hunt, whose heart quietly smoldered, hoping to meet another *kal* to repay over again the wrong done to *Alleehavah*. He didn't bother to look around him, feeling that the *kals* would make themselves known when they were in the vicinity.

Dropping back to where he silently trudged, Tselitel found Hunt's hand with hers in the semi-darkness.

"Rex?" she asked quietly, her voice trembling.

"I know," he said firmly, hoping to firm her up with his tone. "I'm right here."

She smiled and nodded.

"Shouldn't we be busting out the lights?" Milo asked in as loud of a voice as he dared.

"Why?" asked Gromyko. "You got lucky last time keeping yours off. Maybe they won't notice us if we keep a low profile."

"I doubt that," Hunt said more loudly than his brother wished, making him grimace. "*Alleehavah* told me that they can detect our life essence. Apparently they can sense it from some distance."

"And you're only telling us this now?" snapped Milo, shoving his hand into his pocket and pulling out his flashlight. "Do you *want* us to run into them?" Suddenly his eyes grew large. "I could have been *eaten* the night we landed! They must have known I was there the entire time!"

"And yet, you weren't," Gromyko replied philosophically. "Perhaps you don't smell good to them."

"I'm sure any source of life force is good enough for them!" Milo replied. "And with five of us walking together, we must be screaming *buffet* right now! Everyone, bust out your lights!"

"No, don't do that," Pinchon said with quiet authority. "Remember, those things aren't the only ones out here anymore. We've got scout ships searching for us overhead. We don't want to attract attention."

"And *I* don't want to become *dinner*!" retorted Milo. With this he clicked on his light and began flashing it all around him.

The colonel instantly turned around.

"Turn that *off*," he growled, grabbing the light and wrenching it from his grip. Switching it off, he put it into his own pocket.

"Give that back," Milo said in a restrained voice, aware that Pinchon, while older, had at least thirty pounds on him.

"Not until you get some sense back into your head," Pinchon replied, turning and resuming the lead.

"Rex?" Milo asked, as his brother and Tselitel caught up to where he stood.

"He seems to know what he's doing, Milo," Tselitel said. Hunt didn't bother to answer, just keeping his eyes on where he was walking.

"What's got into this group?" Milo muttered under his voice, following up the rear and straining to see everything around him at once.

Eventually they reached another clearing, Pinchon signaling for them to stop as he crouched low and poked his head just outside the protection of the jungle.

"Can hardly see a thing," the pirate said, busting out a canteen and taking a drink. Despite the setting of the sun it was still stifling.

"Any sign of a hangar?" asked the smuggler.

"Mm mm," he replied, shaking his head side-to-side as he drank. "If it's here, it's got to be further on."

"Do we stick to the trees?" Tselitel asked. "Keep under cover?"

"I'd like to," Pinchon said. "But this rock told us due south. That's what we've been doing for hours now, so the ships have got to be close. Who knows, it could be right in the center of this clearing, just like that obelisk was. With visibility like it is, we can't risk missing it by playing it cautious. We've got to head right on out there and hope for the best."

"Hope isn't going to help us if we get jumped by those monsters," Milo said grimly. "Can I have my light back now?"

"Only if you keep it off until I say so," the pirate said.

"You're not the boss of me," he retorted. "If anyone runs this outfit, it's Rex."

"He seems to be taking a backseat role for the time being," Pinchon replied factually, glancing at him in the darkness. "In the meantime, *I* run things, so take it or leave it."

"I'll take it," Milo said with quiet anger, taking the flashlight from the pirate.

"Alright, I'll head out first," the colonel said. "Gromyko will follow up the rear. The rest of you, stick to the middle. Let's go."

Without another moment lost he quietly pressed the branches aside that barred his path and stepped into the clearing. Straightening slowly from his former crouch, he listened carefully to the sounds of the night. Nodding to himself, he began to move, his boots softly brushing against the half foot of grass that covered the ground.

Milo slipped out next, determined to keep the pirate in sight. Hunt and Tselitel could hear him muttering to himself as he moved past them.

"Come on," Hunt said, squeezing her hand and leading the way into the clearing.

Walking across the open ground made them feel small and exposed. Even though the jungle had blinded them with its vegetation, it provided at least some cover against the *kals*. But here, in the open, surrounded by a thick veil of darkness, the only thing that could protect them was the sharpness of their own senses and a half dozen flashlights.

"*And Rex's gift*," Wellesley thought with satisfaction, recalling what he'd done to the *kal* that had taken *Alleehavah*.

"Of course, if there's more than one..."

A light breeze began to blow from the east, gently brushing the grass and causing it to whisper in the night. This masked the sound of their movements, but it made their own ears all but useless. Hunt felt Tselitel squeeze his hand tighter, until finally he began to lose feeling in his fingers.

"You're alright, girl," Wellesley said through their skin contact. "You should have seen what Rex has already done to one of those things. Shattered it like a plate."

"Really?" she asked in a shaky voice, her eyes desperately scanning the darkness.

"Oh, yeah. You couldn't be in safer hands," he replied, not feeling quite as certain as he sounded. But he detected a slight drop in her heart rate, which was all he'd meant to achieve, anyhow.

"They could be anywhere," Milo muttered to himself. Somehow Tselitel managed to hear what he said, and instantly her pulse increased again. In the privacy of his own thoughts Wellesley cursed the younger Hunt in *Kol-Prockian*.

One of *Preleteth's* moons poked over the horizon, casting the faintest possible light upon them. Coating the world in a milky glow, it very nearly made seeing harder. Pinchon held a hand against his brow to keep its faded rays out of his eyes.

"What? Did we miss it?" Milo asked, as they reached the end of the clearing empty handed. "Should we double back?"

"We'll keep going forward," the pirate said. "It must be farther on."

"No, it's here," Hunt said with certainty.

"I don't think we would have missed it," Pinchon replied. "We must have walked right through the middle of that clearing. The planet said due *south*. Alright, we *went* due south and haven't found it. It's got to be farther ahead."

"You don't understand," Hunt said quietly, drawing closer to keep his voice as low as possible. "I just *know* it.

Delta-13 used to communicate through intuitions like that. I'd get an impulse, follow it, and it always turned out right. I'm getting that same feeling now."

"Sometimes people *think* they're getting a message from the outside when they're in danger," Pinchon replied in a slightly didactic tone. "It's just their nerves working on them. You can't pay attention to stuff like that. I say we go on."

"And I say we turn back," Hunt replied, his voice dropping a little.

"Look, I'm the only pilot here. You aren't going *anywhere* without me. So how about we cut this nonsense and proceed. If we don't find it ahead we can always come back."

"No, we're running out of time," Gromyko said. "If Rex says he feels something, I believe him. I saw it too many times back on Delta to doubt him now. The same goes for all of us." As he said this the other two muttered quiet words of agreement.

"Alright, you can recheck what we've already covered if you want. But I'm going on ahead."

"No, you're not," Hunt said.

"Excuse me?"

"As you said, you're the only pilot. I know for a fact that the ships are back there, and I'm not going to waste one minute waiting for you to finish chasing your tail. We all go back together."

"Or what?" asked the pirate, his hand slipping to the pistol in his waistband.

"Remember those people in the cave?" Gromyko chimed in, finding his own handgun in the dark, wrapping his fingers around the handle.

"Killing me won't get you off this rock."

"Who said anything about killing you?" Milo asked. "He'll just acquaint you with your darkest fears. Not a pleasant experience, I'm telling you."

"How would you know?"

"Why, he shot me with his power twice," Milo said, almost proudly.

"You zapped your own brother?" Pinchon asked, a touch of respect entering his voice at the hardness that action implied.

"And believe me," Gromyko seconded, "he will do the same for you. And faster than you can snap that iron out of your belt, I promise you."

Reluctantly the colonel released his grip on the pistol, letting his hand fall easily to his side.

"Alright, Hunt," Pinchon said, a mixture of anger and respect in his voice. "Lead the way."

"Antonin," Hunt said, nodding toward the colonel as he turned back, Tselitel still holding his hand.

"With pleasure," the smuggler said, falling in behind the colonel to ensure his good behavior.

Milo, glad to see the pirate humbled, moved with a decidedly chipper spring in his step to the space beside his brother.

"Get up ahead, Milo," Hunt ordered, gesturing with his free hand. "And keep your ears open."

"On it," he said eagerly, zipping ahead until they could just barely see him in the gloom.

Heeding another intuition from the planet, Hunt twisted their steps a little to the right, nearly losing Milo until he realized that the group had shifted course. Quickly he resumed his position in the van.

After nearly a quarter hour of searching a sudden impulse from the planet froze Hunt where he stood.

"Milo!" Tselitel called in a harsh whisper as he continued to scout. "Milo, come back!"

"You alright?" Wellesley asked as Hunt closed his eyes and felt his temple with his free hand.

"Headache," he said. "Bad one. We must be right on top of it. *Preleteth really* doesn't want us to move from this spot.

"I'll get Milo," Gromyko said as he and Pinchon caught up. "Heyo! Milo!" he called quietly, disappearing into the darkness.

"Well, Hunt, looks like your intuition isn't up to snuff," the pirate said, crossing his arms. "*Now* can we get back on course?"

"It's here," Hunt said, as the other two came back. "Fan out and search for it."

"What are we looking for?" Gromyko asked, as he returned with Milo and moved back to where the pirate stood.

"Anything," Hunt replied, the headache beginning to drown out his thoughts. "A hatch, a door, anything."

"Alright," the smuggler said, nudging Pinchon. "Come along, friend. Two heads are better than one."

With a sour expression on his face the colonel turned from the group and began half-heartedly searching the area.

"Darling, what good will a hatch do us?"

"Bunker," Hunt said, a powerful ringing rising in his ears. "Underground hangar."

"Oh, I see," she said. "Do you need to sit down?"

"No time," he said, shaking his head and instantly regretting the motion. "Let's just get moving. *Preleteth* will back off on me once we find it."

Carefully they searched, though none so energetically as Milo, who wished to humble the pirate yet further by proving his brother right. Soon his enthusiasm was rewarded.

"Hey! I found something!" he said loudly, forgetting himself for a moment.

"Keep it down," scolded Gromyko, as he and Pinchon neared.

"Just listen, will you?" Milo replied. Then he bounced in the air several times. Each time his feet connected with the ground a hollow metallic clang rang out. "It's your hatch, Rex. It's buried under the grass."

"Get it open," Hunt ordered, the pain in his head rapidly receding.

Milo dropped to his knees and began pawing at the ground in the darkness, clawing up handfuls of grass. The others, save Tselitel, followed suit; possessing only one good hand, there was little she could do but watch.

"Come on, boys," Gromyko said encouragingly. "We can't let a little dirt–."

Suddenly a horrific cry rang out a hundred yards to the west. A ghostly wail of cruel triumph, it was followed by two more, one to the south, and one to the north-east.

"They've found us," Pinchon said. "Flashlights, now!"

In an instant they had their lights drawn, shining them in all different directions. The creatures snarled and dashed quickly from side-to-side, trying to find a gap in their defense.

"We can't cover the whole area with just these," Milo said, only half the ground around them illuminated.

"Then I suggest we get that hatch open double fast," Pinchon said. "Give me yours, Junior."

"Don't call me that," Milo said, handing him the light and going back to work with redoubled vigor.

"Rex?" Tselitel asked, starting to crumble now that the creatures were upon them.

"Hold it steady," he said. "Go help with the hatch as best you can. Milo, get that thing open *now!*"

"What do you *think* I'm doing?" he barked.

Twice a *kal*, larger than the rest, slipped between two of the lights and closed half the distance before being driven back. It was a tense, panicky dance to keep them at bay. Soon more cries were heard in the darkness.

"Sounds like we're getting their attention," Gromyko said in a thrilled tone, his adventurous spirit stimulated by the danger. "We'll have a small army of them soon."

"Oh, *fantastic!*" said Wellesley to Hunt. "Rex, don't you think it's about time we thinned their numbers a little?"

"I agree," he said aloud. Allowing one to slip closer than the rest, he froze it with the light just short of the group. As it screeched and covered its face with its thin, crooked arms, Hunt formed a connection with it and poured a few seconds of darkness into it. Its painful howls drew the attention of the others, forcing Hunt to break the connection and shine the light on them to keep them back.

"Close! Very close," Wellesley said, as Hunt's target slinked away from the group, taking refuge just beyond their lights.

"Milo?" Hunt asked over his shoulder, as the *kals* continued to multiply. A dozen and a half surrounded them, and the screeching they heard in the distance promised yet more.

"Almost…got it," Milo said between breaths, his hands working feverishly. "Got it!" he exclaimed, ripping the last of the grass and dirt away. Feeling a loop handle in a recess of the hatch, he wrapped his fingers around it and pulled it upright. "Get off!" he ordered Tselitel, who in the dark had moved onto the trap door by accident. In her haste she used both hands to scoot onto the grass, instantly letting out a little yelp for putting weight on her damaged hand. Hunt flashed the light in her direction to ensure a *kal* hadn't gotten through.

"I'm alright!" she assured him quickly.

"I can't get this thing up!" Milo said, both hands wrapped around the loop, tugging for all he was worth. "It's rusted shut!"

"Fine way for us to go out, Hunt!" Pinchon said acrimoniously. "Led to the slaughter by your pal, the planet!"

"Give me that!" Hunt barked, backing into the group and finding the loop with his free hand, holding the *kals* back with the light he held in the other. "Now *pull!*"

Sweat poured down his forehead and into his eyes as he strained with Milo to open it, blurring his vision. In a snap he wiped them clear with the back of his flashlight hand, the nearly instantaneous movement giving the creatures on his side of the circle the time they needed to close some of the distance. The beam from his light sent them scurrying back.

"We're not strong enough alone, Rex," Milo said, his strength beginning to fail.

"Cover my side, Hunt," Pinchon said, by far the burliest of the group. Hunt took his lights, holding his own light in his mouth and one of the pirate's in each hand. Flashing back and forth like an insane lighthouse, he held down both his and Pinchon's sections through a manic series of quick movements.

"Alright, Junior," Pinchon said, spitting on his hands and wrapping them firmly around the loop, "Give it all you've got!"

With a grunt Milo snapped his legs half straight, straining with his whole body against the rusted hinges.

"Pull!" roared Pinchon.

Suddenly the hinges broke free, the hatch flying upward in their hands and nearly braining Hunt. A reflexive jerk from the colonel stopped it short and he and Milo dropped it on the grass.

"Everyone inside!" the pirate ordered, reaching around and pulling the light out of Hunt's mouth. "You first, Doctor."

As quickly as she could manage with only one good hand, Tselitel positioned herself over the hole. Feeling for a ladder with her foot, she found it and slowly descended.

"Today, Lily!" Milo said. "You're holding us up!"

"Then *help her!*" barked Pinchon, kicking him in the dark as a *kal* reared up before his light, wailed ferociously, and scampered for the cover of night.

Taking the wrist of her damaged hand, he anchored her as she descended. Finally she got out of reach and he had to let go.

"Keep going till you reach the bottom!" Milo called downward, no longer able to see her. Suddenly she screamed.

"Lily!" he bellowed down the hole impotently, unsure what to do.

"Well, get after her!" ordered Gromyko, tossing him one of the lights. "We'll be alright! Just look after our Lily!"

In a flash Milo swung his legs over the side of the hole and disappeared. Moments later they heard a pair of gunshots echo back up the hole.

"You next, smuggler," Pinchon ordered, taking the former's light and pressing his back to Hunt's. "This is gonna be tight," he said, as Gromyko clambered down the ladder like a monkey.

"Go ahead," Hunt said to the colonel. "I'll be right behind you."

The darkness around them undulated with inky black bodies. Like piranhas snapping at a piece of meat held just above the water, the *kals* hemmed them in. They flowed back and forth around them, instinctively searching for the tiniest opening they could exploit. Their mouths hung open, otherworldly moans escaping their vicious lips.

"No dice," the pirate replied, as the *kals* formed a tighter and tighter circle around them. "Get down there."

"Stop arguing and *hustle!*" ordered the AI. "Get moving, Rex. You're mission critical."

"So's he!" Hunt shot back. "We're not getting off the ground without a pilot!"

"Leave your lights on the ground," the pirate said. "They'll help me. Now *go!*"

Reluctantly Hunt did as he was told, quickly positioning the lights for maximum coverage and heading down.

"Alright, come on!" Hunt shouted over the howling of the *kals*, moving far enough down the ladder for Pinchon to fit.

In an instant the heavy yet limber body appeared over the hole, his large boots finding the ladder's rungs and following them down. With a light in his right hand, he used his left to keep hold of the surface until he was low enough to grab the top rung. As he drew back his hand to do so a *kal* dragged its fierce claws across his wrist, digging them deep and severing the muscles in the back of his hand. With a scream he pulled his quickly blackening hand back and tried to climb down the hole. Dropping his flashlight, he grasped desperately for the ladder with his other hand. Missing the next rung with his foot, he slipped several feet, nearly landing boots-first on Hunt before he managed to catch himself with his powerful right. Hauling his body upward several inches, he found the rungs and got himself oriented, clambering down as quickly as he could.

"Keep that light shining upward!" Hunt ordered Milo as he reached the bottom, carefully watching the colonel to offer any help he could. Grasping the latter's belt once it was in reach, he helped him down to the floor.

"Watch out for the snakes," Gromyko said, snatching the light that the pirate had dropped and whacking it against his wrist a few times to make it turn on once more.

"Snakes?" Pinchon asked, sweating profusely as he turned from the ladder, holding the living part of his wrist in his right hand.

"Yeah. One of 'em nailed Lily already," the smuggler said.

"What?" exploded Hunt, instantly taking the damaged light from Gromyko and shining it at Tselitel. She sat atop an old metal vent of some kind, holding her right ankle in her hand, her face twisted with pain.

"Everything happens to me," she said with grim humor, fighting to put a faint smile on her face as Hunt took a knee beside her. Raising her ankle, he saw two angry red holes with blood oozing from them.

"Where's the snake?" Hunt asked as calmly as he could, hoping Wellesley could identify it.

"Over there," she said, pointing over his shoulder. "In the corner. Milo shot it."

Squeezing her shoulder, Hunt stood up and made for the other side of the small room as the other three spoke in low tones to each other. Finding the serpent, its head shattered like an overripe tomato from the bullet Milo had thrown at it, Hunt took hold of its tail and held it up.

"Wells?" he asked, just short of panic as the fear of losing Tselitel filled his mind.

"Don't worry, it isn't lethal," the AI said reassuringly.

"Thank God," Hunt said sincerely, tossing the limp snake back into its corner and returning to Tselitel. "You're alright," he said, taking her good hand in both of his. "Wellesley says it isn't poisonous."

"Well, I said it wasn't *lethal*," he corrected. "But it *can* cause a severe allergic reaction. I can't say for certain what effect it may have on her, since most of my data is sourced from *Kol-Prockian* examples. It's possible that she'll just have a mild fever or something of that sort."

"Worst case?" Hunt asked, squeezing her hand to try and give her some of his strength.

"That's not very likely," the AI evaded.

"Come on, Wellesley," Tselitel said. "I'm a big girl."

"Well, *worst case* is pretty much everything short of death. Feeling ice cold one minute and supernova hot the next; shock; loss of memory; neurological damage; deterioration of the–."

"Okay, even big girls have their limits," she said with an anxious chuckle.

"But, again, that's exceedingly rare. Most likely you'll just feel terrible for the next twenty-four hours."

"Charming thought," she said.

"Better than dying," Wellesley said factually.

"Is she alright?" Milo asked, still by the ladder with the other two.

"Yeah," Hunt said, standing up and turning from her. "She's alright."

"Good, then get over here," Pinchon said. "We've got

another problem to think about."

❖ ❖ ❖

"Krancis, I don't know how much longer I can hold the navy back," McGannon said tensely, her yellow hologram standing in the middle of his small transport ship as he departed the station that held the Omega Project. "A sizable minority of the officers of most of the major fleets are ready to mutiny and defend their homes. Even Von Ortenburg is having trouble holding his in line, though he's managed to quiet them for the time being."

"Von Ortenburg is a good man," Krancis said approvingly, nodding slowly as he thought.

"They all are," she replied. "But this policy of non-engagement is too much for them to bear. Sooner or later they'll break and fight the invaders piecemeal. And when they do, they'll be ripped to shreds."

"Your job is not to hold them in check *permanently*," he said in his thin, precise voice. "You just have to keep them obedient long enough for Omega to be completed."

"But you must understand my situation," she replied. "The only threat I can hold over them is that of action by the loyal elements of the navy. The moment I have to make that threat a reality it will shatter discipline for good! There's no way the officers will tolerate firing on their comrades in arms while the enemy is left to ravage our worlds without resistance!"

"Then you had better hope your bluff keeps them in line for a little longer," Krancis replied with cool indifference. "Soon Omega will be ready, and then their forbearance will be rewarded. Even with the project completed we will need the majority of the navy intact to drive them out. We cannot tolerate emotionally charged heroics, especially by those who have been trained to know better. The only things standing between humanity and annihilation are the navy and Omega. It will take both elements for us to survive."

"I understand that," she persisted. "But numerous worlds have already been reduced. The ships that have destroyed them are now moving toward their next targets. Billions of lives have been lost. That figure will jump to *tens of billions* when they reach the more populated planets. Once that happens there won't be any holding back. I know these officers, Krancis, and I know the people that serve under them. They will not stand aside while our people are *exterminated*."

"Then I suggest you get imaginative in your methods," he replied, his voice growing tighter.

"And just how am I supposed to do that?" she asked. "You can't threaten an entire fleet unless you have forces that are willing to fire upon them."

"You military types always think in such *linear* terms," he said coldly. "When you assault a fortification, do you strike the *strongest* or the *weakest* point you can?"

"The weakest, naturally," she replied, her jaw muscles tightening.

"Then do the same with your officers," he said. "The weakest part of a sailor is not his *body*, but his *heart*. Find those who are important to him and *immediately* place them under arrest. He won't dare act against the will of the emperor so long as those closest to him are in danger."

"You're insane!" she exploded, unable to contain herself any longer. "You're literally insane! How could you even *contemplate* such a soulless, barbaric policy? I shall do no such thing! Even if I–."

"I will be soulless – indeed, I'll be the very devil himself – if that serves the empire," Krancis said grimly. "Nothing, absolutely *nothing*, will stand in my way. I will *break* whoever I have to break. And I will *kill* whoever I have to kill. There are no limits, McGannon – absolutely none. The

Devourers lowered the bar to zero the instant they began indiscriminately savaging our worlds. They will kill every last one of us if they can. Only by matching their ferocity can we hope to succeed. Enact this policy. Guarantee the navy's loyalty."

"You're insane," McGannon said again, shaking her head in disbelief.

"I thought you would prove intractable," Krancis said knowingly. "And that is why I have already carried out this policy against those closest to you."

"What?" demanded McGannon, simultaneously enraged and terrified. "How–."

"If you doubt my word, just try to contact your husband, or your aged parents," he replied with brutal factualness. "I understand that your mother has a rare condition that requires constant attention. The medication she depends upon is both rare and expensive. With the exigencies of war upon us, I cannot guarantee her supply, I am afraid, unless I have her moved to another location."

"You cruel, miserable–."

"But that decision rests with you, Minister," he replied coolly. "Shall I have your mother moved? Or would you prefer that she end her days now, painfully and before her time?"

Trembling with fury, unable to speak, McGannon stared at Krancis with murderous hatred in her eyes. Returning her look with indifference, he slipped one leg over the other and simply waited.

"How can you do this?" she finally uttered, torn between love and duty.

"By knowing exactly where my ultimate loyalties lay, and serving them without hesitation. Now, Minister, where do *your* ultimate loyalties lay?"

Another long interval ensued before she finally spoke.

"Have her moved," McGannon said.

"I thought you would see reason," he replied with satisfaction. "Those who serve under you will see it as well.

The instant I learn that the policy is in motion, I will have your mother moved." Her mouth opened to curse him, but he cut her off. "And not a second sooner. Goodbye, Minister."

CHAPTER 9

"What's wrong?" Hunt asked, joining the other men by the ladder as Tselitel nursed her ankle.

"Just look up," Milo said, pointing upward.

Grabbing hold of the ladder, Hunt swung his head under the shaft that led to the surface. The *kals* surrounded the hole, constantly poking their heads over the side and pulling them back as the light Gromyko held struck them.

"So?" Hunt asked casually, temporarily numbed to all danger now that he knew Tselitel was safe.

"So just what are we going to do?" asked his brother. "There's *one* door in here, and I've already tried it." Milo shook his head. "No good. It's locked tighter than a drum."

"Then we'll get it open," Hunt replied simply, turning to Pinchon. "How does it feel?"

"Like nothing at all," he replied, still holding his wrist just short of the portion that had turned deathly black. "It's gone stone cold numb. I think it'll have to come off. We can cut it just short of the live flesh."

"I agree," Hunt said. "There's knives in the survival kits. Antonin, give Milo the light and help the colonel get set. I'll see about the door."

Silently they did as they were told. Hunt returned to Tselitel and knelt beside her once more.

"Sorry, I have to take this, darling," he apologized, grasping the flickering light that sat beside her. "But I don't think there are any more snakes down here. I haven't seen any, anyhow."

"I have," replied Wellesley, making Hunt glad that he hadn't been touching Tselitel at that moment.

"Still, maybe you'd better stick with me all the same. You'll probably feel better than sitting here by yourself."

"Okay," she said weakly, getting unsteadily to her feet and following him to the door.

"What do you make of it, Wells?" he asked once he stood before it, doing his best to illuminate it with the damaged flashlight.

"Well, that's the funny part," the AI replied.

"Make me laugh."

"It's of *Kol-Prockian* make."

"So?" Hunt shrugged. "We already knew they'd come here. That's how *we* knew to come here in the first place."

"You don't understand," Wellesley said. "We knew the *priests* came here. But that was ages ago. Whoever built this *wasn't* a priest, and they did it *very* recently."

"How recently?" asked Hunt, cocking on one leg as Tselitel took his hand to listen.

"Probably the last two hundred years," he said in a voice that scarcely believed what it said. "Maybe even less. This whole bunker is military by design, not civilian. I'd say a team of *Kol-Prockian* combat engineers built it."

"Then where are they now?" she asked.

"No idea."

"Well, can you open it?" Hunt asked.

"Probably," the AI said guardedly. "Provided the door is still powered. It's been dormant for a long time. There's a little slot beside the door that I can fit into. Put me there."

Mutely obeying, Hunt stepped to the door and found the slot. Sliding the medallion inside, he stepped back and looked. Moments later he heard machinery whirring on the other side, and the door slid sideways into the wall.

"Heh, piece of cake," Wellesley said as Hunt pulled him

from the slot. "No security protocols of any kind. It's almost like we were expected."

"A comforting thought in a place like this," Tselitel said, looking around anxiously.

Stepping inside with her by his side, Hunt flashed the light around. The room was large, with closed shelving units on either wall and a massive table in the middle. A number of rough chairs stood at the table, providing an incongruously homelike touch to the space.

"How do you make sense of this, Wells?" Hunt asked as he moved to the back of the room where yet another door stood. "Your people were lost, destroyed."

"Apparently not," the AI replied with wonder. "Some… some of them must have escaped captivity. That, or they managed to flee before the final end came. But what were they doing *here*? Why come to *Preleteth* of all places? This miserable old rock doesn't even *like* us."

"Maybe the answer is through here," Hunt said, slipping the disc into the slot beside the door. Slowly it opened, revealing a cavernous room that housed a pair of fighters. Hunt emitted a low whistle as he approached the sleek, angular craft. "Nice ships," he said, running his hand along the gray paint which covered them.

"We are glad you like them," a sarcastic voice said from the wall off to their left.

Instantly Hunt jerked Tselitel behind him and drew the pistol from his belt. Moving slowly around the craft, the flickering light held beside his gun, he felt Tselitel's good hand on his back as she followed.

"You don't need that, human," the voice said in a lecturesome tone. "There's no one down here that intends to hurt you. Though perhaps there should be, given how you've led the *kals* to this position. The Devourers will be simpleminded indeed if they fail to infer what is attracting them here. We'll be lucky if they don't put a fighter patrol over this region just for good measure. Though the obelisk is likely enough to draw their attention in any event. There's always just–."

"Excuse me?" Hunt said pointedly, cutting the voice off. "Just who are you, and what do you want?"

"What do *I* want?" the voice asked with a laugh. "What do *I* want? I'll tell you what: some intelligent conversation for a change would be nice. Oh, and perhaps a change of scenery once in a while. I've been stuck down here for so long that I've nearly forgotten what daylight looks like. Do you have the least idea how *boring* it is to hold conversations with *yourself*? Naturally I had to do this to avoid going mad. Although AIs can't actually *go mad*, not in the sense that organics do. Of course–."

"Can you just answer the question?" Hunt cut in.

"I was," the voice replied tartly. "You asked what I wanted, and I–."

"I also asked who you are," Hunt interrupted again, moving closer to the voice and scanning the darkness around him.

"Oh, you're not going to find me that way," laughed the voice. "Ha! You organics are all alike: you think that anything with a voice has a body! Well, technically I do have a body. But–."

"Name," Hunt ordered, as his light fell upon a tall computer terminal that was embedded in the wall. Approaching it, he saw a number of slots for *Kol-Prockian* AI medallions to fit into. One of them was already filled.

"My name is *Merokanah*," the voice said with annoyance. "There, does that satisfy you? Probably not! Oh, I've heard of the unreasonableness of humans, but you sir must truly be the chief of your sort in that regard! After all–."

"*Merokanah*," Tselitel said respectfully, "are you related to the AI *Allokanah*?"

"Related? Related?" the voice snickered. "How could I possibly be related? AIs aren't *born* like you organics. What a ridiculous notion! Just another literalism drawn from your own experience! Ha! How did you ever get into the stars with such thinking? Well, no matter. Besides, the AI *Allokanah* would just be a pile of dust at this point. His day came and went long ago. And if he *could* somehow manage to survive this long, his faculties would be so rusted and decayed that nothing of value could be drawn from them to inspire an AI, especially one as modern as myself."

"How old are you?" she asked, as Hunt walked slowly past the sound of the voice to check out the rest of the hangar.

"I am two-hundred and thirty-seven years old," *Merokanah* replied with audible pride. "I am among the newest and most advanced of all *Kol-Prockian* AIs, which is why I was given this important post. Naturally they could only entrust such a position to one who excelled in every conceivable fashion."

"So, if you're not related to *Allokanah*, why does your name sound so similar?"

"You really know nothing of the *Kol-Prockian* tongue!" the AI exclaimed. "You'd do well to study the ways of my people. We are–."

"Just answer the question," Hunt called from the end of the hangar.

"The task of teaching the rudiments of my language is hardly worthy of my time or effort," *Merokanah* said. "But it's been so long since I've had anyone to speak with, that I suppose I'll indulge you. The mistake you make is in supposing that *kanah* operates like a surname. A natural conclusion, given your limited understanding of naming conventions outside your own. This reflects the general lack of mental breadth common to humans. They tend–."

"Cut the lesson, professor," Hunt said with annoyance, returning to where Tselitel stood and crossing his arms. "Just spit it out."

"How rude!" exclaimed the voice. "Do you imagine that I maintain saliva just so that I can float words in it?"

THE BEAST EMERGES

"What?" asked Tselitel, genuinely confused.

"Your ill temper is matched only–, only by–," stammered *Merokanah*. "Well, no matter. *Kanah* is not anything like a surname. Instead it is a suffix which means *assistant*, *aid*, or *helper*. The first part of my name, *Mero*, means. Well, nevermind what it means."

"Plug me into the system, Rex," Wellesley said with a chuckle. "This is gonna be good."

"What are you doing?" *Merokanah* asked as Hunt approached his terminal. "What's that medallion?"

"An old friend," Hunt smiled, slipping the disc into an open slot.

"Ah, nothing like *Kol-Prockian* technology," Wellesley said. "More chaotic than what the humans make, but a lot more fun to use."

"Who are you?" demanded *Merokanah*. "How dare you enter my system without authorization! I'll expel you *instantly* if you don't–."

Suddenly the lights clicked on, brightening everything from the hangar all the way back to the entrance.

"How did you–."

"I guess my faculties haven't rusted *that* much," Wellesley said. "Now are you going to tell them what *Mero* means, or shall I?"

"You wouldn't *dare!*" exclaimed the other AI. "If you so much as *hint* at it, I'll–, I'll–."

"Ooh, I'm trembling," Wellesley said with a chuckle. "*Mero* means *lesser* or *minor*. It refers to–."

"Stop! Stop it!" cut in *Merokanah*.

"...one of the various orders our military hierarchy was divided into," continued Wellesley imperturbably. "The *Mero* were the bottom rung of the command structure. *Allo*, incidentally, refers to the top rung: admirals, generals, and so forth. Literally I am assistant to the top rung, and our new friend here, well, you can do the math."

"Heh, and you say your faculties haven't *rusted!*"

Merokanah said scornfully. "Only a diseased mind could imagine that math has *anything* to do with language!"

"Remember how I just said that *Kol-Prockian* technology was more fun?"

"Yeah?" Hunt asked.

"Well, not always."

"An insult! An insult!" exclaimed *Merokanah*. "You come stomping into my facility and instantly you assault my character! How *dare* you?"

"It's pretty easy, actually," Wellesley replied offhandedly. "*Kol-Prockian* military science must have really fallen off a cliff since the civil war."

"Oh, if only I had a body! I would–."

"What's all the ruckus in there?" Milo shouted from the entrance.

"How many of you are there?" *Merokanah* asked at once.

"Why don't you just use the cameras in the front room?" prodded Wellesley.

"I can't. They…they don't work."

"Mm, looks like they work just fine," the ancient AI replied.

"How did you manage that?" asked *Merokanah* with shock in his voice.

"Oh, that was simple. Just took a little tinkering while we've been talking. I've been looking over all the base's systems in the meantime."

"I don't understand how you could. The architecture must be wildly different than what they had back in your day."

"Not as much as one would suppose," Wellesley said with a dry laugh. "*Kol-Prockians* never throw anything away. Even when they *should*," he added significantly.

"Yes, that's true," *Merokanah* replied densely. "Wait! You insult me again! How *dare*–."

At this point Hunt drew the younger AI's disc from the

terminal and set it on the desk beneath it.

"Thank you," Wellesley said. "For every sentence that pinhead uttered an extra fifty were pumped into the system. He was thinking out loud in the computer, trying to use it to process his thoughts."

"Why would he do that?" Tselitel asked.

"Because he's fractured," the AI replied. "Terribly fractured. I think he must have been all that the *Kol-Prockians* could spare for this mission, whatever it was. You know, I've got an idea. Plug him back into the system."

"Are you sure about that?" Hunt asked.

"Oh, yeah. I'll block his connection to the audio-visual system and talk to him within the system. Give me a few minutes alone and I'll be able to find out what he was doing here a lot faster than we could through audible dialogue."

"Alright," Hunt said, taking the disc and slipping it back into its slot.

"And furthermore, I will not tolera–," *Merokanah* got out before his voice abruptly stopped.

"Sorry about that," Wellesley apologized. "I blocked the wrong connections. Talk in a few."

No sooner had he said this than Tselitel burst out laughing.

"That was the *last* thing I expected," she said, stifling her laughter as she grew light headed. "Oh, excuse me," she added, putting a hand on her chest and breathing slowly. "I got a little carried away."

"I'm glad to hear it," Hunt said. "I haven't heard you really laugh since we got here."

"Yes, I'm afraid our lives have been short on humor lately," she replied.

"Not surprising," Hunt said meaningfully. "How's the ankle?"

"Getting nasty," she replied, leaning against one of the fighters and reeling up enough of her pant leg for him to see. "It's starting to swell pretty badly. It hurts when I walk on it."

She laughed again, this time dryly. "It's probably going to be thick as a tree trunk by morning."

"Probably," Hunt agreed, bending over for a good look before gently smoothing her pant leg over it. He stood up and put his hands on her waist. "You know, despite being chased by monsters, bitten by a snake, and nursing that hand of yours, you're still just as beautiful as the day I met you."

"You're just saying that," she said with a coquettish flutter of her eyelids.

"Yes, I am. You look terrible right now."

"Wha–," she exclaimed incredulously, her cheeks turning red. "You're not supposed to *agree* with me! You're supposed to deny it and make me feel even *more* beautiful!"

"I cannot tell a lie," he said with boyish purity, clasping his hands behind his back and looking slightly upward.

"Oh, you must have told a *few*," she said, as he leaned on the ship beside her.

"One or two," he said casually. Suddenly his face went heavy as his mind shot back to *Alleehavah* and what she'd been led to believe. "One or two," he repeated quietly, the joy in her blue eyes haunting him like an evil spirit.

"Are you alright?" she asked, breaking his train of thought and causing him to look at her.

"Why do you ask?" he replied, not eager to answer.

"Because you've been quieter, more serious ever since this morning," she said soothingly, drawing closer and wrapping her good hand around his left arm, drawing it limply against her torso. "You seem distant, like there's something distracting you. You're not as…solicitous as usual."

"Oh, that," he said. "I've got a lot on my mind."

"But nothing you want to share with me?" she asked, a little hurt at the idea. "You can tell me anything. You know that, right?"

"Mhm," he nodded, looking at a spot on the floor just

above his feet, trying to process the tumult that was flooding through him at that very moment. The guilt of lying to *Alleehavah*; the regret for not being able to save her; and perhaps more than anything: the achingly trusting naiveté with which she had lived. It made him want to protect her, to lay low everything and everyone that could possibly threaten such a warm, delicate psyche. And he couldn't do it. He'd failed. He knew he could never love her, and that made the memory of leading her on all the more bitter. Though a mature woman by the standards of her clan, she possessed none of the world-weary cynicism by which the Earthborn demarcate adulthood. Though fascinated by her wide-eyed sense of wonder, eventually he would have been bored by it. He could cherish her, appreciating the freshness of her perspective. But he could never respect her.

"Hey, are you coming back here?" Milo shouted from the entrance. "We're still waiting on you for the operation."

Mutely pushing off the fighter, he felt Tselitel pulling gently on his arm as he tried to move.

"It's her, isn't it?" she asked, her eyes soft and sympathetic. "She meant a lot to you."

"It's more than that," he replied. "But–."

"Before you go chopping the good colonel's hand off," Wellesley interrupted, "have him come back here."

"Why? Can we save it?" Tselitel asked.

"No. But there's a small medical facility in this bunker, just beyond this room," the AI replied. "It'll be a lot safer operating in there. *Kol-Prockians* are famous for our medical technology. Should be a walk in the park."

"I'll go get him," Hunt said, pulling away from Tselitel and walking slowly back to the entrance.

"Well," sighed the AI. "Back to my talk with the blabbermouth."

"Just a minute, Wellesley," Tselitel said in a quiet, yet earnest voice. "I have a question."

"About *Alleehavah*?" he asked.

"Yes," she said with surprise. "But how did you–."

"I've been listening the whole time," he replied matter-of-factly. "I've got to do something to keep this nut from talking me out of my mind. Honestly, I'm only half listening to his replies. Do you have any idea how *frustrating*–," he stopped. "Well, anyhow, that's my problem. What did you want to know?"

"Well, what *happened*?" she whispered confidentially. "I understand that Rex is torn up about her death. But I've been working on the human mind too long not to know guilt when I see it. He feels at fault, Wellesley. What's he blaming himself for?"

"I'm afraid I can't help you, Lily," the AI said. "That's something Rex has to tell you about in his own time."

"I don't think he will," she shook her head. "To him it's just a matter of shame. You know the harsh standards these Deltans hold themselves to. Milo did the same thing until I eventually snapped him out of it. But Rex's sense of right and wrong is adamantine. He'll torture himself for this until his dying day. There's no forgiveness to his thinking, Wellesley. He did something wrong, and that's that. There are no mitigating circumstances for a man like that, so there won't be anything to do about it. He won't want to share his shame with anyone else. Even me."

"That's his choice. Every man is entitled to a few secrets."

"Even if they hurt him?" she persisted.

"*Especially* if they hurt him," the AI said, lowering his voice as the others neared. "Those are the secrets that make him who he is."

"I've never heard your speaking voice aloud like this before, Wellesley," Milo said a few moments later. "It was either skin contact or that annoying monotone."

"Yeah, *Kol-Prockian* computers let me synthesize my natural speaking voice," the AI replied. "Take the colonel toward the back of the bunker. You'll find a narrow door with a medical room behind it."

"Right," Gromyko said, leading the group off.

"Don't try and force him, Lily," Wellesley said quietly when they were out of earshot. "You can't change who he is."

"I can't change who *I* am, either," she said. "I can't stand by while someone is hurting and just do nothing."

"It'd be better if you did. Remember, I've known him a lot longer than you have."

"Hey! This door is locked!" Milo shouted from the far end of the hangar. Moments later a loud click reverberated through the space and the door slid open. "Thank you!" he called, heading into the medical bay with the others.

"I've got to go," Wellesley said. "Just leave him be." With that he receded into cyberspace to resume his exasperating discussion.

Tselitel crossed her arms over her chest and paced aimlessly for a few minutes, waiting for the AI to return. When he didn't she wandered back to the entrance, the noises of the *kals* sending a shiver down her spine. Instantly the figures in her apartment came to mind, making her hands tremble and her chest tighten. Determined to be brave, she walked to the ladder and looked up. Small lights illuminated the shaft, running all the way to the surface. The *kals* could be seen peeking their heads over the side and instantly drawing them back. Like mindless automatons they did this incessantly.

"You'd think they'd learn," she said, shaking her head and drawing back from the ladder. A faint hissing sound in one of the corners made her jump. Unsure if she'd really heard a snake or not, she decided to play it safe and scoot back to the main room.

"How's Pinchon?" she asked Gromyko nearly an hour later, when the smuggler walked wearily into the hangar and sat beside her near one of the fighters. She had been sitting with her knees drawn against her chest, her chin resting upon them.

"Oh, he'll be fit as a fiddle in a few hours," he replied, laying back on the cold floor and stretching. "I wish we had a piece of equipment like that back on Delta-13. Can you believe it? They have a laser-based surgical table in there. Just climb into the machine, tell it what you want, and it'll get it done for you." He pointed at her ankle. "Too bad it can't do anything for that wound of yours. But the venom has long since passed into your bloodstream."

"But he's okay?" she persisted.

"Yeah, pretty much. He's kind of shaken up. It's not everyday that you lose an entire hand." He made a saw with one hand and drew it sharply across his lower arm, between the base of his other hand and his elbow. "It took a little while to get the device working properly. It kept insisting that his hand could be saved. I guess it wasn't programmed to understand the kind of instant death that the dark ones can inflict. We needed Wellesley to come in and override its safety protocols."

"*Kals*," Tselitel said moodily. "They're called *kals*."

"Yes, of course," he replied, eyeing her curiously. "Something the matter, Lily?"

"Oh, nothing," she replied, shaking her head and trying to brighten up. "I'm just tired, I guess."

"Well, you've got a right to be," he said, laying his head back on the hard floor and yawning loud and slow. "We've all had a big day."

One by one the others filed out of the medical bay. They assembled themselves in a loose group near the computer terminal.

"Well, I'm *finally* done with our loquacious friend," he said in a voice that was thin with impatience half an hour later. "How are you feeling, Colonel?"

"I'm alive," he replied with a faint smile, unable to help glancing at the capped end of the stump that rested atop his thigh. He sat with his back to the terminal that the two AIs inhabited. Leaning against the cold metal, he shut his eyes.

"What have you got for us?"

"A lot, in fact," Wellesley began. "But first, do me a favor and pluck this moron from the system, will you? Every time I block his access to *one* part of it, he climbs into *another part* and keeps jabbering. I've had about all I can stand."

With a dry chuckle Hunt went to the terminal and drew *Merokanah* from his slot.

"…and furthermore, I must add that without the added difficulties that attended–," Hunt heard through his skin. Surprised, he dropped the disc on the narrow desk that ran along the front of the terminal.

"Oh, goody. I'd hoped he'd forgotten how to do that," Wellesley said, as his friend eyed him for an explanation.

Hunt shook his head at the start he'd received and walked a few paces away, leaning an arm on one of the fighter's wings.

"Go ahead," he said.

"Alright. Now, there *might* be parts missing here and there. I had to piece this together from everything he threw at me:"

"First of all, the folks that built this base belonged to a tiny resistance faction that survived the war that destroyed my people. Escaping to Quarlac, they managed to find a terrible, inhospitable world that no one would ever dream of wanting and established a secret base. They've been quietly nursing their strength at that location ever since. That is, until they received a message telling them to come here and establish an outpost."

"Who sent the message?" asked Pinchon.

"They don't know. But whoever it was, they had *deep* pockets. Along with the message they received the coordinates for a supply drop. With it they were able to replenish their nearly depleted supplies and construct these fighters, along with many others that they have stashed across our galaxy."

"Across the Milky Way?" asked Tselitel.

"Yes, apparently our mysterious benefactors didn't know just which of the so-called *Ahn-Wey* we would end up contacting, so they instructed the *Kol-Prockians* to dispatch vessels to a bevy of different worlds."

"But how could they possibly know about us?" she asked. "You said this facility was built hundreds of years ago. It's not like they could see the future."

"That's one of the gaps I mentioned earlier," Wellesley said. "Somehow or other they knew what to prepare for. I'm sure we'll learn more in time."

"What else?" asked Hunt.

"Well, it turns out our friend *Merokanah* was left here just to keep an eye on things. Apparently when they put him in charge of this place he was already a little shaky, but they didn't have any other AIs to spare. The centuries alone haven't been good for him. Although I might be able to fix him up a bit, given a little time."

"What about the rest of the story?" Hunt clarified. "What about the Devourers?"

"Nothing helpful about them," the AI replied. "All the *Kol-Prockians* were told was that a 'great death' was coming to our galaxy, and that they would be well paid if they did as they were told and planted outposts. Unwilling to look a gift horse in the mouth, they did as instructed and continued to receive supplies and weapons until their task was complete. Then the flow dried up."

"Did they talk to *Preleteth*?" Hunt asked.

"No. They tried to. But the planet wouldn't reply. They never saw *Alleehavah* or any of her glowing kin, either. But they *did* see the *kals*. They left a very detailed record of their encounters with them. Hence why even the shaft down here is studded with lights."

"Alright, so how do we get the ships out of here?" Milo asked. "We can't fly them through the dirt."

"The wall ahead of them is made of a series of sliding doors that lead to a covered space that's been dug out of the ground. We'll be able to fly into, and then out of, this space."

"Oh, good," replied the younger Hunt, nodding with satisfaction.

"Then that's all?" asked Pinchon.

"Not quite," replied Wellesley. "Apparently our mysterious benefactors added a message to their instructions. It's encrypted, and will only open for a human. It is contained in a small cube that is hidden within this terminal. I've tried to get it open, but it seems only *Merokanah* has the key."

"So we have to talk to him again," Hunt said with a roll of his eyes, walking back to the terminal.

"Sadly, yes," agreed the AI.

Hunt reached for the disc and then drew his hand back.

"Anyone want to get in a final word before that chatterbox drowns us out?" he asked, looking across the various faces in the room. "No? Alright."

"...way that it could proceed. After all, how could there be a secondary–," Hunt heard as he picked up the disc and quickly plugged it into the computer.

"Give me a second to talk to him," Wellesley said. "Alright, I'm opening the audio-visual portions of the system to him."

"How *dare* you cut me out of my own system!" *Merokanah* exclaimed.

"We've been over all that," Wellesley replied as patiently as he could manage. "Now, you remember your purpose here?"

"Of *course* I remember it!" snapped the younger AI. And then, as though reciting something he'd learned by rote: "Monitor this installation until the arrival of human forces. Assist them in any way I am c-c-capable of."

"And that includes opening the hidden pocket that contains the data cube, does it not?" asked Wellesley.

"It does," replied *Merokanah* reluctantly. "Although I

must have your word that you will not give the information to the aliens that now float above us."

"You have it," Hunt said. "Now, open it."

"Very well," the AI said.

"Well?" asked Hunt after a few moments of silence.

"I'm getting it! I'm getting it!" *Merokanah* said quickly. "You organics are always so impatient. Probably it's your tiny life spans that cause you to demand that *everything* happen instantaneously. Naturally, if you had longer to live, there wouldn't be–."

"*Merokanah!*" barked Wellesley. "Stop playing for time and get it open."

"I-I can't. It won't budge. I keep issuing the open command but nothing happens."

"Probably stuck," Gromyko said. "This stuff has been down here for a couple hundred years, you know."

"Yes!" *Merokanah* said, seizing his explanation with gusto. "That must be it! I can't be held responsible for mechanical failures!"

"Where's it located?" Hunt asked with annoyance.

"Just beside the slot you put me into," the AI replied. "It's small, only a couple inches high by a couple inches wide, right on the edge of the terminal."

Hunt ran his fingers across the smooth metal and detected the slightest hint of a line; a little gap between the hidden compartment's door and the rest of the terminal. Twisting it outward, the little space opened and a small cube fell on the floor.

"Lucky it didn't break," Milo said, approaching his brother as he picked the device off the floor. "We'd be up a creek without it."

"What do I do with it, Wells?" Hunt asked, holding the cube between his thumb and forefinger, examining it closely.

"I don't know. That's alien tech – something I've never seen before. Maybe it detects human fingerprints?"

"Oh, ho ho," *Merokanah* laughed. "Really?

Fingerprints? Is that what the great *Allokanah* thinks?"

"You got a *better* idea?" he shot back.

"Yes. My instructions included a complex series of actions that were intended to ensure that the recipient of the cube was indeed human. I speculate that the reason for so many actions was to ensure, in the event that I was captured, that the enemy could not torture the information out of me and then open the cube. There would be too many fail-safes for them to–."

"Get on with it," Wellesley cut in.

"Fine. The first action I have already taken. A coded signal was built into the infrastructure of this terminal. I have sent it to the cube."

"Alright, then what?" asked Hunt, still holding it as before.

"Next, you must deposit a small drop of blood upon the cube. It will analyze it for the unique properties present in human blood."

"Anyone got a knife?" asked Hunt, looking around.

"There's a device in the medical bay that will allow you to extract a small amount of blood," Wellesley told him. "A tiny laser will immediately reseal the wound, eliminating the risk of infection. It's pain free as well."

"Be right back," Hunt said, making for the small room. The group could hear him talking to Wellesley and *Merokanah* inside. They couldn't make out what was said. But more than once they heard the older AI utter a sharp word that temporarily silenced the younger. After more than twenty minutes he finally returned.

"Too many cooks in the kitchen?" Gromyko asked with a humorous gleam in his eye.

"You have no idea," Hunt said frowningly.

"Okay, the next step is to utter the following sounds: eeee; aaaaa; oooooo; uuuuu; h'shrath; nu'shrath; vrar'shrath."

"Are you pulling my leg?" asked Hunt.

"I could not *possibly* be pulling your leg," *Merokanah*

replied with a sigh. "Lacking arms, I am incapable of–."

"Just do it, Rex," Wellesley said. "It must be analyzing you for human vocal characteristics."

"Of *course* that's what it's doing," *Merokanah* said. "Honestly, sometimes I wonder–."

"Ooooo, eeeee, aaaaaa?" asked Hunt, raising an eyebrow toward Wellesley's medallion.

"No, '*eeeee*, aaaaa, oooo, uuuuu,'" corrected Wellesley. "Followed by 'h'shrath, nu'shrath, vrar'shrath.'"

"Sounds like a tongue twister," Hunt muttered, eliciting a laugh from Milo. "Alright, oooo, eeee, aaaaa, uuuuu; h'shrath, nu'shrath, vrar'shrath."

"Good," *Merokanah* said. "The final test is the simplest. It will require a number of unique human fingerprints to–."

"Ha! So there *are* fingerprints involved!" Wellesley said triumphantly. "And just what were you so smug about before, *Merokanah*?"

"What do we do, *Mero*?" asked Gromyko, jumping to his feet and heading toward Hunt.

"My name is *Merokanah,* not *Mero*," the AI said importantly. "Please remember that."

"*Merokanah* is much too long to say over and over," the smuggler said simply. "Now, what do we do?"

"Perhaps you would like to assign a number to me instead," the AI said hotly. "That might be easier for your lazy tongue to say *over and over!*"

"Any suggestions?" Gromyko asked good-naturedly.

"How about 'zero'?" offered Wellesley.

"*Merokanah*," Tselitel said in a diplomatic voice as Pinchon joined the rest of them by Hunt. "Please tell us what we're supposed to do. We don't have any time to lose."

"It's simple really," the AI said in the superior tone of a schoolmaster. "All you have to do is apply a unique fingerprint to each of the cube's sides. Then it will open, revealing the message hidden within."

"You want them to apply a unique fingerprint to each

side?" Wellesley clarified.

"Yes," the AI replied. "Really *Allokanah*, you seem to be having a hard time keeping up with this. I suspect that time–."

"Has it occurred to you that a cube has *six* sides, but there are only *five* humans here?" Wellesley shouted, his patience gone. "What kind of *stupid*, *idiotic*–."

"Then we can't open it?" Milo asked, the rest of the group melting away in disgust.

"Nope," said Gromyko, dropping to the floor a few feet away and stretching his arms over his head.

"Then what was all that business with the blood and tongue twisters about?" Milo demanded. "Are you just messing with us?"

"I assure you that those steps were totally necessary," *Merokanah* said. "And now that they are complete–."

"He's an idiot," Wellesley said sharply. "He's not smart enough to mess with anyone."

"How *dare* you–," the AI began once again.

"Someone jerk him out of the terminal!" Wellesley ordered. "I've had enough of him for one day. He can't speak without lowering the intelligence level of the room."

"Such insults! Such–."

At this moment Milo ripped the disc from the computer and tossed it across the hangar. The sound of it bouncing off the far wall and clattering to the floor reverberated back to them.

"I think simply pulling it from the computer would have sufficed," Gromyko said, his eyebrows raised as he watched the fuming Milo stride angrily past him toward the entrance.

"No, it's better this way," Wellesley said. "Maybe he'll knock a little sense into that brainless piece of circuitry."

"Or knock what was left out," Tselitel said with concern.

"Not like it would be any loss," the AI replied. "We've

gotten what we need out of him. Tomorrow we'll take off and find a sixth human."

"We're going to have to head to another planet for that," Pinchon said. "Past the Devourer blockade. I hope those fighters are still in good shape."

"I've already checked them over," Wellesley said. "They're in perfect shape."

"Good, good," the pirate said. "Then I suggest we get some sleep. We've all been on the go since early morning. We can't leave until sunup, anyhow."

"Why's that?" asked Gromyko.

"Because those *kals* are still out there," he said. "If we open the hangar doors now they might jump on the wings like gremlins and tear the ships to pieces."

"Good point," the smuggler nodded.

"Any sleeping facilities in this place?" Pinchon asked Wellesley.

"Far wall. Just a little way past the medical bay."

"Right. Goodnight folks."

"Check for snakes before you settle in for the night!" the smuggler called.

"So there *are* more?" Tselitel asked, looking uncomfortably around herself.

"Who can say?" Gromyko said flippantly, shrugging his shoulders. "Better safe than sorry." With another yawn and stretch he sprang to his feet and followed after the colonel. "Guess I'll give him a hand looking and then turn in, too. Goodnight!"

They watched him walk to the back of the hangar and disappear through a narrow door. Moments later Milo came running into the hangar.

"There's more snakes out there!" he said urgently, pointing over his shoulder. "At least a half dozen of them! Just like the one that bit Lily!"

"I'll shut the outer door for the night," Wellesley said, the workings of the machinery echoing through the cavernous space as he spoke.

"Good," Milo muttered as he walked past. "That just leaves us locked in with however many are already inside." Hearing Gromyko and Pinchon talking, he gravitated to their room and joined them.

"Goodnight, Milo," Wellesley chuckled. "That guy gets too excited sometimes."

"And you don't?" laughed Hunt goodnaturedly. "I've never seen you tear into someone like you did *Mero* a few minutes ago."

"*Mero*?" Wellesley asked, as though jogging his memory. "*Mero*…Oh, you mean *zero!* Heh, you would too, if you'd spent a couple of hours parsing all of his nonsense just to get three and a half minutes of information out of him. I'd rather make a snowman during an avalanche than talk to that numbskull again. As far as I'm concerned he can *stay* in the base once we've finished with it."

"We can't just leave him here!" Tselitel protested. "Who knows how many centuries he might live down here all alone! It would be like burying someone alive and simultaneously putting them on life support!"

"And your point is…?" he asked.

"Wellesley I'm *shocked* by your attitude," she said with revulsion. "I thought you were kinder than that."

"Usually I am."

"Do you agree with this?" she asked Hunt.

"I don't know what I agree with," he said, shaking his weary head and pointing toward the sleeping quarters. "I'm too tired to think anymore. I'm going to turn in."

"Oh, you Deltans are too hard for me!" she growled through gritted teeth once he'd gone. "You're as cold as the world you lived on for so long!"

"Hey, if you want to cast stones, cast 'em at me," Wellesley said. "Rex has no part in this. He's just beat from saving our lives a couple of times over today. Don't forget that."

Flustered, she shook her head angrily and stomped off.

"I'm going to find that poor AI and keep him company," she said over her shoulder.

"Be my guest," Wellesley said.

A couple of hours later Hunt suddenly jerked awake on his narrow cot in the sleeping quarters. Looking around the dimly lit room, he saw the other three cots still occupied by the other men. Quietly Gromyko and Milo snored, oblivious to their surroundings. Only Pinchon lay silent, his arms folded across his chest, sleeping on his side as he faced the door. Even unconscious he seemed prepared for trouble.

Shaking the misty residue of sleep from his mind, he realized that he'd awoken because Tselitel wasn't there. Swinging his feet over the side of the cot, he padded quietly out of the room and cast his eyes across the hangar. In a dark corner he saw her lying on her side, *Merokanah's* disc a few feet away from her.

"Hey," he whispered, taking a knee beside her and shaking her gently. "Are you okay?"

"What?" she asked, half awake. "Oh, you."

"Oh, *me*?" he asked with surprise, his face puzzled. "You're usually glad to see me."

"Usually I am," she replied tartly, laying back down and facing away from him.

"What is this?" he asked, laying hands on her side and turning her onto her back. She crossed her arms over her chest as he did so, avoiding his gaze. "Lily?"

"How could you agree with what that cruel old AI wanted to do to this…this poor…" she trailed.

"*Cruel?*" he asked in astonishment. "I've never known a more genuinely kind AI than that old bird over there," he said, tossing a finger toward the terminal on the other side of the hangar. "He'd gladly sacrifice himself in an instant to save any one of us. Shoot, he put his neck on the line when he detonated those explosives and took out the mind control chamber on Delta, didn't he?"

"And yet he'd leave *Merokanah* here to suffer in silence, all alone," she countered. "And you didn't say one thing against it! Not one thing! What did Delta-13 do to you? Freeze your heart into a solid block of *ice*?"

"Delta-13 didn't do a thing to me," he said bitterly. "Not half as much as you've done to me now." He stood up and eyed her angrily. "You want to know why I didn't say anything earlier? Because Wellesley *didn't mean what he was saying!* If you knew him *half* as well as I do, you'd have known that. The poor guy had to watch me destroy *Alleehavah* earlier today. Oh, don't look so surprised," he snapped as her eyes grew wide. "It was a piece of cake for a man with a frozen heart! But just for your information, she was about to be turned into a *kal*, and begged me to spare her that. Then he comes down here, and for the first time in who knows how many *centuries* he gets to speak to one of his own kind. And he turns out to be an absolute moron! Can you imagine how *frustrating* that would be? Thinking he was the last vestige of his race, he suddenly finds there are more of them, only to stumble into *Merokanah* of all people!"

"Rex, I–."

"No, you've had your chance to speak," he cut her off. "And you've made yourself *quite clear*. Now I intend to do the same. I didn't speak up earlier because there's no way Wellesley would leave that nitwit here alone. He was just blowing off *steam*, get it? And I was too tired to want to get involved and smooth out your feathers. I knew you were mad, but I thought you'd get over it. But apparently I know you as well as you know me and Wellesley!"

She got to her feet and reached out to touch him with her good hand.

"Darling, I–," she began.

"Don't *darling* me," he said, pushing her hand away. "And don't touch me, either. You wouldn't want to get *frostbite*." With this he turned from her and went back to the sleeping quarters.

Tears welled in her eyes as he walked away. She laid back down on the floor and sobbed for a good while, letting the emotion flow out. Slowly getting to her feet, she walked silently across the floor to Wellesley.

"I suppose you heard that?" she asked in a defeated voice, slumping down in front of the terminal and resting her back against it. Rubbing her red, tear-stained eyes with the knuckles of her good hand, she leaned her head back, causing the metal to gently clang.

"I should think everyone did," Wellesley said. "Unless they were too tired to be roused." He went silent for a moment and checked the camera that covered the sleeping quarters. "Nope, they heard you. They're just pretending to be asleep."

"I've lost him, Wellesley," she said in a voice that began to shake. Now that the shock of his painful words had begun to subside her anxious mind made the most of what it had experienced. "I've driven him away. I've made him hate me."

"Nothing could do that," he said soothingly. "I've known that fella for a long time. He's too crazy about you to let you go. I thought he made that clear to you already."

"But the words he used! The anger in his eyes!"

"You spoke more harshly than he did," the AI replied. "Yet here you sit, scared he's gone for good."

"Oh, I was such an idiot!" she said, drawing her knees against her chest and hiding her face against them. "Why didn't I just keep my mouth shut? I know better than this." She sniffled. "Oh, I have no excuse, you know. I'm a trained psychiatrist, after all. I know that people should just bite their tongues when they're angry. Nothing they say is in any way true in a state like that. They're just venting, like you were earlier."

"Indeed."

"But me? Oh, I had to shoot my big mouth off! I had to tear into that poor man and hurt him like no one else can.

I know all about it. You told me, remember? When you said that I had access through the one opening that he couldn't close? The one through which he lets the woman he loves into his heart?"

"I remember."

"Well, it's no good now," she said, shaking her head and wiping her running nose with the back of her hand. "I've hurt him too much. People draw back when you hurt them, you know. They...they cut off the ones who...who hurt them." Her voice getting thick with emotion, she rested her forehead on her knees and began to sob, her chest convulsing.

"Lily, you need to calm down," Wellesley said quietly. "You're feeling worse than things really are. Rex won't leave you. Rex *can't* leave you, anymore than you can leave him. It's just your anxiety playing tricks with you. Remember, you don't have your medication anymore."

"Callous *and* weak," she ground out in self-reproach. "Stupid, stupid, stupid!" she said, punctuating each word by smacking her head against her knees. "Maybe I should just wander out there and let the *kals* have me."

"You don't mean that."

"How do I know what I mean anymore?" she asked in anguish. "Just that poor man's luck that he'd fall in love with someone nutso like me."

"I think a lot of men would consider themselves lucky to–," Wellesley said, stopping himself. "What do you mean by that last remark?"

"Nothing," she said, shaking her head.

"Lily, there's something you haven't told us," the AI said. "That medication was for more than just anxiety, wasn't it?"

"Wellesley, you *can't* tell Rex about this!" she said desperately, turning around and looking at his disc. "Promise me you won't."

"I think he already knows," the AI said.

His comment made her look back toward the sleeping quarters. Hidden in a shadow cast by the nearest fighter stood Hunt, his hands in his pockets, leaning against the wall.

"Oh, I could *die!*" she exclaimed, falling onto her back and sobbing, the tears running afresh down her red and puffy face. "When will I keep my mouth *shut?*"

"What is it, baby?" Hunt asked tenderly, kneeling beside her and drawing her up into his arms. But all she could do was cry. "Wells?"

"I don't know," the AI said frankly. "Just hold her awhile."

Hunt moved her to the terminal and, resting his back against it, drew her head onto his chest and stroked it softly. Gradually her convulsions calmed until she cried in still silence. His mind raced with a thousand questions he wanted to ask and ten thousand assurances he wanted to make. He yearned to tell her he loved her; that he'd never leave her. But he knew he had to let her ride out the wave of emotion she was on, and that it would be selfish to interrupt it. So he gently stroked her head and waited.

"I'm no good," she said at last. "I'm no good for you."

"I'll be the judge of that," he said in a quietly certain voice, kissing her forehead and pulling her tightly against him. "Now what were you begging Wellesley not to tell me? Something about your medication?"

"I can't tell you," she said in a shaky voice. "You'll–you'll stop loving me."

"Never," he said in a low, almost fierce voice. "Now, tell me about the medication. It wasn't for anxiety?"

"No, it was," she assured him. "Believe me, it was. I never lied to you about that."

"Okay," he said smoothly, nodding his head.

"But it's for more than that. The–the pellet also contained medicine for…for a…" she stumbled, unable to force the words out.

"Baby, I'm right here," he said, pulling her head against his cheek. "I'll always be here, no matter what. Don't be afraid. Just let it out."

"M-my family has a–," she paused, struggling to say it. "My family has a g-genetic defect. Neurological problems. Neurological *degeneration*. Several of my ancestors suffered from it. N-no cure. No treatment. Just medication to slow its advance. The symptoms are subtly visible from an early age, but don't usually start getting severe until about forty." She looked up at him and forced a faint smile. "N-now you know why I'm so passionate about birthdays," she said. "I-I've been counting them since I was a child. I knew that once I hit forty I'd start slipping. I'm slipping now..."

"No, you're not," Hunt said stoutly.

"Oh, yes I am," she said, her hands starting to tremble as she slipped her good one around his neck. She drew up the broken one and clasped its wrist. "Why do you think I've been so clumsy?" she asked. "Remember when I tripped over that fence back on Delta, and you had to untangle me? Remember how I fell getting out of the escape pod here? Oh, I kept making excuses, claiming it was because I was 'no good' out of doors. But that was a lie. It's all been a lie. My nervous system is slowly turning to dust, Rex. There's nothing I can do about it."

"But the medication–," he began.

"Was just a stopgap, something to slow things down," she cut him off. "It doesn't work indefinitely that way, either. It's mostly ineffective once you get past forty. I don't know why – nobody does. It has the doctors baffled. They just prescribe it for as long as it works, and then recommend hospice once you can no longer function. When you're as old as I am, it just helps to mitigate some of the symptoms, but it can't help the cause. This disease is the real reason I got into psychiatry. As a child I was in constant terror of the day I would start coming apart. I couldn't sleep, I couldn't function. My life came to an utter standstill the day I was diagnosed."

"When was that?" he asked.

"Three weeks after my eleventh birthday," she said, resting her head against his chest once more. "My mother noticed me having difficulty opening my presents, and she made an appointment with our doctor. She didn't tell me why, just that I needed a checkup. I had no idea my life would end that day."

"It *didn't* end," he assured her. "You're still here."

"Normalcy ended that day," she said. "No child can face a diagnosis like that without being permanently changed by it. The happiness went out of my life. I dreaded the passage of each *minute*, because that meant I was sixty seconds closer to–to the condition that had destroyed my grandparents. I'd seen the effects of the disease before, Rex. I saw *firsthand* what it did to people. They were dead by fifty, darling. Both of them! I spent most of my teen years in my room, reading books and trying to avoid the fear as much as I could. Finally I decided I couldn't live like that anymore, that I had to come to grips with my situation and accept it. So I studied the human mind, trying to learn how to accept the dark fate that had been thrust upon me. I excelled in my studies, but didn't learn to calm my nerves any. As I got older I had to go on anxiety medication too, just to be steady enough to function each day. Combining the meds with a massive workload I managed to ignore my steadily advancing years up until recently. Suddenly I had to act – I had to make some kind of change. When the reports of madness among the prisoners of Delta-13 started doing the rounds I jumped on it with both feet. I thought that fate had given me the chance to squeeze one final achievement into my rapidly shortening life, an opportunity to make up for all the time I didn't have. It's why I threw myself into my work with such abandon. I *had* to make it work. I *had* to help those prisoners. But then I met you, and I was so in love that I didn't care about anything anymore, just spending all the time with you that I could. My heart pushed aside my reason, darling. It made me do things I never should have done."

"You've done nothing wrong," he said, closing his eyes and squeezing her tightly against his body.

"I've done *everything* wrong," she insisted. "I've led you on. Here you thought you were getting a relationship with a woman who had a good forty, maybe fifty years ahead of her. I've cheated you. You'll be lucky to get another twenty-four months out of me before I start crumbling. Why do you think I was so *unreasonable* with Wellesley earlier? This disease works upon the mind, too, not just the body. I'll be a basket case inside of five years. In ten–."

"Stop talking that way," Hunt told her. "You don't measure a love like we have in *years*. I'd consider myself lucky to have you in my life for weeks. Shoot, even days would be enough. When something precious like you comes along, you snatch it up with both hands and thank God every day that you have it. You don't gripe about what you *didn't* get, what you *didn't* have. You appreciate it for as long as you have it. And when it's gone, you pull up the good days in your memory to remind yourself to keep breathing – to remind yourself why you're alive at all. People like you don't come along often, baby. It's mere mortals like me who are just thankful to have you for as long as we do."

"Heh, 'mere mortals.' A mortal chosen for a great fate."

"A dark fate," Hunt corrected her. "One I wouldn't choose on my own."

"Yes, you would," she said, raising her head and brushing her cheek against his neck. "You absolutely would."

"I'm not a healer like you, Lily," he said, shaking his head.

"I'll be the judge of that," she smiled at him, giving him a little peck on the cheek and lowering her head. "You've healed my heart, Rex. Oh, I still fear death alright. But it's because I'll be losing you. I'm not pitying myself anymore."

"I'm going to stop this," he said stoutly. "I'm going to

get this fixed. I can't lose you."

"There's nothing we can do, darling. Even in this age of high technology there are things we can't control. You can't stop death."

"Perhaps not," he said grimly, looking intensely at a point on the far wall, as though in a staring match with death itself. "But you can delay it. If human technology isn't up to the challenge, maybe another race's will be. Wellesley?"

"I'm not aware of any tech from my people that would be able to help," he said quietly. "But there *are* other races. Perhaps our mysterious benefactors will be able to help us."

"Perhaps so," Hunt said. "When we get these fighters airborne we'll make for Quarlac and talk to the *Kol-Prockian* rebels."

"You can't do that, Rex!" Tselitel said with alarm. "We can't abandon our race to the Devourers! You're the only one who can stop them."

"I'm also the only one who can save you," he said. "And if I can't do both, then I'll save you."

"You can't mean that," she said, raising her head and looking at him through wide eyes. "You can't put my life in the balance with billions of other humans and find *me* more worthy!"

"The heart makes choices we can't always justify," he replied.

"No," she shook her head. "Not like this. You can't love me like this. I'd be the greatest curse mankind has ever known, if I took their champion away from them in their darkest hour. I could never bear it. My soul would die the moment we left for Quarlac."

"I'm your champion before I'm anyone else's," he said. "Don't forget that it was humanity that exiled my father, my brother, and me to Delta-13 and left us there to rot. It was *you* who set me free, and showed me I could live after all that. My life had no meaning before you."

"And it will have none if you let your love for me

destroy our race," she argued. "We could never be happy knowing that you abandoned billions of people to a fate they didn't deserve, even if I somehow *do* manage to have my condition healed. It would never work."

"At least I'd have you," he said.

"You'd have my body," she replied. "My soul would be gone."

"Rex," Wellesley cut in. "At the rate the Devourers are working, all meaningful human resistance in the Milky Way will be extinguished within six months. If we fail, there will be plenty of time to get to Quarlac and seek help for Lily before her condition is likely beyond help. And if we succeed, it'll be even sooner than that."

"Can you last that long?" he asked, looking down at her.

"Without a doubt," she smiled. "I'm a tough little cookie, remember?"

"You must be," he said, kissing her forehead again. "You survived running into that tree, didn't you?"

"Hey, you *hit* me with that!" she said. "And don't you forget it!"

"I won't," he chuckled fondly, pulling her close and sighing.

"I'm sorry for what I said earlier," she said after a few minutes. "It was awful. I've never known a man with a warmer heart than you have."

"It's alright."

"No, it isn't," she said, pulling away and looking into his eyes. "Nothing about it was alright. You love me so *tenderly* that only an idiot could say such a thing. I don't know what came over me. It was inexcusable." Her wide eyes fixed onto his as she shook her head back and forth in utter sincerity. "I'm so sorry."

"I forgive you, darling," he said, drawing her close again. "Let's not talk about it anymore."

"Alright."

"We should go to bed. We're going to need plenty of rest for the journey ahead."

"Alright," she repeated. "But one thing? Please don't tell the others about this. I don't think I could bear them knowing."

"I won't," he said. "Now, come on."

Quietly they made their way to the sleeping quarters and climbed into Hunt's former cot. Laying side-by-side, he drew the blanket over them and kissed her. Moaning almost inaudibly, she rolled onto her side and put her arm across his stomach, resting her head against his chest and letting out a sigh. Putting his arm around her, he thanked God that he was such a lucky man and quickly fell asleep.

Silently watching from his bunk, Pinchon smiled in the darkness.

CHAPTER 10

Elasha was quietly walking along the path that ran all around the emperor's retreat deep in thought. Her mind troubled by the deception she had worked against her sovereign, she struggled to quiet a conscience that would not remain still.

"I had to do it," she told herself for the thousandth time. Yet her peace had gone. Using her powers to deceive left her drained and out of sorts. Unable to sleep, she wandered the grounds for hours at a time, scarcely aware of the security forces that dutifully noted her every movement.

"I didn't want to do it!" she burst out suddenly, causing one of the guards in the nearby forest to turn his head and eye her carefully for a moment. Long distrustful of the mystics that the emperor chose to keep near his person, the more prosaically minded sentries constantly suspected them of hatching plots against him. To their style of thought the mystics were just plain weird. And weird people were capable of doing unexpected things. Dangerous things.

Growing self-conscious, Elasha lowered her head, the hood of her long, flowing robe sliding forward on her soft white hair until it hid her eyes. She was glad of this, for tears had begun to flow just moments before.

"Oh, my brother!" she thought bitterly. "Why did you have to die? Why did those envious animals in the military destroy you? Only you could have guided our liege with the steadiness and goodness that the empire requires! Now we must make due with Krancis, and his dark, ruthless ways!"

Connected to the workings of the empire through a thousand hidden sources, Elasha was aware of the terror that had suddenly gripped the navy. She knew of the incarcerations ordered by McGannon almost before the small, sleek transports of the Naval Intelligence Service slipped into warp toward their targets. Though long harboring an intense personal dislike of McGannon, Elasha knew that only one mind could have conceived of such a plan and then ordered its execution: the very man into whose hands she had manipulated the emperor into entrusting the entire conduct of the war.

Torn with doubt, she clasped her hands behind her back and walked through the flowing, ankle-high grass that covered the grounds. She paused and watched as the blades of grass fluttered in the wind. Her tormented visage softened momentarily as she focused on one blade in particular. It was a little smaller than the rest, and a little more weatherbeaten, too. But there it grew, following the impulse to live without bringing harm to any of its fellows. She shook her head and wondered why all living things couldn't be like that – why they had to bring death and envy and destruction to those around them. Her mind raced over the brutalities that the war had already brought to the Milky Way: the billions of dead, to say nothing of the devastation of the last remaining worlds of the *Ahn-Wey*. She wondered how the *Prellak* could have ever brought forth something as foul as the Devourers.

"Ma'am?" a male voice asked from behind her. Wiping her eyes before turning, she raised her hood slightly and saw a bright but disciplined young man of about twenty standing before her. He was one of the countless guards that ensured the emperor's safety.

"Yes?" she asked quietly, trying to hide the emotion in her voice.

"A call has come through from Krancis," he reported.

"He instructed us to find you immediately and bring you back to the main building. He said there were urgent matters that he had to discuss with you immediately. Even now he's waiting on the line."

"I'll come at once," she said, nodding to the young man and following him back to the main building.

The stairs were not kind to a woman of her advancing years. Much older than her famous brother, she was nearly sixty when she first came into the emperor's service. Her seventy-fifth birthday had passed without notice just days before, the threat of the Devourers driving it from even her retentive memory. Slowly climbing the steps, she couldn't help but chuckle as she saw the young man ahead of her trot up them with ease.

"Oh, excuse me, Ma'am," he said, having turned to look when he was halfway up them. "May I offer you my arm?"

"Yes, thank you," she said, wrapping her fingers around the inside of his elbow and pressing on with determination. "Aren't you afraid of me?" she asked a little further up.

"Of you, Ma'am?" he asked, genuinely surprised.

"Most of the people who…guard this place don't…take to me," she said, beginning to pant as she labored upward. "Any more than they…took to…my brother."

"Oh, I'm certain the emperor wouldn't have a person by his side if they weren't worthy of our respect," the young man said with unflinching certainty. "He's very wise, Ma'am."

"Yes, he is," she replied for the young man's sake.

"But they say he's unwell," he added. "We all know of his condition, Ma'am. But rumor has it that it's grown worse since the aliens have come."

She could hear the leading tone in his voice, how he hoped for some little tidbit of forbidden gossip from the inner sanctum. Glancing at his face momentarily, she saw concern written on it. This was no mere tattletale digging around for imperial dirt. Rather he was a young man who ardently believed in the wisdom and power of his sovereign, but through exposure to his fellows had slowly begun to doubt. She decided to put his mind at ease.

"I can assure you that our emperor is daily conducting the war with sagacity and honor," she said once they had reached the top and she had recovered her breath. "It thrills me each day to see a master in his element."

"Thank you, Ma'am," he said sincerely, his face flushing with pride that it was his privilege to ensure the safety of such a great man.

"You may return to your duties," she said, laying a hand on his shoulder and squeezing it gently. "I know the way."

"Yes, Ma'am," he said as she turned slowly away and ambled into the house.

"Another lie," she muttered under her breath in self-reproach. "Wasn't lying to your emperor enough?"

Moving slowly through the large structure, she found the secure room through which the emperor's servants were permitted to conduct offworld communications. She immediately saw Krancis' bright yellow hologram upon entering. Closing the door behind her, she moved to a chair close to where his apparition stood and rested her tired bones.

"How is the emperor?" Krancis asked.

"As you would expect," she replied, unwilling to say more unless it was face-to-face.

"This communication channel is secure, Elasha," he said in his precise voice. "Our people in the experimental technologies department have just finished it. It routes our connection through a warp dimension which is impossible to tap into. And beyond that, it's encrypted. You may speak freely. Now, how is the emperor?"

"Not well," she replied gravely. "His condition worsens day by day. The strain of the war is too much for him."

"He is stronger than you know," he replied with easy confidence.

She turned her head slightly and eyed him.

"I sense you haven't called just to inquire about our sovereign's health," she said suspiciously.

"I have not," he agreed. "Omega is giving us trouble. I want you to speak with Bohlen-7 and learn what it knows."

"I cannot speak to Bohlen," she said, shaking her head. "It's impossible."

"Nothing is impossible," he said in a quiet voice that mingled confidence with menace. "I assure you of that. *Nothing*, and *no one*, is beyond reach. The counsel your 'brother' gave the emperor was good. Now we need more help. Omega must be operational as soon as possible, and our scientists and engineers have exhausted every known possibility. I've been over every scrap of technical material they've produced while rebuilding it. But absolutely nothing has worked. There must be something we are missing."

"I cannot do it," she said. "Bohlen will not speak to me anymore. The risk is too great. Manifesting itself in the image of my brother was already terribly hazardous. I tried to limit the manifestation so that only the emperor could see it. But I'm not certain that it wasn't beheld by – by them."

"We are rapidly approaching the point where we mustn't concern ourselves with what 'they' may do," Krancis replied. "The *Ahn-Wey* must see that their time will end if they do not help us. The Devourers will destroy each and every one of them if we fall. Then it won't matter if the *Pho'Sath* get involved or not."

"Don't use that name!" she exclaimed in fearful urgency. "Don't *ever* use that name!"

"I will use whatever name I see fit, Elasha," he said calmly. "The *Pho'Sath* aren't pulling the strings behind the curtain this time, no matter what the worlds of the *Ahn-Wey* believe. If they let this paranoia continue to guide them, they're going to bring death to us all."

"If you use that name again I will end this communication at once," Elasha said stoutly, rising from her seat and making for a nearby desk. Upon it was a massive keyboard loaded with buttons, most of whose functions she didn't understand. But she knew that the large red one on the upper left-hand side would immediately terminate the call. Her hand hovered above it as she turned to look at Krancis over her shoulder. "Just once more, and I'll close it down."

"And I'll open it right back up again," he said imperturbably, his eyes flitting to where her hand hovered. "But out of respect for your standing with the emperor, I'll humor you for the moment."

Slowly she withdrew her hand and turned toward him once more. Not trusting him to keep his word, she remained by the desk, leaning slightly against it.

"I cannot speak to Bohlen," she said. "It will not answer me."

"Then I suggest you figure out a way to make it do so," he replied. "We need information, and we need it *now*. Ask it how to make Omega function. Or the emperor will shortly find himself in need of a new mystic."

"But I–," she began.

Suddenly Krancis' hologram evaporated, leaving the room nearly dark.

"That man," she muttered, shaking her head and making for the chair once more. Letting out a long sigh as the weight came off her legs, she leaned back and thought. "How can I possibly speak to Bohlen, when it won't speak to me?" she asked herself, slowly putting one leg over the other and bobbing her foot slightly. "Naturally, I could…" she mumbled, unwilling to verbalize her thought. "But it told me never to do that…" she countered. Eyeing the tiny square device in the middle of the floor that had projected Krancis' hologram, she sighed again. "Not like I have much of a choice."

Rising from the chair, she opened the door and made

for the emperor's private chambers.

❖ ❖ ❖

"Rise and shine, gang!" Gromyko said several hours past dawn, sitting up in bed and stretching his arms. "What? Do you all still want to sleep?" he asked, as his enthusiasm was met by a variety of groans and mild imprecations. "Don't you know that an entire galaxy is at war out there as we speak? We must do our part! We must rise and *fight!*"

"I could sleep for another thousand years," Milo mumbled, pressing his face into his pillow as the smuggler turned on the light. "This is the first decent bed I've slept in since…" he paused. "Since I don't *know* when. We've been on the run for so long that I forgot what it means to really *sleep!*"

"Right now monstrous vessels float over our very heads, and you want to *sleep?*" asked Gromyko with surprise. "Where's your energy, man? Where's your fighting spirit?"

"I never fight before breakfast," the younger Hunt said, grabbing his pillow and putting it over his head.

"As a matter of fact, that's not a bad idea," the smuggler said, suddenly reminded of how empty his stomach felt. "There must be an oven or something in this old bunker. I'll go find it."

"Just ask Wellesley, he'll know," Milo said in a muffled voice from under his pillow. But Gromyko was already out of earshot. "Guess I'd better go help him look," he said with exasperation, pulling the blanket aside and putting his feet on the floor. Scratching his thick head of hair vigorously for a few moments, he stood up and walked into the hangar muttering to himself.

"Good morning, you two," Pinchon said in a somewhat friendly tone. He was laying on his side, his back pressed against the wall. "Sleep well?"

Tselitel neither moved nor made any reply, her breathing slow and even despite all the talking.

"I'd say so," Hunt smiled, giving her a little squeeze. "You?"

"Fair."

"How's the hand?" Hunt asked. "Or rather wrist?"

"Strange," the pirate said, pushing off the bed with what was left of his arm and slipping his legs over the side. "I'm not used to feeling no sensations from it." He raised the stump in front of him and passed his right hand through the air where the left should have been. "Even doing that right before my eyes, I still expect to feel my hands colliding."

"Guess it'll take a little time," Hunt said, as the colonel bent over and began struggling to get his boots on.

"Yeah, I suppose," he said.

More than once Hunt felt the urge to help him get them on. But a man as independent as Pinchon wouldn't want to be babied, no matter how many limbs he'd lost. So Hunt eventually turned away. He drew Tselitel a little closer in her sleep, glad to feel her warmth beside him.

"I heard what you two talked about last night," Pinchon said quietly, causing Hunt's head to instantly snap back to the graying pirate. His boots fully laced, he sat on his cot, leaning back on his hand. "Don't look so concerned," he said with a light chuckle. "We're all on the same team."

"So you eavesdropped?" Hunt asked darkly.

"Hard to help it," the colonel replied. "Bawling her eyes out like she was, she didn't notice how loud she was talking. I guess you were too absorbed to notice, either."

"The other two?"

"Yeah, they heard it, too."

Hunt cursed under his breath.

"Hey, don't get so bent out of shape over it," he said. "Those two look at her like a sister. They'd never do anything to hurt her."

"And how do you look at her?" Hunt asked, finally

verbalizing a question that had long flitted between the shadows at the back of his mind. "Like a sister?"

"No, I can't honestly say that I do," he said slowly. "A woman like that only comes along once per lifetime. Too bad it had to be *your* lifetime instead of mine."

Watching the colonel as he slowly strode from the room, he began unconsciously drawing Tselitel harder and harder against his side.

"What is this, a wrestling match?" she asked groggily, her eyes slowly opening.

"What?" Hunt asked with surprise, looking down and seeing he'd drawn her half on top of himself. "Oh, I'm sorry," he said, letting her slide back onto the cot.

"I absolutely refuse to wrestle without a referee," she said in a strident tone. "No ref, no match. Thems be my rules."

"Where's the fun in that?" he asked.

"No ref, no match," she repeated. "I have to protect myself. After all, being so much bigger *and* stronger than you, it would practically drive you to pull something illegal, like kissing me. Then I'd just melt and the match would be over. I know the way handsome devils like you think."

"You do?"

"I hope so. Otherwise all these hints I'm dropping are going to waste."

He gave her a quick kiss.

"Is that all I get for my troubles?" she asked.

He kissed her again, long and slow.

"That's more like it," she purred, laying her head down on his chest. "You know, it's funny. Whenever I'm with you like this, my condition doesn't seem as bad. I guess you relax me, or something."

"I shouldn't think relaxation would make that much of a difference to a condition like that," he replied seriously, sorry that their tender moment should be ended.

"Nor would I," she said. "And yet…" her voice trailed.

"Do you think you give off some kind of aura, or something? A healing glow?"

"I wouldn't know," he said. Then, chuckling, "I'm the last person who'd ever give off a healing glow. That's your bag, not mine."

"Who knows," she said. "It was sweet of you to get jealous over me with the colonel."

"What, you heard that?" he asked with surprise. "I thought you were asleep."

"Ah, that's because I'm a tricky one," she said playfully, ducking her eyes momentarily behind a fold in his shirt. "Truth be told I was only half awake. I thought it was a dream until you started wrestling with me."

"I was *not* wrestling!" he protested with a laugh.

"Say what you want," she replied, half closing her eyes and shaking her head. "But we both know the truth."

"Yeah, just like me hitting you with the tree," he said with a roll of his eyes.

"Ah! So you admit it!" she exclaimed, drawing her arm up onto his chest and pointing an accusatory finger at his nose.

"I admit nothing!"

"Oh, intractable as ever!"

"Yup, that's me," he said, nodding slightly as he lay there.

"Maybe I should go and talk to the colonel instead," she said playfully.

Instantly his face turned to stone as he drew his eyes away from her and looked at the ceiling.

"I'm sorry, that was too far," she said quickly. "I should have known better, especially after all we said last night."

"Yes, you should have," he replied seriously.

"I'm always looser in the morning. I say things I don't mean," she explained. "Forgive me? Please?"

"Sure," he replied, mostly recovered but still a little warm.

"I'll let you beat me at wrestling if you'll forgive me," she said, raising a thin arm and making a tiny muscle. "You'd better accept! This is probably the only chance you'll ever have of beating me!"

"Oh yeah?" he asked with a laugh, snapping his hand onto her wrist and instantly twisting it behind her back.

"I let you do that," she said, her chin against his chest, her head bouncing as she talked. "Next time I won't be Mister Nice Guy."

"*Mister* Nice *Guy*?" he asked, cocking an eyebrow.

"Semantics," she said with a roll of her eyes. "Now, are you gonna let me go, or am I your prisoner? Because if I am, I expect three meals a day and a nice cell to live in. And I want the bars painted lavender. Lavender is such a calming color, much better than the dull steel they make bars out of."

Hunt smiled and released her wrist.

"Well, *that* was easy," she said with mock disappointment. "And here I thought you'd be all gung ho to have me around all the time."

"Can't afford the three meals," he said with a grin. "And I'm all out of lavender paint."

"Well, darn," she said, shaking her head. "Then I guess that's that." Pausing momentarily, she sniffed the air. "Do you smell that?"

"Uh huh."

"I guess Antonin found somewhere to warm those steaks Milo cooked," she said, working herself upright on the narrow cot and setting her feet on the floor. "I've got to say, I'm starving."

"Me, too," he seconded, sliding to the end of the bed and stretching. "Let's go see what they found."

❖ ❖ ❖

"How can you possibly leave me now?" the emperor asked Elasha, his hands beginning to tremble as he sat upon his throne.

"I must, my emperor," she said, her eyes downcast. "Krancis has requested that I perform a task for him, and I cannot delay. It may be critical to our success against the invaders."

"B-but I *need* you here!" he said. "Without your brother beside me, you're all I have left. Oh, Krancis is a great and trusted friend. But he does not have your insight, your connection to the *Ahn-Wey*."

"It is because of this connection that I must leave," she said firmly. "The journey will be long and hard, and I must go at once. May I take a number of your guards with me? I am forced to venture into the forest, and the trip will be hazardous."

"Naturally you may take anyone you see fit," he replied morosely. "But be quick. I may need you very soon."

"I will be as swift as my task allows," she said, bowing deeply and leaving the throne room.

Within two hours Elasha and an escort of three departed the compound, heading north toward the forest. Among her party was the young man she'd met earlier, plus two others who served in the imperial guard. They were well prepared for the long journey, with pistols on their hips and rifles slung over their left shoulders. Their backs bore modest rucksacks filled with provisions.

"Pardon me, Ma'am," the young man asked, whose name was Lieutenant Conan Rede. "But why are we setting out on foot? A transport would be much faster."

"The moment you leave the compound the forest becomes impossibly dense," she explained patiently. "This is the only way to travel."

"I see," he replied. "Is all of Bohlen-7 this dense?"

"Essentially. The livable parts, anyway. By the poles the change in temperature naturally alters the growing conditions."

"Yes, Ma'am," he said.

It was late afternoon when they set out. Though an otherwise bright, sunny day, the trees blocked so much light that it immediately felt like twilight to the small band once they'd penetrated a short distance into the forest.

"Ma'am," Rede said after a little while. "They say that there are fierce animals in these woods. Wouldn't it have been wise to bring a larger party?"

"You are a good shot, are you not, Lieutenant?"

"Oh, yes, Ma'am. One of the best."

"And these two that I asked you to select, aren't they good shots, too?"

"Indeed. That's why I chose them."

"Then what do we have to worry about?"

"But, Ma'am, there are only *three* of us. Indeed, we're very well armed. But if we should come across a large pack of wolves, for instance, or–."

"If three young men with rifles, who by your own admission are crack shots, cannot take care of us, then a platoon wouldn't suffice. We are not at *war* with the creatures living in the forest, Lieutenant. Our aim is simply to scare them off and go about our business. If three rifles aren't enough, then they are determined to destroy us. Their numbers are far too great for a troop of any size we could muster to handle in that circumstance."

"I see," Rede said quietly, nodding to himself as he walked beside her. "You are very wise, Ma'am," he said honestly.

"Thank you," she chuckled. "I try."

After two hours of slow walking Elasha called a stop underneath an enormous tree. Sitting down on one of its massive exposed roots, she took off her shoes and let her feet rest.

"When you boys are as old as I am, you'll understand how I feel," she laughed.

"Yes, Ma'am," Rede said.

"Oh, enough of that 'ma'am' business," she said with a wave of her hand. "Call me Elasha."

"But, Ma'am," Rede said earnestly. "You are an advisor to the emperor himself! How can we possibly address you like–like you're an *equal* of ours?"

"Because I give you permission to," she said simply, reaching down and rubbing her foot with her hand. "Believe me, this trip is going to be long enough without us all standing on ceremony. Now, give me all your names. Oh, I know yours already, dear," she said kindly, stopping Rede before he could speak.

"Pasco Halshan," a tall, nervous looking fellow of twenty-two said. "Corporal."

"Glad to know you," she nodded. "And you?" she asked, looking at the one next to him.

"Algar Plessi," he said. Twenty-one, and with an air of reluctance about him, he avoided making eye-contact with the mystic. "Sergeant."

"Glad to know you, too," she said with another nod. "And you're all crack shots?"

"Yes M–," Rede and Halshan began, stopping themselves.

"Yes," Plessi said in a serious tone, still avoiding eye-contact.

Elasha looked into the distance and found a thin branch that had been snapped in a storm. Hanging by only a few fibers, it was ready to come down at the slightest suggestion.

"Do you see that branch over there?" she asked, pointing with a short, bony finger. "No, a little higher."

"The one barely hanging on?" Plessi asked.

"Yes. Can you shoot that down?"

Without a word Plessi stepped a couple paces ahead

of his fellows. Drawing his rifle from his shoulder, he cocked it, aimed momentarily, and then fired. The birds in the branches exploded upwards at the sound, releasing a cacophony that drowned out all other sounds. But when the forest was quiet once again they all looked toward Plessi's target and found it lying on the ground beneath its tree.

"Excellent shot!" Elasha said with a clap of her hands. "Who's the best of the three of you?"

"Halshan," Plessi replied, his face as serious as ever. "Then Rede."

"What, you're the worst of the three?" she asked with a laugh to which he nodded. "Then I consider myself in very good hands indeed."

"Do you shoot, Ma–," Rede began, stopping himself but lacking the forwardness to call her by her name. "Do you shoot?" he asked at last.

"Me? Oh certainly not," she chuckled. "I'd be lucky to hit the tree I'm sitting on! No, I leave tasks like that to people who are actually good at it and just stay out of the way. It's always fun to watch, though."

"We should get moving," Plessi said flatly, looking into the forest. "It'll be dark soon, and that's when the animals come out in force."

"I think you're right," Elasha said with spunk, putting her shoes back on and sliding off the enormous root. "Best not to dally. Let's go, boys."

❖ ❖ ❖

"So just what *is* our plan going forward?" Milo asked no one in particular. They had finished breakfast a few minutes before and were lolling near Wellesley and the first fighter. "I mean, the whole idea was just to come to Epsilon and find out what plan *it* had, right?"

"Right," Wellesley confirmed. "The one where they collapse a dimension and leave the Devourers to rot. Kind of late for that now."

"Yeah," Milo agreed. "So, now what?"

"We find out what's inside this cube," Hunt said, taking it out of his pocket and tossing it in his hand a few times. "Whoever put the *Kol-Prockians* to work building this base has some kind of plan for us, or they wouldn't have gone through all this trouble. And we know something else."

"What's that?" asked Milo.

"That they're bound and determined not to let anyone but us humans know about it," he said. "That's why the cube is so hard to open. Whatever it holds must be very important."

"I'd say they nearly outsmarted themselves on that one," Gromyko said. "Now we have to get out of here alive and find a sixth human to help us. Failing that, its secrets will die with us."

"Guess they considered it a risk worth taking," Hunt replied.

"Alright, Mister Genius," the smuggler said to Wellesley. "I suppose you've been hard at work all night scouring the computer for our next location."

"I would have been," Wellesley said. "If there was anything to scour. The system was never connected to any kind of communications array."

"So we're blind down here?" Pinchon asked.

"Uh huh," the AI replied. "Naturally I know of any number of human settlements thanks to the computer back on Delta-13. But I can't say what the Devourers have been up to since I last interfaced with it. Any previously safe worlds might be under attack by now."

"So we take a gamble," Gromyko said casually.

"Not a great idea," Wellesley said. "Especially considering Rex's importance in all this. We can't take a chance like that."

"And just what *is* Rex's importance in all this?" the pirate asked pointedly. "I get that he has a power and all. But what good is that going to be against a fleet of ships? He couldn't even finish off one of those *kals* last night."

"*Preleteth* believed that he could become a potent weapon," the AI countered, a little surprised at the colonel's tone. "I think all we can do for now is just follow the trail as far as we see it and hope for the best. We're better off now than we were back on Delta. At least now Rex can destroy those creatures. Given time, maybe he can expand his powers further, or find some other way to magnify them. One way or another, all we can do is keep moving forward."

"Sounds pretty thin to me," Pinchon replied.

"Sometimes that's the best you can do," Wellesley said philosophically.

"Alright, er, another question," Milo said awkwardly. "I've been looking over these fighters and they're each three seaters. With just a single one-handed pilot among us, how are we supposed to get out of here?"

"One of you will have to fly the other one," the AI replied simply. "I'm sure the colonel will be more than willing to share what he knows."

"That's impossible," Pinchon said with finality. "You can't teach someone to fly that fast. They'll just crash and kill whoever is with 'em."

"Then I suggest you do your job well," Wellesley replied, growing annoyed with the pirate. "The exigencies of war are upon us, Colonel. Make do with what you've got."

"And just who am I supposed to train?" he asked.

"Rex has the best temperament for the task," the AI replied with unblinking confidence. "Milo's too jumpy and Antonin's too flashy."

"Thanks a lot!" Milo exclaimed. The smuggler just laughed to himself and crossed his arms over his chest as he leaned against the fighter.

"But you can't teach someone to fly on the *ground*,"

persisted Pinchon, glancing at Hunt and then back to Wellesley. "It takes actual flying time to practice. Head knowledge is no substitute for body knowledge. You need to *feel* the craft you're flying. You can't just be intellectually aware of its controls and whatnot. Besides, half a minute after we take off, those Devourer craft are gonna be right on top of us. A man who has never so much as flown can't survive a dogfight."

"Which is why he'll make a break for the nearest friendly system, dropping into warp within the atmosphere if he has to while you cover his exit."

"Do you have any idea what dropping into warp inside the–."

"Yes, I do," snapped the AI. "I know better than most. Now get moving, Colonel."

"How can I train him on a *Kol-Prockian* fighter?" he asked a little more quietly. "I'd never even seen one before last night."

"I'm quite familiar with the design techniques of my people. Their style hasn't changed that much in the centuries I've been out of contact. *Kol-Prockian* military science pretty much stopped after they were carried into slavery. To be honest, these designs are pretty retro. Go ahead and hop into the first craft. It's connected to the network, so I'll meet you there."

"Fine," Pinchon said. "Come on, Hunt. Let's get to work."

"What's eating him?" Milo asked Tselitel as they moved away from the first fighter. "Does he still have a beef with Rex?"

"I'm not sure," she said, eyeing the pirate carefully as he climbed up on the wing of the fighter and gestured for Hunt to take the pilot's seat. "He said something this morning to Rex about finding me desirable."

"Really?" asked Milo with surprise. "Why in the world would he say that?"

"Well, you yourself felt the same way at one time," she smiled.

"Oh, that's not what I meant," he said with a dismissive wave. "I'm just surprised that he would say that to Rex. You're nearly his religion, you know. It would just about be safer to tell a mama bear that you're gonna have one of her cubs for dinner than to get between you and him."

"No, Rex was very calm about the whole thing. Well, mostly," she said, recalling the wrestling match. "But you're right, something has gotten into Pinchon."

"Well, some people are just weird, I guess," Milo said with a shrug. "Not like we've known him for very long. Any quirks he has haven't had much time to float to the surface."

"That's not much of an answer," she said.

"Well, you're the psychiatrist, not me," he said, tossing up his hands and walking away.

"Yes, I am," she replied thoughtfully, watching Pinchon as he tried to learn from Wellesley how the controls worked. He sat in the front seat of the craft, with Hunt in the seat behind him. Moving to where she could watch them both with ease, she saw the older man's graying head move around as he got his bearings. Leaning against the cool concrete wall, she crossed her arms over her chest, careful not to hurt her left hand as she did so, and settled down to observe. There was nothing from his actions themselves that would enlighten her as to his behavior. But that was not her intent. Keeping her eye on him was meant to be purely a stimulus for the unconscious workings in the back of her mind. She'd long ago discovered that, by keeping a given patient in view, she could focus her intuition until it began to yield subtle wisps of insight.

"Just what are you up to…" her voice trailed in a low mumble as she watched.

Her eyes flitted to Hunt and then back to the pirate. She knew he didn't *really* want her, despite what he'd said, so the simple explanation of jealousy was off the table. What she couldn't square was why he'd appeared so respectful toward Hunt at first, and then soured soon after reaching *Preleteth*. It was as though his priorities had shifted, and the man she loved had become an object of aversion to him. But why…

After nearly an hour she decided to call it quits. Her insight wasn't being cooperative that day, and moreover she'd grown tired of the hard concrete against her back. Pushing off it, she wandered past Wellesley's terminal just as he'd finished with Pinchon.

"He's doing alright now," Wellesley announced without warning, making her jump and stop in her tracks. "Pilots, no matter what race, need to perform essentially the same tasks in the cockpit. Once he was up to speed on which controls did what, his intuitive knowledge of flying took care of the rest."

"How's he treating Rex?" she asked with concern, her eyes flitting to Wellesley's medallion before fixing on the fighter's older occupant.

"He's *still* acting odd, isn't he?" the AI replied, dropping his voice. "I'd had just about enough of him earlier, and then he straightened out. Maybe he just needed to be slapped around a little bit. Some folks are built that way."

"Uh huh," she nodded, half listening as her eyes bored into the back of the pirate's head.

"I know what that means," Wellesley chuckled.

"Huh?" she asked, turning and looking at his disc momentarily. "What do you mean?"

"You're trying to figure him out now," he replied. "A surface answer won't do anymore, so you're going to dig deep."

"Well, I *am* the resident psychiatrist, as Milo reminded me."

"Take a piece of advice from me: don't look too far into this. Pinchon's not a complex man. He's just had his hand chopped off and he's feeling a little out of sorts. It would be strange if he didn't, don't you think? Who could just laugh off losing one of their most important limbs? The guy's got enough skill to fly a fighter with just one hand, but in pretty much every other endeavor he undertakes he's gonna be handicapped. That's not an easy thing to deal with."

"I suppose not," she said. "You know, I feel kind of silly. Here I was getting all geared up to dive deep into his mind, and in a few sentences you deftly explain his condition in purely practical terms. Maybe you should take over my job," she chuckled.

"Nah. What I said was just common sense combined with a *lot* of experience. After a while you learn to stop looking past the obvious and fit it into its proper context."

"Context is always the hardest thing to find," she said.

"Indeed." And then, after a few moments, "How's your hand?"

"It hurts," she said, holding it up and gently flexing her fingers. "Still can't use it for anything."

"Really ought to have a cast for it," the AI said. "Of course! How stupid of me!" he exclaimed.

"What?" she asked, turning around.

"The medical bay! I was so caught up with helping the colonel yesterday that I forgot to check over the rest of its inventory for something that might help you. Just give me a second to look."

She waited for a few moments, quietly drumming the fingers of her good hand on the terminal.

"Okay, turns out the surgical table can help us," Wellesley said.

"I don't want to cut my hand off, too!" she said light heartedly, her voice a little louder than necessary. Glancing over her shoulder, she saw Pinchon scowling at her before he turned back to the controls in front of him. "Someone should tape my mouth shut," she said quietly, squeezing her eyes closed as she faced Wellesley again. "Alright, *what* were you going to say?"

"The surgical table is capable of partially fusing bones together that have been broken," the AI said. "Granted, it isn't perfect. Your bones will still need to heal themselves in their own good time. But as long as you're gentle with it, your hand will be functional again."

"A stopgap, then," she asked, raising her hand and looking at it. "Any risks?"

"A minor risk of infection," he replied. "Naturally the table will have to cut its way through the skin on the back of your hand in order to access the bones. But it'll fuse the incisions back together again the moment it's finished. Just take it easy with your skin too and you'll be fine. Shouldn't take more than a few days for it to be good as new."

"Anything else I should know? Pain? Swelling?"

"*Please*," Wellesley said. "This is *Kol-Prockian* medical technology. It's some of the best in the galaxy. Even the emperor's medical staff would love to get their hands on one of these tables."

"Maybe I should tell Rex first," she said quietly, turning to look at the fighter he occupied.

"I wouldn't. He's got enough things on his mind. But snag Antonin or Milo. We might need an extra pair of hands for this."

"Alright," she said, making for the smuggler.

"Tired of talking to our digital friend?" he asked as she approached. He'd been idly watching the pirate teach his friend, and was glad of a little conversation to break the boredom.

"No, we need your help with something," she said in a low voice, her eyes darting to Pinchon momentarily. "Would you come to the medical bay?"

"Sure," he said, pushing off the wall and following her. "What's on your mind?" he asked once they were there.

"Wellesley found out this table can fix the bones in my hand," she said, laying a hand on the table as she spoke. It was large, about nine feet long by five feet wide. Its surface was covered with little orange squares. Above it hung a large white rectangle made of a very advanced form of plastic. Numerous lasers and other kinds of surgical equipment dangled from it, ready to perform.

"Really?" he asked with enthusiasm. "That's fantastic."

"Well, not *fix* them, exactly," the AI quibbled. "It's only a temporary measure to make her hand functional again. She'll still have to be careful with it until it finishes healing on its own."

"Alright," he nodded. "What do you need me for?"

"Just in case anything goes wrong or we need some help," she smiled. "You don't mind, do you?"

"Not at all," he said, leaning against the wall and settling in to watch.

Once she had gently washed her hand and dried it, she went to the table and awaited instructions.

"Give me a second to program the operation we want," Wellesley said. "Done. Okay, lay your bare arm across the table, spreading your fingers until your palm is flat against it."

"Alright," she said, carefully putting her arm down. She drew a sharp breath as she began to splay her fingers, hot bolts of pain shooting up her arm and into her brain.

"Easy, take it easy," the AI cautioned her. "Nothing about this has to be fast."

Heeding his words, she slowed her pace and gradually flattened her hand.

"What next?" she asked, her teeth clenched in pain.

"Now we start the operation."

Suddenly the small orange cubes near her hand rotated. Little straps shot across her arm, wrist, and parts of her hand and fingers.

"Wellesley?" she shrieked, instantly trying to drag her hand away but finding it stuck fast under the straps.

"It's okay!" he reassured her. "It's just part of the

procedure. You can't risk moving your hand while the lasers are at work."

"You could have *told* me that!" she exclaimed. "I nearly died when those things grabbed me!"

"Sorry. I wasn't thinking," he apologized.

"You guys alright in there?" Milo called from the hangar.

Gromyko pushed off the wall and stuck his head out the door.

"All good!" he said.

"Wait," the younger Hunt said, as Gromyko started to pull his head in again. "Why did Lily shout? Is she okay?"

"Of *course* she's okay," the smuggler said. "She's with Gromyko, isn't she?"

With this he stepped back inside and pressed a button near the door that made it close.

"Try to keep your screams to a minimum," he said in a casual voice, resuming his leaning and digging some dirt from under his index finger nail with that of his thumb.

"I'll do my best," she said with annoyance at his flippancy, her heart slowly climbing down from her throat and back into her chest. "What's next?" she asked the AI.

"Laser time," he replied. "Ready?"

"As much as I'll ever be," she said, bracing herself against the table with her other hand and gritting her teeth. "Go for it."

"Okay."

A beep sounded from the machine, making her jump. She watched as a half dozen lasers descended from above the table and hovered just over her hand. For an instant they turned on, opening as many incisions in the back of her hand.

"Why doesn't this hurt?" she asked, surprised to feel nothing at all as her hand began to ooze blood.

"The straps administered a transdermal anesthetic moments after they made contact with your skin. You shouldn't feel a thing."

"What about bleeding?" she asked, watching as another set of lasers took the place of those that opened the back of her hand.

"The strap across your wrist is acting as a tourniquet. If you look beneath your wrist, you will see that the blocks have formed a small ridge to complete the blockage."

"Thanks, I'll take your word for it," she said, growing nauseous at the sight of her blood running down her hand and onto the table.

Without delay the lasers responsible for fusing her bones together began their work. With mechanical efficiency they performed their task, evincing a chilling lack of hesitation. She couldn't help but wonder how much damage they could do should they malfunction. Taking what heart she could from the fact that Wellesley was overseeing the entire procedure, she looked away and closed her eyes.

"Are you sure you don't want to watch this?" he asked. "It's a fascinating display of-."

"No, thank you!" she said quickly, not wanting to hear more.

Quietly the machinery whirred. Resisting the temptation to look, she did her best to think of other things.

"It's done," Wellesley announced shortly thereafter. "You can raise your arm now."

With surprise she turned to the table and saw that nothing was holding her down. Lifting her arm slowly, she found it was still dead numb.

"I can't feel anything," she said.

"It'll pass shortly. The anesthetic has a very short lifespan, so the straps administer it continually. You'll start getting sensation back in a few moments. Try to flex your fingers."

Cautiously she made a loose fist and then spread her fingers.

"I'm starting to feel something," she said with

growing excitement, her fingers brushing against each other as she clenched and unclenched them. Gently she clasped her hands in front of her and squeezed.

"Ah, ah, ah," Wellesley cautioned. "Go easy with that. The mending is most susceptible to side pressure. Don't squeeze too tight."

"How much of a load can I put on it?" she asked, holding her hand up and resuming her careful clenching.

"Technically, about half of what your hand is usually capable of. But that's the upper ceiling. I wouldn't recommend going above a quarter."

"That isn't much," she said with disappointment.

"It's a lot better than what you had before, which was zero," the AI lectured. "The table also made sure the bones were properly set before it began, so you can be sure that they'll heal right."

"Thanks, Wellesley," she said, eyeing the little scars on the back of her hand for a moment. "Thanks a lot."

"Anytime."

She quickly washed the blood off her hand in the nearby basin and then opened the medical bay door. She saw Milo on the other side, his arms crossed in a huff.

"Done?" he asked tartly.

"Yup," Gromyko replied without further explanation, walking past him toward the fighter.

"Look, Milo," Tselitel said, holding up her hand and wiggling her fingers.

"So?" he asked grumpily. "Why'd he slam the door in my–," he started to say. "Oh! That was the broken one!"

"Indeed it was," she said happily, holding it out toward him. "Not good as new. But pretty darn good all the same."

"Cool," he said with interest, taking her hand in both of his and examining it for a moment. "Rex'll be glad to see that."

"I know," she smiled, pulling her hand away and slipping it into her pocket. "But I don't want him to know yet.

I'll surprise him with it later."

"Sure," Milo said in a low voice, giving her a wink.

"How's he doing with the colonel?" she asked, as they moved slowly toward the fighter.

"I don't know," he shrugged. "I was watching close earlier, but that pirate chased me off. Said I was distracting them. Boy, he's touchy today."

"I know," she said, a hint of concern in her voice. Subtly they turned their heads toward the two men as they walked past the fighter toward the terminal on the other side. Despite Wellesley's pragmatic explanation of the colonel's attitude, something still gnawed on her. She shook her head and dismissed it as a side effect of her anxiety medication wearing off.

◆ ◆ ◆

"Ma'am–," Lieutenant Rede began, catching himself. "I mean, Elasha. I really think we ought to stop for the night."

Continuing to walk long after darkness had fallen, the small group moved through the ancient forest, a tiny dot of light in the midst of thousands of tightly packed trees. Little animals jumped between the branches above them, following their progress and chittering to their fellows. Nearly a dozen times the rays of a flashlight fell upon the large, glowing eyes of otherwise unseen predators in the distance. Night hadn't merely come: a shadow had fallen over the primeval wood. Rede felt it vaguely, as a pervasive sense of unease. Something, he felt sure, was watching them.

"It won't do any good to stop now, Conan," Elasha replied, laboring forward with a crooked walking stick that Halshan had made from a fallen branch. "Any danger we're in will multiply with stillness. Our best bet is to present a moving target. The forest moves slowly, dear boy, and as long as *we're* moving it will have a harder time making sense of us and our purpose here."

"The *forest*, Elasha?" he asked, a faint fear growing in the back of his mind that the gossip he'd heard about the aged mystic was true. Word around the imperial retreat was that she was slowly taking leave of her senses.

"Oh, I know how that must sound," she chuckled despite being short of breath. "To your military mind all phenomena are material in nature. Indeed, you must think that way in order to perform your job well. But there are… things that cannot be explained in this galaxy of ours, young Conan. Things that can only be seen and accepted."

"Sounds like superstition to me," Plessi mumbled to Halshan almost inaudibly, walking several paces behind Elasha and Rede.

"Often it can be," she answered him, her peculiarly sensitive ears picking his words out of the rustling of leaves and the cracking of sticks under their feet. "But reason is a dangerous tool, my dear Algar. Often it obscures as much as it illuminates. We make too much of scientific laws, blinding ourselves to every phenomenon that doesn't bind itself to our narrow set of rules. Arrogantly we approach the universe and tell it what shall and shall *not* be possible. As if the universe cares! It has better things to do than listen to pinhead intellectuals who pretend to know everything in advance. Naturally," she added as an afterthought, "I do not count *you* among that set of people, Algar."

"You're free to count me any way you like," he said sourly, shining his flashlight off to the right, spooking a small animal that had been quietly waiting beside their path. "I'm sure you will, in any event."

"What, do you think my moldy old brains will be unkind to you?" she asked with a laugh. Glancing over her shoulder, she saw that Plessi's face was as stony and cold as ever. That of Rede beside her, however, betrayed growing agitated at the turn the conversation had taken. She gave him a little nudge. "Relax, Conan! I'm aware of the rumors that pass through the emperor's guard. I know the aversion, indeed, outright hatred with which I'm regarded by many. Plenty of your comrades think I'm off my rocker, a real loon."

"The emperor finds value in your presence," Plessi said in a stiff tone. "That's all anyone need know. His will is absolute."

"A very correct, official answer," she replied, digging the walking stick into the soft dirt a little more forcibly as her legs grew weary. "And yet you maintain your own opinion, one that exists quite separately from the niceties of imperial etiquette. Tell me, Algar, in your own words, just what you think of me? What magic influence do you fear I have over our beloved sovereign?"

"What do you want, Elasha?" he asked boldly, unafraid to use her name, unlike the others. "Are you trying to get me to indict myself?"

"Why should I do that?" she asked in a light tone, enjoying the discussion. "If I truly possess the influence you suspect me of, then it doesn't matter what you say. I'll simply pour a potion in his ear while he sleeps and whisper that you have spoken treason against him. Indeed, that you come from a long line of traitors that must be exterminated at once. Naturally, having no will of his own, he'll be forced to destroy you to satisfy my wicked will."

"You're mocking me," Plessi said with annoyance.

"I'm not," she said frankly. "Believe me, I'm not. I'm just showing you how ridiculous the gossip is that you hear about me." She paused for a moment to rest. "And further, dear Algar, consider this: why would I venture into this dangerous forest at night if I didn't have the best interests of our liege at heart? Why take the risk, if I'm merely exploiting him?"

"I never said you were wicked," he replied. "I never said anything, in fact."

"No, you haven't," she agreed. "But you've thought

a great deal. And I should like to know just what those thoughts are, if you don't mind."

"I do mind," he replied flatly.

"That's your right," she nodded, turning from him and resuming her walk.

The next hour passed without a word from any of them. The night seemed to draw closer, hemming them in. A light mist arose from the forest floor, blunting the reach of their lights and multiplying the tricks that Rede's and Halshan's minds played on them. Plessi appeared indifferent to its influence, seemingly too surly to care. Elasha, long used to the mysterious ways of the forest, was calm throughout. Mechanically she raised her staff, sinking it into the ground a couple feet ahead of her. Just as it passed behind her she would draw it out and sink it in once more. As one hand tired she would switch it to the other. Finally the pale light of Bohlen's moon began to slip between the branches above their heads. The mist through which they walked magnified it, producing a dull glow that surrounded them.

Suddenly Elasha stopped. Halshan, who'd been walking behind her, was looking off to his left and collided with her. Gripping the walking stick tightly, she managed to stay upright.

"I'm sorry!" he exclaimed, his nerves taut as a bowstring as he placed his hands solicitously on her back. "Are you alright?"

"No harm done," she said, turning toward him and smiling.

"I-I wasn't watching where I was going!" he continued, still afraid that he'd hurt her.

"She's fine, Halshan," Plessi said gruffly. "Stop fretting."

"Yes, Halshan, stop fretting," she said with good-natured mimicry. "We'll camp here for a few hours."

"Why, because the moon is out?" asked the skeptic.

"Very perceptive, Algar," she said approvingly. "Yes, as

a matter of fact, that's precisely why."

"Superstition," Plessi muttered under his breath, beginning to walk away.

"Where are you going?" Rede asked.

"To get wood," the sergeant replied irritably. "You want a fire, don't you?"

"No fire," Elasha said firmly, the sudden iron in her voice making even Plessi pause and look back at her. "What would happen if you invited yourself into a neighbor's home and began pulling apart their furniture so you could put it in the fireplace?" She paused and looked up into the trees for a moment. "We're in *his* house now, boys, and we must be respectful. No fires."

Plessi snorted and resumed his walk.

"Sergeant, get back here at once," Rede barked.

"Is that an order?" he asked over his shoulder, still moving.

"Yes," he said sharply, causing Plessi to stop. Standing still for a moment, he muttered something inaudible and then came back.

"Is there anything else we ought to do, Elasha?" Rede asked solicitously as the sergeant plunked down on a fallen tree, facing away from the group and searching the darkness with his light.

"No, nothing for now," she said quietly, her sensitive ears carefully examining the night. "For now we can rest. Two, maybe two and a half hours from now we'll have to move again. Until then, recuperate as well as you can. Once we leave this place we'll go nonstop until dawn."

"But what about the animals?" he asked, as she leaned against the large, smooth trunk of a tree and slid to the ground. "Shouldn't we–."

"Normally, yes," she said, laying her stick aside. "But they are his servants, and he will do nothing so long as the moon is upon us. Rest easy, Conan, you're safer than you know."

"Yes, Ma'am," he said automatically. He turned to apologize, but she smiled and waved her hand, showing it was unnecessary. Nodding, he sat down beside Halshan and tried to get what rest he could.

An owl hooted in the distance, but otherwise the fauna of the forest were still. A gentle breeze wended its way through the trees, stirring the grass and rustling the branches. Suddenly an animal shattered the stillness by emitting a fierce, angry call a short distance away. The three young men leapt to their feet, weapons at the ready.

"It's alright, boys," Elasha said, gesturing for them to lower their arms. "It's alright. The Master of the Forest is just reminding us that we are guests in his house, and that as guests we oughtn't to get too comfortable."

"*That* was the Master of the Forest?" asked Rede, his hands trembling as he looked into the darkness.

"That? Oh, certainly not! That was just one of his pets. Now, listen to what I say and take it easy. He didn't mean to threaten us with that little outburst. This isn't my first time traversing these woods. *Relax.*"

Nodding slowly, Rede settled down once more to rest, his eyes fixed in the direction of the animal's cry. Quietly he opened the clasp on his holster, slipped his pistol out and laid it in the shadow his body formed from the light of the flashlights. He glanced at Elasha to verify that she hadn't noticed his action; but she sat looking back at him, a slight smile on her face.

"Never hurts to be careful," he said apologetically, to which she only chuckled.

None of them slept. The night was far too tense for that. No more 'reminders' disturbed them. But the constant anticipation of one kept them on their toes. Finally Elasha groaned and stood up.

"Alright, boys, it's time for us to proceed," she said, looking up toward the moon. "The clouds are blowing in and will soon obscure our protection."

"If this 'Forest Master' is dangerous without the moon shining, then why did he merely warn us earlier?" asked Plessi. "Seems pretty inconsistent."

"The 'Forest Master,' as you call him, isn't governed by a hard and fast set of rules. He has moods, superstitions, irrational beliefs," she said, sinking the staff into the ground ahead of her and beginning to walk. "Just like you, my dear Algar," she added with a slight edge in her voice.

"I'm not superstitious," he said stoutly.

"You apprehend magic damage from me, don't you?" she prodded. "Somehow I threaten the emperor, though you haven't any evidence to prove it. You think me possessed of bad aura, and thus everything I do is suspect. That's superstition, plain and simple."

"No, you threaten the emperor by–," he said, stopping himself short.

"Yes, Algar?" she asked.

"Nothing."

"As you like it."

"Elasha?" Halshan asked, speaking up at last.

"Yes, Pasco?"

"How did you come to know so much about this world?" he asked, a touch of amazement in his voice. "It seems so vast, so mysterious. I don't think I could know half as much as you do, even if I'd been born here."

"Don't tell me you believe this garbage?" Plessi asked scornfully.

"She knows what she's talking about, Algar," Halshan said, almost apologetically.

"That's Sergeant Plessi, *Corporal* Halshan," Plessi shot back.

"Not for this trip," Rede said. "Elasha is right. This is no time to stand on ceremony. We need to be flexible."

"But you're still giving the orders, eh, *Conan*?" Plessi asked tartly.

"Yes," Rede replied with an air of confidence he'd

lacked before. "And don't you forget it."

Plessi humphed and fell silent.

"Elasha?" Halshan asked after a few moments.

"Oh, yes," she said, the argument making her forget his question momentarily. "Well, my brother Taegen taught me most of what I know. He was a great man. Very, very wise. He lived here even before the imperial retreat was built. In fact, it was on his advice that it was placed here. Bohlen has a marvelous capacity to heal those who are ill, my dear Pasco. It was why I finally came here, in fact."

"Then you're unwell?" asked Halshan hesitantly, not wishing to pry.

"Only when I leave Bohlen."

"And the emperor?" he asked. "It helps him, too?"

"Yes, but not so much as one would hope," she said. "Not everyone responds to it in the same way. The planet is not magic, Pasco. Rather it is a being, like you or I. The capacity it has to work upon the human form is something we don't understand. Yet we know from experience that it helps some more than others. I would be dead by now without its help. And yet the emperor continues to suffer from his condition, though in a mitigated form. It is just another one of the mysteries of our galaxy that we have yet to understand."

"I didn't think understanding was important to you," Plessi said acidly. "Slack-jawed amazement, perhaps."

"Sergeant!" snapped Rede.

"That's *Algar* to you, *Conan*."

"No, it's alright, Conan," Elasha said. "I'm glad to hear him speak his mind. Though it would be nice if he employed his obvious talent for wit more productively. The difference between you and I, Algar, is that you reject what you don't understand, and I do not. I accept phenomena whether or not they conform to generally accepted rational laws, so long as they can be proven to exist."

"There's a great deal more that separates us than that,

Elasha," he said caustically.

"Indeed," she chuckled.

"Elasha, what happened to Taegen?" Rede asked after a few minutes had passed. "I remember the emperor declared an entire year of mourning. The news was full of reports about the tragedy of his death, but details always seemed rather thin."

She looked at him for a moment and then stopped.

"I must have the solemn word of each of you that what I tell you shall go no further," she said firmly.

"You have it," Rede said, followed quickly by Halshan.

"Algar?" she asked, raising an eyebrow.

"Sure, why not," he said dismissively.

"Is that how cheaply a servant of His Imperial Majesty holds his word?" she prodded.

At this he stood straight and looked her in the eye.

"Indeed not," he said formally. "Very well, on my word as a servant of His Imperial Majesty, what you say regarding Taegen's death shall go no further."

"Good," she said, resuming her walk. "He was assassinated – murdered by elements in the military that felt him to be a threat."

"I don't believe that," Plessi said instantly. "The military is constantly being blamed for such things. Soft heads like you always imagine we're up to no good, that we *enjoy* killing and destroying because it happens to be a part of our job. But rightly or wrongly, Taegen was the emperor's advisor and friend. No one would dare touch him."

"Unless the conspiracy went to the very top," Elasha countered. "Unless he was regarded as such a powerful threat to the military hierarchy that he had to be eliminated, no matter the risk."

"Such fanatics don't exist in the military," Plessi replied. "You're imagining things."

"Was I imagining this?" she asked, pausing to pull the top of her robe slightly to one side, revealing the nasty scar of an old wound in her right shoulder.

"How did you get that?" Rede asked with alarm.

"The same way my brother met his end," she said, straightening her robe and sinking the stick into the ground once more. "By opposing the military's plans for abusing mind control."

"More nonsense!" Plessi nearly barked. "How can you listen to this–."

"Can it, Algar!" Halshan said, his mild nature finally having enough of the sergeant's outbursts.

"Mind control?" Rede asked.

"Yes," she said in a regretful voice. "It was one of two methods for dealing with the threat of the Devourers. The plan was to knit humanity into one unified block that could fight back with senseless abandon. Through my brother's connection to Bohlen we learned what they were capable of – indeed, how they had once before nearly destroyed all life in this galaxy. It was clear that only the most desperate measures could possibly cope with them. Mind control was a dark method indeed, but it was one of the only options open to us. By producing an empire of fanatics we could possibly turn the tide."

"But humanity–," began Halshan.

"Would become slaves," she finished for him. "Yes, that's true. But we would be alive, and that was the main thing. The spark of freedom that always beats within the human heart would eventually reassert itself. Man is one creature that you can never hold down indefinitely. We just keep springing up, again and again. At least, that's always been my hope."

"But why did Taegen die?" persisted Rede. "What exactly did he do?"

"He tried to keep control of the project out of the military's hands," she explained. "Most of them didn't believe in the Devourer threat in the first place. But they felt that mind control would give them a wonderful weapon for dealing with the fringe independence movement, which was growing in strength with every passing day. For this reason his interference was intolerable, and he was shortly thereafter eliminated while on an errand for the emperor."

"I'm sorry," Rede said, laying a hand on her shoulder as they walked.

"In the end it was all for nothing," she said. "A band on Delta-13 destroyed the facility where the mind control research was taking place. That strange world facilitated the work being done there while simultaneously working with the rebels who destroyed the facility. I don't know, perhaps it was confused, disoriented from the last war. Bohlen has always been suspicious of that planet. In any event, it was the only such place where research of that kind seemed feasible. The *Ahn-Wey*, like humans, have gifts that individuate them. Perhaps there were other worlds in times past who could have supported such work. If there were, they must have been killed during the first war with the parasite."

"Does that mean we cannot cope with the Devourers?" asked Halshan. "Are we doomed?"

"No, my dear Pasco," she said earnestly. "Certainly not. There is another option, one that I cannot speak of. Our hopes now rest with it."

❖ ❖ ❖

"I've taught him everything I can," Pinchon said late in the afternoon as he approached the trio that sat quietly by Wellesely's terminal. "He's got a good memory, so I don't think he'll forget anything vital during flight."

The trio watched as Hunt climbed out of the cockpit and sat on the fuselage for a moment. Scratching his head, he moved out onto the wing and slid off of it to the ground.

"Ready for action, my friend?" Gromyko asked as he

joined them.

"Ready as I'll ever be," he said, stretching after so many hours in the cramped cockpit. "Just how big were your people, Wells? There's barely any room in that thing."

"More or less of human height, but much narrower and lighter. Average male weight was around one hundred and thirty pounds."

"You're *kidding*," Milo said. "I always figured them for being pretty husky fellows."

"You saw their skeletons in that mausoleum you raided," he said pointedly. "It doesn't take much imagination to add a little muscle and skin."

"Well, sure. But I thought they were just skinny academics. You know, never getting any sun or exercise?"

"Nope, they were a pretty representative sample of my people," the AI replied.

"Huh. What do you know…" Milo muttered.

"So when do we leave?" Tselitel asked, looking up at Hunt as he leaned against the terminal beside her.

"Soon as we figure out where we're going," he said. "Any more thoughts on that, Wells?"

"A few," he said. "I've been going over the data I extracted from the computer on Delta. The closest human settlement is twenty-six hours from here. But it seems like a likely target for the Devourers."

"*Ahn-Wey*?" Hunt asked.

"No. But it's got a pretty sizable population. Sooner or later these parasites are gonna have to turn onto humanity proper, and it'll be one of their first targets. They may be there already, in fact. To my knowledge the only Devourers who were held back from reaching their target quickly were the ones right above us now. None of the other *Ahn-Wey* seemed to know how to disrupt their warp travel."

"So some of the fleets in the area could already be en route to their secondary targets?" Pinchon asked.

"Uh huh."

THE BEAST EMERGES

"So, what then?"

"Well, there's one facility in the area that has almost certainly escaped the notice of the Devourers. It's small, hidden, and offers no real inducements for them. But it's a little…questionable," the AI said.

"Like how?" asked Gromyko.

"It's a pirate base," Wellesley replied. "The computer didn't know the name."

"Where is it?" Pinchon asked.

"About forty hours from here. It's on a moon the computer called *Psoo'lafan*."

"That doesn't help," the pirate shook his head. "I don't know your alien names. What kind of planet does it orbit?"

"Lava world."

"Oh," he said, sharply turning his head.

"Problem?" asked Gromyko.

"Well, that depends," Pinchon replied, taking a few steps toward the fighter and leaning against it. "That's a place we call the Black Hole. It's where a lot of our boys go to hide for a while when they've become too hot to handle. Sometimes a Black Fang will get a little…over aggressive, and upsets the authorities in a big way. They put out a dragnet for him, and we hide him there. You're right, Wellesley: that's probably the last place in the Milky Way that the Devourers will have any reason to attack. Who'd bother with a bunch of skulking scum?"

"Then they're a rough crowd?" the AI inquired.

"That's putting it mildly."

"You said that its being a problem 'depended' on something," Wellesley observed. "On what?"

"On whether or not Ivo Kaljurand is still in charge there," he said with a frown.

"Is he a good sort?" asked the AI.

"Is any Black Fang?" asked the pirate dryly. "No, I wouldn't call him good. But he's got two things going for him: he's obsessed with the bottom line, and he's obsessed with order. It's why they put him in charge of that rat's nest years ago. Before he got there it was nothing more than an expensive shooting gallery. All the roughest types in the organization ended up there at some point or another. Well, pirates are pirates: they want to be on the move. You pen them up for a couple of months and you're asking for trouble. Kaljurand brought order to the place, more or less. But even he can't control all of it."

"Sounds terrific," Milo said sarcastically.

"Sounds like our destination," Hunt said.

"You can't be serious?" his brother asked. "What about Lily? You gonna take her into a vermin hive like that?"

"Nobody'll touch Lily," he said with certainty.

"They're not gonna let us keep our weapons," Pinchon said knowingly. "Just how do you intend to guarantee her safety?"

"Oh, he can guarantee her safety," Gromyko said, walking up to his friend and slapping him on the back. "You needn't worry about that."

Pinchon looked at Tselitel.

"Are you willing to take that risk?" he asked.

"Anywhere Rex goes, I go," she said, hopping to her feet and standing beside her man.

"Your choice," the pirate said simply.

"You say it's forty hours away?" the smuggler asked.

"Yes. I suggest we get moving immediately. It won't be too much longer before nightfall. Then the *kals* will be out and they could threaten our takeoff."

"Did the *Kol-Prockians* leave anything like money in the base?" Hunt asked. "Anything we can barter with if we need to?"

"Funny you should ask that," Wellesley began. "The fact is they *did* leave a small stash of kantium behind. Now, it isn't worth a whole lot in Quarlac, but–."

"Did you say *kantium*?" Pinchon clarified.

"Yeah."

"That's one of the rarest elements on the black market today," the pirate said. "Any Black Fang would shoot his mother to get his hands on that."

"It sounds like they would do that in any event," the AI said with annoyance, well aware of its value. "In the event we need to trade, that should prove more than sufficient."

"Just don't mention it unless you have to," Pinchon added. "Or they'll take it by force."

"Yes, be careful, children," Wellesley said tartly, rolling his eyes as the pirate pointed out what he considered to be insultingly obvious.

"We'd better get our kit together," Hunt said. "Wells, where's that kantium?"

"Well, that's another thing," he said reluctantly. "Recognizing its value within the Milky Way, the *Kol-Prockians* knew better than to just leave it lying around."

"You mean it's in the terminal?"

"Uh huh."

"Like the cube?"

"Uh huh."

"So we need *Merokanah*?"

"Uh huh," the AI said with aversion.

"I'll go get him," Tselitel laughed, patting Hunt's arm and moving quickly away. "Boy, he's *not* happy," she said upon her return, holding the AI's disc in a fold of her shirt to break the contact with her skin. "I think he'd bring this whole base down on our heads if it wasn't against his instructions."

"I'll work on *Merokanah*," Wellesley said with resignation. "You guys just get the rest of the stuff together." The AI sighed. "Alright, stick him in the terminal."

"You sure?" she asked, still holding the disc with her shirt.

"Better to get it over with," he said, as though having a tooth pulled.

"Okay," she assented, leaning forward over the terminal and slipping the disc into its slot.

"And furthermore," exploded *Merokanah*, "*never* have I been subje–."

"That ought to keep him quiet for a while," Wellesley said, cutting his connection to the audio-visual system. "Well, what are you waiting for?" he asked, as the others stood around watching. "I'm already doing my part!"

◆ ◆ ◆

"I deserve to be shot," McGannon said, looking at her drawn face in the mirror of her bathroom. Shortly after the Devourers emerged from their prison she had one of the rooms near her office converted into a small apartment. This way she could keep in constant touch with the fleet, never having to leave headquarters for any reason. She eyed the woman in the mirror for a few more moments and then spat viciously into her left eye. The glob hit the glass and slowly streaked down it toward the counter.

Shambling exhaustedly from the bathroom, she went to her small bedroom, turned off the light, and laid down.

"What have I done?" she asked herself, running her hands tormentedly through her blonde hair. Laying her hands on her stomach, she looked through the darkness at the ceiling. In an instant she had become the most hated figure in the entire navy. Though every officer affected was ordered to maintain the strictest secrecy for the sake of their imprisoned relatives, the number involved was simply too great for it not to become generally known. The brutal measure she had been forced to undertake would mar her name in the history of mankind from that day onward. The fact that she had been extorted into doing it, she was sure, would do nothing to mitigate the damage done to her reputation.

But then her mind rolled over to her mother. She couldn't stand by while Krancis left her to die. What a poor woman, McGannon thought, to have birthed a child that would bring shame on her entire family for so long as humanity existed. At the end of her wits, she began to cry the tears of nervous exhaustion.

No sooner had the order been given than an attempt was made on her life. A young officer, Lieutenant Sharon Cruise, snuck a knife in under her clothes and nearly made mincemeat out of her. It was only the instantaneous intervention of a pair of recently appointed bodyguards that stopped her. Their presence was perhaps the greatest humiliation she'd been subjected to, for they were on Krancis' personal payroll. He'd assigned them to her just hours before the order was given.

"Just his stooge now," she muttered bitterly.

Her mind raced back over her long, award-laden career.

"Have I really come all this way just to be the pawn of a sociopath?" she asked herself. Unable to sleep, she arose after half an hour and walked to her makeshift living room.

Its sole window had been covered over with heavy metal sheeting to prevent would-be assassins from taking her out. Another innovation from Krancis reminding her that his roving mind left no possibility unaccounted for. Lifting an empty cup off the table before her, she hurled it at the sheeting, scattering tiny bits of sharp glass all over the hardwood floor. She eyed the mess for a moment, wondering if she should clean it up. Then she shook her head.

"Don't have to worry about that," she said with biting sarcasm, feeling totally out-maneuvered by the master strategist that the emperor had all but handed his throne to. "He will have foreseen that eventuality as well. A cleaning crew is probably already on the way."

CHAPTER 11

"The sun is finally up, boys," Elasha said, pausing beside a large rock and resting her tired bones upon it. "Oh, and not a moment too soon! I don't think I could have gone on another hour."

"I'm sure you could have," Rede said with a pride in their mystic guide that he didn't understand.

"Thank you," she said with a smile. "But when you get to be my age everything takes a little more work. Frankly I'm surprised to have made it through the night. I feared you fellows would have to carry me at some point."

"Not like we aren't already," Plessi grumbled as he moved away from the group. Finding a covered place under the branches of a pair of closely packed trees, he slid the pack and rifle from his shoulders and climbed underneath to rest. Rede opened his mouth, about to take him to task for his remark when a staying hand from Elasha grasped his arm and stopped him.

"Leave him be," she said quietly, eyeing the young sergeant for a moment. "He's got to grapple with things in his own way, and in his own time,"

"He won't grapple with anything," Rede said frowningly. "He's been the same way as long as I've known him. His mind is made up about everything. He's never yet walked into a situation he hasn't already judged in advance."

"It's a common tactic," the old woman said knowingly,

THE BEAST EMERGES

leaning as far back on the rock as she could without tipping off the other side. "People try to box in the world according to an acceptable framework. It helps keep them sane."

"Weak people," Rede said bitterly, cycing his comrade in arms with aversion. Elasha had begun to awaken in him a broader sense of what was possible. Through her words he dimly beheld a universe that was teeming with life; indeed, with intelligences far greater than his own – demigods who days before he hadn't even known existed. She bore the promise of a mystical union between man and something higher than himself. Long a student of mythology – though he hid this fact from his friends – there pulsated within his spirit a primitive impulse that longed to see such beliefs return. Suddenly there were living worlds! Masters of Forests! Ancient beings of incomprehensible intellect and power! The thought both thrilled and terrified him. But it also made him feel alive, blowing a breath of fresh air into a life that had grown arid through overmuch rationalism. But above all this it gave him hope that a way to survive the Devourers could be found. Despite his faith in the wisdom of the emperor, he secretly possessed doubts that anything could grapple with the invaders. The words of Elasha gave him hope that all the players in the galactic drama hadn't revealed themselves yet, and that in their aid mankind might find a rescue. Every snide comment from Plessi only served to undermine this hope. In retaliation Rede scorned his closed-mindedness.

"Not everyone is strong," she said sagely, her eyes falling on Plessi's boots as they poked out from under the trees. "Before my brother Taegen introduced me to the wonders that have always surrounded us, I was as blind and cut off as our young friend over there."

"Not you," Rede said in disbelief, shaking his head. "There's no way that you could have been so – so prejudiced."

"What is prejudice?" she asked. "It's just whatever happens to fall outside our system of thought. Everyone has it, because no mind can encompass the totality of life around us. To possess no prejudice is the same as possessing no mind at all. Indeed, dear Conan, there's no greater insult than to say someone has an open mind – a *truly* open mind. Because it means they've never once formed a solid opinion about anything!"

"You think people should be prejudiced?" asked Halshan, sitting on the ground a couple of feet away as he drew a ration from his rucksack.

"I think they should make up their minds," she replied. "Algar does, though with limited success. He's striving to understand the world around him, but he's made a classic error. Instead of *expanding* his thoughts when they don't fit the facts, he simply rejects the facts. But he *is* thinking, that I assure you. If he wasn't there'd be no conflict within him. I would be little more than an irritation, a fly to be swatted away. Indeed, I would be less than that: I would stir no reaction at all, because his brain would be switched off. His anger and bitterness are an attempt to grapple with what I say. He's also unsettled because he sees that you two are inclined to believe me. The sight of his fellows pursuing something outside his beliefs makes him question them all the more. He wonders if he ought to expand his thoughts, but he's afraid to fall into error. So he withdraws, as you can see," here she tossed a finger toward the boots. "He's trying to figure out what to do."

"But you're no threat to him," Halshan said, his voice incredulous. "You're not a danger to anyone."

"Everything is dangerous that upsets our perspective," she replied, smiling kindly at his intellectual naivete. "The human mind lives in a world of its own making. That's not to say it's *unobjective*. But the slant we put upon things tells us both where events are trending and what our relation to them is. When someone introduces a discordant note, we must have either the security to absorb it, or the bravery to reject it."

"Bravery?" Halshan asked.

"Tell me, does it require bravery to go on a night patrol? Everything around you is unknown; innumerable unaccountable sounds enliven the night. Your impulses tell you to stay inside where it's warm and bright. But your duty sends you out into the cold, and you follow that duty. And yet, the only difference between a patrol at night and one during the day is visibility – knowledge. The former is a deliberate foray into ignorance, and that's always dangerous."

"Well, sure," Halshan replied. "But those are two totally different cases. Shrinking from the truth is mere weakness – something they pounded out of us at the academy. Most of us, anyway," he added, some of Rede's scorn for Plessi taking root in his heart.

"You think the two cases are different," she said, wrapping her hands around her walking stick and leaning forward on it as she sat. "But they aren't. Algar's showing great courage to stand up to someone like me – an authority figure both because of my position with the emperor, and because of the decades of experience I have over him. I potentially possess knowledge that could be useful to him, yet he pushes back because it disagrees with his system. The easy thing would be to acquiesce, to soak up what I say uncritically and then, just as uncritically, to soak up what the next person tells him. Some people really *are* human sponges like that. They lack the courage to maintain their own thoughts." She looked between them. "Don't ridicule him, boys. He's just trying to find his way, like the rest of us."

"He doesn't have to be so disagreeable about it," Rede said, reaching into his own rucksack for a pair of rations and offering one to Elasha, which she gratefully accepted. "He's all but friendless, as far as I know. Pretty much everyone dislikes him."

"Some people are like that," she mused aloud. "Still, he may come out of that in time. Our journey is far from over.

Who knows," she said with a mysterious gleam in her eye, "he may see something that will change his ideas of what's possible and what isn't."

"Like the Master of the Forest?" Halshan asked.

"Perhaps."

"And just who is he? What's he like?"

"I can't talk about him," she said, shaking her head. "You'll just have to see for yourself, if we encounter him."

"But why?" asked Rede.

"Because I made a promise to him once that I wouldn't speak of him. Not in detail, anyway."

"You made a promise to a creature which would have killed you last night had the circumstances been right?" asked Halshan, his eyebrow cocked.

"Indeed."

"Why?" Rede prodded.

"Because he asked me to," she replied simply, to their audible astonishment. "Not everything in this life is self-evident, boys. On the surface I sound off my rocker. But I know the mind I'm working with. You'll just have to trust me."

"How long do we rest here?" Rede asked after a short interval.

"You're leading the troop," she replied. "You tell me."

"Well, I didn't know…" his voice trailed.

"Oh, you didn't want to run an old woman off her feet?" she chuckled. "That's very thoughtful of you. But we need military efficiency on a jaunt like this. We can't concern ourselves too much with a single individual. No, tell me what I have to do and I'll bear up."

"We'll rest for a few hours and then resume. I want to take advantage of the daylight to cover as much ground as possible. We'll rest again a couple hours short of nightfall and then keep moving through the dark. At least until the moon comes out."

"Algar seems to be earnestly on board," she observed

in an amused tone of voice, the sound of the sergeant's snoring wafting toward them on the breeze. "Truth be told we should all be following his example instead of talking. We need rest more than conversation." Carefully lowering herself from the rock to the ground, she laid aside her walking stick and stretched out on the soft dirt between Halshan and Rede, making a pillow with her two hands.

"Do you want to use my pack for your head?" Rede asked, indicating the rucksack he'd just placed under his own.

"No, the simplest accommodations are the best," she said, not bothering to raise her head from her hands as she spoke. "Our ancestors must have slept like this many times in our ancient past. If it was good enough for them, I suppose it's good enough for me." She closed her eyes, and the young lieutenant soon heard her breathing even out as she drifted away.

◆ ◆ ◆

"Maybe you should go with Pinchon," Hunt said quietly to Tselitel, as the other three finished packing the two fighters. "I can take Antonin."

"You prefer his company to mine?" she purred, straightening his collar slightly, a coy smile on her face.

"No," he laughed. "But Pinchon is an ace when it comes to flying. Me – I'm not even a rookie. It's at least even money that I plant this thing in the ground right after takeoff."

"I have faith in you," she said, finishing with his collar and patting her hands on his chest, leaving them there for a moment as she looked into his eyes.

"Wish I could say the same," he replied, looking over his shoulder at the fighter.

"Aw, don't worry, Rex," Wellesley said, just managing to overhear what they were saying a few feet from his terminal. "*Kol-Prockian* vessels are some of the easiest birds in the entire galaxy to fly. The onboard computer should correct for any drastic errors you might make."

"Should?"

"Well, you can never be too sure with dumb AIs," Wellesely said with a touch of disdain. "It's not like they can *think*, you know. They only respond to the environmental factors that they've been programmed to address. And *technically* they've been instructed to respond to errors a *Kol-Prockian* pilot would be likely to make, not a human pilot. Still, it's better than nothing."

"Wells, you have a wonderful way of offering hope just to dash it to pieces with qualifications," Hunt said, shaking his head.

"You say the *nicest* things," the AI replied, withdrawing from the conversation to resume his dialogue with *Merokanah*.

"He's right, you know," Tselitel said, taking his hands. "Don't worry, I know we'll be fine."

"I suppo–," he began, suddenly realizing he held her left hand. Holding it up, he saw the little scars on the back. "What happened?" he asked, surprised that the gentle pressure he was exerting on it wasn't causing her any pain.

"We fixed it," she said happily, flexing her fingers and squeezing his hand with modest firmness. "Well, sort of. Wellesley figured out that the surgical table back there could fuse my bones together. It was a little scary at first, but essentially pain free."

"That was when you yelped earlier?" he asked. "Milo mumbled something about you finding a rat. Or being *with* a rat. Something like that."

"I think he meant Antonin," she said quietly, her pretty gray eyes filled with mirth as she put her hand to her mouth to stifle a laugh. "Antonin blew him off and he wasn't happy."

"So it's good as new?" he asked.

"Not really. Wellesley said I could probably exert half my maximum force with it, but recommended staying below twenty-five percent. Apparently the fuse job isn't a replacement for good old-fashioned healing. But it makes the process a lot easier to bear."

"I should think so," he replied, examining her hand a moment longer and then releasing it. He looked into her bright face for a moment and then dropped his voice. "What about…you know?"

"My condition?" she asked.

"Yeah. I'm sorry to put this so crudely, but will you come unglued if something happens during flight?"

"Honestly I can't promise that I won't," she said. "But wouldn't you rather I was with *you* if something did happen?"

"I'd rather you were with the man who had the best chance of getting you to our destination safely," he said, glancing at Pinchon. "But I'm certain you won't give me any choice on that front. You'd probably just strap yourself across the outside of the cockpit."

"I probably would!" she laughed. "Don't worry, darling. I don't think anything will happen. I've been doing just fine today. That's how this condition works, at least for me. Up and down; up and down. Right now we're on the up. I say we ride it for as long as it lasts."

"Guess that's as good as we can do," Hunt said reluctantly.

No sooner had he said this than Wellesley broke in on them a second time.

"Okay, I've *finally* worked this miserable little ignoramus into telling us where the kantium is."

"What took so long?" Hunt asked.

"Oh, I had to listen to him go on and on about his rights and prerogatives – how we've insulted him and whatnot. That's half an hour of my life that I'll never get back."

"So, where is it?"

"I was going to add that his instructions specifically forbade him to give the kantium to anyone but a human. Naturally having half a dozen of them *all around him* wasn't enough to satisfy his punctilious little mind. He has to be addressing you directly, and you have to ask for it expressly."

"Those were his orders?" Tselitel asked.

"That's his interpretation of them, anyway," the AI replied. "Unfortunately that means I have to hook him back into the audio-visual system."

"Go ahead," Hunt said, walking to the terminal and crossing his arms.

"Alright," Wellesley said with resignation. "Just don't forget that you told me to."

"Hello? Hello? Can you hear me again? I can't tell you how embarrassing it is to be cut out of the system. It's like having your home invaded by burglars, and then having them tell you which chairs you may and may not sit in. I tell you, it strikes me as absolutely–."

"*Merokanah*," Hunt said forcibly, as the others drew near to watch the tete-a-tete. "I want you to show me the kantium."

"Will it only be used by humans? You won't spread it around to our enemies, will you? After all, kantium is a valuable resource."

"We only intend to sell it to other humans. And only then if it is absolutely necessary."

"Do you *promise*?" the AI asked suspiciously. "My orders were explicit, you know. I didn't stay down here for hundreds of years in order to fail my purpose. Now, all of you at once, you must promise to–."

"Your orders said nothing about *everyone* having to promise," Hunt said, quickly growing irritated. "The only requirement was that you give the kantium to a human.

Well, I'm a human. So fork it over."

"And just how do *you* know what my orders are?" he asked in a superior tone.

"You told Wellesley, and he told me."

"He did?" *Merokanah* asked awkwardly. "Oh, well, I suppose–."

"Open. It."

"Yes. Yes, of course," the AI replied solicitously. "I'm, uh, afraid that there's a little…problem," he added moments later.

"What?" asked Wellesley sharply. "Is this compartment rusted shut as well?"

"No, no, nothing like that," he said slowly, dragging out his reply.

"Then what?" asked Hunt.

"Well, heh, it's the funniest thing really," *Merokanah* began. "You see, I'd forgotten that the people who built this bunker, well, they weren't the most *honest* folks in the world."

"Meaning?" Wellesley prodded.

"They, um, stole the kantium instead of placing it inside the terminal."

"They *what*?" exploded the ancient AI. "And you put us through all this rigmarole just to tell us that?"

"I forgot!" *Merokanah* replied defensively. "I-I was confused! You all had me so angry that I forgot that…minor…detail."

"Minor indeed!" exclaimed Gromyko. "What are we supposed to trade with if we need supplies?"

"We could always barter a gently used alien AI," Wellesley said.

"No! Please no!" *Merokanah* begged. "I'm sorry! I-I didn't mean it!"

"I believe him," Tselitel said, walking to the terminal and standing beside the flustered AI's disc. "Anyone could forget after a couple hundred years."

"Yes! Yes, anyone could!" he seconded urgently. "Please, don't sell me to those scum at the Black Hole! I'll-I'll do anything!"

"We'll see," Wellesley said after a moment. "But only if you behave yourself."

"Yes, absolutely."

With an exasperated sigh Hunt turned from the terminal toward the three men who stood between him and the closest fighter.

"Is everything loaded?"

"Everything but the people," Pinchon said.

"Who wants *Merokanah*?" Hunt asked.

"I'll take him," Tselitel said, reaching for his disc when no one else spoke up.

"No!" Wellesley said decisively. "I absolutely refuse to ride with that dimwit. Let one of the others take him. I've earned a respite after all the time I've had to spend with him."

Merokanah, too scared to speak up, was for once silent.

"*I'll* take him," Milo said, walking to the terminal and reaching for the disc. Just short of it he pulled his hand back and bunched up a bit of his shirt, emulating Tselitel's example to avoid direct skin contact. "I said I'd take him," he said with a wink to Tselitel. "I didn't say I would *listen* to him. "

"Thanks, Milo," Hunt said.

"Anytime, brother," Milo replied, walking to Pinchon and Gromyko.

"So I guess these two guys are coming with me?" the pirate asked.

"Uh huh. Take your bird out first. I'll be right behind you."

"Alright," Pinchon nodded, making for the fighter.

"See you out there, you two!" Gromyko said, turning to follow.

"Sure, forget all about me," Wellesley said sarcastically.

"How could I?" the smuggler teased over his shoulder. "You're never silent for more than two minutes at a time!"

"Bah!" exclaimed Wellesley.

"I just realized something," Tselitel said with concern. "If we're taking *Merokanah* with us, who's going to open the hangar doors?"

"You're absolutely right, Lily," the AI replied. "I guess we'll just have to leave him here."

"Wells…" Hunt said in a mild tone of warning.

"I *suppose* I can program them to open on their own," he replied. "Just give me a sec…Done. Alright, you've got five minutes to get strapped in and fired up. *Did you hear that, Colonel?*" he asked in a louder voice.

"Got it," the pirate called from halfway down the hangar.

Pulling Wellesley from the system, Hunt walked with Tselitel to the fighter. Helping her up onto the wing, he watched her climb into the seat directly behind the pilot's and get strapped in.

"All set?" he asked, slipping a pair of fingers under the harness and giving it a gentle tug.

"I think so," she replied, looking it over quickly before looking up at him. "I think I'm the only one thin enough to fit in these things comfortably!"

"You're right," Hunt agreed, reaching into the seat behind her and pulling out a helmet. "Did you forget this?"

"But think of what it'll do to my *hair!*" she said in a humorously whiny tone as he slid it onto her skull. Reaching up, she centered it on her head, pulling the chin strap tight. "It does absolutely *nothing* for my eyes, either," she said, looking up and crossing them at him.

"I'm afraid we all have to make sacrifices on this trip," he replied, bending down and kissing the tip of her nose.

"There's a slot for AIs on the right hand side," Wellesley said as he dropped into the pilot's seat. "Hook me up and I'll help you out."

"Wait, can you fly this thing?" he asked, his hopes soaring at the possibility.

"No. *Kol-Prockian* smart AIs were strictly forbidden from directly piloting military craft after the *Balla'Trovian* incident. The fighter's computer systems would need a complete rewrite to enable it."

"So, you could conduct the logistical work for a civil war, but you couldn't fly a ship?"

"What can I say? *Kol-Prockian* politics were complex and, at times, insensible."

"So just what *can* you do?" he asked as he slid his helmet on.

"I can scream if it looks like we're about to crash," the AI offered.

"How helpful," Hunt replied, taking the medallion and slipping it into the aforementioned slot. "How's that?"

"The infrastructure is a little cramped compared to the base's," Wellesley said. "But at least I don't have to share it. A room of one's own, and all that."

"How much longer do we have?" Hunt asked.

"About three minutes. You'd better get the engines fired up."

"In a space this tight? Shouldn't I wait until the doors are open to vent some of the exhaust?"

"No, this ship is very advanced. The onboard computer will automatically detect our limited room to work and cut the engines' output accordingly. They won't thrust big time until we're ready to move."

"'Big time?'"

"Just speaking in language my audience will understand."

"Hey!" Tselitel objected from the backseat.

"Just kidding."

"Can you read me, Hunt?" Pinchon's voice crackled over the radio.

"Loud and clear, Colonel."

"Good. Wanted to make sure that was working before we took off. Remember, those dogs are gonna be on top of us almost as soon as we leave the base. Stick close to me, and I'll keep 'em off the both of us until we can warp. Have you got the Black Hole punched into your navigational computer?"

"Yes," Wellesley replied, having just plotted their course.

"Good. Now, if by some chance you get there first, *don't* try to land without me. Hopefully old Ivo will remember that time I busted him out of imperial custody and won't have us blasted out of the sky."

"What?" they heard Milo ask over the radio. "You never said anything about getting shot at!"

"It's pretty obvious, isn't it?" asked Pinchon rhetorically. "The place is one of the Black Fang's most secret hideouts. Do you think it's stayed off the imperial radar because we let every wandering fighter land there? The policy has always been to shoot on sight."

"Don't you think that stealing one of their freighters just *might* have turned them off to you in the meantime?" Gromyko asked, flabbergasted by what he heard. "There's nothing a pirate hates more than someone who steals from him."

"Naturally," Pinchon replied easily. "But we don't have any choice. Besides, communications have probably been jumbled by the war. It could be that they don't even know about the freighter."

"You don't believe that," Milo said.

"No, but it's possible. And, like I said, Ivo owes me a favor. We should be fine."

"'*We should be fine*,'" they could hear Milo mutter sarcastically before the radio was switched off.

"Just about go time," Hunt said, glancing over his shoulder. "Not too late to change ships, if you want."

"Nope, you're stuck with me," she replied.

Smiling, he lowered the canopy and started the

engines. Quietly they hummed to life.

"All systems are green," Wellesley said. "Doors open in thirty seconds."

Settling himself into his seat, he looked at Pinchon in the other craft. The latter flashed him the OK sign, and then looked straight ahead, watching the doors. A tremendous rumbling sound suddenly surrounded them, reverberating off the walls.

"What's that?" Tselitel asked.

"It's the doors," Hunt said.

"But they're not opening," she replied, leaning to one side to see around Hunt's seat.

"Give them a sec," Wellesley said. "This machinery hasn't been used in ages. It's gonna grind a little."

Moments later a narrow line of yellow appeared between the doors – the stark rays of the setting sun bursting through the opening that was forming.

"Stay right on my tail," Pinchon radioed, pushing the craft into a hovering position just above the hangar floor. Like a hummingbird it swayed slightly in place, the expert hand of its pilot gently testing the controls in the few seconds of safety he possessed before bolting into hostile airspace. Deftly he moved the fighter into the hollow space adjacent to the hangar and then floated upward into open air.

"Our turn," Wellesley said.

Cautiously Hunt laid his hands on the controls and began raising the craft. Unable to find the sweet spot as Pinchon had, the ship slowly floated toward the ceiling.

"Okay, okay, okay," the AI said, the urgency in his voice growing with each repetition. The fighter continued rising slowly until Hunt found the midpoint in the elevation controls and more or less held it in place. "We're too high," Wellesley said. "We'll shear off the cockpit if we fly out this high."

"I know that," Hunt replied, his palms beginning to sweat. Pushing the controls down, he brought it within a couple feet of the floor.

"Alright, that's good," Wellesley said. "Now just–."

"Can it, Wells," Hunt snapped, pushing the controls forward until the ship floated uneasily inside the subterranean nook. Moving the elevation control forward, the ship emerged from the ground and hovered. "Where are you, Colonel?" he asked, scanning the transparent dome that covered the cockpit.

"Up there," Tselitel said, pointing toward nine o'clock high.

Trying to rotate the craft, he oversteered and spun it around toward the hangar. Grinding his teeth, he carefully turned it back and pointed it upward. Then he pushed the controls forward again, moving it toward the pirate's vessel.

"You're gonna have to move faster than that," Pinchon said as they approached his ship. "The Devourers aren't gonna play this out in slow motion."

"I'll have a handle on it in time," Hunt said in a slight growl. He was already painfully aware of his own ineptitude with the craft and didn't need reminders.

"Let's hope you won't need it," the pirate replied. "I'm not reading any of them on the scope. Could be they're checking out another part of the planet."

"Yeah, hopefully the other side of it," Milo chimed in.

"Come on," Pinchon said, flying past Hunt towards orbit.

"Alright, cowboy," Hunt said, swinging the ship around more precisely than before and taking off after him.

"A pair of Devourer craft just popped up from the south," Wellesley said moments later as he watched the radar. "They must have been on the ground when we took off."

"ETA?" Hunt asked.

"Oh, about thirty seconds," the AI replied.

"Get up here *now*, Hunt," Pinchon ordered.

Pushing the ship to the max, Hunt quickly reached the

pirate's craft and fell in alongside it.

"Alright, we're gonna have to–."

"Rex, look out!" Wellesley said, just as a trio of Devourer blobs shot past his wing from above. "There are three of 'em above us!"

"Evasive maneuvers!" Pinchon barked, rolling his ship off to the left while Hunt peeled away to the right. "Don't try to engage 'em, Hunt! Just get into space and warp to the Black Hole!"

"I'm not leaving you here," Hunt said, swinging the ship around and falling onto the colonel's tail just as the latter opened fire on one of their assailants. A burst of plasma shot from the fighter's wings, searing holes in his target. Instantly smoke began to pour from the craft and it quickly lost altitude.

"Must have hit the engine," Pinchon uttered as he swung onto another target.

Following his example, Hunt broke from his tail and tried to engage. But the alien pilots were too deft for his nascent skills.

"Stop playing fighter ace and get out of here!" the pirate said over the radio. "I'm not hanging around here for the fun of it! I'm buying you time to warp! Now *go!*"

Without another word Hunt ended his pursuit and climbed toward space as quickly as the craft could manage.

"Two of 'em are on you, Rex!" Milo said over the radio, watching helplessly from the backseat of his craft. "Look out, they're gaining!"

A sudden intuition caused him to toss the craft into a wide corkscrew roll to the right. Bright green globs flew past the ship in a long stream, the Devourers barely missing their nimble target.

"Summersault now!" Wellesley barked.

Instantly Hunt obeyed, jerking the controls back and swinging up and over his assailants. As he did this another pair of alien vessels attempted to strafe him from above, casting blobs toward their comrades and causing them to scatter to avoid being hit.

"How many of these guys are in orbit?" Tselitel asked, craning her neck and seeing over a half dozen more pairs on the way.

"Get up here, Colonel," Wellesley said sternly. "They're all over us. You're not doing any good down there."

"Roger," the pirate said, just as he sent another craft screaming toward the ground. "What's the situation?"

"At least sixteen of them," Wellesley said, as Hunt barrel rolled to the left, avoiding another burst of green death. "All we can do now is run."

"I agree," Pinchon said, rocketing past Hunt's craft. "You're over-maneuvering, Hunt! It's eating your speed! Just flick it back and forth and climb, man, climb! Our only hope lies in warping!"

"Look out, Colonel!" the AI radioed, as another group of fingers ascended out of the setting sun and unleashed a flat sheet of green balls.

Shoving the craft's nose downward just before they reached him, he slipped underneath the sheet and gathered momentum. The instant the balls had passed over he drew back on the stick, rocketing upward.

"I count thirty-two," Wellesley said, as Hunt dodged more fire from behind.

"Where are they all *coming* from?" growled Pinchon, looking all around the cockpit's canopy. A wide screen of little dark dots were visible descending into *Preleteth's* atmosphere ahead of his craft. Squinting, he could just make out their outline as innumerable green balls appeared in front of them. Roaring down from orbit, their velocity incredible, they were on top of him before he knew what was happening. Reflexively he twisted the ship's wings vertical, just slipping between the blobs and fighters.

"I count one hundred and fifty-eight," the AI said, as Pinchon's ship disappeared into the angry cloud of attackers.

Bursting out the other side, he spun as a horde of them got onto his tail and spewed their lethal load, lighting up the evening sky.

A trio of vessels were chasing Hunt as he reached orbit. Looking frantically for the colonel's ship, he could see it striving to reach space but forced down again and again by incoming sheets of enemy fire. He was about to radio when a ball shot just over his wing and singed the paint.

"Pay attention, Rex!" Wellesley ordered. "Pinchon has to take care of himself."

"He can't! Not against odds like *that*," he said, twisting the ship as another pair of blobs sailed past.

"Then you can't be any good to him," the AI said pointedly. "I'm warming up the warp drive now." A dot appeared on Hunt's HUD. "Fly toward the waypoint."

"Pinchon?" Hunt asked, maneuvering the ship by degrees toward the dot, trying not to give his pursuers a predictable target.

"I've got dozens of 'em on me," the colonel said through gritted teeth. "Just get out of here! I'll be right behi–."

The instant he was cut off Hunt jerked his head around and saw a blob scrape along the nose of Pinchon's ship.

"Colonel? Colonel?" Hunt asked urgently.

"There's no time," Wellesley said. "The warp drive is ready. Go now!"

Reluctantly Hunt pressed the glowing red button on the panel before him. Instantly a small green rift was torn in space before him, swallowing the ship and closing the moment it was through.

"What happened?" Tselitel asked, fruitlessly twisting her neck to try and see the colonel's ship. But all her eyes beheld was a brilliant shaft of green light. "Did they make it?"

"He was trying to reach space when we warped," Wellesley said. "I don't see how they can make it."

"No!" she cried out in horror. "We can't lose the three

of them! Not all at once!"

"There were dozens of craft on them," the AI said. "Their chances are next to nil."

"If anyone could have made it out of there, Pinchon could have," Hunt reassured her, aware that she was about to start crumbling. "That last shot just took out his radio, is all. We'll probably see them at the Black Hole."

"Probably?" she asked.

"There are no guarantees in war," Wellesley said candidly.

"I understand," she said quietly, suddenly feeling cold. Wrapping her arms around herself she leaned back in her seat, feeling a grim shadow fall over her. Closing her eyes, she saw the three men back in the hangar right before they left. She saw Gromyko swaggering to the craft, Milo right behind him with *Merokanah* held in a fold of his shirt. And she saw the colonel: calm, quiet, ready to get his craft into the air.

None of them had suspected that within a half dozen minutes they'd be clawed out of the sky by an implacable horde.

"You can take your harness off, if you want," Hunt said, hoping to make her a little more comfortable. "Lily?"

"I heard," she said without energy, reaching up with her left hand and unclicking the straps that were stretched tightly over her chest. Automatically they withdrew into the ship.

She felt her mind going numb as the realization of their loss truly started sinking in. She wanted to cry, but no tears would flow. Her emotions frozen, she twisted in her seat to look back, as though to see them one last time. Over the glow of the fighter's right engine she saw the spiraling tunnel of light reach back into infinity. She was about to turn forward once more when a blinding white flash erupted before her eyes, making her shriek.

"What was that?" Hunt asked, twisting in his seat just as an object blazed over their heads and shot off down the tunnel. "Are we under attack?"

"I don't think so," Wellesley replied.

"Did you identify what it was?"

"Negative. But we'll know in a moment."

"Why?" Tselitel asked urgently, gripping the shoulders of Hunt's seat and peering around it.

"Because it's slowing down," the AI replied. "And it's doing it real fast. We ought to know in just a second..."

The object cut velocity so sharply that it shot past them going the opposite way, a tan blur in a tunnel of green. Quickly it caught up and fell in alongside them. It was the other fighter.

"I don't believe it!" Wellesley exclaimed, stunned at what he saw. "But how could..." he began to ask, as the ship flipped over and three gesticulating men became visible.

Gromyko and Milo were waving their arms wildly, mutely shouting at them through the void of space. Only Pinchon kept his head, gesturing exaggeratedly to get their attention. After several moments of trying to make himself understood, he twisted around and barked at his two passengers. Once they'd settled down he looked back at Hunt's craft. He pointed to the microphone that was attached to his helmet and then raised his two hands in front of him, making a gesture as though he was breaking an invisible stick.

"Radio's broken," Hunt mumbled, nodding to the colonel.

"There's a backup," Wellesley said. "I just hope that numbskull *Merokanah* has the sense to mention it."

"I'll try to tell him," Hunt replied. Pointing to his own mic, he held up two fingers. One he pretended to break, while the other he pointed at. Slowly Pinchon nodded.

"I think he gets it," Hunt said.

The pirate looked around the dashboard, trying to figure out which button would activate the secondary radio. Being unable to read *Kol-Prockian*, eventually he looked back toward Hunt and threw up his hands.

Drawing Wellesley from his slot momentarily, he held him up and then pointed at Pinchon. The pirate rolled his eyes and then nodded, twisting to look at Milo as Hunt reinstalled his friend.

"Boy, he's in for a treat," Wellesley said dryly.

For nearly ten minutes they watched Pinchon shout inaudibly at the AI. The other two chimed in occasionally. But the increasingly red faced pirate eventually silenced them as he bellowed at the hapless construct. Finally he nodded exaggeratedly, seeming to say thank you as he began slamming keys on his panel.

"Can...hear me?" his voice crackled over the radio.

"Yes!" Hunt and Tselitel exclaimed at once. She patted his shoulder eagerly, signaling for him to speak. "Yes, we hear you. What happened?"

"I don't...There was at least...All of a–."

"Colonel, your reception is poor," Hunt cut in. "We're only getting bits and pieces."

"Under...," he replied, making the OK sign again and nodding. "...ust be damaged. I can hear you...."

"Guess our curiosity will have to wait," Wellesley said, as Pinchon flipped a switch on his panel and pulled off his helmet. Unexpectedly he jerked *Merokanah* from his slot and tossed him violently over his shoulder, nearly striking Gromyko in the face. The smuggler began shouting at him, and the two quickly fell into an argument. "Now he knows how *I* felt talking to that imbecile," the AI added. "I think they're gonna have a long flight."

"At least we won't," Hunt said, patting the loving hand that still rested on his shoulder. He repeated the words silently, mouthing them musingly. Suddenly his eyes shot open. "Wells, can you read lips?"

"I don't know. I've never tried."

"Has *Allokanah* finally found something beyond his capacities?" Tselitel teased good-naturedly. "Well, besides making breakfast?"

"You promised you'd never tell!" he laughed, glad that the burden of surviving had passed from their shoulders for at least the next day and a half. "But seriously, I've never thought of trying. I don't see any reason why I couldn't. Why do you–," he began. "Oh!"

"Uh huh," Hunt nodded, activating his radio.

"Colonel? Colonel?" he asked, watching as all three men in the other craft argued vehemently with each other. "Colonel!" he shouted, but to no avail.

"He must have switched off the backup," Wellesley said. "Get his attention."

Hunt waved, first with one hand and then with both. When that failed he began flailing his arms above his head. But it was no use.

"I know how to get his attention," Tselitel said, raising her arms over her head and starting to pull her bright blue shirt off.

"Lily!" exclaimed Hunt in surprise, his eyes wide with horror as her shirt climbed inexorably up her body.

"What?" she asked, pulling the shirt over her head and revealing a light beige tank top underneath. "Oh, Rex! You didn't–," she began, her words interrupted by joyous laughter. "Oh, Rex: what kind of girl do you think I am?"

"It's been a long day, babe," he replied, shaking his head as she tossed him her shirt.

"There. That's the only colorful thing in this whole ship. If you wag it around they can't possibly miss it."

Sure enough, within a few moments of waving it back and forth it caught Gromyko's eye. The smuggler managed to silence his companions momentarily and gestured for them to look at the other vessel. When Hunt made sign for Pinchon to turn the backup back on he did so.

"Colonel, I know you can hear me, so just listen. Wellesley is going to read your lips. Just look up here and tell us slowly what happened. I'll respond through the radio."

The pirate nodded.

"I'd crack my knuckles if I had any," Wellesley said. "I make no promises about the results of this experiment."

"Don't worry about it," Hunt said. Then, looking at Pinchon, "Okay, Colonel: shoot."

"*We were under attack,*" Wellesley said slowly, speaking with slight pauses between each word, "*when suddenly a loud tumble–rumble,*" he said, catching himself, "*erupted. The fighters pulled back, and we managed to climb out of the atmosphere and into space. We were about to jump when we were thrown into warp.*"

"Thrown?" asked Hunt.

"*Yes. Just before I engaged the warp drive we left normal space. Judging by our last experience warping near Preleteth, I think the old rock must have given us a little kick. It is probably what caused the rumble and drew off the fighters. Though I can't imagine how.*"

Hunt nodded to himself for a few moments, digesting what he'd heard before speaking.

"Is your ship alright? Can you make it to the Black Hole?"

"*I should think so,*" the pirate replied through Wellesley. "*We suffered only minor damage besides that done to the radio. All other systems are green. I think Wellesley is amazing, by the way.*"

"You added that last part," Hunt said.

"What makes you say that?" the AI asked.

"His lips weren't moving," he smiled.

"Foiled again," Wellesley said, making Tselitel chuckle.

"Alright, Colonel, thank you," Hunt said into the radio. "You can go back to your argument now."

He saw the pirate's eyes narrow as he uttered something.

"You want me to relay what he said?" Wellesley asked.

"Don't bother," Hunt said, pulling off his helmet and

putting it down by his feet. "I've had enough of that pirate for one day." Picking Tselitel's shirt off of his lap, he tossed it back to her. "You can put that back on now if you want."

"Are you sure you want me to?" she asked playfully, tossing the balled up shirt back and forth between her hands for a moment.

"Yeah, pretty sure," he replied blandly, depleted from the battle. It hadn't escaped his notice that her beauty increased as her clothing diminished. But he was unable to get excited about anything after the narrow escape they'd had. There was a heaviness hanging over him, almost a sense of depression. Something felt wrong, out of place. The battle didn't feel right somehow.

"Okay," Tselitel said quietly, a touch of disappointment in her voice as she slipped the shirt over her head.

The thought that he'd hurt her feelings idly floated through his mind, but he was incapable of being stirred by it. Leaning back in his seat, he placed his right elbow on the armrest and pressed his index knuckle against his nose, working it back and forth as he thought.

"Something's wrong," he mused almost inaudibly, shifting his head side-to-side slowly. "Something isn't right."

"I hope those guys put the food somewhere we can reach it," Tselitel said after a few minutes to break the silence. "I'm getting hungry."

"There's a compartment under your seat," Wellesley chimed in. "Some of it should be there."

"Yup, you're right," she replied in a tone that strove to be bright. "Good. I'd hate to fly forty hours without something to eat!"

She was just making conversation, Hunt knew. There was a strain in her voice that she fought to hide. But he'd known her long enough to notice.

"Lily?" he asked finally.

"Hm?" she returned, half an emergency ration bar in

her mouth.

"What's wrong?"

"I was hoping you'd tell me," she said in a frank tone.

"Look, I know you were just having fun," he began.

"No, it's not that," she said quickly, not wishing the conversation to get off course. "Something is troubling you. I can feel it. What's the matter, darling?"

"I don't know," he replied, shaking his head and looking up at the green tunnel as it shot past. His mind returned to the battle, to the sight of over a hundred fighters all around them. Like a cloud of locusts they filled the air. "Why did only a few of them chase me?" he asked suddenly.

"What do you mean?" she queried.

"Wellesley counted over a hundred enemy craft. And yet we only had a few of them on us. Why the kid gloves? Why weren't they hounding us like they were Pinchon?"

"I don't know," she said. "Luck, maybe?"

"No, it was deliberate," he said with growing certainty. "And another thing: why didn't they shoot us down? I wasn't flying half as well as the colonel, and yet we got away practically unscathed while he took damage. We should have caught one of those blobs right in the cockpit and exploded."

"He had a lot more of them on him, Rex," the AI replied. "The real miracle is that he got away with only that much damage."

"I don't agree. The way they flew – there was a *tepidness* about it, like they were uncertain. Now that I think of it, at least twice I saw craft coming at me that didn't fire. I must have been right in their sights, yet they didn't shoot."

"Probably afraid of hitting the guys behind us."

"No, I had just come off a turn the second time. Their ships couldn't have been right behind me."

"What are you driving at?" the AI asked.

"I think they were told to keep their distance," Hunt said. "They were ordered to leave us alone. I felt it at the time, but couldn't make rational sense of it. That's why they piled on Pinchon."

"That doesn't make sense, Rex," Wellesley replied. "The Devourers have no reason to want you alive. Quite the contrary, in fact. I think you must just be having a hard time accepting that you actually got us out of there. You know, rookie pilot and all. You can't believe we managed to survive."

"No, it's not that," he said firmly.

"Look, if they wanted us alive, then why did they fire on us?"

"Probably just poor discipline on their part."

"That's too thin," the AI replied.

"Say what you want, Wells. But I saw it with my own eyes. Those fighters treated us like royalty. Something stinks about the whole business."

◆ ◆ ◆

"It's time to wake up, Elasha," Rede said quietly, gently rubbing her shoulder with his hand.

"What?" she asked groggily, her eyes fluttering open as she ascended out of a dream. "Oh, Conan. Is it time to go already?"

"Uh huh," he nodded, squatting beside her. "I think it's getting set to rain."

"Oh, that's not good!" she said urgently, sitting up and getting to her feet as quickly as she could. "We have to move now, boys. Right now!"

"What's wrong?" Halshan asked. Plessi stood a few feet behind him, leaning against a tree with his arms crossed skeptically over his chest.

"Rain angers the Master of the Forest," she said in a fretful voice, bending over and grabbing her walking stick. "Angers him badly. There's no time to stand and talk. Pick up your things, and let's be on our way."

"Elasha," Rede began, after they'd been walking for a few minutes. "Why does rain anger him?"

"It's a reminder of his past life," she said, the walking stick being inserted and removed from the ground with much greater rapidity than the day before. "I cannot say more than that. Should he hear me…" her voice trailed as her old eyes searched the forest around her. "No, you'll have to be content with that. Even now I can feel his spirit close at hand."

"He's a spirit?" Halshan asked nervously, the hand on his rifle stock unconsciously squeezing it a little tighter.

"Don't ask any more questions about him," she said sternly. "I've already said far more than I should have."

"Yes, Ma'am," the corporal said, unconsciously slipping into the military frame that Elasha had previously nixed. Rede noticed but said nothing, his curiosity about the Master of the Forest absorbing all his interest. He could feel words forming on the tip of his tongue as a thousand questions darted through his mind. Where did the Master come from? How old was he? Why was he a danger to them? Was he a friend of the planet, or an unwelcome, yet tolerated, houseguest? Only a long habit of listening more than he spoke kept his mouth shut. Otherwise, he was certain, he couldn't have helped embarrassing himself by barraging her with a flood of questions she mustn't answer, for her sake as well as theirs. Instead he determined to snap up every little comment she made in order to put together a picture of the Master for himself. He had been destined for a job in naval intelligence before his high marks at the academy won him a spot on the emperor's personal guard, a much coveted position that carried with it immense prestige. What better way to prepare for his post-guard role, he thought, than to set his attentive mind to work figuring out what the Master of the Forest was like?

Drawn from his reverie by a muttered comment by Plessi, he turned to face the disgruntled sergeant just as a massive drop of rain fell through the branches above and struck his nose.

"We'd better hope that the storm is brief," Elasha said, hastening her pace as thunder rumbled overhead. "Or his mood is going to be terrible by nightfall."

All throughout the day the rain came down, soaking them as they ambled through the forest. Gradually the soft soil under their feet turned to sloppy mud that splashed as they walked. The old mystic's walking stick gradually became useless, sinking far into the mushy ground whenever she put any weight on it and fighting her as she tried to pull it out. Her shoes began to stick in the muck, and twice she nearly fell over as she lost her balance. Seeing this, Halshan picked up his pace until he was right beside her.

"Let me help you," he said, offering her his arm.

"Oh, thank you," she said, about to take it when Plessi grabbed his jacket and pulled him back.

"No, let me do it," he said grudgingly, taking the thin corporal's place. "You'll both end up in the mud that way."

"Would you really mind if I fell in the mud?" she chuckled, taking his arm and squeezing it. "You're quite a stocky one, aren't you."

"I take care of myself," he replied gruffly, being by far the strongest of the three. "I just want to show you that normal folks like me aren't afraid of you."

"I never imagined that you were," she said, drawing on the young man's arm as she pulled her foot out of a particularly sticky well of mud. "Why would you be afraid of me?"

"Folks usually are, aren't they?"

"Some are," she replied. Giving up on her walking stick, she grasped it around the middle and carried it beside her. "And some aren't. You're not the type to let fear dominate you."

"Look, I didn't say I wanted to *talk* with you," he said.

"As you wish," she replied calmly.

Rede kicked himself for not offering his arm first. *He* wouldn't have given up his place to the testy sergeant, like Halshan had. But it was too late for that now. A bolt of lighting shot through the sky, illuminating the forest below and reminding the lieutenant how dark it had gotten. Night couldn't be more than an hour away, probably less.

"We need to find some cover for the night," he said. "Somewhere we'll go unnoticed."

"There's no such place in the entire forest," Elasha said between breaths, the muddy ground exhausting her. "You wouldn't expect to hide under someone's dining room table and go unnoticed, would you?" She paused and looked carefully around them, her sharp ears easily discriminating between raindrops and the unseen footfalls of stealthy animals. "No, dear Conan, there's no disappearing from the Master of the Forest. We can only stay one step ahead of him. I'm afraid we'll have to press on through the night."

"But you–," he began, correcting himself. "We can't walk all day *and* all night."

"You boys can," she smiled. "And I'll do my best to keep up. I'm afraid there's nothing for it. We *can't* stop."

"And just what is so blasted important about this little suicide run of ours?" asked Plessi. "What are we looking for?"

"I'm afraid I can't tell you that," Elasha said. "But perhaps when we–."

Her words were stopped by a deep rumble that seemed to come from the trees around them. Instantly Rede's eyes went to the sky, his logical mind seizing upon the only rational explanation despite the testimony of his own ears. For several moments he stared upward, the heavy rain falling on his face and blurring his vision. Lowering his gaze, he wiped his eyes and looked to Elasha just as the rumble sounded a second time.

"*Elasha*," Rede heard in the midst of the rumble, as though spoken by a vast, breathy voice.

"Let's get moving," she said with urgency, pulling

Plessi into motion, for he too was struck by the voice. Reluctantly he moved a few steps and then stopped, still looking around him. The others had only moved a pace or two. "Boys, if you want to be killed, stay where you are now. Otherwise you'd better hurry!"

"What–what *was* that?" Halshan asked, finally shaking off his amazement and falling in behind her and Plessi.

"Fewer questions, more walking," was all Elasha said, determinedly striding forward with all the strength her old bones could muster. "I never thought he was that close," she muttered unconsciously, not meaning for her companions to hear.

Elasha moved with strident urgency. But another hour in the mud was all it took to drain the rest of her strength. By this time it was dark, the only illumination provided by the lights her escorts carried.

"I–I can't go on," she said breathlessly, lowering herself to a log with the help of Plessi's arm.

"Then we'll carry you," Rede said valiantly. "Sergeant, take her left arm. I'll get under her right."

"No, it's no good, boys," she said, waving her hand to stop them. "Don't think I can't see how tired you are. Walking all through the night with an old woman suspended between you is more than you can bear. You have to leave me. Press forward until daylight, then double back and hightail it to the imperial retreat. Don't come back for me."

"We're not leaving you here," Plessi said stoutly.

"I should have thought you'd be the first one to want to leave me," she said, looking up at the sergeant as he leaned over her, his foot resting upon the log on which she sat.

"I don't like you," Plessi said flatly. "It doesn't mean I want you *dead*."

"You're right," she nodded, swallowing to clear her dry throat. "I'm sorry. That was unfair of me."

"*Elasha…*" the voice said again, this time in a haunting

whisper.

"He's getting close," she said, her hand going to her throat, her fingers twitching nervously. "Terribly close."

The sound of a stick snapping twenty yards down their backtrail made them all jump, their lights shooting to the source of the noise.

"Go now," she ordered them, putting her hands on Plessi's knee and trying to shove him off the log. "Go!"

"No dice," the truculent sergeant said, his foot not moving an inch. Twisting where he leaned, he drew his pistol and held it against his straight leg. "We'll meet this Master of the Forest together."

"*Elasha,*" the voice said in an insinuating, singsong manner. "*Who are these who would defy me?*"

"They're just boys," she said pleadingly. "Let them go! They don't mean you any harm!"

"*You lie, Elasha,*" the Master replied. "*They would harm me if they could. Yet I am beyond them, as I am beyond all pain and death. Their weapons cannot harm me.*"

As the voice said this their weapons flew from their hands, falling softly into the mud twenty feet away. The lights still in their hands, the young men darted them all around the forest but saw nothing save falling rain.

"*Do you think I am visible, like one of you?*" the Master asked.

"It was worth a try," Plessi said gamely, the only one of the three of them who could still move his tongue.

"*Don't be tart with me, boy!*" the voice hissed, sending a shiver through them all. "*I could break each of you instantly, if I so wished.*" At this Elasha began to levitate. Stifling a whimper, she clamped her hand over her mouth as tears of terror began to gather in her eyes. "*She knows what I am capable of,*" the Master said, swinging her back and forth above them.

"She is an old woman, weak and frail," Plessi said in a loud voice. "Perhaps you'd like to try your tricks on someone a little stronger!"

"*Are you volunteering, young one?*" the Master asked in a breathy voice, slowly setting down the aged mystic.

"Yes."

"*Such courageous stupidity,*" the Master said, flicking Plessi on the head and sending him tumbling over the log. Instantly the sergeant was on his feet again, vaulting over the log and standing tall. "*You have a great deal of...spunk, for your kind,*" the voice said. "*Humans usually crumble before me. What is your name?*"

"Sergeant Algar C. Plessi," he replied defiantly, blood spilling out of a wound on his forehead and running down his nose and cheek in a narrow stream.

"*Sergeant Algar C. Plessi,*" the voice repeated musingly, as though weighing the words with its tongue. "*And tell me, Sergeant Algar C. Plessi, why is it that you do not fear me?*"

"Because any being deserving of either fear or respect would not limit itself to haunting a forest," Plessi said scornfully. Instantly a blow to the stomach doubled him over. With a groan he dropped to his rear.

"*I am no mere 'being' as you would have it!*" the Master roared. "*I am the unity! The binding of flesh and spirit!*"

"A petty despot," Plessi wheezed, struggling to his feet. "A scourge to weary travelers, nothing more!"

"*Miserable upstart!*" the Master said, plucking Plessi from where he stood and casting him against a tree.

"No!" screamed Elasha, as she watched him fall to the ground and struggle to get up.

"*Your entreaties will do him no good!*" the Master taunted. "*Nor will it save the others from their fate!*"

"Murder is not fate," Plessi retorted, getting to his feet. "You claim superiority. But you're nothing more than a cowering criminal! An invisible highwayman who preys on those weaker than himself!"

"*It is the price of entering my domain!*" exclaimed the voice. "*There is no mercy for those who violate* my *dominion!*"

THE BEAST EMERGES

"In that case," Plessi said, plucking an orb from his pocket and dropping it on the ground, "I think it's time our discussion came to an end." Instantly the orb exploded with brilliant orange light that blinded the four humans. The Master howled with agony as he was paralyzed by the light and his true form was revealed. Standing before them like a dark shadow was a massive *kal*, though even in the light of the orb it was barely materialized. It hovered on the fringe of mind and body.

"*No! Release me!*" it said in a desperate growl, trying to move but unable to.

"We've long sought an encounter with you, *Master*," Plessi said, stepping closer to the beast but careful not to obscure the light. "We're certain that you have many secrets that you could unfold to us."

"*I will say nothing to your kind!*" the kal spat. "*I have not lived these many years to act as a teacher to the Earthborn. You will have to kill me!*"

"As you like," Plessi said, reaching into his coat and drawing a dagger whose blade was darker than death.

"What is that?" Elasha asked, though she already knew the answer. She was merely surprised to see one in the possession of the truculent sergeant.

"This," Plessi said, expertly twirling the weapon in his hand, "is what they call a Midnight Blade. Recognize it?" he asked the Master, slicing the air just ahead of its neck.

"*Why should I?*" it growled, just as its eyes fell upon a small emblem that had been etched into the base of the handle. Depicted was a serpent fleeing from a swiftly pursuing sword. "*Your name is not Plessi!*"

"No, it is not," he agreed, holding the weapon against the creature's throat. "This is your last chance, Master. Give up your secrets, or give up your life."

"*I will never tell you anyth–.*"

Before it could finish Plessi drew back the dagger and plunged it into the Master's chest. A horrified scream burst from its lips as the creature froze and then exploded into a thousand black shards. Calmly Plessi bent over and picked up the orb, switching it off and putting it back into his pocket.

"Who are you?" asked Halshan in amazement, watching as his comrade slid the dagger back into a sheath that had been sewn into the inside of his jacket.

"I think I know," Elasha said, her eyes narrowing as her retentive memory was stimulated by the emblem on the weapon. "Gustav Welter?"

"In the flesh," Plessi replied with a little bow.

"Come on, Algar," Halshan said. "What's all this about? What's with the knife and that light you've got? And how did you know that creature?"

"As Elasha has said, my name isn't Algar," Welter corrected. "I am Gustav Welter, son of Florianus Welter." Stabbing a finger at the pile of black bits that lay on the muddy ground a few feet away, he added, "That creature killed my father, who belonged to an organization dedicated to–."

"The removal of the mystical forces in our galaxy," Elasha finished for him.

"Just the bad ones," he said. "Though I must admit you've caused us doubt at times, Elasha. Your manipulation of the emperor has put you in our crosshairs more than once. As had your brother Taegen. For too long humanity has had its course chosen *for it* by beings who would lord themselves over us. It was just such beings who nearly destroyed us all a hundred thousand years ago. We don't intend to let that happen again."

"It already *is* happening," Rede countered. "The Devourers are spreading across the galaxy like a plague while you're down here settling old scores."

"I assure you, that is being seen to," Welter said with certainty. His eyes fell upon the pile of shards once more. "It's too bad we couldn't have gotten something out of that old beast. He could have shed light on a great many things."

"A *kal* never reveals its secrets," Elasha said knowingly.

"Rarely," he corrected her. "Rarely, dear Elasha."

"So that's what your beef has been with Elasha?" Halshan asked. "You don't like mystical people?"

"To say I 'don't like them' rather misrepresents the matter," Welter said, his manner seemingly changing the moment his name had. He appeared older, more poised and self-possessed than before. The moody dullness of his prior expression had vanished. His eyes were clear, crisp, and analytical. "It was the living worlds that brought this plague upon us. There have been, and always will be, those who are envious of humanity's strength and intelligence. They want to break us down, keep us weak and beneath them. Our lives are in danger now only because the other clans were obliterated by a conspiracy of the *Ahn-Wey*."

"That's not true!" exclaimed Elasha. "They would never do that to us!"

"We have the truth, Elasha," Welter said with cool certainty. "We've heard the words from their very *lips*, if you'll pardon the expression. The proof is irrefutable. Had the other clans survived – had their technological and intellectual brilliance gradually been joined with the hardiness of our people – there is no doubt that with a hundred thousand years of growth humanity would be the unassailable master of this galaxy, to say nothing of those which neighbor the Milky Way. We would have been invincible. Instead we have had to fight our way ahead, taking a step back for every two we made forward. Our progress has been slow, painful, and bought at *terrible* cost. We of the Earthborn have never been the smartest of our race – not by *any* stretch of the imagination. But we are hardy and strong, and could have provided the counterpoise our relatives needed."

"I don't have the least idea what you're talking about," Rede said, shaking his head. "Clans? Earthborn?"

"Elasha can explain it all to you later," Welter said. "My task is done here. I must return at once to the imperial retreat so that I may depart on my next mission."

"You can't leave us now," Elasha said. "Even with the Master dead the forest is still throbbing with danger. There must be other *kals*."

"Of course there are," Welter said. "But they're days from here. You have more than enough time to complete your task and return home. They'll fight amongst themselves to decide who gets to play master now that the original is gone. That'll buy you time."

"No way, Gustav," Rede said, putting a hand on his shoulder as he began to walk away. "We came in here as a team, and we're leaving as one."

"I was never a part of your team," Welter said, eyeing the hand on his shoulder which was soon removed. "I needed this little expedition to lead me to the Master, and it did. Any other dangers you encounter will be infinitely more mundane."

"So it's all been a lie?" Rede demanded. "Everything you've ever told us? All our time together protecting the emperor? You've just been playing your own game?"

"What's truth and what's fiction?" he asked. "I lived those months as you did. But I did it with a secret purpose. Does the fact of my being there cease because you learn my purpose there was different than you supposed?"

"Than you led me to believe!" snapped Rede, growing heated. "Every member of the imperial bodyguard had a single objective, for which we would have gladly surrendered our lives: serving the emperor. We pledged our lives and our honor to him every morning! That was the creed we all lived by, Gustav. How could I believe anything other than that you were sincere?"

"I was sincere," Welter said. "But my devotion was to an authority higher than the emperor himself."

"There is no higher authority than the emperor,"

Halshan said. "Be careful: you're very nearly talking treason."

"Strictly speaking, I *am* talking treason," Welter said factually. "But only against the emperor, who is the servant of humanity. It is in our collective name that he rules, and not for himself alone. The greater treason would be to ignore this fact, and pretend that humanity exists to serve *him*, and not the other way around." Walking to where the Master had deposited his pistol, he plucked it out of the mud and did his best to wipe it off.

"Then you're determined to go?" Elasha asked.

"I am," he nodded, sliding the pistol back into its holster.

"Just one question," Halshan said. "How did that creature take our guns and lift Elasha up into the air? To say nothing of how it kicked you around? It assaulted us like some kind of wind spirit. And yet, with the light on it, it was more or less corporeal."

"It was both," Welter said. "When it first came upon us it was all but mind, intellect. The faintest trace of its physicality was still present, however, and the exposure to the light emphasized it, drawing it into its physical form and rendering it destroyable." Here he tapped the dagger under his jacket. "With the right weapon, of course."

"And what about that dagger?" Halshan asked.

"You said just one question," Welter smiled. "And now I must depart. I wish you good lu–."

As the word was on his lips a shrill cry from a hundred yards away tore the air in two.

"Days away, eh, Gustav?" Elasha prodded, for the sound of another *kal* was unmistakable.

"Looks like I'll be with you all for a little bit longer," he said, ushering them forward. "Keep your lights shining all around. They're fast, and they'll seize upon any opening they find."

❖ ❖ ❖

"What in the world could those three find to argue about all this time?" Wellesley asked, watching as the trio in the other ship continued to tear at each other just ten hours short of their destination.

"Well, Antonin and Milo have never really liked Pinchon," Hunt said. "They've been stuck with him for over a day now. That'd be more than long enough to bring any latent irritations to the surface."

"You'd think they'd have the sense to hold off. This simply isn't the time or place to start chewing on each other."

"They're impulsive," Hunt replied dismissively, trying to make out from his brother's gesticulations what he was yelling about.

"Do we have to watch?" Tselitel asked in a hollow voice. Her mood had been steadily dropping ever since they'd entered warp, and the mute argument on the other side of the tunnel hadn't helped. "Could we twist the ship a little so we wouldn't have to see? Even just for a little while?"

"Well, we really shouldn't, just in case they need to tell us something."

"I can watch for that," Wellesley said. "This ship has cameras all around it to facilitate the dumb AI's operations. Go ahead and flip it over."

"Fair enough," Hunt said, gingerly taking the controls and slowly rotating the craft. Tselitel tried to look over the side of the ship, just to make sure they were really out of view. Then she sat back in her seat and sighed.

"I've just about had enough of all three of them, if I'm being honest," she said in an exasperated voice. "One minute Pinchon is cool and calm. And the next he's casting suspicious glances at you and acting secretive. Antonin hasn't been normal ever since he broke away from Wanda and the Order. And Milo's always jumping at one shadow or the next. I wish they were more like you – calm and collected."

"We can't all be perfect."

"Yes, yes that's true," she chuckled. "Though, you *could* talk a little more. We only speak when there's a problem. What happens when this is all over and we start living like normal people? Will I have to create problems just to hear your voice?"

"Most likely. Though it's hard to imagine ever living a normal life after this. Shoot, what do either of us know about normalcy, anyhow? I've lived on Delta-13 for almost as long as I can remember. Normal for me would be scraping by while living in little more than a doghouse. And you–," he began thoughtlessly, only catching himself at the last moment. "Well, you've worked a lot," he redirected.

"That's true. I've never really known anything beside work," she said, trying to play along with his dodge. But her tone betrayed her.

"I didn't mean to bring it up again," he said. "I'm sorry."

"No, it's my fault," she replied. "I started you off on thinking about the future. I guess all we can really do is take things one day at a time."

"I guess," he agreed, kicking himself nonetheless. Then his eyes brightened with an idea. "Alright, let's start right now. Get up here."

"What?" she asked.

"You heard me."

"But how can I climb up there? The seats are practically packed against the canopy."

"You're a resourceful girl, you'll find a way," he said with amusement. "Now, come on."

She drew her feet onto the seat, careful not to hit any of the handful of buttons around her by accident. Standing up and hunching over, she put her hands on his seat and began to squeeze between it and the canopy.

"A little help, please?" she asked, her stomach pressed against the shoulder of his seat, her hands too far from it to get any leverage. He chuckled at her predicament, unable to help himself. "I'm glad *one* of us is enjoying this," she strained, trying to work herself farther into his part of the cockpit but afraid to tumble forward and crash into the buttons on the panel.

"It's not that," he said, twisting in his chair and putting a knee into it, half standing. "It just reminds me of that first time I saw you sticking out of your apartment. You looked darn cute then, too."

"It didn't *feel* too cute," she replied, as he took hold of her upper half and slowly pulled her into the front of the cockpit, Hunt's strong hands righting her and drawing her into his lap. "Especially when you grabbed my tummy like you did. Sometimes I think I *still* feel the bruises you left behind."

"Let's check," he said, his arms around her as he grasped the bottom of her shirt and pulled it up. "You're looking awfully beige, dear."

"That's my *undershirt*," she said with a flirtatious roll of her eyes.

"Is *that* what it is?" he asked. "Well, let's try again." Taking the thin material between his fingers, he began working it up her stomach.

"What are you doing?" she asked with playful embarrassment, putting her hands on his as the bottom of her tank top reached her solar plexus.

"Tut tut," he said, wagging a finger in her face. "I'm examining the evidence of your claim. Now, *young lady*, you allege that you still feel bruises sometimes. And I," here he paused, carefully examining her soft, comely stomach, "can find no evidence of bruising at all. Thus I conclude that you are needlessly and viciously slandering me. I hereby sentence you to–."

"Objection, your honor!" she said.

"On what grounds?"

"On the grounds that you're acting as a medical expert, counsel for the defense, *and* the judge hearing the case. There's a clear conflict of interest."

"Ah, but I object to your objection, on the grounds that you're interested, too. Moreover, you're attempting to work your wiles within this courtroom!"

"*I*, your honor?" she asked innocently, fluttering her eyes.

"Indeed, are you not presently sitting in the judge's lap?"

"Indeed I are," she said in a dense voice.

"Don't expect any sympathy just because you can't speak properly," he said, wagging his finger again. "Your backward ways will do you no good."

"Your honor?"

"Yes?"

"Is that your hand I feel gently massaging my tummy?"

He looked down.

"No, that's the *medical expert's* hand gently massaging your tummy. He felt that there might be some invisible bruising that he'd missed, so he wanted to make sure your stomach was good and relaxed."

"How thoughtful of him.

"He's a great guy. I could give you his contact information, if you'd like."

"Mm, nah. I'd rather stay here with the judge," she said, leaning back and nestling her head against his shoulder.

"Ah, so you *admit* to working your wiles!" he said triumphantly. "Do you know how many years you could get for that?"

"Actually I don't," she purred.

"Nor do I," he said frankly. "But don't tell the defense counsel," he added in a whisper. "He's always going on about how he knows more about the law than I do. More than me, an actual judge! Can you believe it? Now, where were we?"

"You were about to throw the book at me for working my wiles."

"Oh, it's much worse than that," he said in a lecturing tone. "First, you slanderously accused me of leaving you bruised to this day, which is patently false. Secondly, you attempt to beguile the judge in front of an entire courtroom, demonstrating both that your first claim couldn't stand on its own, and also that you are deliciously bold. How do you plead?"

"Guilty."

"Don't do that! I'm having too darn much fun building the case against you! All that fun will be over in a snap if you plead guilty."

"Very well, I un-plead guilty."

"Good girl," he said, patting her stomach approvingly. "Now, let me see. Ah! Is it not true that you got *yourself* stuck in that window, and that you asked – nay, *begged* – me to help you get unstuck?"

"I have to admit that's true."

"Aha! How can you have the temerity to slander me for simply trying to help you out of a situation you got *yourself* into? How can you be so bold?"

"I guess I'm just a wicked, wicked woman, your honor," she said in a distraught tone, burying her face in his chest to escape all her wrongdoings.

"No guesses in the courtroom!" he said, banging an invisible gavel on the armrest. "I do not tolerate hearsay or guesses. Only cold, hard facts."

"Very well, I'm a factually wicked woman, your honor."

"A factually wicked woman?" he asked. "You sound like just my type. What are you doing later on today?"

"Going to jail, I suppose."

"Why would you want to go there?"

"I don't. Some nasty judge is sending me there."

"Oh, really? Anybody I'd know?"

"Yes, I think so," she said, peeking up over the folds of his shirt.

"Well, I'll have a talk with him," he said with a confidential wink. "I'm pretty sure I can get you off easy. But only if you promise not to be wicked anymore. Do you promise?"

"Uh huh."

"You'll have to do better than that," he said disapprovingly.

"I promise not to be wicked anymore," she said, separating each word with a kiss.

"Madam, why are you kissing the judge?"

"I thought I was kissing the other guy, the one who was going to talk to you about letting me go."

"I'd be nuts to let you go! Forget the other guy, you're coming with me!" he laughed, wrapping his arms around her tight as she giggled.

With a delighted smile she regarded him.

"I never knew you had such a silly side," she uttered appreciatively.

"Oh? Never?" he asked with a laugh.

"You tend to be a little more serious than this," she pointed out.

"Well, I've been under the gun practically since the moment I met you until we entered warp above *Preleteth*. There hasn't been much time for humor."

"That's true," she agreed, laying back against him and watching the green tunnel shoot past them. "Do you suppose they're still arguing in the other ship?"

"They are," Wellesley chimed in before he could respond, making her jump.

"Oh, I'd forgotten about Wellesley," she said, pulling her tank top back down over her stomach and Hunt's hand.

"There's no need for that," Hunt said. "Wells hasn't

been watching. Right, Wells?"

A long pause ensued.

"Wells?"

"Of *course* not," the AI said.

"Wellesley!" exclaimed Tselitel.

"Oh come on, it's not like you guys were necking or anything. Besides, your little courtroom drama was a lot more interesting than watching those three guys pull each other's eyes out."

"What, they're *attacking* each other now?" Hunt asked with alarm.

"Figure of speech."

"Oh. Well, how about you go back to watching them and leave me and this beguiling little thing in peace?"

"Aye aye, Captain," he said with an exasperated sigh.

"I'm honestly not that little," she said, eyeing Wellesley's medallion suspiciously for a few moments before turning toward Hunt. "After all, I'm six feet tall. Although I look smaller because I'm so thin."

"I noticed," he said, taking her wrist in his hand and wagging her skinny stick arm back and forth with a smile on his face.

"Oh, you," she said, raising her hands to his face and pressing her palms to his cheeks. "What am I going to do with you?"

"I don't know. Love me, I guess."

"That's a given," she said, kissing his lips and reclining against him. Suddenly she sat up and looked at Wellesley again. "Did you see *that*?"

"Nope."

"Ha! Then how did you know what I was talking about?"

"I didn't. I turned off the cockpit camera. But I didn't shut off my ears."

"Oh," she said, leaning back again. "Well, good."

"Yes, I thought so," he replied.

She shrugged her shoulders at Hunt and closed her eyes.

"I wish this wouldn't end," she sighed, feeling the tension flow out of her body. "There's something so, so *safe* about being in warp. It's like we're in a universe that's been set aside just for us. Well," she said with a roll of her eyes, "apart from *those guys*. But we can't hear them, so they're easy to ignore."

"Not for me," Wellesley commented.

"Stop ruining my romantic moment!" she said with playful anger, sitting up once more. "Unless you'd like to fly with them next time. I'm sure *Merokanah* would enjoy your company!"

"Don't even joke about such things," he said with a shiver.

"Well, then you should leave us alone," she said, as Hunt drew her back and wrapped his arms firmly around her middle, anchoring her against him.

"Enough talking," he said, pressing his lips to hers.

Quickly she forgot about everything except his embrace.

CHAPTER 12

"Night has passed," Welter said, looking up through the rain soaked branches as a dim glow began to filter through the clouds, heralding the dawn. "The kals are already beginning to retreat to their holes. Another half hour and you'll be safe."

"We won't be safe so long as we're in this forest," Halshan said bluntly, dropping into the mud in total exhaustion. "I thought we'd had it last night, when those creatures started chasing us."

"There were many times that you nearly had it last night," Welter said. "But *kals* are easy enough to keep at bay, provided you have a bright light with you."

"And an expert guide," Elasha added.

"These boys are smart," he replied. "They'll manage."

"Whilst carrying an old woman between them? No, I don't think so. I'm not as strong as I once was, Gustav. Truth be told, I haven't attempted a journey like this in years. At first I thought I was holding up pretty well. As a matter of fact, I *was* holding up pretty well. But then my strength failed to return even after hours of sleep. It's going to take days of solid rest to recuperate, and I can't do that out here. Logically, that means I'm going to need help, both to reach our destination and to return to the imperial retreat. Now, how can you expect these two to keep guard, watching out for *kals* and more mundane forms of wildlife, *and* carry an old goat like me? It's too much to ask, especially for boys who are so green."

"They'll have to bear up as well as they can. And so will you."

"No, Gustav," she said firmly, shaking her head. "If you leave us now we won't be coming back. You'll be signing our death warrants. And my mission is too great to risk failure."

"I am not concerned with whatever mission the emperor has sent you on."

"It wasn't the emperor it was–," she hesitated. "It was *Krancis*."

"Krancis?" he asked, his eyes broadening a little. "And just what's the purpose of your mission?"

"I can't tell you that," she said decidedly. "The ramifications are too great."

"Then I can't help you," he said. "I'll stay by you until the sun is up. Then you're on your own."

Silently he moved off toward the south to watch their backtrail. It posed the greatest threat, since the passing of their bodies would have left a distinct signature that any *kals* in the area would detect in an instant and follow should they happen across it. The chance that danger would come from the front or sides was minimal.

"That's the strangest fellow I've ever met," Halshan said confidentially to the aged mystic. "I never doubted for an instant that he was one of my peers. But now he's so different! I swear he's gained ten years in as many hours!"

"You're right, Pasco," she nodded, her eyes upon Welter's back as he leaned against a tree, a silent sentinel protecting them from the dark beings that lurked behind. "He tricked me, too. Some people have a talent for misrepresenting themselves. They can make you believe almost anything. He's much older than either of you two. Ten or fifteen years at least. That's why he speaks with such authority, such calm."

"What are we gonna do when he leaves us?" Rede

asked. "I hate to admit it, but I was scared stiff when the Master came upon us. And later on, when those creatures were after us, it was all I could do to keep from breaking and running. It was only Welter that kept me together. Something about the assurance with which he dispatched the Master told me he would see us through."

"And you weren't disappointed," she said knowingly to the young lieutenant. "I know. There's a certain kind of man that can make you believe in him no matter what you're up against. Whatever that quality is, our friend over there has it by the bucketful. I should hate to lose him for that reason alone, to say nothing of our diminished chances of survival. Oh," she added, a touch self-consciously, "I hope you boys don't feel that I was running you down before, when I said you were green."

"It's true," Halshan said honestly. "No, you were just speaking the truth. Without Welter, we're toast."

"I just hope I can convince him of that," Elasha said quietly, looking at him once more before laying back to rest on the damp ground.

"Time for me to go," Welter said quietly after an interval, jolting her out of the doze she'd fallen into. She opened her eyes to see him leaning on his knee above her. The two young men rested on either side of her, falling asleep by accident as she had. Lacking her sensitive ears, they hadn't been startled to alertness by the older man's whispered words.

"Has half an hour passed already?" she asked, sitting up with alarm and trying to piece together an argument in her head that might persuade him to stay.

"More like an hour," he replied, straightening up and looking to the east. "There shouldn't be any more storms to get in your way. Sleep during the day and make all haste at night. With luck you should be able to make it." With this he turned and began to walk away.

"Stop," she said, forcing her tired frame vertical and

taking off after him. The young men shifted in their sleep at her words, but otherwise didn't stir. "You *can't* leave us like this!"

"You're not the only one with a mission to pursue," he said, not bothering to stop as he walked.

"But my mission takes precedence over yours," she countered.

"That I doubt very much," he replied.

"Don't kid yourself. I saw the way your expression changed when I mentioned Krancis. You know that if *he* bothered to communicate with me, then it must be something important."

"I only know what I know," he replied sagely. "All you've dropped are hints and inferences. I can't delay my mission for so much as a day without a good reason." He stopped and turned to look at her, casting an eye back toward the two sleepers as he did so. "Do you think I *like* what I'm doing? I fully realize the danger you're all in. But I *can't* allow my feelings to cloud my judgment. The imperial navy is not the only element in this war that has been pressed thin by its many obligations. Three men are doing the work of one right now."

"Then how do you justify eliminating the Master?" she asked when he'd resumed movement. "Surely he didn't–."

"He threatened the *emperor!*" he exploded, his face suddenly red. "He was a danger and an insult to *every* human on this world!"

"But he wasn't an official mission, was he?" she prodded.

"Your insight serves you well," he said, nodding slowly and regaining his composure.

"That wasn't the working of insight," she said. "Just simple observation. You've already expressed the opinion that the emperor is little more than a tool for humanity, and yet you cite him as a reason to destroy the Master. That implies that you are covering up the true reason.

The emotional violence that just erupted indicates a deep personal motive. Simple arithmetic leads me to add the fact that you taunted the Master with the dagger that was about to end his life. You *wanted* him to remember who else had borne that Midnight Blade. You came along solely to avenge your father. Moreover, you did it at considerable risk to your position in the organization you belong to. They must have gone to great trouble to get you onto the imperial bodyguard – forging records, bribing officials, and so forth. To put that all at risk was a terrible gamble."

"Some gambles are worth taking," he replied quietly. "I've striven for years to destroy the Master. But somehow he always intuited my purpose and stayed away. I knew that you had a history with him, and I figured that your presence would preoccupy him so totally that he would pass right over me, which in fact he did. Honestly half of the reason I taunted him was to see if he'd finally figure out who I was. When he didn't, I decided to bring things to a head."

"Such arrogance," she said, shaking her head. "What if he had snapped you in two like a twig? He could have killed you in an instant if he so chose."

"No, I knew my target very well," he replied with complete assurance. "I knew he wouldn't kill me without having his fun first. Why do you think he lifted you into the air before us all? He wanted to show his power, to be *feared*. When I didn't cower before him it only motivated him all the more to keep me alive so he could break my *spirit*. He wanted to see me *beg*."

"And then you destroyed him, plunging that dagger into him."

"He deserved nothing less. Do you doubt that?"

"No," she shook her head slowly. "But I can't help but wonder what kind of man could pursue such a hatred for so many years with calm dedication. It seems that sooner or later he would have to abandon it or it would drive him mad. After all, your father has been gone an awfully long time."

"I'm a patient man, like my father before me. I'll wait my entire life if necessary to accomplish my object."

"And what of them?" she asked, tossing her head toward the young men. "When the *kuls* kill them, will you come to avenge their blood as well?"

"I can't trouble myself with them. Every war has casualties. They're both military men. They understand this."

"They're also human beings, forced into danger by the threat that hangs over us all. Doesn't that move you to help them? Or is human warmth and sentiment something you reserve only for your immediate circle?"

"We feed the people of our own table before seeing to the needs of our neighbors," he replied with self-evident logic. "It would be unnatural to extend the same care we give our families to those who don't belong to us."

"We're all family now – the *human* family. We cannot leave our members to die before strange threats. The *kals* that threaten them are the product of the Devourers as well, when their evil fell upon our galaxy the first time."

"No, they are the work of our so-called allies, the *Ahn-Wey*."

"Even if you are right, the *Ahn-Wey* couldn't have expelled the parasite without the psychic energy of our kin. Many *kals* still would have been produced. There is no way of knowing which is legitimate, if you'll pardon the expression, and which is not."

"That's not my concern," Welter replied. "And I can't waste time by discussing the matter any further. I must go."

"And if I told you my mission?" she asked, halting him again once he was a few steps away. "Would that make a difference?"

"It would depend on the mission," he called over his shoulder. "I would have to hear it first."

"I have no chance of succeeding without you," she said, attempting to justify her course to herself. Drawing near, she looked up into his eyes for a moment and then sighed. "What have you heard about the Omega Project?"

◆ ◆ ◆

"We're nearing our destination now," Wellesley said, breaking the long silence that had ensued ever since Tselitel had returned to her seat. Hours before they had checked in with the trio in the other craft, interrupting their argument long enough to learn that everything was fine, at least materially. Now Hunt watched them sit together in moody silence. "Approximately fifty minutes to go," the AI added.

"This tunnel is so beautiful," Tseltiel said. "Why is it a different color than the one we passed through inside the *Stella*?"

"Human and *Kol-Prockian* ships travel through different warp dimensions," the AI explained. "Some of them have different colors."

"No kidding," she said, looking around her and trying to make a mental imprint of what she saw. "I hope I never forget this. It's wonderful."

"I'm glad you like it," Wellesley said, taking a little pride in the dimensional choice of his people.

"Wells, what can we expect on the other side?" Hunt asked. "Can you give any kind of threat assessment?"

"Not really. The Black Hole is fairly large for a pirate base. It'll have a pretty healthy fighter complement to ward off curious onlookers."

"How well do their craft compare with these *Kol-Prockian* makes?"

"Not phenomenal. I'd say they weigh in at about seventy percent the capacity, though their maneuverability is awfully good. Your main advantage will be in speed and weaponry."

"Yeah, that last one isn't going to help us a whole lot. We're trying to land there, not blow it open."

"I realize that."

"Any advice in that direction?"

"Ask nicely?"

"Anything *actionable?*"

"I'd recommend following the colonel's lead," the AI said, leading Hunt to cast an eye toward the sulking pirate. "These are his people. He'll know best how to handle them."

"You mean the colonel with a broken radio and a half-functioning backup?" Hunt countered.

"I didn't say it was a *good* plan. Just the best one I had."

"Not very reassuring, buddy."

"Consolation isn't my line."

"He…Hello?" they heard crackle over the radio. "This is *Mero…ah*. I've been trying to fix the…dio by rerouting the… within the system. Can you h…me?"

"This is Hunt," he said, activating the microphone on his helmet. "I read you solidly, say ninety percent. Over."

"Really? That's m…ellous! I'm so gl–."

"This is Pinchon," the colonel said, taking over for the AI, who he unceremoniously jerked from the system and tossed to Milo. "I put that…AI onto fixing the radio. Sounds like he did a pr…good job. Over."

"I agree. What's our plan, Colonel? They're bound to swarm all over us the second we drop out of slipspace."

"I know. I'm gonna radio in who I am. With any… they'll let us land and expl…Over."

"Just be aware that your radio isn't perfect," Hunt cautioned. "You might have to repeat yourself a time or two. The occasional word drops out."

"Understood. Thanks for the heads up."

"No problem. Over and out."

"That's it?" Tselitel asked, as he slid his helmet off once more and held it in his lap.

"That's it. Now we wait and see what happens."

"I suppose it's too late to get off the bus now?" she joked.

"Just a bit."

The silence began to grow tense as the time ticked down, Wellesley noting whenever ten minutes had passed. At the twenty minute mark Hunt could hear Tselitel nervously drumming her fingers on the armrests of her chair. Glancing over his shoulder, he saw her looking out of the canopy, watching the lovely stream of green that shot by.

"You alright, babe?" he asked in a low voice.

She turned to him and smiled anxiously.

"Uh huh," she nodded. "Just a little…uptight."

She did her best to hide the shaking of her hands, not wishing to give him anything more to think about. But his sharp eyes caught their subtle trembling as she pressed them against the armrests. Extending his hand a short distance around the seat, she took his meaning and gave him both of hers. Kissing the fingers of each hand, he squeezed them momentarily.

"We'll be alright," he assured her in a whisper. "We didn't come all this way just to get shot out of the sky."

Kissing the backs of her hands, he released them and looked ahead, bracing himself for what was to come.

"Ten minutes," Wellesley announced.

Hunt put on his helmet, Tselitel following suit.

"Five minutes."

"Colonel, all systems go?" he radioed.

"Aff…tive. You?"

"Ready to rock and roll, over."

"Alright. Just stick close to…and we'll be fine. Over and out."

"Three minutes, Rex."

"Anything else you'd like to say before we jump into the fire, darling?"

"I love you more than life itself," she said with feeling, leaning forward in her seat and wrapping her arms around his, her hands just reaching his neck. "More than life itself," she repeated.

"I love you, too," he said, patting her hands. "Now get strapped in. There's no telling what we're gonna run into."

"Right," she said. Moments later he heard her harness click into place. "All set."

"Two minutes."

Hunt dried his sweaty palms on his pants and slowly reached forward to take the controls. Gripping them firmly, he closed his eyes and tried to breathe slowly.

"One minute."

This time was worse than the first time. Then he was more scared of crashing into the bunker than of what waited ahead. Having never flown before, he had been ignorant of how hard it was. But this time he *knew* how hard it was, and that he'd be flying into the teeth of some of the best pilots humanity could offer outside the navy. Everything hung on how they responded to Pinchon. If they failed to accept him, they'd have one chance in fifty of successfully bolting from the system before Black Fang railguns tore their ships to pieces.

"Thirty seconds."

He opened his eyes and glanced into the other ship. At just that moment Gromyko looked his way and winked in his confident fashion. He could have no idea of what was passing through Hunt's mind at that time, for his stony face revealed nothing. Yet this simple gesture did much to reassure him.

"Five, four, three, two, one."

Suddenly the green tunnel vanished, and the two ships dropped into normal space once more.

"This is Colonel Philip Pinchon of the Black Fang pirates," Pinchon radioed the instant they'd left warp. "Repeat, this is C...Pinchon of the Black Fang pirates to Black...base, please respond. I am in a damaged vessel of alien manufacture, requesting immediate perm...to land. I am accompanied by another such vessel. Over."

The seconds ticked by with painful slowness.

"I repeat: this is Colonel...of the...pirates. My radio has been...and I'm using the backup. Requesting immediate assistance, over."

"Rex, I see something," Wellesley said after another short interval. "Looks like fighters coming our way."

"Colonel?" Hunt radioed.

"Steady," he replied. "They're just checking us out."

A group of a half dozen pirate craft approached, breaking into groups of three and surrounding each fighter. The lead fighter of each group peered into the canopy of the alien vessels. Pinchon took off his helmet so they could clearly see his face, certain that his picture would be on file, for better or worse. The pilot he looked at nodded and took to his radio, drawing back slightly while the other two ships hovered close behind.

"They're taking an awfully long time," Tselitel said quietly after a couple of minutes had passed, twisting in her seat to look at the ships.

"They want to be sure of us," Wellesley said. "For all they know we're some rival organization trying to smuggle a bomb onto one of their most secret bases. Lucky for us these fighters are all but unknown in the Milky Way. Seeing them will at least pique their curiosity and make them think. And the sight of the colonel will also make them think twice about shooting us out of the sky, even if he has made it onto their blacklist."

"Do you think he has?" she asked nervously, still eyeing the fighters.

"I can't say. I'd just be speculating."

"Well, I hope–," she began, her words instantly cut off by the sight of muzzle flashes behind them.

"Don't move!" Pinchon barked over the radio, just as Hunt was about to throw the craft into a summersault. "They're not shooting at us. They're reminding us who's in charge."

"You sure about that?" he asked,

"They wouldn't have missed otherwise," he said. "Remember, I know these guys. They're just telling us to play by their rules."

"He's right," Tselitel said. "One of them just winked at me."

"Fantastic," Hunt said sourly. He'd wondered what kind of reception Lily was going to get at the base. Now he felt he knew.

"Hello, Colonel Pinchon," a voice said over the radio. It was an older voice, with a tinge of an accent that neither Hunt nor Tselitel could place.

"Is that you, Ivo?" he asked. "It must be ten years since I last saw you."

"At least that long," Kaljurand replied. "It was aboard the *Justice*, wasn't it? We sure did a job that day, didn't we? Snatching an imperial frigate as it limped home to dock!"

"No, Ivo," Pinchon said with a chuckle. "The last time we saw each other was in the bar aboard the *Munificence*, just before your present appointment. I told you it was a dead end job, and you said it was better than the snowball I'd been relegated to. I was hotter tempered then. I bloodied your nose, remember?"

"I do," the voice said with satisfaction. "Sorry, Philip, I had to be sure it was you."

"Sure. Is it alright if we land?"

"Just as soon as you tell me who your friends are," Kaljurand replied, a slight edge of officialdom in his tone.

"Oh, just some driftwood I picked up on Delta-13. They're all on the run from the government. Did you hear about the explosion that rocked the prison there?"

"Yeah."

"These are the guys who caused it."

"No kidding?" he asked, astonishment in his voice. "I should like to meet them very much. After the usual checks, of course."

"Of course."

"Proceed to the docking bay. Your escorts will show you in."

"Roger, thank you."

"Over and out."

"Seems like a friendly enough guy," Wellesley said. "Though there's something hard in his voice. I don't think he'd hesitate to blast us to bits if he saw cause."

"Nor do I," replied Hunt, watching as the lead fighter of each pirate group scooted ahead and guided them toward the moonbase.

"I'll land first," Pinchon radioed. "But follow close behind me."

"Roger."

Nervously Hunt handled the controls, guiding his craft by wide, slow movements along the path set by his guide. The Black Hole slowly grew bigger. It was a gray, rectangular affair, built on the side of the moon that faced away from the molten world of undulating lava it orbited. A single massive docking bay was visible on the side that faced him. Towards this Pinchon and his escort flew, with Hunt's lagging slightly behind. Had he heard the colonel's message and decided to oblige him? Hunt didn't know. Tensely he watched as the ship ahead of him cut its velocity and began to close in. Sweat gathering on his palms, he reached for the speed control and cut it back just as the guide's engines came worryingly near.

"Good job, Rex," Wellesley said encouragingly, as the gap between them began to grow once more. "Just try to keep a comfortable distance."

No sooner had he said this than the pirate cut his speed again, this time so sharply that the two of them almost collided.

"What does that idiot think he's doing?" Hunt barked, reflexively pushing the craft down and out of formation to avoid hitting him.

"Get back in formation!" Pinchon ordered fiercely. "Do you want to screw this whole thing up?"

"I'd rather not crash into the blockhead in front of me!" he shot back, slipping back between the lead fighter and the pair that followed.

"Just follow their lead," the colonel replied brusquely, closing the channel.

"Why didn't I think of that?" Hunt asked acidly, his trembling hands wiggling the controls and making the craft subtly shake. The lead fighter cut his speed once more as they neared the base, though this time much more slowly.

"Probably got chewed out by his boss," Wellesley opined, as their speed fell to a crawl and the formation around Pinchon flew inside first.

"We can only hope," Hunt said tensely, not really paying attention. His eyes were everywhere at once, trying to take in everything so as to avoid making any mistakes. Overloading himself with information, he almost missed it when the lead fighter eased his way forward and coasted into the base.

"Our turn, Rex," Wellesley nudged him gently, just as he'd noticed.

"I know," he uttered quietly, pushing the speed control slightly forward and following the ship inside. Passing through an atmospheric shield, the pirate vessel set down within a bright white ring that had been painted on the deck. Hunt chose the one next to it and slowly brought the craft to a stop above it, lowering it with infinite care and landing more or less on top of it. "It'll do," he said, modestly satisfied with his first ever attempt at landing a spacecraft.

"Better than most could have done," Wellesley congratulated him, as he shut off the engines. Leaning back in the seat, he closed his eyes and exhaled, letting some of the tension flow from his body. Opening them, he saw that a security team was already on hand to escort them from the hangar.

"Looks like they're pretty organized around here," he commented, unfastening his harness and looking over his shoulder to Lily. "Stay close to me, baby. If anything happens," he said significantly, dark smoke floating momentarily between his fingers and then vanishing.

"Like a glove," she nodded.

"Good girl," he said. He was about to take the pistol that had been packed away under the seat, but thought better of it. One way or another they would take it, so no point in risking offending them. Keeping his hand below the canopy, he drew Wellesley from the system and slipped him into his pocket. "Ready?" he asked, half turning his head over his shoulder.

"Ready as I'll ever be," she replied, trying to keep her nervous trembling to a minimum.

"Alright," he said, popping the canopy and standing up.

"Down this side," one of the hangar staff ordered flatly, wheeling a rolling ladder up to the side of the craft so they could climb down. Hunt descended first, followed by Tselitel.

"This way," a security man said brusquely, leading them toward a door on the far end of the hangar. The security man was supported by two others, both of which moved to the rear of their guests.

"*Seems like three is the magic number for escorts around here,*" Hunt thought, as he put his arm around Tselitel's narrow shoulders and kept her alongside him.

A cross-section of pirate society watched them as they walked through. Mechanics, smugglers, thieves, even professional killers – all bent their eyes upon the visitors with keen interest. Naturally their gaze landed on Tselitel first, for while not beautiful she had a striking cast to her body and features that was destined to catch the eye of anyone who appreciated a finely apportioned woman. But then their eyes moved to Hunt, and to their surprise he

THE BEAST EMERGES

drew – indeed, *compelled* – their attention. There was an aura about the man that made them stop their work and stare, as if hidden within him was some secret that could be discovered by sufficient observation. Once the pair had disappeared with their guards through the door the spell was broken. Looking at each other awkwardly, the occupants of the hangar returned to their work.

"That man means trouble," an old mechanic said to his younger assistant as he slid underneath the nose of a damaged fighter to continue his work. "There's an essence about him that you can smell from a mile away."

"Aw, come on, Becker," the younger man said, wiping his greasy fingers on a filthy red rag and jamming it into the breast pocket of his blue overalls. "You can't tell me that you can read all that from a man just by *looking* at him."

"Mostly not," the old man admitted. "But some folks give you a *feeling*. It's like they reach out and *touch* you somehow. And *that* guy touched me. I can't explain how, but I know it's true."

"I think you've been whiffing exhaust fumes for too long, that's what *I* think!"

"You kids have no sense of mystery anymore," Becker said, sliding out from under the nose and looking up at him. "Everything in this old galaxy of ours isn't *self-evident*, you know. Some things just *are*, whether or not we can make sense of 'em. Ah, there was a time when us pirates had a sense of *art*, you know? It wasn't all pillaging and stealing. Sure, there was that, too. But mostly it was the *life* that drew us in. You were free to follow nature how you saw fit. It was like poetry. And all the things you saw! Why, it was enough to remind you that after all you're just a tiny gnat in a universe too big to care about you. And that made you respect it – made you respect the things that folks said weren't possible, but that happened, anyhow. It showed you the limits of what we can truly understand." Becker paused and looked toward the exit through which the visitors had left the hangar.

"There's something significant about that man. Mark my words: we'll be hearing from him before long."

Hunt and Tselitel were taken down a long, narrow corridor of gray with doors on each side. Twice they were ushered to the side of the passageway by their escorts to permit base personnel to pass by. Bearded men with wide, hungry eyes looked at both of them. The air of inner-world refinement and educated clarity that Tselitel brought to their domain surprised them, though their eyes quickly locked onto the escort who, with possessive protectiveness, kept his arm around her shoulders at all times. The men passed by, stopped in the corridor, and looked back, trying to see more of the unexpected visitors before they disappeared around a corner.

"In here," the lead guard said, standing beside an open door and gesturing sharply for them to enter. Eyeing him skeptically, Hunt slipped his arm off Tselitel's shoulders and ushered her just ahead of him, his hands vigilantly on her upper shoulder blades. No sooner had they entered than the door was shut.

"What is this place?" she asked, looking up and down the dull gray room. She saw a horizontal bar that ran the length of the small rectangular space laying on the floor against the right wall. Suddenly a bright light appeared along its edge, making her jump.

"Don't be alarmed," a female voice said over an unseen speaker. "Please stand away from each other with your legs spread and your arms held over your heads."

"Scanner," Hunt explained, as he assumed the position. "They're checking us for weapons."

"That is correct," the voice said snappily, irritated that Hunt had stolen some of her authority by explaining the process.

The bar moved up to the ceiling and returned to the floor twice. Finally it stopped just at the level of Hunt's pocket.

"You have a small round device in your pocket," she said in a sharp, accusative tone. "Take it out and hold it away from your body for the scanner to examine."

Drawing Wellesley from his pocket, he held the medallion by the chain.

"What is that device?" she asked.

"An alien artifact. A decorative piece."

"No explosives or other weapons detected," she said flatly. "You may return it to your pocket."

Hunt did so and assumed a normal stance, Tselitel following suit.

"Are we done here?" he asked after a few moments.

"We will *tell* you when you are done," she said emphatically.

"*Security types are all the same,*" Hunt thought, stifling a snort with effort. Instead he looked at Tselitel, who merely shrugged and looked at the horizontal bar. As the only interactive part of the entire room, she felt that it somehow represented the woman who'd addressed them so harshly. Nearly ten minutes passed in this silent manner before her grating voice was heard again.

"You may go," she said, dismissing them as though they were last week's leftovers. "You are cleared to access any A level rooms in the base. Should you attempt to enter rooms whose clearance level is B or greater, you will be severely punished."

"Good to know," Hunt said dismissively, wanting to say a great deal more but thinking it unwise.

The door automatically opened, rising upward into its frame almost noiselessly. Tselitel took his arm as he passed by and followed him out. A young woman was waiting for them. Unattractive, overweight, and possessing the entitled demeanor of one who was overly impressed with the meager authority of her position, she gestured roughly for them to follow.

"This way," she said without enthusiasm, turning

before them and ambling slowly down the corridor. She brought them to a flight of stairs and laboriously made her way up them, her charges following her at a crawl. Finally they reached the top, took a left, and then were deposited without another word before a door marked Director.

"I guess we go inside," Hunt said with a shrug once the young woman had disappeared back down the stairs that had given her so much difficulty.

"Shouldn't we knock?" she asked, as Hunt seized the doorknob with his large hand.

"Nah, we're expected already," he said, twisting it and pushing the door open. Within was a sternly appointed room dominated by a large desk and a trio of chairs that stood before it. Behind the desk sat a partially balding man in his fifties. He held himself with the poise of a career military man. His fiery red hair and quick, fox-like eyes gave him the appearance of insatiable, roving intelligence. In front of his desk sat Pinchon, one leg tossed over the other, looking back toward the door.

"These are the two I told you about," the colonel said, standing up and ushering them to the empty chairs beside his as though the office was his own. "Rex Hunt, Lily Tselitel, meet Ivo Kaljurand."

Pleasantries were briefly exchanged as they took their seats.

"I've already had the...pleasure of meeting your other friends," Kaljurand said with some reluctance. "The smuggler can be a handful, can't he?"

"More than a handful," Hunt agreed. "He has enough personality to fill the entire base."

"Of that I have no doubt," the pirate boss replied. His eyes darted between Hunt and Tselitel for a moment. He was sizing them up, comparing the testimony of his own eyes to the story Pinchon had been telling him. A calm, cool customer, he was in the habit of verifying everything that passed under his gaze with a deliberateness that seemed inexhaustible. "I must say, Doctor Tselitel, that we never imagined you'd make up part of our complement of guests."

"Then there are others?" she asked, following the colonel's example and putting a panted leg over the other. Subtly her hands trembled, so she folded them in her lap to keep them still.

"Oh, yes," he nodded. "We always have a few guests on hand for one reason or another. Though we don't publish that fact, and I'll appreciate it if both of you keep it under your hats." He asked this politely, but a hint of warning appeared in his eyes as he momentarily narrowed them.

"You must forgive my friend, the director," Pinchon said with a casual ease born from years of friendship. "He's spent far too much time with the likes of those devils you met in the hall earlier. With folks like that, every request must be paired with a threat to obtain compliance."

"You mean those bearded men?" Tselitel asked. "They looked almost like wild animals. Their eyes were so wide and hungry that I half felt like the next item in a buffet line," she laughed. When none of the men laughed with her she looked awkwardly between them, her eyes finally falling on Hunt along with a querying look.

"You're not too far off," Kaljurand said in a low tone. "They're some of the worst we get here. They certainly would have assaulted you had you not been escorted by our security team." Kaljurand stopped speaking for a moment, absorbed by some inner thought that took his whole attention. When he resurfaced he looked seriously at his guests. "Honestly I'd push them out of the atmospheric shield if I could. They're worthless – no good. And that's saying something on a base like this."

"Ivo is a civilized man stuck in an uncivilized post," Pinchon commented. "It's why he got the job in the first place."

"Among other reasons," he said, a tight-lipped smile on his face. "Someone has to whip this scum into line. And make no mistake: they are *scum*, rotten down to the core. It's why I had you immediately evacuated from the hangar and escorted to the security room. Naturally, I also had to ensure that you posed no threat to the base."

"You mean we were taken away so crisply for *our* sake more than anything?" Tselitel asked uneasily, her assessment of conditions on the base growing darker.

"More or less," Kaljurand said. "Technically this base is meant to give our boys a place off the beaten track to wait while official ardor for their arrest cools. But that's not its only purpose. Commanders of different Black Fang outposts use it as a dumping ground for all their undesirables."

"Cronyism is rampant within the organization," Pinchon elaborated. "Abuse is the norm, not the exception. So when an outpost commander wants to get rid of someone without resorting to homicide, they're sent here."

"It's a simmering pot of filth and refuse that could boil over at any moment. Now more so than ever, given the pressure the aliens have placed on our resources. Every little lost black sheep in the area that knows about us is hightailing it here. One of the unwritten rules of the Black Fangs is that we never turn away one of our own. It's supposed to make us stronger – a tighter knit unit. But in reality it reduces our power to maintain discipline and order. With the flood of refugees has come a massive uptick in crime. Scarcely a day passes without a fight. Sometimes a murder, too."

"Murder?" exclaimed Tselitel, her hands unconsciously parting and finding places on the armrests of her chair. There they shook nervously for a few moments before she became aware of the fact and returned them to her lap. "Are we in any danger?"

"Yes," Kaljurand replied without hesitation. "Why do you think I'm telling you both this? The Black Hole has never been the sort of place for a family vacation. But we've always been able to uphold a basic level of order. That is, until the present crisis. Now I cannot guarantee anyone's safety. Even my own." He paused to roll up his sleeve, revealing an angry red gash in his arm. "That happened eleven days ago. One of my so-called brother pirates decided this base could be better run along anarchistic lines, and took it upon himself to bring such a state of affairs about. Once he was apprehended I gathered all the refugees in the hangar and personally pushed him out the atmospheric shield into space. That bought us nearly five days of subdued, sullen order before his death was forgotten and the antics of these animals resumed."

"I don't suppose we'll be allowed to keep our weapons?" Hunt asked.

"No, you will not," Kaljurand said. "The base has a blanket policy about weapons, given the unique nature of our situation. Because even if *you* behaved well with them, which I have little doubt you would, the risk is constant that they could be taken from you and used by someone else."

"Such as the aforementioned anarchist," Hunt replied.

"Precisely. For this reason only trained security personnel are allowed to go about armed. All the rest of the official staff are prohibited from having weapons of any kind. This place is too much of a powder keg already to risk letting everyone walk around with a personal box of matches."

"Makes sense," Hunt nodded.

"So, for the time being, enjoy our hospitality with caution. The staff is overburdened by the influx and inclined to be surly, so please don't take that to heart. I'm sure you've already experienced a few examples of tartness since you've been here."

"We have," Hunt agreed with a hint of a grin.

"Yes, I thought so."

"Honestly, we're just glad to be out of the fire for a little while," Pinchon said. "We've been on the run ever since those monsters hit Delta-13. It's nice to take a breather."

"Catch whatever breath you can," Kaljurand said. "Just don't do it too loudly."

"Meaning?" Hunt asked.

"Meaning you've got to keep on your toes," he replied, his expressive eyes deadly serious. "Stick with your friends. Travel in pairs. And you," he said, pointing a finger at Tselitel, "don't even *consider* walking the halls alone. Not even to walk a half dozen paces." His gaze dancing between them. "He's your man?" he asked, now pointing at Hunt.

"He is," she replied proudly.

"Good," Kaljurand nodded, seemingly checking off some internal point of concern. "He's dangerous. You can see that at once. And from what Philip tells me," he said, his eyes rolling to Hunt, "you can handle yourself in a fight."

"I manage."

"Do more than manage," he replied, almost as a reprimand. "If you must strike, strike to kill. No mercy, no hesitation. As long as these scum hit first I don't care what you do with them. Frankly I'd be glad if you got rid of some of them for me. Just don't go around starting trouble."

"That's plain enough," Hunt said.

"I like things plain," Kaljurand replied, leaning back in his seat with an overburdened sigh. Once again his eyes danced between his two visitors. "Plain rules, plain people. Plain women, in particular," he said, his gaze falling on Tselitel.

"Thank you?" she asked, her cheeks beginning to redden.

"You misunderstand me," he said with his first hint of a smile in the entire discussion. "I mean honest women, straightforward women. I wasn't commenting on your appearance, which is quite charming."

Hunt shifted in his seat, a look of deadly coldness entering his eyes.

"You're not all man," Kaljurand said, noticing and returning his gaze easily. "You're part wildcat. That's good. I don't think this one can look after herself adequately in a place like this. Nor, one could say, in the galaxy we now

THE BEAST EMERGES

find ourselves in. Her instinct is to heal, not to kill. You've got enough of the latter quality to take out half this base. But," he added, savoring the precision of his own delineation of Hunt's character, "only if you're crossed. You're a snake that only bites when trampled upon. Or, more accurately," he corrected himself, looking at Tselitel once more, "when she is."

The mere verbalization of this idea caused Hunt's left fist to reflexively tighten, a motion that was not lost on the director.

"Good," he murmured approvingly, yet another invisible box in his mind being checked. "Good."

"Just as observant as ever, Ivo," Pinchon said, glad that his old friend was still sharp, given their situation.

"It's the only reason I've held on this long in a post like this," he explained. "That, and because I possess a certain talent for discipline."

"I don't doubt it," Tselitel said, unsure if she should be impressed or a bit frightened. Her ambivalence was apparent in her voice, and drew a faint smile from the director.

"Unfortunately I can't play favorites with you people," Kaljurand said, changing topics after a few moments of silence. "I would like nothing more than to station you near my own quarters because of the heightened security that prevails there. But I'm afraid that's impossible. You'll have to be lodged with the rabble. Though fortunately I can put you on the very edge of their accommodations, so you won't have to venture inside their den, just to the outskirts of it."

"I trust the locks work well?" Tselitel asked with a little laugh.

"Quite well, I assure you," he said, appreciating her spunk. "You and your friends will dine with me tonight. I'll send my attendant to fetch you. In the meantime, keep your wits about you and keep to yourselves."

He gave them directions to their quarters and then dismissed them, keeping his old friend the colonel back in order to reminisce about old times and discuss new ones.

"Quite a character!" Tselitel whispered to Hunt as they proceeded down the hall from his office. "He's so intense! So, so *sure* of himself! It's not often you meet someone who's so completely in his element. And yet he *hates* it so fiercely! I fully believe he would push all the riffraff out of the atmospheric shield if he could."

"A good man not to cross," Hunt said factually, keeping his mind on the practical.

"Oh, sure. But you know me: I can't help savoring the intricacies of a new, fascinating personality."

"Just don't savor them too much," Hunt replied, slipping his right arm across her shoulders and turning down another corridor.

"Why, Rex Hunt, you're not *jealous*, are you?" she asked.

"It's one of my failings," he replied quietly, drawing her a little closer as a pair of sullen-eyed security men passed them in the hallway. "He's intrigued by you, anyone can see that."

"Well, who wouldn't be?" she asked, tipping her head and fluttering her eyes.

They walked in silence for a few minutes, finally reaching a clean metal door with the number twenty-four painted on it in white.

"This is it," Hunt said, inserting the keycard the director had given him into a reader beside the door. The lock clicked open, and when Rex turned the knob and pushed inwards it moved noiselessly.

"Rex, do you *smell* that?" she asked, taking his arm and holding him back for a moment. A stench was drifting their way from down the hall. "What is that?" she asked.

"The refugees," he said scornfully, looking along the passageway just as a rumpled, disreputable looking character came out of his room two dozen paces away. Locking it after him, he stood and watched them for a moment. His hand went lazily to his mouth as he contemplated Tselitel, the palm slowly caressing his lips. Finally he turned from them and shambled in the opposite direction.

"That's enough to send a shiver down any girl's spine," she said, as the man vanished around the corner.

"Come on," he said in a low voice, still watching the corridor as he gently pushed her inside the room and closed the door.

◆ ◆ ◆

"This is the place," Elasha said, long after her explanation to Welter of her mission. Before her and her companions loomed an obelisk of *Keesh'Forbandai* manufacture. Of modest height but very broad at the base, its emerald colored sides gleamed beautifully from the rays of the setting sun. "And not a moment too soon," she added, feeling several *kals* in the area. They were under cover, waiting for darkness to fall so they could strike. One, she felt sure, was little more than two hundred feet away, likely skulking inside some burrowing animal's den.

"What now, Elasha?" Halshan asked, lowering the heavy pack from his shoulder, glad for the break. "Do we stay here for the night?"

"Only I can go inside," she said reluctantly. "The rest of you will have to wait out here."

"I didn't come this far to stand in the waiting room," Welter said decisively. "If you're going in, so am I."

"Don't be ridiculous. The planet only speaks to those it *wishes* to speak with. My brother often communed with it, and over time he introduced it to me. The living worlds do not take to human contacts easily, Gustav. Not since the last war. They're cautious and afraid."

"Fear is a luxury they can't afford anymore," Welter

replied. "They've had their heads in the sand long enough. Come on, boys."

The eyes of the young men shot between their two older companions as Welter moved toward the structure's door.

"Elasha?" Rede asked quietly.

"Come on," she said, growing flustered. "We can't leave you two alone out here with the *kals* around."

To Welter's surprise the door opened with perfect ease, almost of its own accord. The space inside was dark, though it somehow illuminated itself when Elasha entered.

"Close the door, Pasco," she said to Halshan, who was the last inside. "It cannot speak so long as any opening to the outside remains."

"Why?" asked Rede, as his comrade carefully pressed the ancient door shut.

"They will hear," she said in an ominous tone that told him not to inquire further.

"Elasha," a deep voice breathed slowly. "Elasha, I feel your presence. And that of others."

"Yes, Bohlen, I am sorry," she said respectfully, bowing low to the floor. "The one insisted, and the others could not be left on their own to brave the dangers of the forest."

"It is well," the voice said in tones of sadness and regret.

"And why is that?" asked Welter in a straightforward manner that horrified the aged mystic.

"Bohlen, I must apologize for my associate," she said quickly. "He is–."

"His presence is welcome," Bohlen said. "I am refreshed by his candor and directness."

Welter shot Elasha a self-satisfied smile that made her eyes roll.

"I have come here for a special purpose, Bohlen," she began, taking several steps away from the small group and lowering her voice. "I must ask something of you."

"Speak."

She looked over her shoulder at the two young men who had not been initiated into the secret of her mission.

"Boys, I must ask you to stand by the door and cover your ears for a moment," she said. "What I must say to Bohlen is of the utmost secrecy."

"It concerns them as well," Welter countered. "Their lives have been put on the line just as much as yours or mine have. They've earned the right to know."

"No one *earns* the right to knowledge like this," she replied. "Boys, it relates to the greatest secret now possessed by the imperial navy. For any number of reasons I cannot enlighten you. Please, do as I ask."

"Yes, Elasha," they both said, following her instructions.

"Now, what is it you wish to know?" Bohlen asked, as Welter approached the mystic and stood beside her.

"I have been sent to you by special request of the emperor's chief servant, Krancis."

"And what does Krancis desire?" Bohlen asked, long aware of both the man and his nature.

"He wishes to know why the Omega Project has failed to activate," she said in a whisper. "They have bent all the energies and talents of the smartest minds in the empire upon it, and yet it will not function. Repeated examinations reveal that the device has been fully repaired. Nothing, it seems, is out of place."

"And yet it does not function?" Bohlen inquired.

"That is correct."

"The fault lies in your assumption of its functionality," the planet replied. "The tools of the *Keesh'Forbandai* are not the hollow shells that your people now make. They are not mere mechanical husks wrapped around their bodies. Rather they join the material with the immaterial. These two, bound in one, give them their power."

"But, Bohlen, how can we possibly emulate them?"

she asked, anxiety filling her heart as she spoke. "Our people are not like the *Keesh'Forbandai*. They are great architects, master builders. They blend together matter and energy in a seamless unity that is beyond our people. We are but children, standing in their shadow."

"Children that must mature," Bohlen replied sagely.

"We cannot mature in time," Elasha said with a shake of her head. "On all fronts we retreat before the invader. Everywhere that they appear we are defeated, scattered to the wind like ashes. Once the worlds of the *Ahn-Wey* fall they will turn their attention onto humanity with singular focus, finishing the work they began ages ago. They will hunt and consume us with relish. No, Bohlen, we cannot mature. We shall die long before then."

"The maturation is ongoing, desultory, chaotic – a true reflection of your people. Some have matured but many have not. It is in the few that you must find your rescue."

"I don't understand," she replied.

"I think I do," Welter said, taking a step forward. "There's a man who we've been watching carefully. Immense darkness resides within him. The powers of the *Prellak* were bent upon him from an early age, twisting him to their purpose. But he was broken from their grasp and protected from their influence."

"Your people possess great darkness," Bohlen replied. "In this he is an archetypal expression. I know of this man. As a diamond is mere base matter compressed into a precious form, so it is with this man. He is the broad power of your people pressed into a single being. He is the one that you seek. Within him resides your only hope of activating the Omega Project."

"But how can one man possibly activate it?" Elasha asked in astonishment. "It is enormous – gigantic!"

"You underestimate the skill of the *Keesh'Forbandai*," Bohlen said in a chiding tone. "It is little with them to produce such a machine. Many more have they made, and far greater. Of this you may be certain."

"Very well," Elasha said. "But how shall we locate this man?"

"One of our men has been carefully tracking him ever since he emerged as a force on Delta-13," Welter said. "You know of the destruction of the ancient facility under the prison?"

"Of course."

"He was largely responsible for it. Once the Devourers came upon us he sought assistance, along with his friends, from the pirate base on Delta-13. Our man, Philip Pinchon, made contact with him and shortly afterward disappeared."

"A *pirate?*" asked Elasha.

"Merely a cover," Welter replied. "He's very nearly a renegade among our members. But he has the necessary cunning to survive inside the Black Fangs. When the rumors of a wielder of darkness began to circulate on Delta-13, we naturally became interested and looked for any opportunity to stick a tail on him. And then he fell right into our laps."

"And now you've lost him," Elasha said.

"Only temporarily."

"How can you be so calm when all our hopes reside with him alone?" she snapped. "Our fate rests in the hands of a man who could well be dead by now."

"Oh, he's not dead," Welter said with certainty.

"And how can you be so sure of that?"

"You heard Bohlen," he said, nodding toward the center of the room, where the voice had emanated from. "He represents everything we are as a people, compressed into a single being. And man is nothing if not a fighter, a survivor. I have no doubt that he'll turn up."

"What can we do in the meantime?" she asked neither of them in particular.

"Inform Krancis of what I have told you," Bohlen said. "Let him know that a visitor will shortly come to him who is the key to the Omega Project."

"But how will he reach Omega?" she asked. "It's kept in a secret location in the middle of empty space. Not even I know where it is."

"He will reach it," Bohlen said decisively. "Of that you may be certain. Many hands have been at work ensuring this outcome, Elasha. Invisible hands, working in secret. Now it is time for you to depart. Pass to Krancis what I have told you, and remain close to the emperor. He will need all the strength he can muster for the struggle ahead, and will lean heavily upon you. Be his strength, Elasha. Be his pillar."

"I will do as you say," she replied, bowing low once more and retreating slowly from the center of the room toward the door.

◆ ◆ ◆

"Our neighbors seem to be getting restless," Hunt said several hours after they'd reached their room. The modest accommodations included a single bedroom, bathroom, and a tiny sitting area. Quite forgetting Wellesley in his pocket, he climbed into the narrow bed that was his and Tselitel's to share, waited momentarily for her to climb in half atop him, and then instantly fell asleep.

"I feel like I could sleep for days," she replied groggily, the dim light of a small corner lamp casting long, frightful shadows from the meager furniture that reminded her of past troubles. Lying on her stomach, she closed her eyes and pressed her face against his chest. "When's dinner?" she asked in a muffled voice.

"I have no idea. He said we'd eat 'tonight,' whatever that means in outer space. They must have their clocks tuned to some kind of day-night cycle to maintain their sanity."

"I suppose," she replied, drumming the fingers of her left hand on his upper arm. "Wellesley!" she suddenly exclaimed. "We've forgotten all about him!"

"I thought it seemed unusually quiet around here," he said with a laugh, shoving his hand awkwardly into his pocket and pulling out the medallion. "Still alive in there?"

"Oh, is it okay if I talk now?" he asked tartly. "Or would you prefer to keep things 'quiet?'"

"Of course you can talk, Wellesley," she said soothingly, though her consoling manner was spoiled by a laugh she barely stifled. "You must have plenty to say. We've seen an awful lot since coming here."

"No, *you've* seen an awful lot," he corrected. "I'm dependent on a companion for sight, remember? All I could do was hear things. Though that might be an advantage, now that I think about it. You humans always give too much precedence to sight, anyhow. You miss the things that only an attentive ear can pick up."

"Well, then it's a good thing you're here to compensate for our failings," Hunt replied. "Please, hold forth. Enlighten us, wise teacher."

"You keep up that attitude, pal, and I'll just clam up and leave you to your own devices."

"Please, Wellesley," Tselitel said. "We really want to know."

"Well, since you asked so nicely," he replied grudgingly. "Just understand one thing, bucko: I'm telling *her*, not you. Understand? Anything you happen to overhear is just…dumb, silly human luck. Got it?"

"Loud and clear," he chuckled.

"Fine, well, good. Now that that's out of the way, there are several things I'd like to mention. First and foremost, Ivo Kaljurand is a dangerous man. Don't cross him."

"I think we know that," Hunt replied.

"I'm not talking to you, remember?" he said in a petty voice that finally began to betray the good humor he felt despite his exasperation at being cut out of the loop for so long. "Kaljurand is someone dominated by powerful drives. There's a subtle note of cruelty that runs through his 'well oiled machine' mentality. The coldness, the hardness with which he acts, speaks, and thinks, implies a nature that distrusts the human element and sees it as responsible for all the imperfections that exist in his otherwise sterile world."

"That's an awful lot to draw from one discussion," Hunt replied dubiously.

"I've seen his type before, alright? You run into them in managerial positions quite frequently. Their obsessive drive to put everything in its proper place includes humans as well. There's a faint, ever-present irritation with anything organic because it doesn't fit seamlessly into their framework. Anything asymmetrical has got to go. That's why he hates the riff raff that's been dropped on his doorstep."

"I think anyone would hate people like them," Hunt replied.

"Naturally," the AI agreed. "Anyone with the slightest regard for decency or personal hygiene couldn't help being offended by their presence. They live like animals and have no respect for proper structure or authority. But," he paused dramatically, focusing their minds on his next point, "he carries it into a different sphere entirely. He despises them. That's why he personally executed the anarchist. Naturally it had the dual purpose of showing all the others who's boss. But a subtle note of personal satisfaction entered his voice as he said it, as though an inner tension had been relieved by the act. Of course, you sight-dominant humans–."

"Missed that crucial point," Hunt finished with a roll of his eyes.

"Just so. He's driven by a compulsion for cleanliness and order. These people are dirty and he wishes them gone. He'd exterminate them like cockroaches if he could. At least that's his inner fantasy. Ultimately his personal set of rules would prevent him from undertaking any such act. He could only move against them if it's justified by his ethics, such as when he acted against the anarchist. It's why he encouraged you to solve his problem for him: his ethics restrain *his* hand, not yours. But even in that case he had to meddle in it somewhat."

"You mean when he said that I shouldn't go picking fights?"

"Exactly. His system bleeds over onto other people and he has to manage them. Why do you think no more than a few minutes of exposure to Antonin was enough to turn him off?"

"Too much of a free spirit?" Tselitel asked.

"Uh huh. Inwardly his nature is fierce, consumptive, aggressive. But it's held in check by a counterpoise of rationally adopted rules that keeps him from degenerating into the kind of animal that he scorns so visibly now that they've been dumped on his doorstep. In them he sees a sort of kin, though of a lowly, inferior quality. He secretly envies them whilst at the same time he looks down upon them. Embracing the nature that he holds constantly in check, they represent a kind of animal brother, the sort of creature he would be if his personality hadn't taken a different, more civilized, course. But this very development has left him divided, conflicted. It produces a massive amount of psychic tension that must be unleashed in some way, else it would swallow him up. So he takes it out through a painfully punctilious attachment to the rules. It's a combination of self-reproach for even possessing such a fierce inner nature; a sort of testament of faith in a higher, more ordered way to live; and an outlet through which he can channel the conflict that constantly pulls at him."

"I'm a little confused," Tselitel said. "We don't have any plans to cross his personal ethics or the rules of the base. Why is he dangerous to us?"

"Because he's a man tied in knots who's suddenly been placed under an immense strain by both the refugees and the broader problem of the Devourers. Anytime you place a conflicted person in a situation of high, indeed, *incredible* pressure, you're asking for something unpredictable. He's taken a fancy to you, Lily, so I doubt you have anything to worry about so long as you don't probe too far into his nature and make him feel like a bug under glass – a perennial temptation for a psychiatrist. No, the real danger lies with Rex."

"Me? What did I do?"

"Absolutely nothing. But it relates to what I said before. Begging your pardon, old buddy, but you're not the most civilized person in the world. Kaljurand clearly felt the force and power you have at your disposal, the animalistic willfulness with which you will destroy anyone that threatens what you hold dear. There's a primitive, elemental quality to you that reminds him of the ferocity of his own inner nature. And yet it isn't coupled with the senseless, obsessive appetites that cause him to hate the refugees and distrust himself. At present you seem to be the perfect weapon: violent and destructive if necessary, and yet not driven to excess by uncontrollable impulses. You appear, in short, to be a bomb that can control both when it goes off and how far its destructive power will reach."

"But, if Rex appears to be the perfect balance…" Tselitel replied, her voice trailing as she failed to grasp his point.

"Oh, how could he make Kaljurand dangerous to us?" the AI asked.

"Uh huh."

"Because he stands on a knife's edge. If he were an animal like the refugees then Kaljurand would know what to do with him and would immediately put him in the 'hated' column within his mind. And if he were dominated by a constrictive set of ethical rules, then he would instantly place him in the 'safe' column and more or less forget him. The fact that he stands outside this polarity confuses and intrigues Kaljurand. He respects it, for the moment, because it appears that Rex has found a third path that has somehow always escaped the director. A core of vital strength has allowed Rex to be both good and by and large unregulated by the kind of obsessive personal accounting that drains Kaljurand of his enthusiasm for life."

"So he's a prisoner of his own nature?" clarified Tselitel.

"Exactly. Usually such people don't rise to any particular height because they self-sabotage themselves. When they *do* make it a good distance up the chain of command, their nature is typically riddled with hidden compulsions and eccentricities that allow them to balance out the obsessive drives that would otherwise destroy them. That, or they find someone to lean upon. Who knows, perhaps in a subtle way he's already trying to do that with Rex."

"I'm not the 'lean on' type," Hunt replied.

"He doesn't know that – yet. And I wouldn't disabuse him of the idea unless you have to."

"I'm no good at misrepresenting myself," Hunt said, a little alarmed at the idea of trimming his sails. "I can't read people and tell them what they want to hear."

"No, your nature is too frank and honest for that. All I mean is, don't come right out and cross him on some point during our stay here. Just be yourself and otherwise nod along to his policy decisions."

"Has it occurred to you that my independence of thought, my *lack* of 'nodding along' as you call it, might be just what disposes him towards me in the first place? Kaljurand is no dummy, Wells. He'll know if I'm pulling something over on him."

"Well, maybe you're right. I guess you'll have to play the cards how they've been dealt and hope for the best."

"I imagine," Hunt agreed. "Besides, it's not like I can't tip the game in our favor if anyone starts to misbehave," he said, holding up his left hand and flexing his fingers.

"I wouldn't count on that, not against the entire base."

"Just a backup option," he replied, lowering it to Tselitel's back and giving her a little rub, for which she kissed him.

"Before you two lovebirds start cuddling," Wellesley said, "I *do* have a thing or two more to add."

"Go ahead."

"Okay, I might have led with my comments about the director, but this is what I *really* wanted to talk about, so pay attention," he said a touch chidingly, as they'd begun playfully kissing each other.

Hunt sighed and leaned his head back against the thin pillow that lay underneath it.

"Thank you," the AI said. "There's something wrong about this base. It doesn't sound right. There's a pall, a shadow that's been cast over it. The people are subdued, angry, irritable. Yes, I know you're about to jump up with the obvious objection," the AI commented, stopping Hunt who had indeed just opened his mouth for that purpose. "I know the refugees have put a massive strain on everyone, even themselves. But it's more than that. I've seen enough of war and turpitude to know the difference between an external and an *internal* disturbance. There's an aura about this base which is unhealthy. Don't ask me to explain what it is – I'm no soothsayer. But the signs are unmistakable. You humans are uncommonly sensitive to such influences, though in an unconscious fashion. Your behavior betrays its presence even if you're unaware of it most of the time."

"What do you suggest we do about it?" Hunt asked, simultaneously stretching out his intuition to try and pick up some trace of what his friend had inferred.

"Be careful and stick close. Don't expect normal, rational behavior from your fellow man. Something is working upon them that might make them act far differently than you'd anticipate."

"Understood."

"And the third point?" Tselitel asked, just as a knock

was heard on the door.

"Enjoy dinner," the AI replied, as she rolled off the narrow bed so Hunt could rise.

Slipping the medallion around his neck, he moved cautiously to the door and paused momentarily, trying to hear how many people were on the other side.

"Who's there?" he asked in a half growl.

"The director's steward, sir," a man replied in a thin, nervous voice. "I've come to fetch you to dinner."

Hunt opened the door a few inches and saw a single man standing before him. About fifty, with closely cut hair and a narrow, bony figure, he appeared distinctly uncomfortable to be standing in the same hallway as that the refugees occupied. Twice during the brief moment that Hunt examined him his eyes shot along the corridor, carefully watching for threats.

"Come on in," Hunt said, laying a hand on his thin shoulder and pulling him inside.

"Really, sir, I didn't mean to trouble you," he said with embarrassment as the door was shut behind him and relocked. Nevertheless he was clearly relieved to be out of sight of the refugees for a few moments.

"Don't worry about it," Hunt said. "Take a seat," he added, pointing to the sole chair in the small sitting room. "We'll be ready in a few minutes."

"Of course, sir," he replied, sitting awkwardly on the chair indicated and doing his best not to draw attention to himself.

"Not very pleasant company," Hunt called from the other room.

"Sir?" the steward asked.

Hunt stuck his head into the sitting room and threw a thumb in the direction of the quarters down the hall.

"Them – not very pleasant people to be around."

"Oh, certainly not," he agreed quickly, nodding his head vigorously as Hunt's receded. "One encounter with them is enough to last a lifetime," he added, his boldness growing.

"How many have you had?" Hunt asked.

"I've lost count," he replied frankly. "Honestly I'm not sure why the director sends just one man down here to fetch dinner guests when he knows their reputation for violence. A platoon of imperial marines would scarcely be enough to cope with them all." Suddenly the man's cheeks went red and his eyes widened. "Y–you won't tell him I said that, will you?"

"Of course not," Tselitel said from the other room, instantly making him jump to his feet.

"Oh, I–I was unaware there was a lady present. The director simply told me to fetch 'room twenty-four' to dinner. My apologies, Ma'am."

"For what?" she asked, entering the sitting room and looking as pretty as she could manage in slacks, a blue shirt, and dirty, beaten up shoes.

"I–I don't know," replied the man in a fluster.

"We don't bite," she reassured him, gesturing for him to retake his seat.

"Not hard, anyway," Hunt said from the other room.

"Your husband?" the man asked discreetly.

"No, not yet," she replied quietly. "Perhaps some day, when all this business with the Devourers is over and done with."

"Yes, Ma'am."

"Ready?" Hunt asked, joining them.

"Ready as I can be in this getup," she replied.

"You look charming, Ma'am," the steward said politely, rising from his seat and making for the door. Reflexively he pressed an ear to it and listened for a moment. "All clear," he said, pulling it open for them.

Instantly upon entering the corridor their noses were struck by the scent of sweat, bad breath, and dried human feces wafting past their door. Tselitel and the steward both gasped, covering their noses and moving quickly up the hallway. Hunt strode heavily behind them, his face like stone as he mentally rejected the testimony of his nostrils. Hearing footsteps and rowdy voices around an upcoming corner, he instinctively placed a hand upon the shoulders of his two companions.

"You should have seen his face when I lit them on fire!" exclaimed a young ruffian to a trio of older, fatter scoundrels. "Well, well, well, *well!*" he said, as his eyes fell upon Tselitel and he rubbed his hands together. "Boys, it's been a long time since I've seen a woman who looked so *fine* in this miserable rathole. Yes, sir, a long time."

"These two are guests of the *director*," the steward said, nervously interposing between the two groups, hoping to inspire some respect by invoking Kaljurand.

"When I want to hear from *you*, little rabbit," he said, seizing the man's nose in his small yet powerful grip, "I'll ask for it." Jerking his arm off to the side, he sent the frail steward tumbling headfirst against the wall.

As he did this Hunt moved in front of Tselitel.

"And just who are you, friend?" the ruffian asked in a light, challenging tone.

"Nobody in particular."

"Well, Mister Nobody, I'll thank you to get out of the way so I can introduce myself to this *charming* lady," he said.

"Take your thugs and get out of here while you can still walk," Hunt said coolly.

"Please, sir," the steward interjected. "The consequences for interfering with the director's guests–."

"Are nothing like the ones you're gonna get if you don't keep your mouth shut!" snapped the renegade. "Boys!"

One of the heavy thugs seized the steward, clapping a hand over his mouth and wrapping an arm of iron around his stomach.

"Let him go!" Tselitel said urgently. "He hasn't done anything to you!"

"A *fine* voice to go along with that *fine* body," he said

approvingly, moving down the corridor to eye Tselitel more freely while his other two friends took his place beside Hunt. "We're gonna get along just fine, sweetie. Just fine." His eyes went to Hunt's. "Do the math, friend. Four on one is bad odds."

"For you," he replied coldly.

"Oh, tough guy, eh?" he laughed. "Well, friend, I'm a sporting man, so I'll tell you what: I'll take you on solo. Mano a mano. Whoever wins…" his voice trailed, his eyes running up and down Tselitel. "Well, you get the idea. Deal?"

"No dice."

"No? Well, in that case," he said, nodding to the thugs. Instantly all four of them drew hidden knives, two of which were held just inches from Hunt's abdomen. "I gave you a chance," the fiend said whimsically, taking a step toward Tselitel and grasping her wrist with his hand. Twisting it behind her back, he held the knife against her throat and released her arm. His free hand moved to her side and then her stomach. "She feels as good as she looks," he said wickedly, Tselitel shuddering as he spoke into her ear. "Now, why don't you go for a little walk with my friends while me and her get to know each other?"

The lights began to flicker as a dark haze fell over the hallway. The thugs looked around them, trying to understand what was happening. One of them gasped when his eyes fell upon Hunt's, and he saw they had turned midnight black.

"What's wrong with you?" he asked in shock, the knife wavering in the air.

Instantly streams of smoke sprang from Hunt's hands, striking the thugs and sending them scrambling up the hall in terror. Slowly Hunt's head rotated to the young ruffian.

"You let me go," he said, the knife trembling in front of Tselitel's throat as he backed slowly down the corridor. "Let me go, or I'll kill her! Right here, right now!" As Hunt inexorably approached the renegade, the latter pressed the knife against Tselitel's skin, exerting just as much force as he could without cutting it. "This is her last chance!"

"No," Hunt said, raising his hand and pausing where he stood. "It was yours."

A great stream of darkness burst from Hunt and soared past Tselitel. With a shriek she closed her eyes. Suddenly the knife fell away from her throat and clattered to the floor. An impossibly cold sensation washed across her back and enveloped her. She opened her eyes and saw that the arms that still held her had turned to black, like charred wood. In a panic she fought free of their hold, the limbs instantly snapping as she pressed against them. Leaping into Hunt's waiting arms half a dozen steps away, she gripped him close and turned back to look.

The form of the young ruffian stood before her. But his skin had turned to flakes of dark ash. His mouth agape with terror, his eyes wide in disbelief, the last thing he saw in this life was an incomprehensible shadow descending upon him. In an instant it was over, and his life was extinguished.

"How–," she began, unable to finish.

"It was what *Preleteth* taught me," Hunt said, stepping toward the inert figure and flicking away part of his shoulder with his finger. "Darkness and light must live in balance with each other. Too much of one or the other and the organism terminates. I increased the dark energy within him until it consumed him. All it takes is an instant, provided the right volume can be reached."

"Why didn't he shatter?" Wellesley asked.

"Because I didn't want him to," Hunt said, eyeing the statue implacably. "I wanted to see his fear one more time before I broke him forever." With this he kicked the statue in the abdomen, casting coarse dust up and down the walkway. He turned to Tselitel who stood shivering with nervous strain a couple feet away. "Are you alright?" he asked, grasping her upper arms.

"I'm okay," she said in a hollow voice, her eyes upon the dusty pile that once had been the ruffian's feet. "Why did you wait so long?" she asked in confusion moments later. "Those goons could have cut you to pieces."

"I had it in hand," Hunt said simply, putting an arm around her quivering shoulders. "Besides, I had to build up enough of a charge to take him down in an instant. I didn't have time to let it build up once I'd started pouring it on. But there's something else, too," he added, raising his head a little and glancing around. "Wellesley's right: there *is* some kind of aura being cast over this place. It made it harder to access my gift at first, like I was confused. Otherwise I probably could have cut loose right as they grabbed the steward."

"The steward!" she said with alarm, breaking free of his grasp and hurrying up the hall to where he lay, blood running down his shirt. Dropping to her knees, she raised his head into her lap and stroked it gently. "Are you alright?"

"I–I think so," he groaned, as Hunt joined her and ripped the buttons of the steward's shirt open. "I don't think they hit anything vital."

"No, just sliced his shoulder," Hunt commented. "The goon that held you must have drawn his knife across it when he turned to run. You're lucky."

"I don't feel very lucky."

"He could have cut your throat," Hunt clarified.

"Oh."

"He needs medical attention right away," Tselitel said, looking at Hunt.

"I agree." Hunt seized the steward's hands and pulled him upright.

"What are you doing?" she asked with alarm, as the older man's head was jerked from her lap.

"His shoulder got sliced, not his legs," Hunt replied matter-of-factly. "Come on, friend: you can reach the medical bay under your own power."

"If you say so," he replied weakly, shambling between

Hunt and Tselitel as they moved slowly up the hallway.

Half an hour later Kaljurand joined them in the base's hospital. Greeting them briefly in the waiting room, he conferred with the medical staff before returning to speak with them.

"Thank you for looking after him," he said appreciatively. "This never should have happened."

"Is he alright?" Hunt asked.

"The doctors say he'll be fine. But they'll have to keep him for a few days just to be safe. That gash in his shoulder is nasty."

"It would seem your no-weapons policy isn't very effective," Gromyko said. He, along with Milo and Pinchon, had already been at dinner with the director when they heard the report from the hospital. "Perhaps you might consider letting the few decent people on this base carry something they can defend themselves with. This wouldn't have happened if Rex and Lily had been armed. Four knives don't compute against two guns."

"That's out of the question," Kaljurand said with finality. "Besides, it appears your friend is more than capable of taking care of himself."

"He shouldn't have to resort to arcane arts to protect himself!" Gromyko insisted. "We came to this base to find a little temporary safety – not to be assaulted in the halls. What kind of a base is it that cannot even guarantee–."

"That will do, smuggler," Kaljurand ordered sternly. "And I'll thank you to address me with respect, when you address me at all, which, I earnestly hope, will be infrequently."

With a scowl Gromyko crossed his arms and leaned against one of the hospital's pristine white walls.

Satisfied with this grudging expression of acceptance, Kaljurand drew closer to Hunt and dropped his voice.

"What happened to the other three? The ones you mentioned before?"

"Turned tail and ran," Hunt said tersely.

"Because of what you did to their leader?"

"No, he was the icing on the cake. I gave the first three a taste of a different brew that I keep on hand for lesser offenders."

"Philip told me you had a gift," he said, shaking his head slowly in disbelief. "But I never imagined it was something so powerful."

"Do you regret my using it?"

"Not in the slightest. That contemptible little miscreant has been on my blacklist for a long time. He was one of the first ones to come here when the Devourers broke upon us and immediately set about causing trouble. Nothing I could justify to the higher command, naturally. He was too slick to get caught. But I had indirect evidence linking him to two murders and at least six assaults. I would have eliminated him long ago if I could have managed it without fingerprints." Suddenly the director stopped himself. "I may have spoken a bit hastily there."

"I won't spill," Hunt said with a chuckle, the idea amusing to him. After all, he thought, who could he possibly tell it to?

"Thanks," Kaljurand said, with more feeling than Hunt had expected. "Well, dinner is cold by now and the evening is ruined," he said in a louder voice, addressing the rest of the room. "Still, I would appreciate it if you and the good doctor could join me for at least a light refreshment."

"Darling?" Hunt asked, looking at her.

Like Gromyko she leaned against one of the walls. But her arms were wrapped tightly around her midsection in a self-hug through which she attempted to calm her nerves. She was totally absorbed by her thoughts, barely cognizant of what was going on around her. The image of the ruffian turned to ash had engraved itself into her memory. Even in the bright lights of the hospital she could see his terror-stricken face before her. It wasn't until Hunt crossed the small waiting room and put a hand on her shoulder that she was shocked out of her reverie.

"What?" she asked, dimly aware after the fact that someone had addressed her. She turned and looked at Hunt, who eyed her with concern. "Did you ask me something?"

"The director would like to have us up for something light to eat," he said quietly in her ear. "But if you're not feeling up to it–."

"Oh, no," she said, shaking her head. "I feel alright."

"Baby…" his voice trailed significantly. "Why, you're shaking like a leaf," he added after a moment. "Are you cold? Do you want to head back to our room?"

"No!" she said, more loudly than she'd wished. "I mean, I don't think I can pass through that hallway again. Not yet, anyway."

"Why don't you two come and have a little supper with me," the director said, intuiting what bothered her from across the room and deciding to intervene. "In the meantime I'll have you assigned to different quarters. Somewhere farther away from the refugees."

"I thought you couldn't play favorites?" she asked blankly, her fearful condition robbing her usual politeness.

"On this occasion I think I can make an exception," Kaljurand replied, a slight gleam in his eye implying a hidden purpose in his sudden kindness. "Please, it's the least I can do after what you've been through. After all, Doctor, you shouldn't be forced to revisit that scene any more than necessary."

"I suppose you're right," she replied with a nervous nod. Hunt's hand supportively squeezed her shoulder. "What about our friends?"

"They'll have to make do," the director replied, his tone immediately formal as he looked at the smuggler. Beside the latter stood Milo, who had been roped into Gromyko's camp in Kaljurand's mind.

"Don't worry about us, Lily," the smuggler said with a

touch of his old flourish. "Gromyko will never perish at the hands of such ruffians. His death shall be as his life has been: glorious!"

The director eyed the smuggler with confusion for a moment, scarcely believing that any man would speak of himself in such a grandiose manner. Shaking his head, he turned back toward Hunt and Tselitel.

"Well?"

"We accept," Hunt said.

"This way," Kaljurand replied, ushering them toward the door.

Along with a security team of six, Kaljurand escorted the couple back to his quarters. They found the table had long since been cleared, the various foodstuffs packed away for preservation.

"I'll have something small sent up," he said, lifting a phone off the wall and speaking into it quietly for a few moments. "Some sandwiches and a bottle of wine will join us shortly," he said, rejoining them. "Come, take a look at the view," he added, ushering them to a long horizontal window.

Before them stretched incalculable miles of gray, pockmarked dust. Above and beyond it twinkled innumerable stars, whose silent guardianship of the vastness of space brought a little comfort to Tselitel as she began to lose herself in its contemplation. Standing between the two men, Hunt's hand still on her shoulder, her breathing began to calm; and the shaking, caused by her condition and aggravated by the trauma she'd just experienced, lessened considerably. The director looked at Hunt behind her back and nodded slightly, indicating that such a result had been his purpose in bringing them there.

Soon a gentle knock at the door brought Tselitel out of her near-trance. She turned from the window and watched as the director took a small plate of fare from an attendant and closed the door.

"Give me a hand moving this table," he said to Hunt,

indicating a small rectangular affair just large enough to seat the three of them. "Over by the window," he nodded, once they'd seized it.

Quickly enough a trio of chairs were placed around it, Tselitel's positioned in the middle facing the window so she could continue to watch the stars without twisting her neck.

"The beginning of this evening has been a disaster," Kaljurand said frankly, pouring rich red wine into three glasses and serving it to his guests. "But perhaps we can redeem a little bit of what that rabble took from us."

"Why are you being so solicitous all of a sudden?" Hunt asked point blank, unable to contain himself any longer.

"Direct," Kaljurand said approvingly. "To the point. I like it."

"Okay," Hunt said, still wanting an answer to his question.

"Mister Hunt, it's not very often that I meet a man who can do more for me than I can do for him. I'm always being besieged by the cronies of a thousand bosses within the organization. And they *all* want something. Typically it's something I can't provide, so I have to find some way to send them off satisfied without gratifying their desires at the same time. Do you have the least idea how *frustrating* it is to tapdance with the kind of refuse that is common to the Black Fang pirates? All those grasping, grubby little hands. Each of them wants something they haven't earned – something they don't deserve. They come to this little dot of order that I've managed to chisel out of the otherwise worthless organization that I belong to, each intent on carving a slice of it off for themselves."

"You haven't answered my question," Hunt replied, grabbing one of the sandwiches and taking a bite. "Though in a way you have. Clearly you want something from me. You had an inkling of what I could do before, and it impressed you. Having seen me in action, you now wish to carve a piece of *me* off for yourself. Isn't that right?"

"Precisely," the director said with a chuckle, pouring himself more wine. "We always accuse others of what we ourselves do, don't we? Perhaps I should have saved some of my moral outrage for another time, when it couldn't come back so elegantly upon my own head."

"Just what do you have in mind for him?" Tselitel asked, concern for her man in her voice.

"A simple trade," he replied. "One of your vessels is damaged. Philip has been twisting my arm for hours, trying to get me to have it repaired. So far I've rejected his pleas. The craft is exotic, unknown to my mechanics. It would take several times longer to get it fixed than one of our fighters. That is the kind of largesse I simply can't afford, especially when you throw in the price of replacement parts. You see, everything I do must be justified to the broader organization. I would immediately be hauled up for review if I started giving away our man hours and equipment. I would have to get something in return."

"Such as?"

"There is an individual from whom I must obtain certain information. She is a member of the fringe independence movement. We captured her nearly a week ago but haven't managed to get any information out of her despite our best efforts. She knows where a number of military supplies have been stashed that are extremely valuable to us. So far our more sophisticated interrogation techniques, which involve the use of alien artifacts, haven't proven effective. Sometimes they work and sometimes they don't. It depends on the individual. In any event, soon we'll be forced to resort to more primitive methods of breaking her. And that is where you come in."

"You want Rex to beat her up?" Tselitel asked.

"It does sound like that, doesn't it?" Kaljurand asked with a light chuckle. "No, I want to use your powers to get inside her head. Your capacity to inspire fear is incredible, and will save us the trouble of breaking her body. If you could send three hardened thugs running for the hills, I have no doubt that you can get what we want out of her in short order. The Black Fang organization values this information very highly. In addition to repairing Philip's vessel, we would be willing to accommodate any reasonable requests you may have during your stay with us."

"Better lodgings for our friends," Hunt said instantly.

"I said any *reasonable* request," the director replied, his face souring at the thought of Gromyko.

"How badly do you want that information?" Hunt countered.

"Very well," he said with a restrained nod.

"Rex, you're not actually going to *torture* that poor woman?" Tselitel asked.

"If I don't, they will," he said pragmatically. "This way she won't be smashed to bits from the experience. Besides, I'll have you on hand to drain the shadow from her once we learn what we need to. It'll be a bitter memory, but nothing more once we've finished."

"How can you talk this way?" she asked, her healer's heart tormented by the very thought. "We have nothing against the fringe independence people."

"Perhaps we ought to," he replied, growing a little heated. "One of their sympathizers nearly got you killed, remember?"

"Even as we speak they are working to establish a confederation separate from the empire," Kaljurand inserted calmly. "The imperial navy is reeling and can't hold them in check for long. Only the squabbling and infighting of petty would-be despots has kept the fringe from uniting under an independent government. And this at a time we cannot possibly afford to be divided."

"As I understand it, you pirates have been exploiting the situation ever since it emerged," Tselitel said with agitation, her hands beginning to shake again. "Colonel

Pinchon told me all about it."

"Yes, we have continued to ply our trade," Kaljurand admitted. "But we have not tried to tear entire worlds out of the emperor's hands. These imbeciles are as shortsighted as they are self-seeking. They preach freedom and prosperity. But what they really want is to gain power for themselves. A moot point, I might add, if the Devourers keep annihilating our planets."

"And you're somehow better? What right do you have to judge while you hide out here doing nothing?"

"A bystander is infinitely more just than a murderer, even if he only stands aside and watches the crime. His hands are clean."

"A very narrow distinction," Tselitel replied.

"But an accurate one."

"All of this talk is beside the point," Hunt said. "The fact is we need those repairs, and pumping information out of that woman is the price. One way or another I'm going to get it out of her. The only question is whether or not you're going to ease her suffering by drawing the terror out when I'm finished. Like you did for Milo."

"Wait, you've done this to your *brother*?" Kaljurand asked, genuinely surprised.

"Twice," Hunt replied offhandedly, his eyes still fixed on Tselitel.

"This is wrong, Rex," she said, shaking her head slowly side-to-side.

"It takes courage to do wrong for the right reasons," he replied. "Our backs are against the wall. We need to do this, for the greater good."

Her eyes shot between Hunt and Kaljurand. The latter, leaning back in his chair, watched with an air of cool detachment as Hunt aggressively made his case for him. Finally she sighed.

"Alright," she nodded, looking defeated.

"Good," Kaljurand said. "The Black Fangs won't forget

this."

"No, but *I'd* like to," she said quietly, pushing back from the table and standing up. "Where are our new quarters?" she asked in an exhausted tone.

"Ask one of the security personnel outside the door to escort you," Kaljurand replied. "Tell them I said to."

"Alright," she replied, as Hunt began to stand up. "No, stay here," she said, putting a hand on his shoulder and pressing gently downward. "I'm sure you two have a lot to discuss." With this she made for the door and left.

"She's a gentle soul," Kaljurand said when she'd gone.

"And a better soul," Hunt replied, his heart sinking in his chest as he continued to eye the door through which she'd left. "Better than mine, anyway."

"Someone has to get their hands dirty," Kaljurand replied knowingly, pouring himself yet more wine. "The idealists won't, so the *unidealists* have to."

"When do I break this victim of yours?" Hunt asked dryly, not wishing to discuss the matter further.

"Tomorrow," Kaljurand replied, not appreciating his characterization. "You both deserve a night's rest after what's happened today."

"Alright," he said, pushing out of his chair and making for the door. "Where are you putting the other three?"

"The room next to yours," he replied, putting a foot up on Tselitel's vacant chair and looking out the window. With the discussion over he withdrew into a world of his own.

With this Hunt left, escorted to his room as Tselitel had been.

"Sure you want to head inside?" Wellesley asked as the guard left him to return to his post. "I don't think she's in a very amiable mood."

"Neither am I," he replied, twisting the knob and finding the door locked. "Hey, guard!" he called down the hall, hoping he had a key. But he was already out of earshot. Muttering under his breath he turned back to the door and rapped loudly. "Open up, Lily," he uttered, pausing to listen. "I said open up," he ordered more loudly.

"Maybe she's in the bathroom," Wellesley offered.

"Very likely," he replied sourly. For a moment he looked at the door, tempted to break it down. Then he remembered Milo and Gromyko. "Might as well spend the night with them, if that's how she's going to be," he murmured, moving to the neighboring door and opening it. The lights were off and the room was perfectly still. They hadn't been moved in yet. "Of course," he thought, remembering he had only given the director his ultimatum minutes before. "Well, they'll be here soon enough," he mused.

"Rex?" he heard Tselitel say from out in the hall. "Are you there, Rex?"

"Funny, she doesn't *sound* upset," Wellesley observed, as Hunt left the room.

"Sorry, I was in the bathroom," she said upon seeing his sullen looking face. "Are you alright?" she asked, moving aside in the doorway as he pressed past her.

"Just fine," he replied, as she closed the door and locked it.

"What's the matter?" she asked, padding across the floor in her bare feet to him. "More trouble with the director?"

"It's nothing," he said, dropping into a chair and rubbing his brow. "Nevermind, it's too silly to mention."

"What is it?" she asked, slipping to her knees and resting her forearms on his legs, looking up into his concealed eyes. "Something is on your mind."

"I thought you were blaming me for this torture business and locked me out," he said, feeling stupid.

'What?" she asked with a chuckle. "No, of course not."

"You know I don't want to do it, right?" he asked. "I don't take pleasure in that kind of thing. It really is the only way. You heard Kaljurand: the repairs aren't gonna be cheap.

We could have paid for them if the *Kol-Prockians* hadn't made off with that kantium. But with things as they are we have to make the best deal we can. And at bottom this really is much kinder than doing nothing and letting them resort to knuckles with her."

"Oh, I know that," she assured him.

"Then why did you tell me to stay behind when you left? Kaljurand got the message just as clearly as I did. Started going on about idealists and whatnot."

"I was stupid," she said, shaking her head and resting it on his knee. "You're right, I *did* blame you. But only until I got outside Kaljurand's door. Once I was in the hall the spell was broken, and I came to my senses. I was going to turn around and take you with me. But I figured I'd made enough of a muddle of things and decided to tell you here. I was going to wait up for you, but just dashed into the bathroom quick because I didn't expect you so soon."

"Funny how this all started just so we could get a sixth set of fingerprints to press against this cube," Hunt said, pulling it out of his pocket and holding it up.

"How did you get that thing through the scanner?" she asked. "I thought you'd left it in the fighter."

"No, I forgot it in my pocket until they locked the security room on us. When I realized we were going to be searched my heart jumped into my throat, but it was too late. Luckily they didn't think anything of it. Must have thought it was some kind of trinket."

"Well, what are we going to do about it?" she asked. "We still need a sixth set of prints. And I gather you don't want to trust Kaljurand with whatever secret it holds."

"I haven't made up my mind yet," he replied wearily. "Who knows, it might open his eyes to what's really going on in this war and make him help us more. That, or drive him to become an active participant. You know as well as I do that the empire needs all the help it can get right now just to stay on its feet."

"Well, let's not think about it anymore tonight," she said, climbing into his lap and wrapping her subtly trembling hands around his neck, drawing his head against her chest. "Let's just relax and forget there's a galaxy outside this room."

Feeling the tips of her fingers tremble against his skin, he drew back, taking her right hand in his left and kissing it.

"Are you alright?" he asked. "I mean really?"

"No," she said, shaking her head. "I'm not. I've been getting worse ever since we came here. I think that pall Wellesley mentioned is working on me, too."

"All the more reason to finish up our business here and get on our way."

"I agree."

With a faint smile on his lips he kissed her. Slipping an arm behind her knees, he stood up and carried her to bed.

CHAPTER 13

Part way through the night Hunt awoke. All around him was darkness. He could feel Tselitel's tall, thin form pressed against the right side of his body. Her arm lay across his chest, her fingers unconsciously wrapped around Wellesley's medallion.

The air in the room was perfectly still. Too still, in fact. Without knowing how he was aware of another presence. Its essence quieted the myriad nearly inaudible noises that filtered through the walls from all sections of the base. The sound of mechanics working the night away in the hangar; feet shuffling to their bunks in the hallway. But most pointedly missing of all was the lightness in the air that allows a man to position himself by his ears alone. The air was heavy, dense, almost solid. He felt certain he could drop a paperweight over the side of the bed and only hear half the report of it clanking to the hard floor.

Instinct told him to be frightened. But he'd experienced too many strange things since his first meeting with Ugo Udris to be shocked by things that were merely unusual. Gently he raised Tselitel's unconscious arm and laid it along her side. Slipping down the mattress, he put his feet on the floor and left the bedroom, quietly closing the door behind him.

"What are you doing?" Wellesley asked.

"Where are you?" Hunt asked in a whisper.

"Right down here, obviously," the AI replied. "Are you fully awake? It so–," he stopped mid sentence. "You're not talking to me, are you?"

Padding across the cool floor on bare feet, he slid the deadbolt aside and looked out the door. Nothing to be seen along either side of the hallway. Puzzled, he pulled his head back inside and relocked the door.

"Something is wrong," he muttered, turning back toward the room.

"Why don't you turn on the light?" Wellesley asked, wondering at his friend's strange behavior.

His eyes searched the darkness, trying to find any kind of outline they could. His unconscious mind painted half a dozen frightful shapes onto the shadowy canvas before him, trying to bring palpably to life notions that floated dimly in the back of his mind. Suddenly a face loomed in front of him, and he vaulted back reflexively, smacking into the door.

"Rex?" he heard Tselitel call from the other room. "Are you alright?"

The face vanished at the sound of her voice. Moments later the bedroom door opened, bathing half the front room with light from a lamp she'd turned on.

"What's the matter?" she asked, walking to him slowly as he leaned against the door, his eyes fixed on the point where he'd seen the face. She took his arm in both her hands and shook him gently, as though he was in a stupor.

"I heard you," Hunt replied in a distracted voice, still not looking at her.

She moved to the space beside him and followed his eyes, searching the room for whatever it was that fascinated him so completely. At last she gave up and shook her head.

"Darling…" her voice trailed, hoping he'd explain. When he continued to stand silently she put her hand to his cheek and rubbed it slowly. "Rex…" she said in a slow, soothing tone, "what's the matter? What have you seen?"

"You," he said at last, breaking away from the memory

of his vision and looking at her. " I saw you."

"Oh, well, it's always nice to be thought of," she said, giving him a little kiss and taking his hand to draw him back to bed.

"You were dead," he said with blunt astonishment as she tugged on his arm, instantly stopping her. "Your eyes were closed, and you were floating in the air. Mute, pale, and lifeless."

"So? Everyone dies sometime," she said, trying to lighten his load despite the sense of dread his words evoked within her heart. "It's nothing, darling. Just a bad dream. A nightmare."

"A waking nightmare?" he countered. "I don't think so."

"Well, I can't imagine what else it could be," she said. "It's probably just mental residue from that run-in we had with those goons in the hallway. You were scared to lose me then, and the fear bubbled up again just now. I wouldn't worry about it."

"This was more than that," he said musingly, drawing out of the conversation as he reflected once more. "It felt…"

"What?" she asked, her voice suddenly louder. "Like a vision? A premonition? Things like that don't happen, Rex. There's a logical, simple explanation for this."

Hunt looked at her, drawn from his reverie by the force of her words. Her hands had started to shake again, and her eyes were wide with fear. His vision had struck too close to home for her, and she was unsettled. He paused and looked away for a moment, as though in deep thought.

"I suppose you're right," he nodded. "I guess I wasn't fully awake." Putting his arm around her he guided her back to the bedroom and shut the door.

"Are you just saying that?" she asked from beside the bed, not quite convinced by his act.

"Well, it's not like I've got a better answer," he replied truthfully enough, climbing back onto the bed and patting the space beside him. "Come on: enough of this for one night. We should be sleeping right now anyway."

She raised his right arm and laid down beside him, draping it across her shoulders and down her back as she rested her head on his chest. He felt her trembling hand just above his stomach, the fingers twitching back and forth as her eyes fell upon a spot on the wall.

"Rex, do you…" she began, swallowing hard and gathering her courage. "Do you think I'll…make it?"

"Yes, I do," he replied stoutly, more from inner necessity than actual belief. In truth the dreadful sense of her mortality had been slowly rising within him ever since they'd reached the base. She'd seemed tired, vulnerable, somehow older than ever before. For the first time since meeting her he sensed the outline of wrinkles beside her eyes. Drawn and weary, he saw the effort with which she controlled her emotions. Something was taxing her. He feared it was the next stage of her condition manifesting itself. "I'm not gonna let anything happen to you," he added, for his sake as much as hers. Kissing her forehead, he flicked off the light.

Hours later they were in the small detention block of the base, standing before a window of one-way glass with the director.

"There she is," he said, nodding toward a rather lean woman in her early twenties. With chestnut hair and a dull brown pair of overalls, she looked more like a mechanic's apprentice than an interstellar revolutionary. Her face was nothing special, though a slight gleam in her eye implied quick intelligence. The interrogation room was bare of furnishings. She freely paced up and down its length.

"So what do you want me to do?" Hunt asked acerbically. "Just go in there and snap her mind in two?" His opinion of the director had dropped somewhat since learning the price of repairs for the colonel's ship. But more than anything he was a target to throw his anxiety over Tselitel against. Channeling fear into anger helped him manage it.

"I'm not a barbarian, Mister Hunt," Kaljurand replied disapprovingly. "As I have already told you, this is the most humane way to extract the information we need. Besides, the good doctor can 'draw the shadow' out when you're done, as you said last night. Really, there's no reason to be unfriendly."

"I'll keep that in mind," he said flatly, turning from the director and making for the interrogation room's door. He was blocked by two sentries, both of which looked at the director. Once he nodded his consent, they stood aside and allowed Hunt to enter.

"Another pirate lackey?" she snapped when the door was shut and he'd stood looking at her for a moment. "What's your story? More artifacts? Or is it time for injections?"

"There won't be any need for injections," Hunt replied, shoving his hands into his pockets and walking toward the one-way glass. Seeing nothing but his own reflection and that of the woman, he watched her shift back and forth between her feet, her eyes darting up and down his body as she tried to figure out who he was.

"You're different than the others," she said after a moment. "You don't have their attitude."

"I'm no pirate."

"Then what are you doing here?" she asked, her eyes bouncing between the back of his head and his reflected face in the mirror, trying to figure out which one to watch.

"What's your name?"

"You already know that," she retorted.

"They do, I don't. I'm Rex Hunt."

"Is that supposed to matter to me?" she asked.

"No," he replied, shaking his head as he crossed his arms and turned around, leaning against the mirror behind him. "But this'll be a lot simpler if you cooperate. I'll get the information I want out of you sooner than you think, and at a price you can't imagine. I don't want to do it, but they've forced my hand."

"What, am I supposed to believe you're a prisoner too?" she laughed scornfully.

"In a sense I am," he replied, his gaze steady and unblinking.

She eyed him for a moment, her head tilting slightly to one side. Slowly she nodded.

"Louise Van," she said. "I'm part of the fringe independence movement."

"I already know that part. What I don't know is where certain supplies are that our hosts," here he jerked his thumb over his shoulder toward the glass, "want very badly. They're willing to break you in half to get the truth. Before resorting to that step they've agreed to let me talk to you."

"What, are you some roving humanitarian?" she cracked.

"Look, I don't have the time or the inclination to kick this back and forth with you," he replied. "I'm trying to give you a chance to–."

"Wait," she said, her eyes growing wide with realization and then narrowing. "Just wait a moment," she said, drawing a little closer and examining his face. "There's something about you," she uttered, more to herself than to him. "Something in your...aura." She reached out and touched his arm, instantly drawing her hand back as though zapped. "You're him!" she exclaimed, gripping her hand with the other and stumbling backward. "But that can't be. Only a handful got off of Delta-13 before the Devourers destroyed it." Her eyes narrowed again, as they shot between him and her hand. "You're the dark one."

"What do you know about me?" he asked in surprise, taking a step towards her as his arms uncrossed.

"Just what I was told," she replied, moving further away. "You were Ugo's great hope."

"You know Ugo Udris?" he asked with surprise.

"Knew him," she corrected. "He never made it off Delta."

"Then you know what I'm capable of," he replied, regaining his self-possession.

"Yes, yes I do," she nodded, moving back until she bumped against the wall. Turning to look at it, she slid along it, angling slightly away from him. "You stay away from me."

"There's nowhere you can go that I won't reach you," he said, raising his hand, smoke beginning to dance between his fingers. "I don't want to do this to you, Louise."

"He trusted you," she said, shaking her head. "You were like a son to him. He knew there was something special about to take place on Delta-13. For years the organization pleaded with him to get off of that snowball and put his talents to use elsewhere. But the planet told him to stay put, so he did. It was watching you, waiting for you to mature before handing you over to him. But once you got what you could out of him you turned your back, wasting all his years of sacrifice. It broke him in the end."

"A fate he deserved," Hunt replied stonily.

"How can you say that?" she snapped. "After all he did for you? He took you out of the worthless life you led before and set you on the path to greatness. All he asked you in return was that you help us recapture our liberty from the emperor. He was true to the human spirit. But I suppose a miserable dog like you wouldn't understand something like that."

"I understand life and death," he replied, losing his patience as he advanced, backing her into a corner. "That's all that matters in the end."

"You *would* think that," she said bitterly as she shrank into the corner. "It's what drove your father into serving the empire, too. Now you're following in his footsteps, helping to shore up Rhemus' tyranny. Your family has forgotten the sweet taste of liberty."

"You can't taste liberty with a dead tongue," he replied

coldly, standing over her cowering form.

"Machines," she uttered derisively. "That's all you Hunt's have ever been: machines. As long as your wheels spin and your motor whirs, you imagine everything is fine and well. You've always ignored the *spirit* of man. It was something Ugo saw from the very first time he met your father. There was power and greatness within him, as there is within you. But he was soulless, materialistic. There was no counterpoise within him to prevent the abuse of the great strength of our ancestors. You are greater than him, but no greater than your family. In the end you serve the same idol."

"How does she know all this?" Wellesley asked.

"Wanda was not Ugo's only granddaughter," she replied caustically.

"What?" Hunt asked in astonishment.

"And here I was hoping never to meet another Udris," the AI retorted.

"There's more of us than you'd think, *Kol-Prockian*," she replied. "A lot more. We've embedded ourselves into every layer of the fringe independence movement. A confederation *will* rise from the ashes of the empire. I assure you of that."

"If the empire falls, humanity goes with it," Hunt replied with certainty. "The Devourers will consume every last human in the galaxy."

"Don't you simpletons understand?" she asked. "The Devourers are only here because of our arrogance. The *Prellak* simply want to lay low the power and pride of the emperor. That done, they'll return the aliens to their prison. A peaceful coalition of worlds presents no threat to anyone."

"It's more personal than that," Hunt replied. "The *Prellak* wants us dead, plain and simple. And the Devourers want to finish what they started long ago."

"Do you think we're special? That this is some kind of grudge? The universe is much broader than the little patch of space we occupy. Only in placid coexistence can we hope to survive. The higher lights of the independence movement have always known this."

"Ugo didn't seem to," Wellesley replied. "He seemed to think this was all about taxes and imperial power in the Milky Way."

"My grandfather was only allowed to know so much," she replied reluctantly. "His position on the frontlines made him vulnerable."

"And yours didn't?" the AI countered.

"Just who do you think I am?" she asked pointedly. "I'm not some low level drudge. They didn't pluck me off a passing freighter. I was kidnapped by the pirates from the planet Erdu-3. The only reason they stashed me in the Black Hole was because almost no one knows where it is. At this moment freedom fighters are scouring the galaxy looking for me."

"Erdu is one of the biggest hotbeds of rebel sentiment," Wellesley said to Hunt.

"That's right," she replied proudly. "We're going to lead the rest of the fringe against his so-called Imperial Majesty. Now that his servants are falling back before the scourge we have the chance to strike and be free. Humanity will once more taste liberty."

"They will taste death," Hunt said with finality. "Nothing more. Now, where are the supplies that the pirates want?"

"You'll have to kill me," she spat, her eyes filled with defiance.

"No," he said with a shake of his head, raising his hand as it was engulfed by smoke. "I won't."

Fifteen minutes later Hunt left the interrogation room.

"The second moon of Yoria-4," he said to the director. "There's a hidden base two hundred miles north of the southern pole. Defenses are minimal. They're relying on stealth mostly."

"Excellent," Kaljurand said, clapping his hands together. "Mister Hunt, you've accomplished in half an hour what we couldn't manage in weeks."

"Better get in there and straighten her out," Hunt said to Tselitel, ignoring the director.

"Okay," she said in a near whisper, rising out of a chair she'd been sitting in and walking past the sentries to Van's whimpering form.

Hunt watched through the glass as she approached the terrified young woman. She bowed low as she approached, getting down to her level and slowly extending her hands as though trying to corral an injured and frightened animal. Gently taking the revolutionary's head between her hands, she quickly drew the shadow from her.

"Who are you?" Van asked a few moments later, uncertain as to what had just happened.

"I'm Doctor Tselitel," she said kindly, modestly extending a trembling hand that was not accepted.

"You look like the one who needs a doctor, not me," Van said, instantly forgetting her past state as she shot to her feet.

"You'll be alright now," Tselitel said reassuringly, gradually straightening up. Slowly she turned and began to walk away.

"Yes, I will," she said under her breath, leaping forward and seizing Tselitel around the neck. "Stay back!" she barked, as the occupants of the observation room flooded in. "I'll crush her windpipe if you try anything!"

The two sentries flanked Hunt and Kaljurand with their pistols raised toward the prisoner and her hostage. Being shorter and smaller than Tselitel, Van easily concealed most of her body behind her frail form. Barely able to breath, the doctor pleadingly eyed Hunt as the revolutionary's knuckles ground against her neck.

"You can't get off the base like this," the director said, completely unmoved. "You'll never make it to the hangar.

Security forces will take you down the instant they have a free shot."

"Not if her boyfriend over there takes 'em out for me," she said acidly. "How do you like that, Hunt?" she laughed. "Looks like I've turned things around on you."

With an annoyed sigh the director took the pistol from the guard next to him and pointed it at the tiny portion of Van that was visible just behind Tselitel's ear.

"Enough theatrics, Director," she said as he closed one eye and carefully aimed. "Put the gun down. I know you'd never risk hitting this poor little–."

Suddenly a deafening report rang out in the small space. The arm around Tselitel's neck went limp and slid off her shoulder as Van's body collapsed to the floor. Shocked almost to death by the sight of Kaljurand seemingly firing straight at her, Lily stood in petrified silence for several moments and then collapsed in a faint, Hunt only just catching her before she hit the floor.

"Witless fanatic," Kaljurand said, shaking his head at the corpse as he handed the guard back his pistol. "She didn't have the least hope of escaping. I'd never allow her out of here, even if I had to sacrifice half the personnel in the base." His eyes rolled over to Hunt, who still held Tselitel. "She'll be alright when she wakes up. Just a little surprised, is all."

A shadowy wave flooded through Hunt, his eyes turning dark as he regarded the director. He was about to put Tselitel down and introduce Kaljurand to every repressed fear he'd ever possessed when Wellesley stopped him.

"Not now, Rex," he said firmly. "Think of Lily first. You need to look after her."

With a scowl on his face he jerked Tselitel up into his arms and carried her back to their room. The blackness only faded from his eyes once he'd gotten her back inside and laid her out on the bed.

"I've never wanted to *crush* someone more..." he growled to the AI. "Of all the high handed, arrogant, *dangerous* things he could have possibly done…"

"I know. A man like that is built to be offensive. But he *did* resolve the entire situation with one elegantly simple solution. And he's clearly a crack shot. I don't think he would have fired unless he was certain of missing Lily and hitting his target."

"I suppose," Hunt said grudgingly. Heading to the bathroom he wetted a rag with cold water and pressed it against Tselitel's perspiring forehead. Suddenly she came around.

"Rex!" she exclaimed, her mind picking right up where it had left off. She sat up and frantically looked around for several moments, trying to understand where she was.

"It's okay," he said, laying his hands on her upper arms and gently pressing her back down against the bed. "It's alright. You're safe now."

"Oh, Rex," she said, covering her eyes with her hand and letting out a long, ragged sigh. "When he fired that gun… I thought I was a goner. Even now I almost think I'm dead, and I'm talking to you in some spirit-dream." She drew her hand down her face and held it above her neck for a moment, looking at him out of the corner of her eyes as he knelt beside her. "This *is* reality, right? I'm not dreaming or something?"

"Nope, no dream," he said. "I almost wish it was. I could have lost you back there."

"You and me both," she replied, covering her eyes with both hands and then immediately pulling them away. "Nope!" she said to herself with a dry, nervous chuckle.

"What?" Hunt asked.

"When I close my eyes I see the muzzle flash. It must have been burned into my eyes. I didn't notice it until now. I guess I was in a daze at first."

"You're okay," he repeated, stroking the back of her hand.

"You didn't…do anything, did you?" she asked, the look on her face indicating she didn't really want to know.

THE BEAST EMERGES

"Almost," Wellesley answered for him. "Naturally I, the voice of reason, prevailed. I can only imagine what assaulting the director of a pirate base would have brought upon our heads. I'm sure they would have struck back without hesitation. And that would have brought our little adventure to an end pretty quick."

"That it would have," Tselitel agreed. "Oh, Rex," she said, laying the back of her hand against his cheek, "you can't always go off whenever something happens to me."

"I'll do it whenever the opportunity allows," he said, in the fervent tone of a solemn promise.

"I know," she mouthed silently, as touched by his devotion as she was disturbed by what it might bring upon him some day.

"At least now the colonel's ship will be repaired," Wellesley said. "And the sooner the better. I want to get out of this place as quickly as possible. There's something wrong with it, like I told you yesterday."

"Yeah," Hunt said, the image of Tselitel's dead face hovering before his mind's eye once more. Shaken to his bones by the horrifying sight, he pushed it away just as the AI spoke again.

"Not that I haven't minded the peace and quiet. But doesn't it strike you a little…odd, that we haven't seen Antonin or your brother yet today?"

"Honestly, with everything going on, I'd forgotten all about them," he said, suddenly concerned. "I'll be right back," he said to Tselitel, leaning over and kissing her lips. Quickly he got to his feet and made for the room next door. He tried the knob but found it locked. Banging several times he received no response.

"Maybe they're out stretching their legs," Wellesley offered.

"Yeah, could be," Hunt said without satisfaction, returning to Tselitel's side.

"Nothing?" she asked, already reading the answer

465

from his expression. Wordlessly he shook his head. "Well, they're probably alright."

"I can't assume that. Not on this base." He began to turn to leave and then hesitated, his eyes finding hers as he thought.

"You can go ahead," she smiled faintly. "I'll be alright now."

He knelt beside her once more and took her hand, kissing her fingers.

"I'll be back as quick as I can," he assured her.

Locking the door on his way out, he made it halfway down the hall before stopping.

"But where do we look?" he asked Wellesley and himself in equal measure.

"Hangar? It could be they went with Pinchon to check out the damage to his ship."

Having no better idea Hunt shrugged and bent his steps toward the hangar. Thrice he got lost in the labyrinthine base and had to ask directions from gruff and unwilling passersby. By the time he reached his destination he was short of patience. Stopping at the entrance, he cast his eyes over the sprawling bay, scanning for their ships. Though they'd only arrived the day before he couldn't remember even roughly where they were.

"Wells?"

"Don't ask me. I was blind when we showed up, remember?"

Grumbling under his breath he struck off toward the left, faintly recalling coming from that direction. Walking slowly, he carefully examined the ships around him. A wide range of vessels were present, reflecting the variegated nature of the refugee population: tiny single-engined scout ships; converted freighters; stolen imperial fighters. But no *Kol-Prockian* craft.

"Wells?" he asked suspiciously, his eyes narrowing as he began to smell a rat.

"I'm thinking the same thing. But we'd better be sure before we start pointing–."

"How can you possibly claim to have lost them!" they heard a familiar voice explode from a short distance ahead. "They are not the sort of vessels that one misplaces!"

"Looks like we're not the only ones on the trail," the AI said, recognizing Gromyko's voice above the din. "Turn to the right a little and then head straight."

"I see him," Hunt said in a low voice, his temper steadily rising.

"Look, pal, I said the ships aren't here," a mechanic said, his dirty thumbs hooked in the breast pockets of his overalls. "Now, I can't make 'em reappear, can I?"

"You made them disappear quickly enough!" Milo said hotly, standing beside the smuggler.

"Look, son," the mechanic said, running a hand through his thinning hair. "Before you start throwing accusations you'd better take a look around." As he said this the handful of pirates who were within earshot put down their tools and slowly formed a circle around him and the two Deltans. "Maybe you ought to think about taking back what you said."

"I'll do no such thing!" exploded the younger Hunt, clenching his fists as his face turned deep red. "First you steal from us, and then you want me to swallow my words?"

"I think you'd better," he said in a low tone.

"No, I think you'd better tell us where our ships are," Rex said from outside the circle, roughly shoving his way through and stopping just short of the man.

"Or what?" sneered the mechanic. "I count eight against your three, friend. Maybe you'd like to think about that for a minute."

"Strange, I count nine against your eight," the voice of the director called out from a short distance. Instantly the circle evaporated, each man recalling a pressing matter elsewhere that required his attention. The mechanic visibly shrank as Kaljurand and his entourage of security personnel approached. The director's eyes scanned those around him before landing on Hunt. "What's wrong?"

"Our ships have gone missing," he replied, crossing his arms. "We were just asking him where they were."

The director's eyes shifted to the mechanic, whose dirty hands were now held respectfully at his sides.

"Where are they?" he asked pointedly.

"Well, sir," he stammered. "Some of the boys thought, since these gents aren't Black Fangs…"

"Thought *what*?" Kaljurand asked, his eyes tightening along with his voice. "Go on, man: speak. Tell us what you and the others thought."

"I, um…That is to say, the boys…"

"The vessels will be returned to the hangar immediately," Kaljurand said crisply. "Within the hour. Should they fail to return, I will conclude that they are no longer within the confines of the base."

"But they'll just sit on them until the hour–." Milo began to complain.

"At which point," Kaljurand continued, stepping closer to the mechanic over whom he towered and leaning slightly downward, "I will dispatch several teams to locate them. *Without spacesuits*. Do I make myself quite clear?"

"Ab-absolutely clear," the man said, nodding vigorously as sweat began to gather on his brow. "I'm sure we'll find them, sir. N-no doubt about it."

"Good," the director replied slowly, straightening up. He turned toward the Deltans. "Gentlemen, perhaps you'd like to have some breakfast with me while they go about repairing your ships," he said in a tone both polite and that brooked no opposition. Reluctantly they nodded and fell in with his security team. Turning back to the mechanic he put his arm around his shoulders and walked a few steps toward the atmospheric shield. "Tell the boys," he uttered in a low voice, his mouth next to the man's ear, "the next time they take liberties with my guests I'm going to hold a little contest to see which one of them can last the longest with his head sticking out through that." The mechanic swallowed hard as Kaljurand pointed at the shimmering barrier. "Is that understood?"

Unable to speak, the mechanic simply nodded his understanding.

"Make sure the others understand it as well. It would be bad for morale for the men to have to watch their comrades' eyes boil out of their sockets in the cold vacuum of space." Turning from the stunned grease monkey, Kaljurand gestured for his entourage to follow and led the way out of the hangar. Dozens of curious onlookers waited impatiently for the moment they could dart to their friend and ask what had been whispered into his ear.

"Your men are thieves," Gromyko said disdainfully as they left the hangar and moved as a mass down the corridor.

"Of course they are," Kaljurand replied with a dismissive wave of his hand. "They're pirates."

"Where's colonel Pinchon?" Hunt asked Gromyko and Milo after a few moments. "I thought he'd be with you two."

"I haven't seen him all morning," Milo replied with a shrug, as the group turned a corner. "He must have left our room sometime during the night."

"Antonin?"

"Me, either," he said with a shake of his head.

Hunt eyed the director for a moment, but he seemed reluctant to comment. Letting the issue drop for the time being, he shoved his hands into his pockets and walked in silence.

"Makes you wonder," Wellesley murmured, as the group's feet pounded along the narrow walkways.

Occasionally they would encounter someone coming toward them. Instantly upon seeing the director's squad of protectors the individual in question would press himself against the wall or duck into a doorway, expecting to be trodden underfoot if he failed to move. Heedlessly the entourage moved forward, apparently willing to do just that. Shortly after leaving the hangar they arrived at Kaljurand's quarters.

"Please go inside, gentlemen," he said, one of his men opening the door for them. "I'll be with you in moments."

"I'd better check on Lily first," Hunt said, turning from the door and beginning to walk.

"I'd rather you stuck with your friends," the director said sternly.

Hunt stopped, his left fist clenching as darkness enveloped it.

"And I'd rather check on Lily," he said in a low voice without turning around.

"Of course, if that's what you wish," Kaljurand said with as much charm as he could muster through a tightened jaw. "You won't mind if we begin without you?"

Not bothering to answer, Hunt resumed his steps, reaching his door in short order and unlocking it.

"The director likes to have things all his own way," Wellesley said as Hunt closed the door behind him. "Even in petty things."

"He can have his own way just as long as he stays out of mine."

Walking into the bedroom, he was about to explain what kept him when he saw Tselitel. She lay on her side facing the wall, hands flattened under her head, her abdomen slowly expanding and contracting. Her eyes softly closed, her lips gently parted, she looked like a sweet drop of morning dew poured into human form and laid out upon the thin, uncomfortable mattress. Hunt leaned against the doorway and crossed his arms over his chest, slowly drawing a breath and contentedly letting it out.

"That's what makes this all worthwhile," he whispered to Wellesley with deep satisfaction. "All of it."

"I agree. You couldn't find another girl like Lily."

"Nope," he agreed quietly, watching her for several moments and then withdrawing.

"So," Wellesley said portentously as Hunt returned to the hallway and locked the door, "what do you think has happened to Pinchon?"

"I can't imagine," he replied.

To the surprise of them both the pirate was present at breakfast when they arrived. Talking in a light, friendly manner, he devoured the food before him with relish. His good humor even infected the director, who after a stony twenty minutes of ignoring Hunt finally found it within himself to recognize his existence. After that the meal passed off pleasantly enough, though the occasional barb from Gromyko toward Kaljurand nearly knocked it off course several times.

"I've got to talk to you," the colonel whispered to Hunt once the meal was over, standing with him before the window that had so fascinated Tselitel the night before. The others were further back in the room, standing and chatting in a desultory fashion as servants cleared the dishes.

"Go ahead," Hunt murmured, his lips barely moving.

"Not here. Ivo's watching me. I'll run into you later sometime. Keep your eyes open." With this the pirate chuckled loudly as though Hunt had made a joke and, shaking his head, wandered slowly from the room.

"And so the plot thickens," Wellesley said.

"Enjoying it?" Hunt mumbled.

"Yeah, actually. Believe it or not I'd prefer a little bit of petty human intrigue to all the existential stuff that's been going on lately. At least a mistake in these surroundings isn't punished by instant death – or worse."

"Worse?"

"Remember what *Alleehavah* almost became?"

"Got you."

"You know, I never really thought about it before, but I wonder if those *kals* could turn an AI dark. Does it even work that way? It's not like I have a normal organic form. I'm not sure how I participate in the whole light-dark economy."

"Your guess is as good as mine."

"I can see you're not in the mood to ponder such things at the moment."

As he said this Milo and Gromyko approached, forestalling a response.

"What's our next move, boss?" the smuggler asked, his slim form approaching the window and leaning against the left side of its frame. "Not a bad view," he commented.

"Can you believe those guys in the hangar?" Milo asked, his hackles still up. "Just who do they think they are?"

"Pirates," Hunt answered self-evidently. "They're not used to following the rules."

"Yeah, you saw how Kaljurand handled them," the smuggler added, nodding toward the director as he left through the door behind them. "He kicks them around 'cause that's the only way to keep 'em in line. Anything less than that and they'd get completely out of hand."

"They're out of hand now, stealing ships and whatnot," Milo said.

"What do you mean *whatnot?*" Hunt asked, his voice sliding into the accusatory tones of an older sibling.

"I can't find *Merokanah*," Milo admitted with quiet reluctance.

"What?" Hunt and Gromyko asked in unison.

"Hey, don't look at me!" the younger Hunt said defensively. "I had him with me when I left the ship. Sometime between then and breakfast they stole him."

"And how do you suppose they managed *that*?" Gromyko asked skeptically.

"One of 'em must have picked my pocket when I wasn't looking," Milo said with an exasperated shrug. "Maybe when we were arguing with them earlier. I don't know. He was there when we went to bed."

"Why didn't you say something when Kaljurand had

them bent over his knee in the hangar?" Gromyko prodded. "At least then they were scared enough to cough something up. Now we'll never find out what happened to him."

"Oh, sure, you *really* want me to admit that we smuggled an alien AI onto the base?" he retorted in a sarcastic whisper. "Don't you think that might encourage him to look for any *other* items we might have snuck in? Like maybe that little moron's older brother?"

"I object to that characterization," Wellesley said to Hunt.

"It'll be all the same when Kaljurand finds out that he's here," the smuggler countered. "Nobody else could have brought something that exotic onto the base. He'll put two and two together in a second."

"No, he won't find out about it," Hunt said with certainty.

"Why?" his brother asked, eager to get out of the corner Gromyko was painting him into.

"For just the same reason: nobody but us could have brought him in. After what happened in the hangar this morning every pirate on this base knows the price of stealing from the director's guests. They're not about to indict themselves by parading something they took from us. They'll keep *Mero* under wraps for the time being."

"Well, at least we have that working in our favor," Milo replied with some relief. "I still can't believe I lost him."

"Forget about it," Hunt replied, turning away. "Had to ditch him sometime."

"Where are you going?" Milo asked.

"I've got to find something," he said as he made for the exit.

"What?"

Hunt paused, his hand on the doorknob.

"I don't know," he replied with an incredulous grin, looking at them for a moment and then departing.

Milo turned to Gromyko with inquiring eyes.

"Don't ask me," he shrugged.

"Do you think we ought to go with him? The base is loaded with that trash."

"Oh, sure, you heard him *begging* us to come, didn't you?" the smuggler replied. "He can take care of himself. He's more dangerous than both of us put together, with Pinchon thrown on top. No, whatever it is, he wants to poke around on his own. Best to leave him be."

Slowly Hunt walked down the corridor from the director's room, following some inner light that seemed to be guiding him.

"Where are we going?" Wellesley asked, a touch of concern in his voice as his friend's feet carried them inexorably toward the refugee quarters.

"I've got an intuition," he replied cryptically.

"Have you ever noticed that your intuitions always seem to get us into trouble? Remember that night we broke curfew in Midway because you had a notion that an artifact was nearby? All we ended up with was–."

"This is different," Hunt replied with quiet certainty. "It feels…."

"What?" the AI probed after a moment of silence.

"Urgent. Almost like a distress call."

"Tell them to call back during business hours."

"Wells," Hunt said chidingly.

"Okay, fine. Go ahead. Leap to the rescue of some forlorn maiden, or whoever it happens to be. Just remember: each time you stick your neck into danger, I'm still right down here, dangling from it. You might consider what *I* think about these adventures every once in a while. It's the polite thing to do."

"Do you want to go back and wait in the room?" Hunt asked, still walking.

"What? No. *Someone* has to keep you out of trouble. But a fella likes to be *asked* once in a while, you know? Even AIs have a limit for how much danger they like to court."

"I'll keep that in mind," Hunt grinned, picking up the pace as the signal grew stronger.

Unfortunately, it wasn't the only thing to strengthen as he pressed on. A powerful stench wafted up the corridor toward him, souring the air enough to make him gag. Trash began to gather along the walls as he moved farther inside. Following the intuition around a corner, he saw low walls of rubbish on either side of the hallway, a narrow path of hard floor visible between them. Ruffians stood at odd intervals, watching him with cautious, hungry eyes that seemed to take in everything at once. As he advanced toward them they pressed themselves against the walls.

"Looks like word of yesterday's little fracas has gotten around," Wellesley observed as Hunt moved with slow confidence down the narrow path.

Instinct screamed for him to stop and turn around. Any one of them could be carrying a knife, just waiting to plunge it into his back the moment they were behind him. But the intuition was too strong to be ignored.

At the end of the corridor he turned right. Instantly he saw three large men standing before him, their bodies blocking the path. Bearded, with arms folded just above protruding bellies, they eyed him with surly indifference.

It was the trio he'd sent running the day before.

"Out of the way," he said, pausing just short of them. When they failed to move he held up his right hand as darkness enveloped it. "Move," he ordered crisply.

"Go for it," the one in the middle sneered. "See if it works."

"I don't like this, Rex," Wellesley said, as Hunt stepped back and cut loose with a smokey blast. Instantly it recoiled onto him, throwing him against the wall, fearful images flooding his mind as he fell face first onto the disgusting floor. Before his eyes he could see a *kal* dragging its long, cruel fingers along the bare skin of Tselitel's exposed stomach. She was tied backward over an altar of some kind, about to be sacrificed to an enormous face which hung over the dark scene, looking down upon it. A crooked dagger lay in a stone basin beside the altar. This the *kal* picked up, waving it in the air before her face in a ritualistic dance.

"How do you like the taste of your own medicine?" the middle thug asked, as his two comrades reached down and pulled Hunt off the ground, grasping his wrists and ankles in their powerful hands. Hunt fought to resist the nightmare unfolding before him, but its hold was surprisingly resilient. The chief thug grabbed a fistful of his hair and pulled his face upward. "Now you're going to see the Mistress."

He writhed against their iron grip, his attention split between them and the vision. Unlike the others he'd experienced, it seemed to have a life of its own. No matter how hard he pushed against it it continued to unfold, an autonomous production within the theater of his mind. The *kal* continued to dance before Tselitel, several times swooping the dagger within inches of her soft, vulnerable flesh.

The men carried him along a series of corridors before stopping at an unmarked room. The lead tough knocked thrice and promptly opened the door. It was dark within, only the light from the hallway casting a meager glow inside. The thugs who held Hunt lifted him over the back of a chair and deposited him in it. The vision instantly became opaque as they released him, plunging him into a dream world that prevented his escape until they were out of the room and the door had been locked. Then it cleared away completely, and he was left in total darkness.

"I have waited a long time to meet you, Rex Hunt," a strange female voice uttered from ahead of him. "A long time. Ever since the *Prellak* failed to turn you to their ends I have been consumed by curiosity. How could a mere human resist their power? Especially a descendant of the *least* of all the clans?"

"Who are you?" Hunt demanded, his eyes fruitlessly

searching the darkness.

"Who I am is not important," the voice purred, moving to his side and speaking into his ear. "All that matters is the purpose that brings me to you."

"And that is?"

"To warn you," she said. "To move you from the course you now pursue. Your futile efforts will cost you the lives of everyone you love. You cannot stop the Devourers. You can only slow their advance. But if you return to your purpose, Rex, you can spare the lives of your friends. You can spare the life of your love."

"Shut your mouth!" Hunt barked instantly.

"She's dying, Rex," the voice said with smooth certainty. "You know that as well as I. There is nothing in the science of your people that can prevent that. The Earthborn are wise to destroy, but not wise to heal. A thousand forms of death have been invented by your kind for every *one* form of healing. Your mighty emperor can snap his fingers and have his fleets annihilate an entire planet's population in hours. But he cannot even save himself from the ravages of disease. Nor can the most brilliant of your scientists present a cure for your love's condition. That requires the skills of a people practiced in healing, Rex."

"What people?" asked Hunt.

"A people not to be named by your kind," she replied. "A watchful, patient people. Long have they been the custodians of the universe. They have set in motion a plan to return balance to all life. Recalcitrant humanity stands in the way, and must be brought low. For this purpose you have been cultivated. You cannot stop this plan, Rex. You can delay it, but at the cost of all those whom you love. But should you return to the course that has been chosen for you, their lives will be preserved. Join with the *Prellak* and finish the work that they have started. It is for this reason that the Devourers were instructed to spare your ship in the battle above *Preleteth*. We wish to draw you back into the fold, Rex.

Join with us, and complete your destiny."

"To destroy humanity?" Hunt asked incredulously.

"Humanity is sick," the voice replied. "Plagued with darkness. They are a blight upon the universe; a blight to be removed. I do not expect you to understand or accept the necessity of this action. But I am well aware of your loyalty to your friends. Only by serving your purpose can you save them."

"You're lying," Hunt snapped. "If humanity must go, then they'd have to as well. You can't tolerate any exceptions."

"Humanity as a mass obstructs our aims," the voice replied in a tone of superior patience. "Four men and a barren woman present no threat to us. Did she tell you that, Rex? That her condition all but precludes pregnancy? Unable to procreate, you would be permitted to live out the extent of your natural lives. Then you would pass from the galaxy as a shadow retreats before the rising sun. The plague of your existence would be ended."

"She sure knows how to sweet talk a guy, doesn't she?" Wellesley quipped.

"Silence, *Kol-Prockian!*" she roared. "The insolence of your people is what destroyed them. Do you imagine that their enemies fell upon them all at once by accident? Did you never perceive some *design* in that coincidence? The humans are weak. But your people were far weaker. It was easy to keep them divided until their adversaries could annihilate them. Now the handful of them that remain perish daily in the mines of hostile races. After all," she said with wicked pleasure, "your people break so *easily*. Manual labor was never their gift."

"I'll kill you!" shouted Wellesley. "I'll–."

"What, *you*? You're nothing but a *trinket*, an impotent chatterbox. Your pathetic people have passed from this galaxy, and all they've left behind is an argumentative *bauble*. Now keep silent before I snatch you from his neck and destroy you."

"Nobody lays a hand on Wellesley," Hunt said stoutly, standing up in the darkness.

"He, along with all your friends, will perish if you persist in this ridiculous resistance. It is only a matter of time before the Devourers finish with the *Ahn-Wey* and pursue your fleets. A handful of engagements is all it will take to shatter them beyond all hope. Then your worlds will lay helpless at their feet."

"If that's so, then why does it matter what Rex does?" Wellesley countered. "Why not wait for the Devourers to finish them off in their own sweet time? Seems to me there's some holes in your story, Missy."

"You dare speak down to me?" she exploded. "Silence him, Rex, or I will destroy him right now."

"Me? I'm just an argumentative bauble, remember? Surely *I* don't warrant the kind of anger that you're–."

"Can it, Wells," Hunt said.

"Only because you asked so nicely."

"It was a glorious day when his people were wiped from this galaxy," she said quietly, trying to regain her composure. "All of humanity will be extinguished once the Devourers turn against you. But it will cost the custodians time, valuable time, in a struggle that is beyond your comprehension. For this reason they are willing to spare you and your friends if you carry out your original task."

"To destroy humanity?"

"Yes."

"I can't. *Preleteth* never finished my training. I cannot oppose the forces of the emperor in my present state."

"I will finish your training," she replied.

"Rex, you can't be serious!" exclaimed Wellesley. "This miserable witch is lying! She'll never let us live! Besides, Lily could never forgive you if you do this. *You'll* never forgive yourself if you–."

"Silence!" the voice ordered. "I warned you what

would happen if you continued to speak. Rex, I will spare your friends. I will also see to it that your love is healed. But you must turn the AI over to me now. I will not tolerate another moment of his interference."

"Like he'd ever hand me over to the likes of you!"

"He will, for the one he loves," she replied with certainty.

"Shows what you know."

"She's right, old friend," Hunt said reluctantly, reaching into his shirt and grasping the medallion. "Lily has to come first. Before you, before me, before *anyone*. I can't leave any stone unturned that might see her healed."

"Rex, what about all we've been through together?" the AI pleaded. "We've been closer than brothers. I've shared every triumph and every tragedy of your life. You can't throw me to the dogs now."

"I'm sorry," he said, drawing the chain from around his neck and wrapping it around the disc.

"Give it to me," the voice said, snapping her fingers in the darkness.

"First finish my training," he said, holding the AI against his side.

"I could just take him, you know," she shot back testily.

"You could try," he assented. "But I'd fight back, and then you'd have to injure your weapon, wouldn't you? Just finish what *Preleteth* started, and then you can have him."

The room was silent for a moment.

"Alright," she said with a superior chuckle. "I guess I can give you that."

At once the room began to illuminate, and he saw before him a robed figure. Her body seemed to be covered by a thin, tightly clinging garment. A gloved hand reached out and touched his chest. Suddenly his entire inner world was illuminated and visible. He saw images flash before his eyes; long forgotten memories that astonished him; memories that reached all the way back to the womb. He was aware of a man talking to his mother; a man with a dark aura who laid his hand on his mother's pregnant stomach. Instantly he felt a fracture within that blinded him with pain and made him cry out.

"So *that's* how you've resisted for so long," the robed figure said. "You've had help."

"Help?" he asked, as he felt her healing touch correct the agonizing fracture.

"Many have known that your family was destined for dark deeds. Forces on both sides have striven to support and halt your development. This man stepped in before you were even born to place a separation between you and the shadow within. It limited its power until now. Surprisingly, had he not done this, the efforts of the *Prellak* likely would have overwhelmed you and left you a mere vegetable. His success in stopping them has proven his undoing in the end. He has doomed your race to extinction." With this she withdrew her hand. "The hold placed upon your power is now removed. You may access it freely." The light continued to glow as she looked down at the disc in his hand. "I'll take that now. Payment is due."

"Yes, it is," Hunt said, seizing her by the throat with his free hand and shoving her against the wall. Before she could react darkness flowed from his hand and paralyzed her body from the neck down, leaving only her head unaffected.

"Don't be an imbecile," she strained. "This is your only chance to save your friends. And yourself."

"We'll take our chances," he replied grimly, as the shadow began to crawl up the neck of her garment toward her jaw.

"You don't understand," she said in a voice that grew distorted, as though it came through a malfunctioning speaker. "The *Prellak* know that you're here. A detachment of the Devourers' craft are waiting on the far side of the planet for the order to strike. If you turn against us they will instantly set out for this base and destroy it. Scarcely twenty minutes will be required for them to reach us."

"That's impossible," Wellesley said. "How could the *Prellak* possibly–." Realization struck him halfway through his words. "I don't believe it! I should have seen it before! The pall made it obvious!"

"What?"

"The moon this base is built on? It's orbiting a *Prellak* world!"

"Yes, it is," the figure sneered. "You thought you were one step ahead of us, but you've been under our watchful gaze the entire time!"

"What is this world's name?" Hunt asked through gritted teeth, his face inches from hers.

"*Cho'Tath*. It was the one who sent you the intuition that brought you here in the first place. Why do you think this base has been a scene of chaos ever since the Devourers arrived? It was in order to keep the director's hands full so that I could slip in unnoticed and bring you back into the fold. There are other agents like me spread across the galaxy, each of us waiting at strategic points to intercept you."

"So much for that plan," Wellesley shot back.

"It doesn't matter," she replied scornfully. "Soon you will be destroyed. Regrettably the great plan will be delayed. But nothing can stop the Journey."

"We'll see about that," Hunt retorted, increasing the flow of darkness until it flooded her entire being. In a moment she was just a statue. With a slight push of his hand her clothes disintegrated, showing her to be hollow inside. A bright cloud of energy ascended into the air and evaporated.

"She was just a shell," Wellesley said, as the room went dark, her peculiar essence no longer lighting it. "Her body was just a containment vessel of some kind. How did you know?"

"I felt it the moment she touched me and began the healing process," Hunt replied, as he slipped the medallion back around his neck.

"What was she?" he asked, as Hunt turned around and felt his way out of the room.

"No time for that now," he replied, finding the doorknob and twisting it. "Locked."

"Well, go on: use your magic powers to open it."

Gripping the knob with both hands, he poured his power into it momentarily and then twisted it sharply to the side, snapping it off.

"That didn't work," he said, holding up his half of the knob, the door still locked.

"Well, zap the entire door then," Wellesley replied. "Our twenty minutes are ticking."

"I've got a better idea," he said, standing back. "Open the door," he said in a loud voice. "The Mistress wishes for me to leave."

"Why doesn't she call out for herself?" asked the lead thug.

"Because she doesn't wish to speak to scum such as yourself!" retorted Hunt.

Believing that it had been her power that had sent Hunt's shadowy assault back onto him earlier, the thug felt certain she was still in control of the situation in the room. He waited a few moments for a contradictory word from the Mistress, just to be on the safe side. When he heard none, he felt that Hunt must be speaking on her orders and opened the door. Instantly upon doing so Hunt grabbed the front of his shirt with both hands and rolled backward, kicking the goon over him and sending him crashing against the far wall. The other two filled the doorway, their eyes adjusting to the dark when a sharp blast of terror struck them both, sending them running as at their first meeting.

"Get moving, Rex!" Wellesley barked, as his friend stepped into the doorway and blinked in the blinding light for a few moments.

"But which way?" he asked, looking up and down the

garbage-filled corridor.

"Take a left," the AI replied. "I was keeping track as they carried you down here."

"What would I do without you?" Hunt said, bolting as quickly as he could down the trash-strewn path.

"Die an agonizing, premature death, I'm sure."

Tearing past refugees who simply stood aside and gaped, Hunt soon reached the director's quarters and breathlessly ripped the door open. He scanned the room but saw no one.

"Where is he?" he asked desperately, bending over and putting his hands on his knees to breathe. "We have to…alert the base."

"Why?" asked Kaljurand from behind him, standing in the doorway.

"We're going to be attacked in less than fifteen minutes," Hunt said, standing up straight and speaking as clearly as he could under the circumstances. "There's a group of Devourer ships on their way here now."

"And how do you know this?" he asked, cocking a suspicious eyebrow.

"Because I spoke to an operative who was in league with them. She tried to turn me to their service. When I declined the order went out for their ships to attack."

"We would have detected them if they were in the system," Kaljurand said dismissively. "Our ships regularly patrol the entire area to ensure that we're alone. They couldn't have missed them."

"They planned this far in advance," Hunt said, shaking his head. "They must have slipped them in a little at a time to avoid drawing attention."

"Mister Hunt, I really don't see what you're trying to achieve with this nonsense," the director replied, walking past him into the room. "If the Devourers were in the system they would have attacked us. Everywhere they've appeared they've immediately assaulted the local garrisons. They're not ones to sit back and wait. They're aptly named: they go at whatever is lying before them."

"They're not mindless parasites," Hunt countered. "They're clearly intelligent, and capable of working according to a plan. You have to put the base on full alert immediately. Scramble your fighter craft and prepare for the worst. They've been scouting out your defenses ever since those refugees arrived."

"Mister Hunt, I will not tolerate any further instructions from you," he said sharply, his temper rising. "Now, your ships are being repaired as we speak. That was part of our deal. But I'll not stand aside while you assume control of this installation and–."

"Incoming ships detected," a voice called out over the PA system to the accompaniment of a warning siren. "Repeat: incoming ships detected. Scanners indicate Devourer vessels. All fighter craft launch immediately and prepare to defend the station."

"Is *that* good enough for you, Director?" Hunt asked, jerking his thumb toward the sound of the PA speaker out in the hallway. "You've got around twelve minutes before they're all over this place. And make no mistake: they intend to burn it to the ground."

"Gather up your people and get out," Kaljurand ordered. "I've got to coordinate the defense."

"With pleasure," Hunt retorted, turning on his heels and making for his lodgings.

"How are we gonna find the guys?" Wellesley asked as he shot along the corridor.

"I have no idea," Hunt said, skidding to a stop before his door and reaching for the key to unlock it. "We'll just have to hope we run into them."

Before he could unlock it Tselitel opened it.

"What's going–."

"We're under attack," he replied, grabbing her hand and jerking her into the hallway. He stepped to the room beside theirs and knocked furiously to ensure the others weren't inside. Receiving no answer he pulled Tselitel into a run and made for the hangar.

"I couldn't hear the announcement through the closed door," she explained quickly. "I just heard the alarm."

"Devourers are on their way here," Hunt replied tersely. "Explain to her, Wells."

"In brief, we encountered a figure who was working with the Devourers. She tried to turn Rex to their side but naturally that didn't work. Their backup plan for that eventuality was to bring the base down around our ears. And that's just what'll happen if we don't get out of here in the next ten and a half minutes or so."

"But what about the others?" she asked.

"They'll have to meet us in the hangar."

Base personnel crowded the hallways, blocking their path. Moving to the wall, Tselitel right behind him, he shoved his way through anyone unlucky enough to be caught in his path. Suddenly he felt Tselitel's thin hand jerked from his fingers, and he turned around to see she'd tripped over a woman who had fallen in the walkway and was in the process of being trampled.

"Help her!" Tselitel said, as he doubled back and pulled her to her feet.

"No time," he replied with certainty, leaving the woman to her fate and racing for the hangar. The sea of bodies resisted their progress despite Hunt's strenuous efforts to thrust them aside, slowing their pace maddeningly.

"Four and a half minutes," Wellesley announced when they reached the hangar.

Fighter pilots darted to their vessels as the duo raced along the grease stained floor. Ships' engines roared deafeningly to life around them. One by one they rose to a hover above their heads and bolted through the atmospheric shield into space.

"Over there!" Hunt said to Tselitel when he spotted

their ships. The main radio compartment on Pinchon's ship was laying in charred pieces beside the craft, the mechanics who'd been working on it long gone. "Pinchon!" Hunt shouted over the noise. "Milo! Antonin!"

"It's no use, Rex," Wellesley said. "They've got to look after themselves. Get us out of here."

Without another word Hunt dashed for the second fighter. With no ladder in sight he climbed onto the wing, helping Tselitel up after him. They slid into their seats just as the others arrived.

"Leaving without us?" Gromyko asked in a jaunty tone, as he and Milo followed their example and scrambled up the wing of Pinchon's fighter. "That's not very friendly of you, Rex!"

"Got room for one more?" the colonel asked in an urgent voice, helping a young woman of twenty-two onto the wing and making for his own craft.

"Who's she?" Tselitel asked, as the woman climbed past her and dropped into the rear seat.

"She's our sixth set of fingerprints," Pinchon winked, expertly slapping half a dozen switches and bringing his ship to life. "Get a move on, Rex!" he called, his ship rising into a hover as the canopy descended around his head. Quickly he turned and shot out of the hangar.

Looking down at his controls, Hunt slowly flicked the necessary switches and heard the engines rumble. Carefully adjusting the elevation control, he put the ship into a hover and twisted it toward the shield.

"Don't forget the canopy," Wellesley advised, though his hand was already reaching for the button. "There you go."

Pushing the controls forward, he eased out of the hangar and into space.

"Rex, keep your...open for–," the colonel began over his damaged backup radio. But his words were cut off by over a dozen angry green orbs that flew up from behind the base, pursued by half as many fighters. "They're on us! Move!"

Hunt threw his craft into a somersault as a trio of balls made for him. Instantly a pair of Devourer fighters were on his tail, casting their blobs after him and narrowly missing.

"Don't worry, I've got 'em," an unknown pirate said over the radio, falling in behind the craft and discharging a burst of shells that drove them off.

"More are incoming," Wellesley announced, another dozen alien craft emerging from behind the base and joining the fight. "They must be creeping up along the moon to stay off radar as long as possible."

"Colonel, we've got incoming," Hunt radioed.

"I see 'em," he replied, a burst of plasma shooting from his craft and striking one of the attackers, sending it careening into the ground next to the base in a fiery explosion. "Kaljurand had better get his boys out…double fast!"

Seemingly in answer to this comment another group of pirate vessels departed the base, giving them a temporary advantage in numbers.

"If we can keep this up we've got 'em whipped," another pirate said, as more of his comrades took to space. "There's no way they can–."

Suddenly a Devourer frigate lumbered over the base and slowed to a stop just above the hangar entrance. A pair of massive tentacles shot from its hull and crashed into the top of the opening, sending pieces of it crumbling to the ground.

"Hit that frigate!" Pinchon shouted into his radio. "If that shield falls, everyone in that hangar is dead!"

Straight away three dozen pirate craft abandoned their targets and made for the frigate. A withering hail of shells from their rapid fire railguns tore into it, shearing pieces off the organic vessel.

"Forget the hull," Pinchon ordered, as the tentacles continued to dismantle the top of the hangar's entrance. "Aim for the arms! Take 'em down!"

Instantly a pair of pirate craft exploded, their obvious

target making them easy prey for the swarming parasites.

"Don't fly straight at it!" Pinchon shouted. "This isn't a simulator: those are real bullets!"

The enemy fighters fell in behind the defenders and cut loose with their weapons. A blizzard of green balls lit up the sky, several of them overshooting their targets and striking the frigate. A handful of pirate craft were struck, one of which lost control and crashed into the base.

"Take down those arms now!" Pinchon bellowed, the evasive maneuvers of the pirates cutting their effectiveness drastically. "Form up in three squadrons, one covering the other, and *hit those arms!*"

The skilled pilots quickly formed up in separate groups, slicing into the frigate's tentacles in a pair of waves that severed them and left them floating dead in space.

"That's how you do it!" Pinchon cheered.

But his joy vanished as the frigate began to turn its front toward the Black Hole.

"Look out! It's gonna ram the base!" he shouted, jerking his ship in the frigate's direction. "Pour everything you've got into the engines! Try to cut its speed as much as possible!"

As one body the craft swarmed around the frigate's rear and poured an incredible amount of firepower into it. Assaulting it in cyclical waves, a fire soon broke out which produced an enormous explosion that ripped the hind quarter of the frigate off the main body. The front section, thrown off course by the force of the explosion, narrowly missed the base and crashed into the moon's surface.

"Colonel, we've *got* to take out some of these fighters!" a pirate pleaded over the radio, as a trio of his comrades were hit by green orbs and exploded. "They're chewing us up!"

"Go for it!" he ordered. "Pinchon to base, we have got to…every last fighter you've got out here!"

"What do you *think* we're doing, having a picnic in here?" roared Kaljurand. "Your last wave of backup will be out shortly. We're pulling craft out of storage."

"Understood."

During this time Hunt had concentrated on simply staying alive, though a lucky shot at a passing fighter had damaged it enough for another vessel to take it down.

"Two more frigates incoming," a pirate announced over the radio. All eyes shot to the base to watch as the dreaded pair rumbled over top of it and set to work finishing what their predecessor had started. "We can't stop 'em this time," the pirate opined.

"Can it!" ordered Pinchon. "Rex, time to earn your keep. The plasma cannons on these ships will work better than the railguns against large targets. Just…your approach. Alright, everyone, pour it into their engines! Start with the leftmost…and let 'em have it! Follow Rex and me in!"

Nervously Hunt fell in alongside the colonel, his hands trembling with adrenaline. Opening fire a second after Pinchon, together they lit up the sky with bright glowing plasma shells that struck the engines and began melting through the armor that shielded the powerplant that resided directly ahead of them.

"Hit it, boys!" Pinchon shouted, pulling a somersault with Hunt and doubling back the way they'd come as a swarm of pirate craft rocketed past. Hundreds of tiny railgun shells struck the ship's armor, tearing into it. "Another pass is all we need," Pinchon announced. "Cover us, boys. We're gonna make this one good."

Suddenly a green glob sailed over Hunt's craft and struck the colonel's vessel on the tip of the left wing, burning it clean off and sending him into a spiral.

"Colonel?!" Hunt yelled into the radio, breaking right as more globs chased after him.

"Get 'em off us, boys!" Pinchon ordered. "These ships are our best chance against those frigates!"

Obediently the pirate vessels twisted around like a swarm of locusts and perforated a pair of them. The rest got the message and pulled off.

"Alright, Rex," Pinchon said, holding his craft steady with effort. "We've only got time for this one pass. Then it's on to the other one."

The atmospheric shield flickered as he said this, powering being rerouted away from a damage section. The tentacles savagely tore at the structure, depositing a shower of parts on the hangar floor below.

They lined up on the damaged frigate and unloaded a devastating stream of plasma into it. Halfway to their target a group of Devourer craft cut across their line of attack, casting green shells into their teeth that they narrowly missed by shoving their ships into a reckless dive.

"I said keep 'em off us!" Pinchon roared into the radio, as pirate vessels soared overhead and intermeshed with the attackers. "No time to line up again, Rex. Just make for the target and hit it as hard as you can!"

Doing as he was told, Hunt pulled the ship up and flew underneath the storm of dogfighting craft. As he got the target in his sights he saw a yellow ooze pouring out of one of the damaged engines and vaporizing in space. Aiming for this spot, he opened fire with everything he had. A small explosion rocked the engine compartment, followed moments later by an enormous blast that split the frigate in two. The front half of the vessel slid sideways into its comrade, knocking into it with tremendous force and ripping it away from the base just as the shield began to flicker.

"Pour it on! Right now!" Pinchon yelled. "This is our… chance!"

The frigate, though damaged, began to right itself and approach the base once more.

"Where are those extra fighters?" the colonel demanded, as he and Hunt fell in line behind the Devourer vessel.

"Quit squawking!" Kaljurand barked over the radio.

"They're here!"

At that same moment a dozen heavy strike craft emerged from the hangar, armed with missile racks. They made a beeline for the frigate and cut loose with their armaments, dozens of warheads crashing into the front of the ship. The force of the explosions was immense, slowing its advance and blowing the tentacles clean off the hull.

"Time for us to do our part, Rex," Pinchon said, as the last of the alien fighters were mopped up and the remainder of the pirate craft fell in behind them. "Let's show 'em how it's done."

Lining up behind the ailing vessel, Hunt and Pinchon poured a steady stream of plasma into its engines. Before their eyes they began to crumble and come apart, the incredible heat of their projectiles burning through them.

"Come on, come on, come on," Pinchon whispered into the radio, willing the frigate to explode without another pass. Already he could see it was accelerating toward the base, determined to ram it. He knew in another few moments the heavy craft would unleash another salvo of missiles that were sure to destroy it. And he wasn't about to share his glory with the newcomers. "Come on."

Just as he said this a colossal explosion ripped from the back to the front of the frigate, severing it into two halves that fell off to each side, floating harmlessly away from the base.

An enormous cheer went up over the radio as every pirate in the area exploded with glee. Hunt felt Tselitel reach around the seat and squeeze his shoulders, unable to do more because of the harness that held her in place. With a smile on his face he put the craft into a slow celebratory barrel roll.

"Radar is clear of hostiles," Kaljurand announced. "You did good, boys. Real good."

"Thanks, dad," an irreverent pirate replied, somehow eliciting a laugh from the uptight director.

"Bring 'em home," he said with a chuckle before

hanging up the microphone.

"Go ahead, Colonel," Hunt said, falling in alongside him. "You're the one who got us through this."

Pinchon smiled at him through the canopy and nodded, guiding his vessel inside.

"You go next, Hunt," one of the pirates said. "Without you two those frigates would have torn the Black Hole apart."

"Thanks," Hunt said, unsure what else to say as he fell in behind the colonel. Slowly he guided his craft through the shield and returned it to the white circle that had been painted on the floor, though this time with a little more certainty. Cutting the engines and releasing his harness, he leaned his sweat soaked head back and exhaled.

"Had enough excitement for one day?" Wellesley asked.

"For the day? How about for the whole year?"

"Who are you talking to, darling?" Tselitel asked insinuatingly, for the benefit of the woman behind her.

"Oh, just myself," Hunt replied, shaking his head and popping the canopy.

The hangar began to cheer as he and Pinchon emerged from their craft. Ladders were quickly wheeled to their ships. Though the engagement had been short, they were both exhausted. With weary legs they climbed onto the ladders and slowly descended, a dozen hands reaching up to pat them as they did so. Turning around into the crowded hangar, they were met by innumerable people who wanted to shake their hands, hug them, and in every conceivable way make a fuss over their victory. Quickly growing awkward at the attention, Hunt turned to the ladder to ensure Tselitel and the young woman got down alright, and then pressed his way through the crowd toward Pinchon.

"Great flying out there, Rex!" he said, extending his sole hand and gripping Hunt's firmly.

"It was nothing compared to yours!" Hunt said with exuberance, his usual reticence leaving him for a moment.

"And with one hand, no less!"

"Ah, we all have our small talents," he said with a modest grin.

Milo had just reached the floor behind them when he dropped on all fours and threw up every last thing that had been in his stomach. Getting shakily to his feet with Gromyko's help, he shuffled to his brother and shook his hand weakly.

"I'm never flying with you guys again!" he said emphatically. "Never, ever again!"

CHAPTER 14

"Call it what you want, Director," Gromyko said loudly, standing over the table in Kaljurand's quarters and toasting the victors for the fifth time. "Gromyko considers this a magnificent victory!" Tossing back his head, he downed the contents of his glass in a single motion and gestured for a refill from the servant who stood nearby for the purpose. The man looked timidly at the director, who nodded wearily for him to comply. "Pour, man! Pour!" the smuggler said, growing ever more joyful.

The director, in stark contrast, was moody and withdrawn. He had pointed out, quite rightly, that the location of the Black Hole was compromised, and that it would likely draw hostile attention in the future. As his guests celebrated their victory, his mind was occupied with problems of logistics and personnel.

"Yes, sir," the smuggler continued, dropping into his chair as his head began to buzz. "Quite a victory.

"What will you do now?" Tselitel asked the director, trying to move the attention from Gromyko in the hope it would quiet him down.

"Naturally we'll have to find a new location for our base," Kaljurand said, watching the smuggler out of the corner of his eye, his lips cast in a sour mold. "There's no telling when those parasites will attack again. We have to–."

"You know what we *have* to do?" Gromyko asked, his

voice even louder than before. "We have to *strike! At once!* Why, if the pirates joined with the navy, we could drive the Devourers out of the galaxy for good!"

"I don't think they'd accept our help," Kaljurand said in a tight voice. "Even if we were inclined to offer it."

"*Inclined?*" Gromyko asked, leaning his elbows on the table and looking hard at the director. "What other inclination can you have? We're at war! Now is the time for all hands on deck! Humanity needs every pilot and every ship on the frontlines now!"

"The Black Fang organization is not a military body," Kaljurand said precisely. "Our purpose–."

"Dash your purpose!" exclaimed the smuggler, suddenly bolting out of his seat and standing awkwardly, his eyes searching each face for agreement before fixing on the director. "It is time for the criminal underbelly of humanity to recognize its responsibilities! You won't have anyone to rob if we're all lying in a mass grave! The Devourers don't discern between pirates and normal, productive citizens. They're after all of us!"

"I'll be sure to pass that along to my superiors," Kaljurand said acidly, watching Gromyko with narrowed eyes. "They'll be ever so concerned with the strategic opinion of a backwater, has-been artifact smuggler."

"How dare you insult Gromyko!" he exclaimed, throwing aside his glass with a crash.

"*Get him out of here!*" Hunt whispered sternly to his brother, who sat beside him.

"Come on, Antonin," Milo said, standing up and patting the smuggler's back. "Time for–."

"Time for this renegade to eat his words!" Gromyko shouted, pushing away his friend's hand and shaking an accusatory finger at the director. "How many lives have you taken while plying your trade, pirate? You may spit upon Gromyko now, but he never took an innocent life. Never! It's no wonder that–."

"Antonin," Hunt said sharply, rising and pushing his brother aside. "It's time for you to leave. Now."

The force of his words penetrated the smuggler's hazy mind. He eyed him for a moment and then nodded.

"Right, boss."

Milo took hold of him and guided him out from the maze of chair legs that surrounded the table. Opening the door, he was about to usher him into the hallway when the smuggler turned and spoke.

"I leave out of regard for my friend," he said grandly, regaining some of his poise but none of his sense. "Gromyko does not *yield* before criminals!"

With this Milo pushed him out the door and pulled it shut behind him.

"For a man who was once a criminal himself," Kaljurand said, his tone lightening as a faint smile crossed his lips, "he's certainly high and mighty on the subject of lawfulness."

"He's a dramatic personality," Pinchon replied, gently sloshing the drink he held in his hand. "You should have been with him on *Preleteth*."

"*Preleteth?*" the director asked, cocking an eyebrow.

"Epsilon-4."

"Ah. And what took you there?"

"Long story," Pinchon said, a slight gleam in his eye as he grinned his unwillingness to divulge more than he had to. Kaljurand eyed him disapprovingly and gestured crisply for the attendant to refill his glass. "I've been meaning to ask you, Doctor," Pinchon said, turning to Tselitel who sat between him and Hunt, "just what, in your professional opinion, makes Gromyko such a handful? He's got enough personality for at least three people."

"Naturally I've never had him under analysis," she began cautiously, covering her bases.

"I'm sure none of us will hold anything you may say against you, Doctor," Kaljurand said, aware that the colonel was just changing the subject but intrigued to hear Tselitel's answer. "Please, expand."

"Well, – and you understand this is *speculation*, not hard fact – I suspect that it is a coping mechanism for the powerlessness commonly felt by residents of Delta-13. Living on a world bound by ice, hemmed in by nature and the government, they quickly despair of ever improving their lot and fall prey to fatalism. Such behavior is common in human history whenever a totalitarian system of government prevails."

"Are you insinuating that our glorious empire is anything less than perfectly just?" asked Kaljurand, a sly grin on his face that mocked the official propaganda. "That's very nearly treason, dear Doctor."

"I'm simply drawing a parallel between the powerlessness of the captives of Delta-13, and the powerlessness generally experienced when people have no capacity to influence their surroundings," she replied officially, turned off by his undercutting style of humor.

"Of course," he replied with a nod. "Please, continue."

"Individuals in that state generally have two courses of action open to them: they can accept, with soul-crushing results, their utter inability to control their own fate. The result is indifference."

"A trait that your friend very clearly lacks," Kaljurand uttered, taking a sip from his drink.

"The other option is to place one's faith in something greater. Some people turn to God; others to unseen political forces that will shortly rise up from the shadows and tear down the oppressor; and still others place their faith in a superman. Naturally there are many other possibilities. Sometimes this faith is channeled into abstract ideas or groups, like freedom or 'the people.'"

"And your friend Gromyko?"

"Has decided to become the superman himself," she replied.

"Remarkable," Kaljurand replied. "How could a man living on that snowball arrive at such a ridiculous notion?"

"Objectively it *is* ridiculous," Tselitel replied seriously. "But not *subjectively*. It grew within his mind as a compensation against his surroundings. Compensations often get a pass from rational critique because we recognize that they're just crutches, and not to be taken too seriously. They calm our nerves and help us remain upright, so we leave them alone to do their work."

"He's gone far beyond what could reasonably be called compensation," commented the director. "He fully believes it."

"He half believes it," Tselitel corrected. "The other half is for show."

"Why didn't anyone shoot him down on Delta-13? Fatalists tend to be cynical people."

"Because they wanted to believe in him." Tselitel's eyes darted to Hunt's chest, where she imagined Wellesley was raising a strenuous objection at just that moment. "Some of them, anyway. Truth be told, most of his movement was made up of naive young people and a number of dreamy, lovestruck females. Although I suspect most members of the population got the occasional kick out of seeing his propaganda painted on walls that had been whitewashed just hours before by the authorities. Even if they thought he was silly, his rebelliousness gave them a little bit of hope."

"A dim light flickering in the night is better than none?"

"Precisely. With the downfall of the Underground he's lost his way. Without the clamor of his adherents to hold up his exaggerated persona, doubt has begun to creep in. He's no longer a superman in his own eyes, though he's maintaining the act for the time being. Eventually he ought to settle into something more stable and mature."

"Mature?" probed the director.

"Wouldn't you consider it childish to place your faith

in yourself to such a degree that your will is imbued with magical powers? That's very nearly self-deification."

"I suppose I would," he said quietly, looking withdrawn. He sat for a moment, reflecting on her words. Then he arose and made for the door. "Please stay and enjoy the wine for as long as you wish. I have some tasks to do."

With this he left the room.

"What did I say?" Tselitel asked, looking between Hunt and Pinchon.

"My old pal Ivo feels like a bit of a superman himself," the colonel said, grasping his glass from the table and leaning back in his chair. "Your words hit a little too close to the mark."

"Him?" she asked incredulously, pointing with her thumb toward the door. "How could anyone so sensible possibly imagine that about himself?"

"Why do you think he's so touchy about being crossed by his men?" the colonel asked. "Every time they resist his will, he's shown to be less than the total master of this station. It's probably why he hasn't left this assignment after all these years: he's intent on bending it *completely* to his will. He won't give up until it is. I'm *certain* that other positions have been offered to him. But none of them would give the kind of free reign he enjoys here. The importance and secrecy of this base forces the higher ups to give him near-autonomy. A big fish in a small, though very important, pond."

"Sounds more like a big deity in a small temple," she said with surprise, wondering why the idea hadn't crossed her mind before. "I hope I haven't offended him by what I said," she added with concern. "I don't want to turn him off to us."

"Nah, he'd be less than a deity, as you called him, if he let mortals like you offend him," Pinchon reassured her. "That's probably why Gromyko gets on his nerves: the guy is so full of himself that he has no headspace left to be filled by Ivo. His lack of adherence makes him a threat."

"Maybe you should be the psychiatrist instead of me!" she exclaimed with a laugh. "I sure never figured that about the director."

"No, you have a talent for it," the pirate replied with a smile. "I've just been around Ivo long enough to know how his mind works. I don't have a head for the kinds of theories that are your stock and trade."

During this conversation Hunt had been aware that the young woman Pinchon had found earlier was watching him from behind. Sitting by herself near the window, an untouched glass of wine in her hand, she observed them carefully without offering the slightest comment. Attractive, with light red hair and freckles on her cheeks, she looked somehow fresh and unspoiled. It was rare for him to see a woman of her few years who hadn't spent most of her life on Delta-13 and subsequently been aged by it. She seemed spritely, a touch ethereal. While Pinchon and Tselitel exchanged psychological insights, Hunt rose from the table and carried his glass to where she sat.

"Mind company?" he asked, as she looked furtively up at him. After a few moments of awkward silence she shook her head side-to-side. "Thanks," he said, taking the chair on the other end of the small table. An empty seat stood between them, facing the window. "Why didn't you join in the festivities?" he asked, nodding toward the empty bottles of wine and the half-eaten plates of food.

In lieu of a reply she shrugged, tilting her head and avoiding eye contact.

"Let's leave her alone, Rex," Wellesley said. "She must have a screw loose."

Instantly her bright blue eyes fixed angrily onto the medallion hidden beneath his shirt.

"Better bite your tongue, Wells."

"Oh, not another one!" the AI exclaimed irritably. "You know, I've been a good boy about this whole magical hearing thing up until now. I really have. But this is the limit.

I'm done having my words listened to constantly from the outside. Why do you think I was designed without a speaker? It was so I could give counsel without regard to wider opinion! This is a violation of my privacy! And yours, too, as a matter of fact. Doesn't that bother you? Rex?"

Hunt could hear him but didn't bother to respond. Something about the young woman's eyes drew him in, and the last thing he wanted to do was break contact. They shimmered like blue crystals, portals into another dimension. A deep sense of ancient wisdom emanated from them, as though a venerable, aged being had taken up residence in her body and transferred all its knowledge into her youthful frame. Her spirit seemed to flow on some broader wavelength, its frequency in tune with the long, slow rhythms of the universe. Suddenly Hunt's life felt small and terribly short – a mere blinking of the cosmic eye.

"Can you talk?" he asked at long last, the crispness of his own voice surprising him, unaware that he'd slipped into a meditative state gazing into her eyes.

"Y-yes," she said mildly, watching the floor. "But," she began, looking up at him appealingly for a moment, willing him to understand without words before looking away again.

"But what?" he probed, his eyebrows raised.

"It's hard," she whispered, as though admitting a guilty truth.

"What's your name?"

"Soliana."

"That's a very pretty name," he said, trying to encourage her to speak. Shyly she darted a smile at him and then looked away again. "Do you have a last name?"

"Just Soliana."

"A girl as pretty as you only needs one name, anyhow," Wellesley said. Instantly her eyes locked onto the disc, suspicious that he was trying to pull one over on her given his previous words. "What? Look, I'm sorry for what I said earlier, okay? I was just surprised, is all. I didn't mean to hurt you."

She eyed him briefly and then slowly nodded, accepting his explanation and returning her gaze to the floor.

Hunt leaned back in his chair and looked at her for a moment, trying to figure out how to get her out of her shell. Before arriving at an answer she sat up straight and her eyes glassed over.

"Are you alright?" he asked, slowly rising from his chair and taking a knee beside her, resting his elbows atop it. "Soliana?" he asked, reaching out and touching her hand.

The instant skin contact was made a vision flashed through his mind that caused him to jerk his hand away and stand up.

"What is it?" Wellesley asked, as Soliana came out of her trance and smiled up at him.

"I, uh," Hunt replied, looking into her eyes as he thought. "I-I don't know," he said.

"Well, it must have been *something*," the AI probed, unconvinced. "What did you see?"

"Just drop it, Wells," Hunt said, confused as he turned from the girl and saw Tselitel and Pinchon approaching.

"You alright?" she asked, reading the confusion on his face at once. "You look upset."

"I'm fine," he lied, putting a hand on her shoulder and turning back to the girl.

"I see you've been getting acquainted with our number six, here," Pinchon said, taking the seat beside her and patting her knee like an affectionate father. "Doesn't say much, does she?"

"Doesn't have to," Hunt said quietly, watching her now gently smiling face.

"Yeah, looks like she's always got some kind of big thought on her mind that she's trying to digest. I don't know, she's probably been through a lot. Sometimes people quit talking for a while when they've had a bad experience."

"Where'd she come from?" Hunt asked.

"I don't know. I ran into her near the refugee quarters."

"The *refugee quarters?*" Tselitel asked, alarmed to think of such a gentle creature near that hotbed of savages.

"Yeah. She was hanging around with a pilot named Higden. He didn't know where she'd come from, either. Just wandered into his company one day here on the base and stuck by him. He didn't know what to do with her, especially with all the riff raff around, so he was glad to get her off his hands. For a small fee, of course."

"A fee?" Tselitel asked with disgust. "What was she, his slave?"

"No," he chuckled, amused by the leap her mind had taken. "But these *are* pirates, so they expect to be compensated for everything they do, even good deeds. He'd been looking after her for nearly a week, and in that time had had a pair of scrapes with some of the refugees. No matter how many times he warned her, she'd eventually head off in the direction of their quarters when he wasn't around. She owed him for that, in any event, but didn't have any money. For that matter I didn't, either. So I traded with him instead."

"What did you trade?" Hunt asked.

"Nothing of value to us," the colonel grinned.

"Nothing of value to..." Tselitel trailed. Suddenly her face lit up with realization. "You gave him *Merokanah?*"

"Keep your voice down," he cautioned, glancing toward the attendants who were clearing the table. "We don't want word to get around that–."

"How could you do that?" she persisted, growing agitated.

"Look, he was the only thing of 'value' that I could part with. I couldn't let this girl wander around the base on her own half the time. And," he added, drawing near and dropping his voice, "we need a sixth we can trust. I don't know much about this girl, but I know an innocent face when I see one. There isn't another on this entire base, let me assure you. I've been scouting around ever since we got here."

"But to trade *Merokanah* to a *pirate*," she said, shaking her head.

"What do you want me to do, return her to Higden and get that idiotic disc back?" he asked, annoyed at her persistence. "A choice had to be made, and I made it. I'd do it again to get this poor little thing out of trouble. Look at her," he said, standing up and placing his hand on her shoulder. "She can't take care of herself. It's a wonder she's made it this far. I can't imagine how she ended up on the base."

"Of course I don't want you to take her back," Tselitel said, calming down. "I just," she began, unable to find the words. "I don't know. He's just so helpless."

"He'll be alright," Pinchon said. "Those AIs are tougher than they look. Besides, he held out for years inside that bunker, didn't he?"

"Guess that explains how Milo lost him," Wellesley commented, as Pinchon took Soliana by the hand and escorted her toward the exit. "Pinchon snatched him while he was sleeping."

"Yeah," Hunt agreed quietly, watching as the pair reached the door. The colonel opened it and stood aside for her to leave first. She hesitated, turning back toward Hunt and looking into his eyes for a moment. Then she lowered her head and stepped into the corridor. "Yeah," Hunt repeated in a mumble as the door shut.

"What's on your mind, handsome?" Tselitel asked, taking his hand which he instantly withdrew. "What is it?" she asked with alarm.

"It's nothing," he replied.

"Rex, I don't want any secrets between us," she said firmly. "If there's some kind of trouble…"

"No trouble," he said, shaking his head. "No trouble at all."

"Then what *is* it?" she asked.

"I can't tell you now," he said, taking her hand again

and making for the door.

Hours later the six of them gathered in Hunt's and Tselitel's cramped quarters. Assembled in a loose circle, the ladies sat while the men leaned on or against a variety of objects.

"How's your head?" Hunt asked Gromyko after a few moments of silence.

"Fine," he said, a touch of apology in his voice. "I hope I didn't cause any–."

"Forget about it," Hunt said with a wave of his hand. "Although I wouldn't expect any birthday cards from the director."

"A hardship I shall attempt to endure," he said humorously.

"Shouldn't we get underway?" Milo asked, shifting from one foot to the other, his arms crossed over his chest.

In truth no one was in a hurry to get the cube open. They didn't have the least idea what it contained, and their imaginations began to circle around dark possibilities. Reluctantly Hunt drew it from his pocket and held it up. Instantly the girl gasped, jumping out of her seat.

"*Keesh'Forbandai!*" she said.

"*Keesh'Forbandai?*" confirmed Wellesley, to which she nodded vigorously. "Well, that's interesting."

"What?" Hunt asked.

"Well, it's nothing too definite. I've just been wondering who these mysterious benefactors of ours are. If this cube is of *Keesh'Forbandai* manufacture, perhaps they're the ones who contacted my people and had them build the bunker on *Preleteth*."

"Could be," Hunt said, more interested in the cube at that moment than Wellesley's suppositions. Pinching it between his thumb and index finger, he held it out towards the others. "Alright, let's do this."

Slowly they gathered around, the original five applying a finger to each side.

"You too, honey," Tselitel said, gesturing for Soliana to join them. Hesitantly she watched, unsure if it was really alright. "Come on," she reiterated. "It's okay."

Soliana nervously approached the group, looked at each of their faces and then gingerly reached out her hand. Extending her forefinger, she pressed it to the top of the cube.

The instant contact was made it floated autonomously out of their grasp to a position five feet above the floor. The six sides opened and a dense emerald green cloud dotted with tiny points of light filled the room.

"It's beautiful," Tselitel said, stepping back with the rest of them so as not to obscure it.

"It's a map," Hunt said, relaying Wellesley's words. "A map of the Milky Way."

"We went through all this trouble for a *map?*" asked Milo with profound disappointment. "Every two-bit freighter has a map aboard. Probably two."

"But not a map with *that* on it, I wager," Pinchon said, pointing at an orange disc in the middle of empty space. Suddenly a half-transparent white line darted from their location toward the disc, landing right in the middle of it. "Looks like the *Keeshes* want us to go there."

"But why?" Tselitel asked, stepping around the cloud and drawing close to the circle. "It looks like there's absolutely nothing there. Just an orange ring."

"Maybe the target is too small to represent on a map like this," the pirate offered. "It's not like there's space to render things in any real detail."

"Could be," Tselitel admitted.

"Anyway, that's our target," Hunt said. "Wellesley has already drawn coordinates from the map."

"It's an awfully long trip, Rex," Tselitel cautioned, turning her back to the glowing green map that floated behind her head. "Are we really sure we want to jump that far? What if the map is wrong and there's nothing there?"

"Then we'd better pack enough supplies to last," he

replied, looking over her white hair at the cloud of little dots. "Colonel?"

"I'll get to work twisting Ivo's arm," he said. "He still owes us plenty for saving the base, though he'll squawk about it all the same. Should have them ready by tomorrow."

"Good. I'll check the condition of our ships in the meantime and make sure the repairs are on track." He looked up at the map. "How do we shut this thing down?"

Stepping into the map's cloud, Soliana cupped her hands underneath the cube and uttered a single word: "*Vreesh*." With this the six sides closed and the device dropped into her hand. With a smile she handed it to Hunt. He eyed her curiously for a moment and then slipped it back into his pocket.

"What'll the rest of us do?" Milo asked, as Pinchon opened the door.

"Just stay out of trouble," Hunt said, slipping out after the pirate.

"Heh, that's a tall order for those two guys," Pinchon chuckled once the door was shut. "Talk to you later," he added, striding quickly down the hall to find Kaljurand.

"Okay, so *now* do you want to talk about what happened with Soliana?" inquired Wellesley.

"Nope," he replied, heading down the hallway in a slow, thoughtful stride.

"Whatever it was gave you quite a start," persisted the AI, consumed by curiosity.

Hunt didn't reply. Instead he shoved his hands into his pockets and turned down a hallway that led toward the hangar. Reaching it, he saw mechanics hard at work on the vessels that had participated in the battle. Crews were standing on scaffolds that reached the top of the hangar's outer opening, working quickly to repair the damage done to it by the frigates. The debris on the floor had already been gathered up and carted away.

"Oughta have this place fixed up in short order," the AI

commented, shifting topics for the time being. "To be honest I'm surprised the atmospheric shield held. There can't be much holding it together."

"Nope," repeated Hunt, his eyes downcast as he walked toward their ships. Moving with calm deliberateness, he'd hoped to avoid attracting attention as long as possible. Given the reception he'd received earlier, he expected a fuss to be made over him the instant he was recognized. This he wanted to avoid, for the wide-eyed admiration of the pirates made him uncomfortable. Somehow his actions in the battle had suddenly made him acceptable to this lot of underworld rabble who hours earlier would have kicked him out into space on the slightest provocation. Now all this was forgotten, and an almost doglike affection prevailed. Essentially a private man, Hunt didn't appreciate such advances from anyone. To receive such fawning attention from pirates he found almost loathsome.

"Hey, it's one of the frigate-busters!"

Hunt reflexively snapped his head around to see who had spoken. But by then two dozen pairs of eyes were upon him, with more looking up from their work each second. The hangar quickly erupted in applause, their earlier show of adulation not enough to satisfy them.

"You've gotten popular," Wellesley said, with characteristic understatement.

"Lucky me," he replied sourly, turning his head back toward the front and looking down at his feet.

But his attempt to shut them out didn't do any good. A concourse of bodies quickly formed ahead of him, blocking his path to the fighters that stood just beyond in a state of partial repair.

"Mister Hunt," one of the mechanics said, taking his small cloth cap in his hands and holding it nervously before his belly, "I want to apologize for what the boys did earlier, taking your craft and all. It was awful good of you and your friends to hang around and save our necks when you could have bolted."

The mechanic, a good foot shorter than Hunt, stood before him with grease on his cheeks and a dirty red handkerchief tied loosely around his neck. Revolving his cap slowly in his hands, he looked into Hunt's eyes with difficulty, only glancing at them momentarily before darting to other parts of the hangar.

"Why don't they apologize themselves?" Hunt asked frowningly.

"Afraid they can't," he replied, still rotating his cap and looking down at his feet. "They didn't come back."

"Oh," Hunt replied, his attitude smoothed somewhat by this fact.

"Reckon you've got plenty of right to be mad at us," the mechanic went on, Hunt's annoyance heightening his own sense of shame until his cheeks began to glow despite the grease. "Frankly, I can't understand why you bothered to stick it out with us at all, after the way we've treated you."

At this moment Hunt became aware that the applause had ceased. Looking over the head of the short mechanic, he saw dozens of quiet faces watching him. They each bore the same question in their eyes: why hadn't he bolted?"

"Oh, the colonel sticking around makes sense enough," he added, still avoiding his gaze. "He might be a scoundrel like the rest of us. But he's a Black Fang, too, and that counts for something. But without the added firepower of this fine ship of yours," he said, tossing a hand toward the sleek *Kol-Prockian* craft a dozen paces behind him, "it wouldn't have mattered. That shield barely held. We'd all be dead right now if it'd fallen."

"Let the man talk, Gene!" someone called from behind him. "He can't get a word in if you keep filling the air!"

Embarrassed further, the mechanic withdrew into the crowd and watched with the rest of them as Hunt stood before them, his hands still in his pockets as he tried to figure out what to say.

Then a sudden inspiration struck, and words began to flow off his tongue.

"You want to know why I didn't run?" he asked rhetorically, sliding his hands into view and beginning to pace before them. "I didn't run because I couldn't save my own skin while others of my kind went up against a savage enemy. Like a shadow they've spread themselves across our galaxy, intent on destroying us. Until now we've been divided, the empire bearing the brunt of the attack. The pirates have stood aside and watched, as have the fringe independence people. But that can't go on any longer. From now on we must stand as one. We are all under the mark of death from these creatures. Only a single solid force can oppose them. We must all recognize our common humanity, and not spare any effort so long as one of us is under threat."

Then his inspiration went dry. He looked at the mute faces which surrounded him, hoping they would explode into applause and dedicate themselves to the broader cause. But they simply watched him. After a few awkward moments he pressed on toward the ships, the crowd parting for him. He inquired briefly about the state of repairs and then doubled back through the subdued hangar.

"It can't have been *that* bad," Hunt said under his breath, turning into the corridor that led into the rest of the base.

"I thought it was good," Wellesley said. "Especially off the cuff like that. Public speaking isn't easy."

"Apparently it isn't one of my talents, anyway," Hunt replied, dropping his head and walking slowly back to his quarters.

That evening Hunt sat in the lone chair of his front room, the sounds of light breathing flowing in from the bedroom. He'd generously donated his half of the bed to Soliana, the two girls sleeping side-by-side. Leaning his head over the back of his chair, he looked up at the dark ceiling and thought. Wellesley lay on the table beside him, his persistence about the episode with Soliana finally wearing down Hunt's patience and driving him to break skin contact. Agitatedly he shifted in his seat, trying to find a comfortable spot to settle into and finally get some sleep. Yet it continued to elude him. Despite the enormous strain of the day his brain wouldn't shut off. It was busy processing all that had happened: the fight with the robed being; the battle in space; the vision…

No. Hunt *refused* to think about that. It couldn't be true. It *had* to be some kind of fakery – a projection from the planet or something. Or Maybe Soliana was pushing his buttons for some kind of hidden purpose. What did they really know about her, anyway? So Pinchon had taken pity on her and traded that annoying little ferret *Merokanah* for her. Shoot, she could even be a spy of some kind, an infiltrator sent to destroy them little by little.

No, that was a stupid idea. Anyone could see in a flash that she was innocent. Beyond innocent, in fact. She appeared untouched by the slightest hint of guile, as though she'd grown up totally separate from the influences that tend to twist even the best people toward self-serving dishonesty. Possessing no filter of any kind, her only defense mechanism seemed to be withdrawal. Maybe that's what made the vision seem so meaningful…

Hunt angrily smacked his skull with the heel of his right hand, trying to knock some sense into it. The vision was *meaningless*. It just played into his fears, was all. That was why it was so persistent – why he couldn't shake it despite his best efforts. Exasperated, he slid out of the chair onto the hard floor beside the wall, hoping to mimic the posture, if not the comfort, of bed.

Gradually he slipped into semi-consciousness.

The events of the last few weeks played themselves over, starting with the last time he'd seen *Selek-Pey*. Slowly they reached the present, culminating in the vision he'd spent all day fighting. He tried to awaken but couldn't, the dream forcing itself upon his mind. In it he saw Tselitel dead, her cold body resting atop a massive stone coffin in the middle of an open field of waving grass. The scene was dull, gray, hopeless. A storm brewed overhead that threatened to burst at any moment. Too heartbroken even for tears, Hunt simply stood over her and gazed upon her still face. Desperately he wanted to reach out and touch her, hoping that by some miracle he'd find her merely sleeping instead of gone. But in his heart he knew the truth. Never again would he feel the sensitive tips of her fingers upon his skin, or the warmth of her slender body beside him as she slept. She had passed beyond him.

Falling to his knees in grief, he rested his arms on the coffin and hid his eyes.

It had been at this point that he'd rejected the vision earlier in the day. Now it continued despite his efforts to halt it, determined to make him watch.

As he knelt beside the coffin he felt another presence enter the scene. It was warm, generous, sun-like. A sense of youthful vitality flowed from it. Its aura began to penetrate his body and fill him with life. Full of hope, he raised his head to see if the same effect was working upon Tselitel. But she was gone, as was the coffin. Somehow he'd been resting his elbows on mere air.

It was then that the gentle sound of humming behind him caught his attention. A woman, dressed in white, stood a short distance away. The sun had begun to shine brightly just over her shoulder, blinding him to all but her silhouette. With serene movements she brought her hands together before her chest, pressing the palms together and shifting back and forth between her bare feet in a meditative rhythm.

"The one is gone," a female voice said from above him. It was harsh, stern – the voice of duty. "Now you will join with this one."

"I will join with *none!*" shouted Hunt, jumping to his feet and ripping at the sky above him with his fingernails.

"None! Do you hear me? With Lily gone I give my heart to no one!"

"Your heart has already been promised," the voice replied inexorably. "On your behalf."

"You have no right!"

"We are not concerned with your rights…" the voice trailed, as the vision began to fade. Just before it vanished he saw the woman's face. It belonged to Soliana.

With a jerk he suddenly awoke, his body covered in sweat. His heart ready to burst, he began to rise but bumped into someone laying beside him. Quickly getting to his feet, he made his way to the door and flicked on the light. It was then that he saw Soliana's lovely form curled up on the floor right next to where he'd been sleeping.

"Rex?" he heard Tselitel call from the other room. "Is something wrong?"

Immediately upon hearing her voice the vision of her lying dead atop the coffin pressed itself into his mind once more. Desperately he unlocked the door, ripped it open, and tore off down the hallway. Dropping to his knees a hundred paces away, he desperately gasped for air as panic seized him. His body red with blood, his breaths short, hurried, inadequate, he felt his limbs begin to tremble. His heart beating in his ears, he didn't hear footsteps approaching behind him.

"Rex, are you alright?" Tselitel asked, causing him to jerk around and look at her. Losing his balance, he tumbled to the floor and struggled to get back up. "What is it, darling?" she asked urgently, reaching out with her subtly trembling hands to hold him. This evidence of her condition, and the end it promised, merely served to reinforce the dreadful memory of the vision.

"What's going on?" Pinchon asked from behind her, as he, Gromyko, and Milo came into view.

"I don't know," Tselitel said, nearly panicking herself. "He just bolted from the room."

"Delayed reaction," Pinchon said decisively, taking a knee beside Hunt and looking at him. "All the fears he'd repressed during the battle finally came roaring back when his guard was down. When that happens, and you're asleep, you feel like you're under attack and fight or flight kicks in. Evidently it was *flight* this time. Once you're awake enough to push back it passes off soon enough."

"It wasn't…the battle," Hunt gasped, trying to get control of himself, his body quavering. "I saw," he began, his eyes shooting up to Tselitel's anxious face and making him stop.

"What?" she asked earnestly. "What did you see?"

"I saw," he repeated, trying to fight the words out of his mouth but finding himself unable to. "I saw the atmospheric shield fall, and everyone killed," he lied at last. "We came so close to failure."

"Delayed reaction," Pinchon nodded with finality. "Come on, Rex: let's get you back to your room." The colonel helped him to his feet. "I'm sure the good doctor would rather treat you there than in a hallway."

"I'm alright," he said, wiping the sweat from his brow with the back of his hand and swallowing hard. "I just need a few minutes to get myself together."

"What you need is a good night's sleep," Milo said, as they reached his quarters. "You've been under more strain than any of us since this journey began."

"No, I'm alright, really," he said, stepping into the room and moving a few steps away from the group. "Just leave me be. I need to gather my thoughts."

"Darling," Tselitel began in an appealing tone, drawing closer.

"Just give me a chance to breathe, alright?" he snapped at them all, making her jump back. Snatching Wellesley off the table, he pressed through the group toward the door. Soliana stood beside it, watching him with wide, sympathetic eyes. Her gaze touched something inside that made him pause. Shaking his head to clear it, he slipped past her and strode quickly down the hall.

"What's happened to you?" the AI asked, as Hunt slipped the disc's chain around his neck and dropped it down the collar of his shirt.

"I saw her dead, Wells," he confessed in an anguished tone. "She was laying there like a statue. There was nothing I could do."

"Just hold on, Rex," Wellesley said. "Now, let's get on the same page about this. What happened? What did you see?"

As well as he could in his distressed state he related the vision.

"And then I awoke to find Soliana lying right beside me!" he exclaimed, pacing the halls between the hangar and his quarters.

"It's like she knew what was going on," Wellesley mused.

"No kidding!" Hunt snapped.

"Look, just take it easy," the AI said calmly. "You've got to keep your head if we're gonna figure this out."

"What's there to figure out?" Hunt demanded. "You and I both know that Lily is gonna die. And soon. There's no hope of a cure for her within the Milky Way. Maybe somebody in Quarlac could help her. But that place is too dangerous to send her alone. Even with me along I wouldn't say we had anything better than even odds of coming back."

"Now just hold on a minute," Wellesley said firmly. "We don't *know* anything of the kind, except that you're scared to death that it might happen. We've gotten out of so many tight scrapes already that it's pure nonsense to bet against us. You're just gonna have to keep it together and wait."

"Then why the vision last night?" he asked. "And why this fresh vision from Soliana? You want to tell me that they're just coincidences?"

"The first vision was an attack from one of your *enemies*," Wellesley replied. "You think they're gonna tell you the truth? It was meant to play on your fears."

"So? Soliana isn't an enemy."

"We don't know what Soliana is," Wellesley replied. "She could be a friend, or a foe. More than that, she could just be a mess, or a kind of psychic magnifying glass. We know she can hear me talk, and she's capable of forcing visions on people she touches. But what's to say she has a gift for prophecy? To my *considerable* knowledge nobody can tell the future. She might just be adept at bringing up people's fears. So far that's all we know for a fact that she's done."

"Then how do you explain the dream? The voice I heard? That whole bit about having to 'join with her?' I know for a fact I'm not afraid of her."

"Maybe you are, deep down," the AI replied.

"Oh, come on," protested Hunt. "That little thing? What could she possibly do to me?"

"I can't say," Wellesley replied frankly. "But she seems to exist on an entirely different plane from you. Maybe that's–."

"Maybe this, maybe that!" growled Hunt. "Do you really expect me to–."

"*Get ahold of yourself!*" the AI ordered, his voice filling Hunt's mind. "She's a weird little goose, but that's all we know for now. Otherwise nothing has changed. Lily's the same girl she was twenty-four hours ago. The plan is still to get treatment for her as soon as possible. Everything is proceeding according to plan. Just keep your cool and we'll come out of this alright."

"And if we don't?" he asked. "If I lose Lily it'll destroy me. That's what I can't handle, Wells. I can't live without that woman. My heart will shatter the instant hers stops beating."

"A lot of people feel that way," Wellesley replied. "But they go on living."

"Not me," he shook his head. "There's no future for me

without her. I couldn't bear it."

"You will," the AI said with certainty. "I've known you too long to doubt that, even if you do."

Despondently Hunt paced the corridors for another half hour before finally turning his steps back towards his quarters. He was nearly there when a sudden realization stopped him.

"Why did she say 'we?'" he asked aloud.

"What?"

"The voice in my vision," he explained. "She said, 'we aren't concerned with your rights.' Who's 'we?'"

"Really, Rex, you need to calm down about the whole–."

"No, hear me out, Wells," Hunt said, turning away from his door and walking back down the hall to give himself space to think. "Why did she say 'we?'" he mused aloud. Suddenly he snapped his fingers. "The *Ahn-Wey*."

"What about them?"

"They've been sticking their fingers in my life right from the start," Hunt said. "Look at how *Preleteth* had me dancing at the end of its string with *Alleehavah*. Or take how Delta led me around by the nose. Those turkeys have a bad habit of manipulating people. Soliana must be one of their agents.They want her to manipulate me. Shoot, I probably only had the vision again because she was lying next to me. She must have been touching me again like earlier to make it happen."

"I don't know, Rex," the AI replied uncertainly. "It doesn't seem to add up somehow. There's something kind of…flat-footed, in the way the *Ahn-Wey* makes use of people. When they want to manipulate people they just cut them out of the loop. Like how *Alleehavah* simply declined to answer some of our questions. *Preleteth* did the same thing. In fact, they did that as a mass when they instructed the Order on how to develop gifts without telling them how to *really* bring them out in force. I don't get that feeling off of Soliana at all.

Oh, I don't trust her any more than you do," he added quickly, as Hunt opened his mouth to comment. "But I don't sense *Ahn-Wey* when I look at her."

"We'll find out soon enough," he said determinedly, quickly striding for his door.

Opening it, he found Tselitel and Milo quietly talking. Soliana was sitting on the bed in the next room. Without a word Hunt went in and shut the door. She looked up at him with wide eyes but said nothing. Taking a knee in front of her, he stared hard into her face for a moment.

"What are you doing here?" he asked. "What really?"

"I don't know," she struggled to say.

"What do you mean you *don't know*? You must have come here for a purpose. Now, what is it?"

"If I knew that, I would tell you," she replied with gentle earnestness. "Truly I would. But…."

"But what?" he prodded.

"But I don't know," she replied, shaking her head back and forth, her eyes full of mystery. "I was brought here by someone," she said, narrowing her eyes to try and remember. "They were curt with me."

"What kind of person?" Wellesley asked, trying to focus her mind. "Man or woman? Old or young?"

"I can't remember," she said after a long moment.

"Look here, honey," the AI began, "you want us to believe that someone just dropped you off without any explanation at all? And in a place as rotten as this, no less? Why would they do that?"

"I–."

"Don't know!" exclaimed Wellesley. "This little innocent act is only going to–."

"Hang on a minute, Wells," Hunt said, the pleading air of innocence in the young woman's eyes capturing his sympathy. Sitting down beside her on the mattress, he looked into her curious face for a long moment. "You really don't remember?"

"I do not," she said emphatically, shaking her head once more. "I wish above all else that you would believe that."

"I would like to," he admitted. "But I don't know you well enough for that. Why all this mystery?"

"Yeah, why this 'orphaned little waif' routine?" inserted Wellesley.

"But I am not trying to deceive you!" she asserted. "I would *never* try to deceive you," she added in a softer tone, her eyes falling mournfully from his as she drew into herself. Pulling her feet together and tightly crossing her arms over her chest in a self-hug, she looked on the verge of shivering. "You don't believe me," she said sadly. "You won't believe me."

"I'm not a man for blind faith," Hunt said. "I must have facts – something I can lean on."

"I have no facts," she murmured. Then, in a more strident tone, "I am as ignorant as you are, Rex Hunt. My life before this, if I ever had one, is lost to me. My body is mature, but my mind is blank. It is as though I have been born again."

"You can talk," Wellesley observed. "And you clearly know your way around alien technology. That bit with the cube yesterday proved that."

"But I don't know *how* I learned such things!" she said. "They are just *there*, somehow present in my mind but with no indication of how they got there. Oh, I wish I could make you believe me!" she groaned, about to cry. "I don't know how I got here, where I came from, or who brought me. My first days were spent in a haze. Dimly I perceived a signal reaching out to me, drawing me towards it. I-I was helpless to resist it in the state I was in. If it hadn't been for that nice man…" her voice trailed, trying to remember his name.

"Higden," said Hunt.

"Yes, Higden," she nodded. "If it hadn't been for him, I would have been destroyed shortly after coming here. The being that called me wished great evil against me – that I knew at once. But I, I couldn't *control* myself."

"I know what you mean," Hunt replied.

"Then you have felt this sensation?" she inquired hopefully, eager to find some kind of common ground.

"I felt it speaking to me," he replied simply. "It led to me being ambushed. A being spoke to me, trying to turn me against humanity and toward the cause of the *Prellak*. I rejected her proposal and destroyed her."

"What is a *Prellak*?" she asked with confusion. "And how is humanity under threat?"

"You don't even know *that*?" asked Wellesley skeptically.

"I do not," she admitted. "There is so much that I don't understand." She looked at Hunt, appeal written in her eyes. "Will you teach me?"

"Soon," he consented. "But first you must answer one question."

"Yes, anything," she said eagerly.

"What is the meaning of the vision you showed me? And *why* did you put it into my head?"

"I do not know," she said hesitantly, her words making Wellesley sigh with exasperation. "Oh, I know that you must be weary of me saying that. But it is the truth. I can't remember anything about it. I wasn't even aware of it until you saw it that first time. I felt a strong urge to communicate something to you, but I didn't know what. When we touched I saw it as well. Likewise when we lay together on the floor, I shared in your dream. I know neither its meaning nor its origin. I am simply a vessel for it."

"This doesn't add up," the AI opined after a few moments of silence. "You're mature, but you have no memory of your past; you end up in one of the worst pirate dens in this half of the galaxy with only the dimmest recollection of how you got here; you possess both psychic powers *and* a knowledge of ancient alien technology–."

"It isn't ancient," she cut in abruptly.

"I'm sorry?" Wellesley asked impatiently.

"The *Keesh'Forbandai* cube is of relatively recent

manufacture."

"How do you know that?" Hunt inquired.

"I don't know," she said after a moment of racking her brains. "I just do."

"I can see this is gonna be just a barrel full of giggles going forward," Wellesley murmured with annoyance. "Intermittent memory loss! Or is it *selective* memory loss, perhaps?"

"I do not understand why you're being so hostile to me!" she exclaimed at once. "I have done nothing to you. I've only tried–."

"Twice you've shown my friend a vision that has rattled him to his very core," snapped the AI. "Moreover, you've attempted to insinuate yourself into his life, stepping into a place that is already occupied by Lily Tselitel. I'd say you've done quite enough to warrant my present attitude."

"I have not tried to push aside his woman!" she pleaded.

"Then why'd you snuggle up to him last night on the floor? Call it whatever you want: that's a pretty intimate posture to take."

"But I don't know *why* I did that!" she said, to which the AI scornfully laughed. She bolted from the bed and stood angrily looking down at Hunt and the medallion he wore, her fists clenched at her sides and her feet spaced wide. "*I tell you I didn't!*" she reiterated, her voice growing otherworldly deep as a green glow emanated from her eyes. "*My purpose here is too great to bandy words with the likes of you!*" she growled. In an instant the light faded and her mild expression returned. With confusion she looked around, as though to find where the voice had come from. "What happened?" she asked, her stance growing meek and withdrawn once more.

"I don't know," Hunt said, reaching up to take her hands and drawing her to the mattress again. "But whatever it was, it's convinced me that a great deal is going on inside your mind that you're not aware of."

"Then you believe me?" she asked hopefully.

"No," Wellesley cut in instantly.

"Yes, I do," he assured her, patting her hands and then releasing them.

"I'm so glad," she said with relief. "I almost didn't believe myself until this moment. This is all so strange. So wrong. I can *feel* that this is not where I ought to be. And yet here I am."

"Indeed," Wellesley said skeptically.

"What will it take to convince you?" she asked, still disturbed by his hostility but calmer now that Hunt believed her. "How can I prove to you that I'm speaking the truth?"

"You could fake it if I told you," he replied.

"There's no call for that, Wells," Hunt chided him.

"Fine, just answer me this, orphan girl."

"Anything," she said earnestly.

"Why are you suddenly so talkative? Earlier you said that it was difficult to talk. But somehow you're holding down a conversation just fine now. How do you explain that?"

"It *was* hard to talk earlier. Terribly hard. I could barely find the words to convey my thoughts. As time goes by language becomes clearer, easier to employ. There is not such a gap between my vocabulary and the notions I wish to convey. Though I realize that my style of speaking is different from yours."

"It is," agreed Hunt. "You sound sort of archaic. But that'll probably pass as you get more familiar with us."

"Then you'll keep me with you?" she asked, her expression indicating that this was another point of anxiety for her. "I'll be allowed to journey with you?"

"Yes. There's no way we'd leave you in a rathole like this. You couldn't last a week here on your own."

"I feel so naive, so helpless," she said, putting her fingers to her temples and shaking her head momentarily. "I am so ignorant of everything that I need to know to look after myself. Will you take care of me until I remember who I am, and where I've come from?"

"Oh, *please*," Wellesley sighed in total exasperation. "If you laid it on any more thickly–."

"I'll take care of you, Soliana," Hunt cut him off. "We all will. Right, Wells?"

"Sure, why not," he said flippantly. "Not like she's a plant or anything like that."

"Obviously she's a plant," Hunt replied, his words alarming Soliana who searched his face urgently. "But not a plant from our enemies. She's been sent to us by friends, though ones we haven't met yet. Probably the same ones who paid your people to scatter ships and supplies across the galaxy for us."

"That's pure assumption," the AI replied.

"If she wanted to hurt us she could have done that by now. She could have stabbed me in my sleep instead of laying down beside me. And the way she was drawn to the refugee quarters shows she's no enemy. The being in that room wanted to destroy her, or at least turn her against us."

"Who's to say she hasn't been turned?"

"Wells, you're jumping at shadows," Hunt replied.

"Okay, fine. Just let the record show that I don't buy this."

"I'm no enemy to you," she said with earnest sincerity, reaching out and gently touching the disc under Hunt's shirt. "Please believe that."

"Time will tell," Wellesley replied skeptically, as she withdrew her hand. "Time will tell."

◆ ◆ ◆

Later that day Hunt entered the hangar with Tselitel

and Soliana in tow, each of them with a bag of supplies slung over their shoulders. Hunt held two, one in each hand. A number of the hangar's occupants eyed them as they passed. The occasional whistle went up at the sight of the supple, graceful Soliana.

"There you are!" Gromyko said, sitting on the recently repaired wingtip of the colonel's fighter. "I almost thought you guys decided not to come!"

"All vacations come to an end sometime," Hunt replied humorously, depositing his bags on the wing of his fighter near the fuselage. He paused and looked around for a moment, struck by a peculiar hush that had come over the hangar. He saw a group of a dozen pilots standing a short distance away, their flight gear already on. "What are they doing?" he asked the smuggler in a low voice.

"No idea," he said with a shrug. "They've been chatting like that for almost ten minutes now, just glancing this way occasionally. It's a cinch there's something on their minds."

"Tell me about it," Milo said suspiciously, eyeing them with aversion as he rested his arms on the wing Gromyko sat upon. "I'll be happy to put this place behind us, that's all I know."

"Yeah," Hunt muttered, taking the girls' bags and putting them up on the wing. Climbing up the ladder next to his craft, he began depositing the supplies inside when a sudden commotion caught his attention.

"Hunt!" called Kaljurand from across the hangar. "Hunt!"

"He doesn't look too happy," Gromyko observed, his legs dangling carelessly in the air as he watched the director approach with his entourage. The pirate's angry footfalls grew audible as he approached.

"What was the idea of giving a speech to my men yesterday?" he demanded, as Hunt descended the ladder to face him. "Is that how you repay everything I've done for you?"

"What are you talking about?" Hunt asked. "They just asked why I stuck around to fight the Devourers and I told them."

"You did more than that!" exclaimed the director, as the group of pilots approached.

"Sir?" one of them asked, a tall, handsome fellow in his mid twenties. The rest, a rough hewn, scraggly looking bunch, stood behind their chosen spokesman.

"I'll talk to you when I'm finished with him!" snapped Kaljurand.

"Begging your pardon, sir, but I was talking to *him*," he said respectfully, pointing a finger at Hunt. "What you said yesterday, well, it kind of put some things in perspective for us. We'd be proud to fly with you, if you'd let us."

"Absolutely not!" barked the director. "The first man who makes a move for his craft I'll order shot. This is a Black Fang base, Captain Michaels, *not* a recruiting station for the imperial navy."

"Maybe it ought to be," Milo said, ducking underneath his brother's fighter and standing beside him. "They seem to be the only ones making a stand for all of us at this point."

"That's the way we've got it figured, too," the captain said.

"Oh, that's how you have it figured, eh?" Kaljurand asked acidly. "Guards!" With this his entourage drew their weapons and leveled them on the assembled pilots. "Now, you'll *all* be escorted to the prison facilities to await judgment."

"No, they won't," a voice said behind him, instantly followed by the cocking of innumerable weapons.

Kaljurand's head snapped around to see half the hangar's population armed and aiming at him. Slowly his bodyguards lowered their guns and raised their hands.

"It's mutiny, then," the director said from between gritted teeth.

"Well, they *are* pirates, Ivo," Pinchon chuckled, walking through the firing line toward his ship and stopping beside the director. "Can you really expect anything else?"

"You stirred them to it!" he exclaimed angrily. "You snuck in here like a friend and turned my entire installation against me! And you smuggled weapons into their hands, no less!"

"As a matter of fact, I did," Pinchon replied easily, pleased with himself. "Although it wasn't really clinched until Rex's little speech yesterday. The time has come for every skilled pilot to get into the fight. I don't know why you can't see that. If the Devourers succeed, there won't be anyone left to rob, Ivo."

"I'll kill you," he said savagely. "No matter what I have to do, I'll find you and I'll *kill* you!"

"No, you won't," Pinchon replied. "There's some people here who have scores they want to settle with you. Believe me, I tried to talk them out of it. But they wouldn't budge."

"So you've killed me as well as robbed me!" he growled.

"No," Pinchon said, shaking his head. "You did that. I merely opened the floodgates, is all." The colonel snapped his fingers and nodded toward the director and his men. "Get them out of here." Instantly a dozen men surrounded the small group and ushered them out of the hangar.

"They'll kill him," Tselitel said with concern as she watched them go.

"Had to happen sooner or later," Pinchon replied with a philosophical shrug. "Pirates never die peaceably."

"So the entire base wants to join us?" asked Milo.

"The whole base?" laughed Pinchon, leaning on the wing and looking at him. "Certainly not. Only this dozen here wants to fly out," he said, jerking his thumb over his shoulder toward the scraggly bunch and their spokesman. "Some of the others are gonna get in contact with the other pirate bases in the area, trying to spread the good word about human unity. The rest are gonna break for it and make out however they can. They just joined up so that we'd get Kaljurand off their backs long enough to escape."

"So only a fraction are actually gonna help us fight?" asked Gromyko with disgust.

"You don't join the Black Fangs because you're a good citizen, Antonin," Hunt replied. Turning from his friends he approached the group, who still stood in respectful silence watching him. "I appreciate the offer, men. I really do. But our mission is going to take us far from here. Honestly, we don't even know what's waiting for us at the other end. But we hope it's something that will help us turn the tide of the war."

"We'll go with you anywhere!" an older man growled from behind the spokesman, leading to a general tumult of assent from the other ten.

Hunt turned from them momentarily and went to where Pinchon leaned.

"Can we trust them?" he asked.

"As much as you can trust anyone," he replied with a faint grin. "These men have severed their ties, Rex. They've put a mark on their heads by breaking with the Black Fangs, and they know it. They wouldn't do that without being utterly sincere."

"But why?" Hunt asked.

"Guess you've got a way with people," he shrugged. "One way or another, you can count on 'em. Especially in a fight. They won't break."

"Wells, how's the logistics of a long distance flight?"

"Well, our fighters use a different slipspace dimension to travel, so we'll be out of contact for a while. Additionally, due to the sophistication of our ships, we'll be moving approximately seven percent faster than they will. It'll give us a chance to scout around ahead of time. But we'll be up a creek if we run into anything really dangerous. I recommend grouping up a short distance from the target and making a brief jump to our final destination."

"I agree," Hunt said. "Cook up a rally point," he added, turning from Pinchon and heading back to the group to give them their instructions.

Half an hour later the two *Kol-Prockian* ships were packed and ready to go.

"You reading me alright, Rex?" Pinchon confirmed over his newly repaired radio.

"Loud and clear," Hunt said with satisfaction. "Those mechanics didn't disappoint."

"Nah, the Black Fangs have always had the best. Alright, let's get a move on. I'll head out first." With this he raised his craft into a low hover and twisted it around to face the shield. Pushing forward the controls, he shot out into space.

"Our turn," Wellesley said, as Hunt switched on the engines and hovered his ship. Turning more slowly than the colonel, he guided it out of the base and joined him outside.

Because of their longer travel time, the pirate group under captain Michaels had already departed for the rally point.

"If we warp at the same time we can keep each other company," Wellesley said over the radio. "Just try not to fall to arguing again, like last time."

"Hey, Milo started that!" Gromyko said quickly.

"I did *not!*" he replied. "I just said–."

"Good enough," Hunt cut him off. "It'll be a long trip for all of us. Just keep a level head. Now, are you guys ready?"

"Ready as we'll ever be," Gromyko replied.

"Colonel?"

"We jump on your word," he replied, his hand hovering over the warp switch on the control panel.

"Alright. Three, two, one."

Suddenly both ships dropped into the *Kol-Prockian* slipspace dimension, a beautiful tunnel of green light surrounding them.

Hours later Gromyko shifted in his seat, trying to make himself comfortable as the tunnel of light shot past. The younger Hunt slept soundly behind him, his shorter frame fitting more easily inside the cramped space. Moving his legs from one side of the back of Pinchon's seat to the other, he accidentally kicked it.

"Watch that, will you?" the pirate asked calmly, his voice half asleep.

"It's not like there's a lot of room back here, my friend," the smuggler replied, finishing his maneuver and settling in once more.

"We've got a long way to go," the colonel said. "Try to sleep more and fidget less."

"You're in a fine mood," Gromyko replied pointedly, raising his voice a little. "What's bugging you?"

"Milo will be, if you don't lower your voice."

"Fine," he whispered, shaking his head at the pirate's ill humor. Crossing his arms over his chest, he closed his eyes and tried to relax. Moments later they reopened. "Why have you suddenly backed off on Rex?"

"What?"

"Rex – you were hounding him almost the entire time we were on *Preleteth*. You cast aspersions on him and hated to let him out of your sight. All that changed once we'd reached the Black Hole."

"That should be obvious to you," the pirate replied.

"Well, it isn't. So why don't you enlighten me?"

With a sigh the colonel shifted in his seat.

"As long as we were on *Preleteth*, Rex was a risk to us all. He could have turned either way, given the influences he was under. That was a dangerous time for him. I could have minimized that danger if I'd been able to keep an eye on him. But *someone* wouldn't let me. So I had to put you all on your guard, trying to keep as many eyes watching him as possible. You'd all known him longer than I had, so I'd hoped that you might catch some change in him that I wouldn't have been able to notice. Once we'd blasted off there wasn't any risk of him turning."

"Makes sense," the smuggler said.

"Does it?" asked Pinchon, genuinely surprised as he'd expected a flurry of objections.

"Sure. Although your concern indicates something that you hadn't intended it should."

"And what's that?"

"That you're no mere pirate," Gromyko said with a sly smile. "There's more to you than meets the eye, Colonel. Now that I think of it, you mentioned something when we sat beside that little stream back on *Preleteth* that should have caught my attention at the time. You said you'd volunteered to pilot us in order to keep an eye on Rex. I can't imagine how I didn't put two and two together until now. Why would a pirate care about monitoring Rex? Only if he had yet another allegiance, besides that to the Black Fangs, would he feel that way."

"Very good," Pinchon said.

"Not hardly," the smuggler replied. "It shouldn't have taken me this long to figure it out. So, just what organization *do* you belong to?"

"I'm afraid that's not something I can discuss. We've kept off the radar for this long by keeping perfectly secret about our members and our intent. But you may rest assured that we are on the side of humanity in this conflict."

"Just tell me one thing," Gromyko said.

"If I can."

"You're *not* with the Order, are you?"

A disdainful laugh escaped the colonel's lips.

"No, I'm certainly not a member of *that* gang of fanatics. Their thinking was contaminated by their hatred for the empire. Even now many of them are working to undermine it in order to help the fringe independence movement. I've never seen a more highly intelligent gaggle of imbeciles in my life."

"Well, that's a load off my mind, anyhow."

"Why?"

"Because we've got a nice little team put together now," the smuggler explained. "I'd hate for that to end because you turned out to be an Order member, and Rex snapped you in two."

CHAPTER 15

Thurston McGannon walked slowly beside his wife toward the transport that waited to whisk her off Earth to the Omega Project.

Fifteen years older than his wife and possessing a slight stoop, he held a small overnight bag in his hand that bore the few items she would need for the trip.

Wearied by the demands of her position, she appeared to have aged ten years in as many weeks. The constant risk of assassination hung over her like a heavy cloud. Throughout the trying first days of the invasion up until the present, Thurston had never been far from her thoughts. A quiet, reflective man, she'd found him the perfect counterpoise to a career that invariably pulled her every which way. Quite fat and nearly bald, he bore the demeanor of an old judge.

"I'm sorry to leave you like this, Thurston," she said quietly, holding his hand as they approached the transport.

In reply he squeezed her hand a little harder, but said nothing.

With concern in her eyes she looked up into his heavy, sagely face. He caught her glance and gave her a faint, reassuring smile.

The morale of the navy had grown so brittle that it was on the verge of snapping. She knew that within the next few weeks she would be forced to make good on Krancis' threat against the families of mutinous officers. The very idea tormented her night and day, robbing her of the cool self-assurance she'd long been accustomed to.

The pair stopped just out of earshot of the transport's ground crew and looked at each other.

"Are you going to be alright?" she asked him.

"I'll be alright," he nodded, squeezing her shoulder.

Never a terribly affectionate couple, there nevertheless existed between them a degree of respect and understanding that onlookers found difficulty to understand. Not once in their twenty-seven year marriage did she raise her voice to him, though literally everyone else in her life, beside the emperor himself, had felt the lash of her temper. Something about his character made him immune to her demanding nature. She simply accepted him as he was, as he did her. More than once they had been likened to siblings, and the comparison wasn't far off the mark.

"You'd better go," he said, slipping the overnight bag into her hand and gently kissing her lips. He looked down into her eyes for a moment and squeezed her upper arms, sensing her reluctance to go.

"I never wanted to do it," she whispered desperately. "I need you to understand that. I never wanted to. He didn't give me any choice."

"I know," he assured her in a whisper. "I don't blame you. Nobody who knows the truth does."

"The truth," she scoffed. "What is the truth? That the empire has been subverted by a power hungry maniac? That the emperor is too–," here she hesitated. Looking around, she saw the pair of minders that Krancis had assigned to her for protection a dozen paces behind them and dropped her voice. "That he's too *feeble* to fulfill even the most basic requirements of his office? That–."

Without a word he drew her lean form against his protruding belly, holding her tight for a moment and then releasing her.

"There's no use catastrophizing," he said. "You'd better

go."

"You're right," she nodded, looking down at her bag momentarily and mentally running through its contents to ensure she had what she needed. Then she looked up at him one more time. "I hope those who survive this war forgive me for all that I've done."

With a nod he put his hand on her shoulder and gently turned her toward the transport. Drawing a deep breath, she walked up the ramp into the vessel without looking back. She could hear the bodyguards' feet clank up the ramp behind her. Two other agents were already in the vessel, seated up toward the front of the passenger area. Finding a window seat in the middle of the ship, she stowed her bag beneath it and settled in.

"What does that maniac want with me now?" she reflected within the privacy of her thoughts, not daring to so much as mumble a negative thought about him with his watch dogs surrounding her.

One week prior he had ordered all the heads of the various imperial departments to relocate to the site of the Omega Project. His official reason was that Earth and the systems surrounding it could no longer be considered safe. The Devourers had decimated their primary targets and were in motion toward their secondaries. Some, indeed, had already finished these objectives also.

Omega, it was true, was guarded by the majority of the imperial navy, though that force was spread out across the nearby systems so as not to draw attention to the Project. They could easily warp to its defense should any Devourer craft be detected en route to it.

And so far they had failed to do so. Apparently ignorant of its existence, they moved methodically toward their nearest targets at an almost leisurely pace.

"That, or they realize it's nothing but a useless hunk of metal," she thought acidly.

Believing that Krancis' true purpose in drawing all

the heads together was so he could hold them captive, she resisted his order to relocate as long as possible. Only after a certain piece of secret business had been taken care of did she yield to his authority and instruct that a transport be made ready.

At that moment she felt the vessel tremble as it hovered off the landing pad, twisted to the left, and lifted up into the sky.

She looked out the window at the place just short of the pad where she and her husband had taken leave of each other. Thurston had already disappeared from sight.

◆ ◆ ◆

Krancis was walking to his office within the station that housed the Omega Project when a young female officer approached and saluted.

"Krancis, a pair of alien vessels are approaching via subspace," she informed him.

"Devourer?" he asked, though he already knew the answer.

"No, sir. Their signature is similar to certain *Kol-Prockian* relics we've found throughout the galaxy."

"Good," he replied. "Scramble a squadron of fighters to meet them. But order them not to open fire."

"Sir?" she asked, confusion on her face.

"They're friends, Lieutenant," he said self-evidently. "Now get moving."

"Yes, sir!" she said, saluting once more and hastening back down the hallway.

"It's about time you got here, Hunt," he thought, looking out one of the spacious outer windows at the sparkling stars. Floating deep in the void of space, there was no local sun to dim their luster. Moments later the small radio in his ear beeped.

"Krancis, Minister McGannon's ship has just left warp and is requesting permission to land."

"Grant it," he said, resuming his walk.

◆ ◆ ◆

"Well, Rex, old man, looks like we're about to find out if this little jaunt of ours has been worth it," Wellesley said, a touch of uncertainty in his voice.

"What, you getting nervous?" Hunt asked, trying to stretch his burning, aching legs in the cramped cockpit.

"I wouldn't say *nervous*," the AI replied. "Let's say suspicious. Fate seems to have a twisted sense of humor. Sending us halfway across the galaxy for nothing would be right up its alley."

Hunt burst out laughing at this explanation.

"Glad one of us is having fun," Wellesley said tartly.

"I'm sorry, Wells," he said, trying to control his mirth. "But the last thing I ever expect from you is mysticism. You're getting superstitious!"

"So would any normal being, after all we've been through," he replied with annoyance. "Talking planets; people made of light; shadow monsters; and whatever that chick in the Black Hole was. It's enough to make anyone goofy."

"Goofy?" Hunt asked, trying not to chuckle. "Is that a technical term?"

"Oh, shut up," Wellesley replied, which only served to make Hunt burst out again. "I'm telling you, Lily, this one is cracking up. The strain of the trip has been too much."

"The only thing this trip has been is *boring*," Hunt replied. "I'll be glad to never see the inside of a fighter again."

"Who knows, you might have your wish granted," the

AI said, his voice growing serious. "We're about to drop out of warp."

"Get strapped in back there, girls," Hunt said, following his own advice. "Colonel, you boys ready for this?"

"Ready as ever," he radioed gamely.

Suddenly the ships dropped out of the green tunnel back into normal space.

"What in the…" Milo's voice trailed, as his eyes fell upon an enormous oblong station floating in space. A half dozen imperial battleships, dwarfed by the monstrosity, were on guard around it.

"Can it, Milo," Pinchon said. And then, "Rex, how do you want to handle this?"

"This is Rex Hunt to imperial station," he radioed instead of answering. "Our intentions are peaceable."

"I'm quite sure of that, Mister Hunt," a thin, authoritative voice replied. "A squadron of our fighters are on their way to escort you in."

"Who am I speaking to?" Hunt asked, his eyes narrowing. Something in the man's tone, his manner, struck a chord within him. He seemed almost familiar.

"We'll meet soon enough, Mister Hunt. That will be the appropriate time for introductions."

"There's more," Hunt said quickly, before his interlocutor shut down the connection.

"Yes?"

"I have an escort of vessels incoming," Hunt began cautiously, unsure what effect his next words would have. "Pirate vessels. They've broken with the Black Fang organization and have joined up with me."

"Then it appears that it's not in vain that we've awaited your arrival, if you've managed to sever some of those reprobates from their old allegiance," the man replied.

"They've dedicated themselves to the human cause," Hunt explained. "They're ready to fight with us against the Devourers. You can trust them."

"I'll be the judge of that," he replied, as the squadron of imperial fighters approached. "Follow your escort into the base. I'll be with you shortly."

"Yes, sir," he agreed, signing off.

"*Yes, sir*?" queried Wellesley. "Don't tell me you're getting respectful on me now, Rex."

"Just seemed appropriate somehow," Hunt shrugged, falling in behind the imperial fighters and flying beside the colonel's vessel.

Halfway to the station the pirate ships dropped out of warp.

"Mister Hunt, are you alright?" Captain Michaels radioed urgently when he saw the *Kol-Prockian* vessels heading toward the station under guard. "Gun it, boys!" he ordered, his vessels darting through space toward the leisurely traveling craft.

"It's alright, Captain," Hunt said. "We're expected. Disable your weapons and wait for instructions from the station."

"But, sir," Michaels began to protest, surrendering to imperial forces being the last thing he'd ever expected to do.

"Do as I say, Captain," Hunt ordered sternly. "Or they'll blast you out of the sky in two seconds."

"And don't you doubt it," Pinchon seconded. "Just relax."

"Stand down, boys," Michaels reluctantly radioed his squadron.

A trio of squadrons quickly surrounded the pirate fighters and held them back from the station until the first two craft were within docking range. Then, slowly, they allowed them to advance.

"This place is enormous," Wellesley said, as Hunt guided his craft into the gaping maw. Innumerable decks were visible in the massive opening. Countless fighters and other larger craft could be seen, docked safely behind an atmospheric shield. Hunt's nerves were tense as he followed his escort, afraid that the slightest mistake in his piloting might be interpreted as a hostile act. Glancing through the canopy of the ship beside him, he saw that the colonel's face was just as red as his own. The pirate noticed him looking and winked him a little reassurance. "I've never seen anything this large," the AI uttered, his awe increasing by the moment.

"Didn't your people ever make things this size?" Hunt asked in a distracted tone, trying to make a little conversation to ease his nerves.

"No," was all Wellesley could manage. And then, a few moments later, "I don't think they could have."

Drawing back on the stick to follow the imperial vessels upward, Hunt and Pinchon climbed the side of the station until they reached deck twenty-six.

"Proceed to land," the squadron leader ordered them. "Take a place toward the back. We have other vessels landing here today."

"Understood," Pinchon replied, looking at Hunt. "Go ahead, Rex."

Reluctantly Hunt pushed the controls forward.

"I never knew anything so big existed," Tselitel said from behind him.

But Hunt didn't hear her. Trying to watch everything at once, his perception nevertheless shrunk into an awkward tunnel vision. Vessels were coming and going around him, threatening to collide with him at any moment.

"You're doing fine," Pinchon radioed, flying a short distance behind him. "Just keep pushing on. They'll part around you."

The pirate was right. The local craft quickly sensed that there was something special about the exotic fighters in their midst and moved to a respectful distance.

"Does this hangar ever end?" asked Wellesley, as the two ships moved deeper and deeper inside.

"Looks like it," Hunt said, as the back wall finally drew

near.

Spotting an open space near a group of landed fighters, Hunt drew his vessel to a stop and descended onto a pad next to them. The moment he touched down he released the controls and cut the engines.

"Good job, Rex," Pinchon said over the radio, as he casually dropped his fighter onto his pad and powered down. "You'll be an ace in no time."

"I doubt that very much," Hunt replied, pulling off his helmet and stowing it by his feet. "You girls alright back there?" he asked, twisting around in his seat to look.

"Yes," Soliana replied distractedly, gawking in every direction as she tried to take in everything.

"Mhm," Tselitel nodded, a faint, anxious smile on her face. "Where do we go now?"

"Search me," Hunt replied. Slipping Wellesley out of the ship's AI slot and putting his chain around his neck and his golden disc down his shirt, he popped the canopy and climbed out onto the fighter's wing. Putting his hands on his hips, he looked up at the ceiling. "Gotta be a hundred and fifty feet," he said.

"At least," Wellesley replied, as a ground crew approached their vessels. They were led by an imperial officer and followed by a half dozen security personnel.

"Mister Hunt?" the lead officer inquired. "I'm Colonel McClain. Would you and your associates be good enough to come with us?"

It took nearly twenty minutes of walking for them to leave the hangar and enter a large elevator. Riding it upward, they reached an immaculate, sternly decorated level that bustled with personnel. Following Colonel McClain's lead, the group made their way to a trolley that facilitated horizontal travel and piled into it.

"Where are you taking us?" Milo asked, as the trolley began to move.

"To see the overseer of this facility," McClain replied.

Hunt glanced around the vehicle and saw that the security personnel had taken positions in the front and back.

"Makes you wonder if we're guests or prisoners, doesn't it?" Wellesley inquired, reading the drift of his thoughts. Silently he nodded.

"How big is this place?" Tselitel asked.

"I'm afraid I can't divulge that information," McClain said in an official tone.

After fifteen minutes of travel the vehicle came to a stop. Filing out of it, they entered another elevator and rode it downward. When it stopped with a ding, the doors opened and a sole man stood before them, his hands clasped behind his back. He was dressed in a black suit.

"Who are you?" asked Milo suspiciously, the man rubbing him the wrong way the instant he saw him.

"I am Krancis," he replied, as the group left the elevator and formed a half circle around him.

"Just Krancis?" Gromyko inquired, raising an eyebrow.

"Indeed."

Hunt looked at him, casting an eye up and down his gaunt face for anything that might remind him of who he was. There was something in his manner, in the aura that he cast off, that made him certain he'd known him somewhere before.

"And you're Rex Hunt," Krancis said, a subtle smile on his lips as he extended his hand to the Deltan.

"That's right," he replied, cautiously taking his hand. Instantly a whirl of images passed through his mind; images reaching from that moment all the way back to his childhood. Hunt jerked his hand from Krancis' grasp.

"Don't be alarmed," he replied in his thin voice.

Before Hunt could respond Soliana stepped to his side, her blue eyes wide and ethereal, as though she was watching the happenings of another realm.

"Your name is not Krancis," she said after a moment. "Your birth name is far different."

"My birth name is of no significance," Krancis replied sternly.

Soliana got the hint and withdrew into the group without another word.

"Just what are we doing here?" Hunt asked.

"I have something to show you all," Krancis replied. "Please, come with me." Ushering them down the corridor behind him, Krancis stepped to the side so as not to obstruct their view at the end of it.

"What's with all this theater?" Wellesley asked Hunt as he reached the opening. "You'd think–."

The AI's words were stopped by the sight of an enormous, ancient warship resting in dock before them. Dwarfing even the largest imperial carriers, it bore enough firepower to shatter an entire fleet by itself. Long and broad, the front portion of the vessel was divided into a pair of wings that left a gap, one which housed some kind of weapon. Spread all across the vessel were many large turrets and innumerable smaller ones meant for targeting fighters. Clearly of alien manufacture, it nevertheless had something recognizably human about it.

The group viewed the warship from a suspended walkway that ran around the entirety of the ship's berth. It stood halfway up the vessel, providing a perfect view of it.

"What is this?" Hunt asked in awe, approaching a handrail and leaning upon it, his mouth agape. Suddenly an engineering ship the size of a Devourer frigate roared through an opening in the wall beneath the walkway, making Hunt jump away from the railing. He watched with fascination as it approached the warship, gradually shrinking in size until it was a mere gnat beside it.

"This is our salvation, Mister Hunt," Krancis said. "This is the Omega Project."

End of Book II

THANK YOU!

I hope you enjoyed The Beast Emerges!
If you did, please leave a review so others can enjoy it too!

Printed in Great Britain
by Amazon